A WAKE-U
THE TAUREG

The edge of the desert sun ..... over the top of the cliff, blinding Stapler briefly as he cupped his hand over his eyes. He shut them for a moment as they grew accustomed to the morning rays. When he opened them a few seconds later, it seemed to Stapler that the rocks surrounding the encampment were moving.

"Here they come!" shouted Corporal Heights from the other side. The rocks weren't rocks. Tauregs had curled up on their sides and draped their Abas over their bodies so that in the shadows of the night they blended into the rocky terrain of the Wadi.

"Hold your fire!" Stapler shouted. "Make each shot count." The Taureg charge was several hundred yards away and uncoordinated. Now that the battle had begun, his anxiety eased. The years of exercises, training, and combat experience burst forth within him.

"Get down, Gunny!" the LT shouted from the Humvee.

Stapler raised his M-16 . . . flipped the safety off and fired as several Tauregs reached the perimeter. The Marines and riggers, who waited for the Gunny's command, opened fire together, sending a wave of bullets out to greet the Taureg horde.

Don't miss
the previous novels in this epic combat series . . .

The Sixth Fleet
Seawolf

Berkley titles by David E. Meadows

THE SIXTH FLEET
THE SIXTH FLEET: SEAWOLF
THE SIXTH FLEET: TOMCAT

THE
SIXTH FLEET
TOMCAT

DAVID E. MEADOWS

B
BERKLEY BOOKS, NEW YORK

THE SIXTH FLEET: TOMCAT

A Berkley Book / published by arrangement with the author

PRINTING HISTORY
Berkley edition / February 2002

Visit our website at
www.penguinputnam.com

ISBN: 0-425-18379-3

BERKLEY®
Berkley Books are published by The Berkley Publishing Group, a division of Penguin Putnam Inc.,
375 Hudson Street, New York, New York 10014.
BERKLEY and the "B" design are trademarks belonging to Penguin Putnam Inc.

PRINTED IN THE UNITED STATES OF AMERICA

10 9 8 7 6 5 4 3 2 1

To all the innocent victims and their families of September 11, 2001, and the people of New York City who rose in the face of terrorism to show the world the spirit of America.

Acknowledgments

My love and thanks to Felicity for her advice years ago that I should write what I know about. From her suggestion came the first manuscript for *The Sixth Fleet*.

This series would never have occurred without the sage advice and professional encouragement of Mr. Tom Colgan.

My thanks to my fellow classmates in the class of 2000 at the Industrial College of the Armed Forces who answered my myriad technical questions. I appreciate my friend Colonel "Slick" Katz, USMC, and the no-nonsense time he spent ensuring I understood the Marine Corps perspective on the Navy–Marine Corps team. *Whew!* Commander (retired) James Hamill, former commanding officer Fleet Air Reconnaissance Squadron Two, provided technical support on EP-3E flight characteristics. And to CDR Joseph Beatles for his aviation experience. My thanks for the support and technical guidance provided by Ms. Sharon Reinke, Mr. Art Horn, and Lieutenant Colonel David "Skull" Riedel, United States Marine Corps, in the Office of the Assistant Secretary of Defense for Public Affairs.

Any technical errors or mistakes in this novel are strictly those of the author.

CHAPTER 1

⚓

GUNNERY SERGEANT STAPLER PEERED OVER
the oil barrels in front of him, ready to jump down if the
shooting started again. Five minutes of quiet didn't necessarily mean the end of a battle. His heart pounded against
his flak jacket. Sweat poured between the T-shirt under
the jacket and his chest, spreading around the belt line,
soaking his skivvies. The ringing in his ears, caused by the
clanging and ricochets of bullets hitting the empty oil barrels around him, was slowly disappearing.

Two hundred yards away, rolling black smoke from
two burning CH-53 helicopters rose straight into the hot,
dry, Sahara sky. The air above the ground simmered from
the midday heat and seemed to leap around the scarlet
flames roaring over the fuselages. The burning silhouette
of the pilots appeared and disappeared as clouds of black,
oily smoke whipped around the broken cockpit windows.
"Damn," he said under his breath through gritted teeth.

Three Marine Corps Cobra gunships had escorted the
Super Stallions across the Moroccan hills and a hundred

miles farther inside Algeria before turning back because of low fuel. Homeplate knew it was taking a chance sending large troop transports into hostile territory without escort, but Intel argued this far south into Algeria was clear and safe. Well, hell . . . it wasn't, it ain't, and what the hell were they going to do now? G2 screwed up. Ain't the first time, either. He'd bet his ass the colonel in G2 would shrug his shoulders and say something about the "fog of war." Hell, this hadn't been fog; it had been a goddamn thunderstorm. Dead Marines . . .

He counted twenty bodies, including enemy, scattered across the plain between their position and the helicopters. Two of the bodies on the plain were Marines. Well, one was a Marine; the other was a Navy corpsman. Every platoon had a Navy corpsman, and the Navy corpsman was special. He—and now, sometimes she—was their doctor, the difference between life and death when wounded. It was an unwritten Marine Corps rule that every Marine had a responsibility to protect that Navy corpsman from harm. This time, Stapler had failed.

Gunnery Sergeant Leslie Stapler of Concord, North Carolina, refused to include the two in his battlefield count. Six members of his platoon and the six Marine Corps Sea Stallion crew members never made it out of the 53s. The slight Saharan wind rippled the loose Bedouin clothing of the dead enemy to wave like sleeping flags. Stapler recalled their Arab translator in Morocco called the long flowing robes *thobes*.

He twisted his M-16 slightly, pulled the magazine out, did a quick count; eight cartridges of the thirty remained. He shoved it back into the weapon until he heard the familiar click as the magazine on the nine-pound rifle was set.

Another shot went off to his right. Stapler bobbed his head back and forth, trying to see around the empty barrels where his Marines had sought position. A second three-burst volley erupted farther to the right. Satisfied that the sporadic fire was coming only from his Marines, he pumped his left hand up and down and shouted, "Cease fire! Cease fire!" He scrambled crablike to the left, nearer a Marine rifleman crouched behind a couple of barrels.

Stapler reached over and patted Joe-Boy Henry on the shoulder. His longhaired cowboy private from Texas. Of course, long hair in the Marine Corps still meant it was shorter than a half inch. "They're gone, Cowboy Joe-Boy. Save your ammunition. You're gonna need it." Stapler took his helmet off and braced it under his knee. With his handkerchief, he wiped the sweat from his forehead.

Private Henry looked up. "Are they gone, Gunny?" he asked with a slight tremor in his voice. "Gawl damn, Gunny. That was shit, wasn't it? That was pure shit. You sure they gone?"

"I doubt it, Cowboy Joe-Boy. I really doubt it, but remember, you are a Marine. I think we were as much a surprise to them as they were to us." Stapler saw fear in the young man's eyes. Cowboy Joe-Boy's knuckles were white where he held a death grip on the M-16. Stapler smelled fear on himself, too: a sharp, ammonia smell, almost like urine but not quite as strong.

"You remember when we pulled into Jamaica a few months ago, Gunny?" The Marine's eyes kept glancing at the gunny, then staring at the battlefield, as if expecting the dead to rise and charge at any moment.

"Yeah, Cowboy. It was a fun time on the beach," Stapler replied, his eyes combing the open sand to the front.

"Well, I want you to know that I will never look at a Jamaican reggae band the same way again." The Marine's voice nearly broke.

The ringing from the barrels had finally cleared. "Me, either." He slapped the Marine on the back. "Good job, Marine. Keep a sharp eye out." Stapler rose waist high and, at a crouch, started to ease around the Marine, ready to roll to the ground if shots came his way.

"Gunny, I can't help but be a little scared." Cowboy Joe-Boy lifted one hand away from the M-16 and wiggled his fingers; then he shifted hands, doing the same with the other. His gaze focused on the dry, white Sahara desert between them and the burning helicopters. Gunny knew the young rifleman was concentrating hard to hide the moisture in his eyes.

Stapler patted him on the shoulder again. "Ain't we all, Private. You stay here and keep alert. And keep an eye on those bodies. Just because they're still don't necessarily mean they're dead."

"Gunny, what about Butt and Stan? Are they dead?" Cowboy Joe-Boy asked, referring to the Marine and the Corpsman lying on the battlefield. He pointed toward the burning helicopters.

Stapler looked out at the bodies, thought for a few seconds, and then said, "Yeah, Joe-Boy. They're dead. We'll bring them in after we've secured the perimeter and are sure the enemy has departed the battlefield." Hell, what was he going to tell the young Marine? *Shit, Private. They're alive, but they're not making any noise, so we'll leave them alone for the time being.* The pool of blood beneath Butt's head and the dark-stained sand surrounding Stan's body showed the damage done to the two. You put your life on the line for your fellow warriors when they were alive because you expected them to do the same for you. He'd do it now, if he thought they were alive. They were quiet. They had remained motionless since the ambush and never moved from the position in which they fell. Stapler looked for movement from the two even as the firefight raged and the attack faded from the battlefield.

The wounded scream, they cry, they moan for help, and you fight to rescue them. He thought this without it being a negative conjecture, just a "Stapler fact." Stapler had been in enough battles to know that those who are alive or are going to live let you know they need help. Most times, vocally and loud. The quiet ones were dead or dying. "Water" and variations of "Mom" were the two most common cries that filled the dreadful, after-combat silence.

The smell of cordite mixed with the sickening odor of burning flesh and fuel confirmed the stories Top Sergeant MacGregory told. Top Sergeant MacGregory said the smell of human flesh was like burnt bacon. The top enjoyed passing on such important tidbits of information during senior NCO poker nights, preferably when someone was eating. Woe to the poker player who showed a weak stomach around the top; MacGregory had a host of stomach-turning descriptions from his experiences in combat, always augmented with the stink of raunchy cigars. The top said human flesh tasted like pork. Stapler wondered where he had gained that tidbit of information but never asked because he didn't think he wanted to know the answer. Right now, he wished the old veteran—gross or not—was with them. The devil himself avoided Marines like Top MacGregory.

A crackling sound of the metal in the helicopter twisting from the flames drew his attention for a moment. The burning pyre filled the wavering desert air with black smoke. For a fraction of a second, the dark outlines of the pilots still strapped in their seats appeared through the flames. Stapler glanced up at the sky, his eyes tracking the smoke plume that rose above the helicopters. Not much danger of hiding their location.

Yeah, he was scared, but never let your Marines see it. Fear is contagious, and he had to be the rock with the captain gone. Damn good thing he hadn't drunk that third cup of coffee before they left Homeplate. He would have wet himself the past few minutes. Still, he needed to take a leak real bad. He glanced at his watch. Ten minutes! They had been fighting only ten minutes? Seemed much longer.

Leslie Stapler walked behind his Marines manning the haphazard line of defense made during the battle. Twenty-two years Stapler had been a Marine. He loved the Corps, but had kept secret his plans to put in his retirement papers next year. He wanted to wait till the last moment before he slapped those papers down on MacGregory's desk. His wife had given him an ultimatum before this assignment: retire or find a new wife. Stapler didn't have too strong a position on whether he had a wife or not. He did have a strong position on not having a third wife. Two were enough in any man's lifetime. Another wife was definitely out of the question. What did worry him were those credit cards Carol had. It had taken three years to pay off the last rampage she went on.

"Gunny," First Lieutenant Nolan said, causing Stapler to jump.

Stapler started to salute, then realized the gesture would identify the officer to anyone observing. "What's the situation on your end, LT?" Stapler asked, drawing out the *L* and *T* with a Southern accent to make it sound like *El Tee.*

"No casualties, Gunnery Sergeant. And yours?"

"We've got two casualties out there: Butt and Stanhope. Until I take muster, I won't know how many or who, made it. But I know we lost those two. I don't know how many failed to make it out of the choppers," Stapler said somberly. He took a deep breath and looked the young officer in the eye. "You know you've got it, LT. The captain didn't make it. He never made it out."

The lieutenant's eyes widened. The young officer held his M-16 loosely in his right hand and with his left reached up and pushed his helmet back slightly. The loose straps hung down. The first lieutenant had only been with the company four months. Twenty-four years old, Stapler recalled. An ROTC graduate from University of Maryland. The dark black hair and light blue eyes made the lieutenant look more like a high-school teenager than a Marine officer. *Lieutenant Malcolm Jeffrey Nolan may as well shave that mangy-looking mustache off,* thought Stapler.

"Gunny, I'm a communicator. I'm not infantry." The LT licked his lips and glanced around nervously. "I just came along for the ride. You know, a chance for experience. I'm just a first lieutenant. You'll have to take charge," Lieutenant Nolan finished almost in a whisper. His eyes searched around the two, making sure no one heard what he said.

"I beg the LT's pardon," Stapler said slowly, pronouncing each word distinctly. "I'm the gunnery sergeant. You're the officer. The Marine Corps made it that way for a purpose. You are a Marine, and every Marine is a rifleman and, if you are a rifleman, then you're infantry. Now, sir, you're in charge."

"But, Gunnery Sergeant—"

"I'll be here to advise you, LT. You can handle it, and you know it." Stapler grinned at him. "Much younger men than you in Marine Corps history have risen to the occasion."

Stapler saw several Marines rise from behind the barrels and begin to move toward them.

"Don't you dare!" shouted Stapler. "Get your butts back in position. This ain't no field exercise and no second chances when you screw up! They're still out there. They may be gone for the moment, but they'll be back, so get your asses down and quit making yourselves easy targets."

The Marines turned in midstep and ran back to their positions. Stapler shook his head. How in the hell was he was going to keep this bunch of fresh-faced young grunts alive until rescue arrived? If rescue ever came. *Stop that. No negative thoughts.* Top MacGregory would jerk him up by the short hairs for those kind of thoughts.

"You're right, Gunny," Lieutenant Nolan replied, rubbing his chin. "But I will definitely need your help, and if you see me doing anything that may endanger us, stop me or give me some options. Any recommendations right now?"

"Yes, sir. I would shave that puny-looking mustache off." Stapler smiled. When the LT failed to smile and ran his fingers over the mustache, Stapler shook his head, tugged his ear, and said, "I'll complete my circuit of the perimeter, LT, and report back to you." He paused and then added, "You'll do fine, Lieutenant."

Lieutenant Nolan watched as Stapler moved off. He ran his fingers across his upper lip again and wondered briefly if they had a mirror inside the office. A small explosion from the burning helicopters caused him to duck instinctively. He started after the Gunny.

Stapler walked slowly, taking in the surroundings of

the oil company compound while glancing toward the
desert, expecting the enemy to return at any moment.

He made a defensive assessment as he surveyed the
site. They had been damn lucky the barrels had been
nearby when they landed. They were ambushed as they
exited the helicopters. Noises behind him drew his attention. Several civilians stood up behind other empty barrels
located closer to the office complex. Several crawled from
under the vehicles parked to the left. He would have a
closer look at the vehicles when he got to that side of the
compound. He was surprised when he turned around to
find the LT walking several paces behind him.

"Looks as if our evacuees are beginning to show themselves, LT."

Lieutenant Nolan looked to where Stapler pointed. He
shaded his eyes from the glare of the sun. "I hope they
have more than those peashooters, Gunny."

Gunnery Sergeant Leslie Stapler grunted in reply. A
few of the oil riggers were holding pistols. He pulled a
cigarette from a pack crammed into his flak jacket. This
was supposed to be an easy evacuation, not like the one
his fellow Marines encountered in Algiers two weeks ago.
The Marines were *still* in Algiers trying to find the American hostages captured during that evacuation. Oh, no,
they said. This would be a cakewalk. Long-ass flight, too;
shove the thirty or so evacuees into the two helicopters,
twenty minutes max on the ground, and fly the hell back
to the temporary base established in southern Morocco.
Instead, what happens? The twenty minutes on the ground
turned into ten minutes of hell with them fighting for their
lives. What in the hell were they going to do now?

Those two CH-53s burning out there were the only two
the USS *Kearsarge* off-loaded before continuing its journey through the Strait of Gibraltar. Backup called for the
Army to come in from Mauritania. Mauritania wasn't
even near this portion of the border with Algeria. According to what he heard yesterday, the Army helicopters had
not even arrived yet at Base Butler. The only thing at Base

Butler was a forward Army headquarters element setting up the operation.

Nineteen—two squads and a squad leader—flew out of Homeplate. They sent him along because of his experience. He figured nine, maybe ten of them remained alive: one squad, three fire teams. If lucky, eleven, counting the LT. He had the fresh-faced lieutenant and himself with the next guy in line being Corporal David Heights. The platoon sergeant was still in the helicopter.

Stapler took a last drag on the cigarette and flicked it in front of him, grinding it into the sand with his boot as he stepped on it. Just like they'd grind him, if he didn't figure a way for them to get out of here. He patted his shirt pocket. He only brought one spare pack of cigarettes with him.

The prefabricated office building at the rear of the compound reminded Stapler of a West Virginia double-wide trailer. *How did that joke go? What does a hurricane, a tornado, and a divorce in West Virginia have in common? No matter which one happens, someone loses a double-wide.*

The prefabricated building fronted a low hill. Stapler figured the craggy hill provided afternoon shade for the complex. The front windows had been shot out. Jagged edges of glass protruded from the bottom, and one large piece, like a guillotine blade waiting to fall, hung from the top. Hundreds of empty oil barrels encircled the complex, leaving a small space about a hundred feet between the building and the barrels. Almost as if someone made a fort from discarded rubbish. *Don't bitch about it, Leslie,* he said to himself. *That rubbish fort saved our lives when we landed.*

Stapler and the lieutenant had been the first two out of each helicopter as soon as the behemoths set down, leading the platoon toward the compound. They were running in dispersed formation, in accordance with Marine Corps training, when the two helos exploded, knocking most of them to the ground. Probably saved their lives, because intense gunfire erupted from the surrounding dunes at the same time, followed by a horde of *thobe*-clad Bedouins charging down on them.

If—and *if* is a very big word—they had landed and loitered near the helos, the rocket-propelled grenades—RPGs—fired by the attackers would have gotten them. They'd all be dead now. Moreover, Carol would still be out there with those damn credit cards.

A burly man in a short khaki shirt and a jungle helmet approached Stapler and Nolan. Beer gut, no neck, and thick arms, observed Stapler. About same height as the lieutenant and a couple of inches shorted than Stapler. If he weren't out in the middle of the southern Algerian Sahara desert, the man could easily pass for a Philadelphia steel worker.

"I'm Chuck Jordan, better known as Bearcat," the man said, shaking hands with Lieutenant Nolan. He turned and shook Stapler's hand. "I'm the supervisor here."

"What the hell is going on, Mr. Jordan?" Stapler asked, wiping the moisture from the handshake on his cammie trousers.

"Your guess is as good as mine. We had no idea anyone was within miles of here until you landed, and then all hell broke loose. Where'd they come from?"

"Wasn't just hell that broke loose," Stapler said. "We just lost a lot of good Marines. You had radio communications with us. Why didn't you tell us you were under attack? We would have approached differently and probably saved the lives of those who died out there!"

"Sergeant—"

"It's Gunny or Gunnery Sergeant."

Bearcat leaned forward, his eyes contracting into tight, angry slits. "Gunny, they attacked as you landed. I would have *fucking* called you if we had had time, but you landed at the same *fucking* time that they *fucking* attacked. Does that make any sense to you?"

Several seconds of silence passed before Stapler nodded, ignoring the anger. "Those two helicopters were the only means of getting us out of here. Without them, we're stranded like Robinson Crusoe until the Army can get here. How many are there of you, sir?"

"I have twenty-two riggers here and another ten at Alpha site."

"Alpha site?"

Bearcat nodded. "Alpha site is our group of rigs about ten kilometers to the northwest. I talked with Charlie when we got word you were on your way. That was before sunrise this morning. They are waiting for us to pick them up. I told them we'd go get them after you landed."

He didn't like this. "You were supposed to be ready to depart when we landed, sir."

"That may be, Sergeant—Gunny, but it's hardly safe to go tramping around the desert in the dark. Especially the way things are in Algeria right now. Plus we still have a contract to keep pumping. I've gone through overnight changes of government before in Third World nations and have yet to see it change the oil contract."

Stapler kept the thought to himself that those ten at Alpha site might already be dead. No need to upset anyone yet. If Alpha site had been surprised, too, he doubted there would be anyone to pick up. He ran his hand across the top of his head, felt the heat through the sparse hair, and suddenly realized that somewhere around here he had left his helmet. Another stupid mistake. He glanced around and saw it in the sand near Cowboy Joe-Boy. Too many stupid mistakes since they landed. He needed to calm down and take charge, like the Marine Gunnery Sergeant he was.

"Joe-Boy, bring me my helmet!"

Cowboy grabbed the helmet and ran to Stapler.

"Thanks, Joe-Boy, now get back to your position. What in the hell do you mean leaving it, just because I told you to?"

Cowboy grinned slightly. "Sure thing, Gunny." The young Marine turned and hurried back to the barrels, shaking his head on the way.

Stapler took the helmet and jammed it down on his head. He would need the helmet. Everyone would need their helmets. Even the oil riggers wore ball caps or jungle hats. They'd need their helmets not only for combat protection but as protection from the sun already baking the morning sands. Sweat soaked his belt line, causing the top of the trousers to rub with every step. It would not be long before he had a raw area around his waist. Stapler undid his shirt and removed the flak jacket. He knew the importance of the flak jacket, but he also knew that he wouldn't survive wearing it. Each breath was hot. Hot! No other word for it. Hot and dry. The other Marines were watching the gunny. He had experience. He had been in combat. None of them had ever fired a piece in anger.

Stapler put his shirt back on and noticed the other Marines, including the LT, removing their flak jackets.

Stapler pulled his handkerchief from his back pocket and wiped the sweat from his face and forehead. A bad case of chicken pox as a boy and an inability to leave teenage acne alone had left Stapler's face heavily pockmarked. A thin, sandpaper-rough face that seemed appropriate for a tough Marine. He put away the handkerchief and pulled out a pair of sunglasses, tangled around his spare pack of cigarettes, from his shirt pocket. The relief from the glare of the sun was immediate.

"Gunny, I think we should contact Homeplate and let them know what has happened. Need to also contact the Army at Base Butler to send in backup."

"Yes, sir, we should do both. But the Army will be unable to help. They—"

"Why?"

"They got nothing there yet, sir. Even if they had, they would be Army Forty-sevens; not, Marine Fifty-threes. Chinooks don't have the legs our CH-Fifty-threes have. The bad news is, I think we are too far away for them to come get us and be able to return to Base Butler or divert to Homeplate."

Behind Bearcat, three people, who looked nothing like oil riggers, approached.

"What is the Army doing in Mauritania?" Bearcat asked.

"I'm not sure," Stapler answered, watching the three approach. "I think it has something to do with this little war with Algeria and Libya; this new country they announced at the United Nations several weeks ago."

The gray-bearded man, leading the three, looked to be in his late fifties, early sixties. The jungle hat jammed down on his head made his ears stand out. Other than Bearcat, he was the only one in the compound wearing a jungle hat. The others had ball caps for the most part. Stapler noticed a pronounced limp in his right leg, which explained the cane the man carried in his hand.

A young lady pranced behind him. *Prance* was the only word he could think to explain her walk. Her head tilted at a high angle, exposing a smooth chin. A sandy blond ponytail stuck out the back of a red Atlanta Braves ball cap, swishing with each step, brushing her shoulders. *How in the hell did something like that find its way out here?* Stapler thought. He looked at her feet, half expecting to discover high heels. He grinned at the thought. No high heels, but leather-laced Timberland walking boots with pink socks turned down on top showed she had some sense of where she was. She belonged on a boardwalk somewhere rather than in the middle of the desert. He looked up at her face to discover her returning the stare, aware of his appraisal.

He turned his attention to the young man beside her. The thin black man looked angry, as if he wanted to take on the world. A white shirt with the top two buttons undone exposed a firm, smooth chest that glistened with sweat. The man's eyes shifted from her to Stapler, as if expecting someone to mug him at any moment. His hair, at one time, had been arranged in nice cornrows, but the desert heat had untangled most to give the man a look as if he just stretched from a rough night of humid sleep.

Bearcat glanced over his shoulder to see what caused the gunny sergeant to frown. He grinned and pointed at the three as they neared the group. "Lieutenant, Sergeant, this is Professor Harold Walthers from the University of Mason and his assistants—"

"It's George Mason University, Mr. Jordan," the professor corrected, smiling. He placed his cane in front of him and crossed both hands over the top of it. "Pardon Mr. Jordan. He is determined to associate us with every university but the right one."

"Oh, yeah, George Mason University," Bearcat corrected, scratching his head as he tried briefly to recall where the university was located.

"I can't tell you how good it is to see you Marines. I have been trying to tell Mr. Jordan for the past couple of days that something was up. Our guides—both of them Tauregs—disappeared two days ago, after delivering enigmatic warnings for us to leave, also. Knowing the history of these nomadic people, I should have guessed something like this was going to happen."

Professor Walthers stuck his hand out and shook Lieutenant Nolan's hand. He did not offer the same to Stapler.

Just what we need, thought Stapler. *A bunch of eggheads to complicate this mess we're in.*

"But who listens to academia anymore? These are my assistants," Walthers said, pointing to the lean black man beside him and then to the young lady who, through narrow eyes, glared back at Stapler. "This fine gentleman is Mr. Karim Abdul Washington from the University of Pennsylvania, a graduate student studying anthropology. This is Miss Sheila Anne Forester, a senior at my own university, George Mason. She is our assistant at the dig, without whom we would be hard-pressed to write our results when we return. I don't know if Mr. Jordan has had time to tell you why we are here, but we are surveying cave paintings that the Loffland Company discovered a few months ago. You do not find—"

"Sorry, Professor," Stapler interrupted. "I don't mean to be rude, but we'll have do the life stories later." He looked at the desert surrounding the compound. "We need to get organized in the event those out there return."

"Quite right, Sergeant," Professor Walthers replied unabashed, straightening up, and tucking his cane under his arm.

"You military types are all alike, you know, Gunny Sergeant," the young assistant, Sheila, said. "You don't have to be rude, and it doesn't matter how long a life story takes; the point is that it is a life story." She stood with her hands braced against her hips. "So let me continue with our life story, because now it is yours, also. We didn't ask to be put in the middle of this. And now that we are, it is your responsibility to get us out. So? When do you intend to airlift us out of here?"

"As soon as we can, ma'am."

The right side of her lip turned up. Nodding her head, she looked at Professor Walthers and Karim. "Stands to reason. Send in the military, and they come with only one plan." She took a couple of steps forward until she stood in front of Lieutenant Nolan and Stapler. "We are American citizens, and our lives are endangered. You are Marines. You are what *Newsweek* and *Time* magazines say you are; the nation's nine-one-one force. How many did they send to protect us? Five? Six? I don't see many here."

"Miss Forester, I am sure—" Professor Walthers interrupted.

"Professor," she snapped. "Their job is to protect us. Our job is to be protected. I, for one, intend to live up to my expected role in this endeavor." She paused and stared at the lieutenant. "And I expect them to do theirs."

Stapler noticed her ponytail bounced up and down, punctuating each word, as she spoke. *How does she do that?* he thought. Her accent sounded almost British.

"I can do my job quite well. I expect them to do theirs *equally* as well. Right now? It does not look like they are doing such a great job. Look out there," she ordered, pointing past the two Marines. "Are those the only helicopters the calvary rode when they came charging over the horizon? Those are the only two helicopters I see, and from what I see, those two are not going to be flying us anywhere."

Stapler stepped forward, his face leaning toward the young woman. "Ma'am, those helicopters contain the bodies of our Marines. I think—" he continued, his voice rising with each word.

Lieutenant Nolan touched Stapler lightly on the shoulder as he interrupted. "We will do everything we can, miss, but please be patient, and we'll do our job. We are here and, as you pointed out, our job is to protect not only you, but everyone else. If you will do your job as you have already defined, listen to us, and do what we ask, then we'll get you out of here."

"Safely, I hope?"

Stapler grunted, thinking, *Let her walk back,* hardly realizing how prophetic this would become.

"Safely, of course," Nolan replied with a smile creeping across his lips.

Stapler caught a soft twinkle pass through her eyes. "Come on, LT. We need to finish our survey and arrange defenses."

"I'm talking, *please!*" she said arrogantly.

Lieutenant Nolan pulled his helmet back down. "Okay, Gunny. What first?"

"Ammo, guns."

The two turned to leave.

"I'm still talking, and you're ignoring me," Sheila Anne Forester said petulantly.

"Come on, Sheila. They're just as trapped as we are," Karim said, pulling her lightly by the arm, glaring at the lieutenant.

"Oh, shut up, Abdullah," she said, small furrows appearing across her forehead as her light eyebrows bunched in anger. She shook off his hand, causing her ponytail to flip over her left shoulder. She reached up and flicked it back.

She drew her foot back to kick the sand, suddenly thought better of it when she saw Stapler's eyes narrow, and instead turned and stomped off. A few steps away, she turned and gave Lieutenant Nolan a quick glance and a smile. The bright glare of the sun darkened the shadow under the LT's helmet lid, obscuring his face, but Stapler thought he detected the young officer blushing. *Shit! Just another annoyance to add to this mess. Raging hormones. Where's a bucket of water when you need it?*

"It's Karim, and you know it. Quit calling me Abdullah!" the Afro-American student shouted after her. Without turning, she stuck her hand up with her middle finger extended and continued walking away.

"Guess I'd better go after her so she don't do something stupid like marching off across the desert," Karim said. Shaking his head, he ran after the woman. "Sheila, wait up!"

What she needed was a good walloping across the bottom, thought Stapler. He wondered briefly if he put her across his lap and taught her some manners would the Marine Corps take his pension? *Yes, in a heartbeat, they would; the Marines don't pay you for having fun.*

He watched her out of the corner of his eye as the young black man caught up with her. He turned his attention to Bearcat.

"Mr. Jordan, what kind of weapons do you have?" He saw the LT staring after the young woman. "LT," he said, his voice loud, "We need to know what weapons they have, don't we, sir?"

The oil rigger slapped the holster he was wearing. "I have this Colt, and we have a small locked armory with ten M-Sixteens. They're protection against raiding bands of Tauregs who periodically ride through here. Most times, they just trade, but the guns keep them honest. At least, as honest as Tauregs can be when you're looking."

"Tauregs? What are they?"

Professor Walthers interjected, "If I may, Tauregs are the desert nomads of the Sahara, Sergeant. An anachronism from another age, actually. They have lived in the Sahara desert for centuries, plying the ancient trade routes between sub-Saharan Africa and the north coast. They were famous eons ago as the only means of bringing valuable goods from the legendary Timbuktu to Barbary. Their religious and cultural beliefs center around a portion of the Sahara running from Mauritania, northeast to the coastal areas of Libya. This is their homeland and intrud-

ers—which we are to them—have always been fair game.
They have a warrior ethic that would rival you Marines;
they just don't have the weapons or modern training you
do nor do they work well together. Fiercely independent,
I must add . . . almost to the point of belligerence. I would
submit that the Tauregs are the primary reason the French
never tamed the Sahara desert in the nineteenth and early
twentieth centuries. In fact—"

"Could this attack have been the work of them?" Stapler asked.

"Some of those dead out there are Tauregs," Bearcat
jumped in. "The Tauregs who visited here and who we got
to know were always poorly armed. They may have a few
old Russian Kalashnikov rifles, but not the automatic
weapons used against us today."

"Then it looks as if someone has armed them," Lieutenant Nolan added.

"You said you had M-sixteens. How much ammo do
you have? All we have is what we carried when we left to
come here."

"I can look, Sergeant. I don't think we have much . . .
never expected to fight a war out here. But, I know we
have a crate with loaded magazines in it."

"Good, Mr. Jordan. I need to know how much you've
got, and I'd like to check out any other boxes of ammo
you have." The magazines should be interchangeable with
their weapons, but Stapler would feel better if he checked
it personally. One box wasn't going to last them long if
they had to fight a couple of more battles like they just
did.

"No problem, Sergeant. We can do that."

Stapler watched the big man motion another oil rigger
toward him. Jordan walked toward the approaching rigger.

"Lieutenant, with your permission, I'll finish my survey of the area."

"Very well, Gunny."

Stapler turned on his heel and walked away from the
growing crowd. Ought to be somewhere a man can take a

leak. He hated crowds. He hated them even when they didn't make good targets. Stapler noticed that two of the riggers were women, or at least they had what looked like tits under those T-shirts. It was hard to tell with those masculine tattooed arms and short haircuts. The earrings helped. He heard one of them in a gruff voice tell the other, "Dot, quit worrying. It'll be all right." But he didn't turn to see who said it because right now it wasn't all right—not by a long shot.

Stapler advanced to where the Marines guarded the front of the compound, saying a few words of encouragement to each, and with professional competence, mentally counting the amount of ammo and weapons they had. He also mentally took muster.

Ten minutes later, when he finished, he had a good idea of what they had to fight with and who survived the attack. With him and the lieutenant, they had eleven Marines to get thirty-two civilians to safety. At least there would be thirty-two if the ten at Alpha were still alive. This was not going to be easy. He hoped the oil riggers lived up to their reputation of being brawlers. Better brawlers than a bunch of whining techno-nerds like he helped evacuate from the U.S. embassy in Senegal last year.

The compound provided an adequate defense against small arms. Old oil barrels, most of them empty, had been stacked one and two high around the perimeter. Whether done intentionally or not, the barrels formed a nice, man-made perimeter around the area. The prefabricated, three-room building braced against the low, rocky hill made him think of the movie *Fort Apache,* but in the movie, the buildings had been against the back fence of a wooden fort. Fort Apache wouldn't have survived a rocket-propelled grenade attack. This place wouldn't, either. Stapler could watch old Westerns nonstop when the opportunity presented itself. He preferred the movies with John Wayne or Randolph Scott in them—great Americans. It wasn't the movie *Fort Apache.* What movie was it?

Twelve feet away, Corporal Heights caught his attention as the young noncom stretched his legs to reposition himself behind a group of barrels. He'd recall the name of the movie eventually.

"Corporal Heights!"

"Yes, Gunny," the short, wiry Marine responded. The corporal pushed his helmet back so he could see Stapler better.

"Take one man and get up there on those rocks above the building! Make sure you watch your exposure. I don't want you shot. Do a quick look-see, and then one of you come back and tell me what you see."

Corporal Heights stood and jerked his thumb toward the burning helicopters. "What about them, Gunny?"

Stapler looked at the helicopters. The fires seemed as intense now as thirty minutes ago. "Not much we can do for them right now, Corporal. Let's think of the living, and we'll take care of the dead later. Now, get up there and assess our situation. I want to know if there are any places where those sneaky bastards can approach us without us seeing them." He slapped the young man on the shoulder. "Go! And, for Christ's sake, be careful."

Corporal Heights shouted, "Hank, let's move out!"

A tall, black Marine with a darker tattoo of the Marine Corps emblem on his right bicep grabbed his M-16 in a cross-arms position and ran after Heights. "Where we going, Corporal?" Jones asked with an inner-city accent that flowed in the river of a deep bass voice.

"Up there, Jonesy. We ain't good targets down here. We're going to draw the fire away from our fellow Marines."

"Oh, thanks, Dave. Just what I need. More white men shooting at me."

"Ah, Jonesy, how you know those were white men shooting at us? They looked black to me. Should make you feel at home. Besides, you know the only reason I'm taking you is because you're bigger than me and a better target."

"Gunny, what's the one eight hundred number for the NAACP out here?" Private Jones shouted good-naturedly as the two friends hurried to the back of the compound. "You know why I know they white men, Dave? Because I come from the dark side of Baltimore, and if they'd been black, they wouldn't have missed."

Stapler would have grinned if the situation were not so bad. Humor was how warriors hid their fear. He glanced around the compound, taking a quick assessment of his Marines. A couple were staring at the helicopters, but most focused their attention away from the conflagration and what it represented to each of them. He doubted the young lieutenant or his Marines had any appreciation of the precariousness of their situation. He was the only one with any combat experience, and that had been years ago in Liberia with two thousand other Marines to keep him company.

Two riggers walked by, mumbled a greeting, and continued toward the back of the compound. The civilians would be looking to the eleven of them to save them, and Stapler had no idea how they would do it. The lieutenant was barely old enough to shave and, with his platoon sergeant dead, that left Corporal Heights as his number two.

Corporal Heights had nearly three *whole* years in the Marines. *Damn! Wish I had taken her credit cards,* invaded Stapler's thoughts. It would be one less worry out here. At least his Servicemen's Group Life Insurance of $250,000 should cover whatever she runs up.

He walked past the end of the line and scanned the high dunes from where he thought the attack originated. The simmering air above the hot sands of the Sahara desert waved above the bodies lying motionless on the battlefield. He closed his eyes for a few seconds while he organized his thoughts, balancing what they had against what he thought they'd need. After five minutes, Stapler nodded a couple of times, satisfied with his assessment. He turned toward the three civilian white high mobility multipurpose wheeled vehicles, commonly called humvees. This was a piece of luck. Humvees he knew and, even if they were the civilian variant, they could endure the sands.

For a short moment, a vision of them fleeing across the Sahara, crowded inside these humvees, running for safety, terrified him. It vividly brought to him the odds against everyone here escaping with their lives. Stapler ran a hand under the lip of his helmet and wiped the sweat from his brow. The idea that they might have to drive out seemed far-fetched, but the Army CH-47s lacked the legs to both reach them and safely return to their base. Right now—*at this very moment*—an alternative option was staring him in the face—one that was not very appealing.

He rubbed the sand off the window and pressed his face against the glass. The interior looked clean. He ran a hand across the hood, bringing away a film of fine dust. The fourth vehicle, partially hidden behind two of the humvees, was a large ten-and-a-half-ton flatbed truck with a metal pylon fence surrounding the bed. Already his mind was weighing how they would convoy out, if the situation warranted them abandoning this stronghold. The truck would be where the bulk of their supplies and most of the evacuees and Marines would have to ride.

Stapler did a quick calculation in his head and realized they could not fit forty odd people in the four vehicles. He looked around and saw no one. He unzipped and peed on the back tire of the truck. Stapler sighed. A good pee always felt good. *"An empty bladder frees the mind, so never pass up an opportunity to drain the lizard."* A quote from the Emily Post battlefield etiquette espoused by Top Sergeant MacGregory. Combat is best fought with empty bowels and dry bladders, or you run the risk of them being empty and dry when the fighting stops.

Stapler looked over his shoulder as he walked around the side of the truck, causing him to nearly collide with one of the oil riggers coming the other way. Two inches separated Stapler from a rigger who leaned to the side, bracing an elbow against the back of the truck. *Weight lifter,* thought Stapler as he stepped back. White T-shirt with the sleeves rolled up with a precision match on both arms, stretched by the large biceps of the man. The man's rugged, sun-scorched face broke into a large grin, revealing polished white teeth.

"Oh, sorry," the oil rigger said, his German accent easily detectable. "I hope you feel better now." The man straightened and clasped his hands in front of him.

"Who are you?" Stapler asked, involuntarily taking another step backward.

"I am Heinrich Wilshaven, *mein klein* man. They are *mein* babies," he said, patting the side of the truck. "I take care of them and keep them running." Heinrich sighed, ran his hand under his cap and through thick blond hair that seemed to flop everywhere when freed. Heinrich shoved the hair back under his hat. Several seconds of awkward silence followed.

Heinrich propped his wrist on his hip. "I am good at keeping things running." He winked.

"Are they ready to go? Any problems with them?" Stapler asked, touching the truck.

"What is ready to go? Me?" Heinrich pointed at himself. "I am always ready to go, American soldier."

"Marine."

"Marine?"

"Yes, we are United States Marines, not Army."

Heinrich nodded. "You are one of those they call the Devil Dogs?"

"We've been called worse."

"Excellent. Marines are far superior to soldiers; don't you think?"

Stapler sighed. "The vehicles, Heinrich? Are the vehicles ready to go, if we need them?"

Heinrich nodded. "Yes, the vehicles are in excellent shape, even if, *mein Gott,* they are not German. I work on them every day. They have a full tank of petrol, and I change the oil every two weeks." He turned with a lopsided smile, the left lip coyly higher. "Wherever you want to go, they will take you there."

"Two weeks?" Leslie could not remember when he last changed the oil on their ten-year-old Ford Mustang.

"Of course. With this dust," Heinrich waved his hand

around the site, "you must change the oil regularly, or the engines get grit into them."

"Gunny!" came a shout from the lieutenant.

"Thanks, Heinrich. Get them ready to go in the event we need them."

"Of course, Marine, and if you need to use my truck again . . ." Heinrich winked. "Let me know. It helps keep the dust off the wheels."

Great, thought Stapler. *Just what I need. Enemy surrounding me, stranded in the desert, wife running amok with credit cards, and now a man twice my size daydreaming about my hips.*

Stapler walked to the end of the truck and waved at the lieutenant, who was walking around the center of the compound, searching for him. *And baby-sitting a brand-new officer. What more can God send me? More sand?*

Seeing the gunnery sergeant, Lieutenant Nolan hurried over.

"Gunny, we need to get those riggers at Alpha site over here. I just talked with Mr. Jordan, and he is concerned about leaving them out there any longer than we need to."

"Yes, sir, LT. But we need to wait until we secure our position. We also need to report our situation to Homeplate before we do anything else. And then we can see what we can do about those stranded at Alpha site."

Lieutenant Nolan pointed at the burning helicopters. "What are we going to do about them?"

Stapler shrugged his shoulders. He knew the lieutenant meant the dead Marines. "Not much we can do, LT. If we go out now, we expose ourselves to any snipers left behind. We'll have to wait for the fire to burn down. Probably tonight sometime. Then we'll recover the bodies. Until then, we live with the smell and the sight." Stapler tugged his ear. "LT, you know there are no rescue helicopters that I know of, which really complicates our problem of evacuation. It also means that if choppers can't get in here to rescue us, those bodies will have to be buried here."

Lieutenant Nolan stared for a moment and then said,

"Bearcat says they have a radio in the shack we can use to contact Base Butler and Homeplate."

Stapler nodded, wondering if the lieutenant heard what he had just said. Their only radioman and the radio was part of the funeral pyre in the troop compartment of the lead CH-53.

Stapler's eyes roamed the compound as they walked toward the office building. He marked the Marines' positions while surveying the surrounding desert landscape. They'd be back, he knew. He didn't know when, but he knew they would. Too many of the enemy and too few of them. A couple of the headdresses—called *ghutras*—worn by the dead attackers rolled across the blinding white sands, pushed by a brief but strong gust of desert wind. The shimmering hot air, radiating a couple of feet above the desert floor, gave the headdresses a fluid appearance as they danced across the sands. Just as suddenly as the wind whipped up, it disappeared, and the *ghutras* fell back onto the battlefield amid the dead bodies. If they didn't bury them tonight, the stench would be horrific by tomorrow morning. He looked up, half expecting to see buzzards or crows. Stapler shielded his eyes. Only the ever-present sun in a cloudless sky burned down. A sky marred by whiffs of dark, oily smoke boiling straight up for about fifty feet where a slight west wind caught it, spreading the smoke like rolling dark clouds as it disappeared out of sight toward the horizon.

Bearcat Jordan stood in the doorway, holding the screen door open for the two Marines. Worry lines, Stapler called them. Scrunched forehead, searching eyes that never seemed to focus, and a nervous twitch. Worry etched its lines across the supervisor's face. *Well, join the crowd, big man,* Stapler thought. *We should be more than just a little worried.* As he walked by, Stapler smelled whiskey on the man's breath. Oh, well, fear affected different people different ways. For him, he found he ate less, drank more water, and had no desire for alcohol and sex . . . though how one has sex on the battlefield was another story, one that MacGregory seemed to know by heart.

Stapler recalled the moment when they ran out of the helicopters. As the lead CH-53 exploded, everything seemed to shift into slow motion, like swimming in thick soup; too slow sometimes, exacerbating the fear gnawing at his stomach. Along with the other survivors of the ambush, he had made the oil barrel barrier, firing at the unseen enemy in the surrounding dunes. He had found himself surprised to be alive and unwounded. Miraculously, none of the other Marines who survived the attack suffered a wound. Either they had been extremely lucky, or those Algerians were notorious bad shots.

"Gunny," Lieutenant Nolan said, snapping Stapler back from his thoughts. The lieutenant flopped down in the chair in front of the console and tossed his helmet on the floor beside him. "That feels good," he said softly, wiping the sweat from his brow.

The squeak of the metal office chair as the lieutenant rocked back and forth made Stapler think of fingernails being dragged down a chalkboard. He shivered involuntarily and moved away.

Lieutenant Nolan spun the chair around to the communications suite and tuned through the frequencies as he fired up the radio. Another office chair lay on its back near a metal desk shoved against the far wall. Stapler figured Bearcat or one of the other riggers had knocked the chair over, diving for cover when the firefight broke out. Under the bullet-shattered window, a half-full coffeepot perked, the orange light still on. On the opposite side of the trailer where a calendar hung, Stapler noticed a rolled-up map. He moved to it, grabbed the small metal grip and pulled it down. It took a couple of tries before the map caught and stayed down. Behind him, the rise and fall of radio noise told him the lieutenant was still searching for the Homeplate frequency. He hoped the young officer remembered the frequency; he sure didn't.

Stapler looked at the map. He tugged his ear. Must be

a geological chart. It didn't look familiar to him, other than that he could tell it was Algeria.

Bearcat saw him looking at the chart. "This is where we are, Sergeant," the oil rigger offered, leaning forward and putting his finger where a red dot had been stuck on the map. "It's a hard chart to read unless you can imagine yourself five miles down. Look here—" he started.

"Where is Alpha site?" Stapler interrupted.

"It's too close to have two red dots, so we just use the one for both of us. Look here," Bearcat said, opening a drawer and pulling out a folded National Geographic map.

From outside, a large commotion interrupted the two men. Another attack was the first thought that crossed Stapler's mind, though he heard no gunfire. He grabbed his M-16 with both hands and burst through the door.

The lieutenant looked up. "What's going on, Gunny?"

Stapler shouted over his shoulder. "Don't know, sir, but I'm going to find out! You get through to Homeplate." Stapler shoved his helmet back on as he jumped down the steps.

A quick observation showed him no enemy in front of them. He stopped running and realized how bright the sun seemed after only a few minutes out of it. He put his sunglasses on.

Bearcat Jordan followed, folding the map and tucking it in his back pocket.

Across the compound, three Marines faced Sheila Forester and Karim Washington. From the hillside, Corporal Heights worked his way to the floor of the compound. Stapler watched the corporal for a couple of seconds and, satisfied the Marine wasn't going to fall and break his fool neck, he turned his attention to the commotion. He couldn't make out the words at this distance, but the tone told him they were arguing.

Stapler walked hurriedly to where the five stood. Voices rose and fell as the Marines argued with the woman until only the sound of Sheila's voice could be heard.

"What are you trying to do? Get yourselves shot?" Stapler asked as he drew near. Sheila stopped, turned, and faced Stapler.

The three Marines stepped back.

She spread her legs slightly and put her hands on her hips. "I am asking when we are going to get out of here. But, obviously, none of you know. Since you seem to be the leader of this bunch, then maybe you can answer the question, *which the whole world wants to know: When* are we getting out of here?"

"Please, Sheila," Karim said, reaching out to touch her on the shoulder.

She shrugged away from the man, narrowing her eyes as she glared at him. "Keep your hands off me, Abdullah."

Stapler remembered he had one of those Afro-American first names . . . then it came to him: Karim Washington. Her name, on the other hand, he remembered with no effort. Sheila Anne Forester. A man would have to be a eunuch not to notice her. Pert nipples shoved the white cotton shirt out slightly, stretching it so the darker areola surrounding each were easily discernible. She had tied the tail ends of her shirt into a knot just above her pierced navel, and the unbuttoned top two buttons revealed a wide cleavage. *No Sophia Loren,* he thought, *more a Jamie Lee Curtis.* He let an audible "Huh huh" escape, but no one noticed.

"But, they need some time to get—"

"Shut up, Karim. I do not need your patronizing. You're scared of anything that smacks of authority, even if it meant . . . if it meant you were going to die. Which we may, if we don't get out of here. You heard what the professor said about the Tauregs. And to think, I wouldn't be out here now, if my Daddy didn't think this was a character-enhancing trip and remember, Abdullah—"

"Don't call me Abdullah!" Karim interrupted angrily.

"—he funded the grant," she finished.

Stapler realized he was staring and turned to the Marines.

"What seems to be the problem?" he asked, ignoring Sheila and Karim.

"Gunny, this *woman* threw rocks at us. Called us a bunch of cowards," Private Sterling, one of the three Marines said. The other two Marines, Private Cathy "Catsup" Kellogg and Cowboy Joe-Boy Henry, stood slightly behind Sterling.

"They weren't rocks. They were pebbles, and all I was trying to do was to get them to stand up and fight."

"Let me show you, lady, what the difference is between a pebble and a rock," Catsup offered, stepping forward. Sterling put his arm out and stopped her.

"Leave her be, Catsup," Sterling said to her. "She's a civilian."

"You know it only takes three muscles to smile, girl," Sheila sneered.

"And you know it only takes eight for me to make a fist and beat the shit out of you," Catsup retorted, stepping forward, handing her M-16 to Cowboy who, not expecting the nine-pound weapon, nearly dropped it.

"Can it, Catsup," Stapler ordered.

"She's a bitch is what she is," Catsup Kellogg said. Catsup was the only one of the two female Marines to survive the crash. Cathy was her real name, but everyone called her Catsup because she was the slowest runner in the squad and always having to *catch up* with them. She was a private with nearly eighteen months in the Marine Corps. She was a tough nut for one so young.

Stapler felt his face growing red. "Okay, that's enough." His face turned red when he got angry. The Marines knew it, and he saw them step back. He took a couple of deep breaths to cage the anger before he faced the young lady. Early twenties, he figured. Designer shorts and a Hilfiger label on her white, short-sleeved shirt. Timberland boots with pink socks and sun-bleached blond hair that obviously had taken a lot of time spent for a *just-right* ponytail arrangement. The sweat stains under her arms caused the shirt to be transparent there, also. Where did she find the time to shave? The gleam on her face told him she had sunscreen tucked away somewhere.

No wonder his Marines were distracted; even he was.

"Ma'am, these Marines work for me. They do what I tell them to do. Do not throw rocks at them. Do you understand?"

Sheila Forester took a couple of steps back, bumping into a smiling Karim. She jerked away.

"And just what is it you'll do if I don't?" she asked petulantly.

"Madam, do not throw rocks at my Marines." He pointed toward the helicopters. "Out there, they have just lost some of their fellow Marines in a battle. They are uptight and trigger-happy, which means if you should throw a rock at the wrong time, they may—accidentally, of course—shoot you. Personally, I would hate for that to happen. A lot of paperwork is involved when we accidentally shoot a civilian—not to mention the inevitable letter from some Congressman. Plus, if they should kill you, then they'll have to bury you, and that's a hell of a lot of work for tired Marines. So, please, we are working as hard as we can to arrange a backup rescue. It will take time, and during that time, you can help us by staying out of our way."

"Yeah, that could happen, Gunny. I know I am sure uptight right now and can't seem to keep my finger off the trigger of my gun," Private Sterling added.

Stapler glanced and saw that Sterling had his gun across his chest, its barrel pointing upward.

"They wouldn't dare shoot me! *You are telling him to shoot me.* Wait until I get back home. I'll have your nuts for garters! Karim, you hear that? He wants another of your kind to shoot me."

"Sheila, you're making this hard on them and us. You're making yourself look foolish. He didn't say they were going to shoot you. He said that they are so uptight right now that they could accidentally shoot you."

"Oh, shut up!" She stepped forward toward Stapler, cutting her eyes toward Sterling, who stared unabashedly at her face, trying to look mean with his eyes deliberately wide above pulsating nostrils. Sterling shifted his M-16 slightly. The movement was not lost on Sheila Anne

Forester. Sterling looked as if he was waiting for any opportunity to use his weapon. Stapler knew better.

Sheila's lips curled in disgust, her blue eyes disappearing as she narrowed them beneath scrunched brows. She stepped back. "You wouldn't dare! I'd have you in a court of law and in jail within a day."

"I am really feeling uptight, Gunny. Is this how they said it would be just before you go off your rocker? Your fingers twitch. Your mind wanders from one fantasy to another . . . all of them involving killing something or someone."

"I know you're scared, miss. We all are to a certain extent. But screaming and hollering at us isn't going to get us out of here any quicker. Look around you. We're all in the same boat. We have a lot of things we need to do right now, and I would consider it a personal favor if you would leave my Marines alone while we do them. When we know how we are going to get out of here, I will ensure you are one of the first to know. Until then, would you mind directing your questions to me or the lieutenant? Okay?"

She looked around and started to say something, thought better of it, and stayed silent but angry. She stamped her foot. "Oh, screw it! You don't understand!"

She turned and stomped off toward a tent Stapler had failed to notice earlier. The tent had been set up under a small ledge that stuck out near the left side of the office.

After a few steps, Sheila stopped and looked over her shoulder. "Hey, bitch!" she shouted at Private Kellogg. "It only takes four for me to flick you off." She raised her middle finger at Catsup before resuming her angry steps toward the tent.

Catsup jumped forward, only to have Sterling and Joe-Boy grab her by the arms. "Let me go! Let me go! Just give me ten seconds with the bitch!"

The two M-16s slung across his shoulders bounced back and forth against Joe-Boy's head. "Damn, Catsup! You're hurting me."

"Ignore her, Catsup," Stapler cautioned in a low voice,

shaking his head. "The same goes for the rest of you. She's a frightened young lady, and probably once she calms down, she'll regret this incident." Stapler didn't believe a word he said, and he knew they knew it.

The two Marines released Catsup, who took her M-16 back from Joe-Boy.

"Guess I better not shoot her right now," Sterling said, a hint of humor in his low voice.

"You're a sick man, Private Sterling, but I think we got our word across," Stapler said, continuing to watch the two civilians as they headed toward the tent. *Now, why didn't he notice that tent earlier?*

"Let me," Catsup muttered.

Karim trotted to catch up with *Sheila Anne Forester. Why is he her shadow?* Stapler asked himself. He hoped the young black man could keep her out of trouble and off their backs. About halfway to the tent, he saw Karim reach out and grab Sheila by the arm. Whatever the young woman said to him as she shook off the man's hand caused Karim to touch his chest as if he had been accused of something.

"Guess not, Private Sterling."

Stapler turned and faced the three Marines. "You three get back to your positions, and don't leave them for a bunch of small rocks. I'd rather have you fire a few rounds over her head than leave your positions and give someone a chance to blow your head off. Understand?"

"Thanks, Gunny. That is definitely something I would like," Catsup Kellogg said, laughing.

"Catsup, get back to your position."

Sterling hung back as the other two left.

"Good work, Gunny," the Marine said. "Most would have lost their cool and joined the argument."

"Thanks, but you did your part, too, Sterling." Sterling was part enigma and part stability. Older—about twenty-eight—than the rest of the squad members, Stapler had developed an affinity for the junior Marine. Even so, Sterling remained a mystery. The few times Stapler tried to dig some additional background out of the older private, searching for things not normally found in a service record, he discovered Sterling was never evasive, but neither did the he volunteer anything about himself. Sterling had not been in the squad long before other members treated the older private like a father figure or an older brother. When they hit the town or the club, Sterling usually hit the library or curled up with a good book. In Jamaica, the man disappeared only to resurface later with a sack full of museum literature and several books on Jamaican history. Sterling never seemed to receive letters, nor could Stapler remember ever seeing the Marine write one. But the Marines were America's equivalent to France's Foreign Legion. Some joined to disappear. Maybe Sterling was one of those.

Sterling smiled and departed, heading toward the three barrels he had grouped together for his makeshift barrier.

The slight wind changed, carrying Sheila's words ". . . one time. A fluke. It will not happen again. So, you . . ." And the wind shifted again.

"Gunny," shouted Lieutenant Nolan from the door leading inside the office.

Stapler glanced at the soap opera near the tent, watching the young man stare after the hot-tempered woman as she stormed the last few feet toward the tent. Her tight cheeks moved the sides of her shorts up and down like a well-oiled set of pistons. "Damn," he muttered, breaking his stare and looking to see if anyone had noticed.

Bearcat slapped Stapler on the shoulder. "She affects everyone who first sees her like that, Sergeant. A nice eyeball orgy, but the baggage of her personality brings it more into the right perspective. Reminds me of a black widow. Look what she's done to that young black stud."

Corporal Heights ran up. "Gunny," he started, his breaths coming in short, quick gasps.

"Gunny!" shouted the LT louder, motioning Stapler toward the building.

"Come on, Corporal, walk with me as you catch your breath. Then you can brief me."

The three strolled toward the office building. A wall of

smoke whiffed down and through the compound for a moment, engulfing the two men. They emerged on the other side, wiping the tears from their eyes.

"Stuff really burns."

"Yeah," Stapler replied. "What you got?"

"Not a thing, Gunny, for two to five miles in all directions. There is nothing out there. There should be, but neither Jones nor I see anything." Heights pointed past the burning helicopters. "There are two hills that way about a half mile. They're covered in rocks. I think that is where our attackers fired on the choppers. Wouldn't surprise me if some are hiding in there, watching us, waiting to see what we're going to do."

Stapler pulled his binoculars out of the leather satchel and scanned the area where Heights pointed.

"You see the rocks, Gunny?"

"I think I do, Corporal. You could be right. Keep an eye on them. Regardless of what we think, we're being watched. I think when we landed, we surprised them. They weren't expecting us, and we weren't expecting them, so most likely they've gone back to decide what to do now. Let's hope they decide to leave us alone. "

Stapler put away the binoculars.

"The only other thing we saw was a road on the other side of the hill leading through the cliffs. Looks as if it has been used recently."

The two reached the door to the office.

"Gunny, get in here," the LT said, shutting the door and hurrying back inside the main office area.

"Corporal Heights, I'll be with the lieutenant, helping him contact Base Butler. You get with the oil riggers and outfit them with the weapons they have here. Get a count on the ammo available. Detail two from the perimeter to get water and food for the men. I want each Marine to drink a liter of water right away. It's too hot to stay out here. Stagger fifteen-minute breaks for each of them. After everyone has had a break, initiate a two-hour rotating watch. Keep the troops busy. Keep their minds occupied. We are going to have to stay here until rescue comes.

Tonight, I am going to take a couple of Marines and go bring Alpha base back—if they're still alive."

"Will do, Gunny," Heights replied, raising his hand to salute before remembering this was a gunnery sergeant.

As Heights turned to leave, Stapler reached out and touched Heights on the shoulder. "Corporal Heights."

"Yes, Gunny?"

Stapler removed his hand. "You're number two, now. There's the LT, me, and then there is you."

Heights nodded. "I know, Gunny," he said somberly and then ran off to take charge of the perimeter.

Good Marine, thought Stapler. *Take care of the men and women under you first, and they'll take care of you.* He knew the thoughts of every Marine here were haunted by the faces of their dead comrades out there. Those emotional thoughts would haunt them even after they recovered the bodies and buried them. To do it before dark would endanger those still alive. Before he departed for Alpha site, they would recover the bodies.

Stapler opened the door and entered. The lieutenant was rising from the console.

"What happened?"

Nolan shook his head. "Gunny, we got a problem. I mean a big one. The Army says we are three hundred fifty to five hundred miles too far for them to send in their Chinooks. They don't even have this site on their charts. And they don't even have their CH-47s yet. The helicopters aren't scheduled to arrive for another two days." He paused and then, in a disbelieving voice, continued, "Gunny, they want us to move closer."

Stapler nodded. From the corner of his eye, he saw Bearcat move. The man bent over the desk to reach across the top and pull a drawer out. He removed a pint bottle of Jim Beam whiskey. Bearcat didn't try to hide the tilt of the bottle as he took a deep swig.

"Well," Bearcat said. "Looks like we may have to drive out." He coughed twice and took a another swig.

"Drive out?" Lieutenant Nolan asked.

"Yeah, drive out. It won't be the first time we've driven

out of here. About a hundred miles southwest of here is a small oasis. We have enough provisions to get to it and, once there, we can replenish our water supply. We'll have to be careful about the gasoline. Humvees get about twelve miles to the gallon, and that old beat-up Volvo truck of ours is about the same. We have two. This one and a flatbed at Alpha site. Speaking of Alpha site, Lieutenant, what are we going to do about my men stuck out there?"

Lieutenant Nolan looked at Stapler. "Gunny?"

"I'll have to go to Alpha site tonight, sir, and bring them in," said Stapler. "Do you have a rigger who can show us the way?" he asked Bearcat. Then, before the oil rigger supervisor could answer, Stapler added, "Before we go, Mr. Jordan, have you established contact with them to make sure they are still—" He nearly said "alive." "All right?"

"Yeah, I did that before you and the lieutenant called your people. They have not been attacked and haven't seen any signs of anyone near them. But if we wait until tonight, they could be overrun by then."

Stapler reached up and tugged his left earlobe. After several seconds, he dropped his hand. He saw the two men staring at him. He had to stop that habit. Stapler cleared his throat and said, "There is always that possibility, but if we go now and they are watching, I doubt we'd make it back. Let us hope they don't know about them being stranded out there. If we do it at night, then we stand a chance of avoiding contact with them. I recommend you give them another call and tell them to keep down and out of sight until we get there."

"Okay, Sergeant, I'll do that." Bearcat screwed the cap back on, started to put the bottle in the desk drawer, but stopped. "I better keep this with me," he said and slipped the half-full bottle into his back pocket. "Never can tell when someone might get wounded and need a nip."

"They have any arms at Alpha site?"

"A couple of pistols are about all, Gunny. One or two of them may have one of the company's M-sixteens. We really don't check on who is carrying weapons and who isn't out here."

Stapler grunted and turned to Lieutenant Nolan.

"Lieutenant, we have an observation position on the hill behind us. Jonesy is manning it. Corporal Heights is taking care of the men, rotating them through a stand-down long enough for water." He looked at the rig supervisor. "Mr. Jordan, I have asked the corporal to break open your weapons and issue them out to your men and women. If you can help him with that, I would appreciate it. You have a better idea who would be the best to have the weapons, since we may not have enough for everyone. It would help if we had the status of water and food on hand. We don't know yet how long we're going to be here before they send more helicopters."

Bearcat pulled out a small notebook from one of his shirt pockets and as Stapler talked, he made notes. Finished, he flipped it shut and tucked it back in his pocket.

"We can do that, Sergeant," Bearcat acknowledged. His eyebrows bunched together forming a V as he talked. "We're in a pretty tight mess, aren't we?"

Stapler nodded. "Yeah, we are, Mr. Jordan. We surely are."

"Thanks for being honest. It will take a couple of hours to get this information together. Let me know if you think of anything else. We are more than just a rough bunch of riggers. Got a lot of talent for such a small group, and we're close knit—have to be to live out this far from civilization. So, whatever you need, you let me know."

"Thanks, Mr. Jordan," Stapler replied. He motioned the lieutenant to one side.

Bearcat nodded a couple of times before he motioned to the nearby riggers to come outside with him. They stopped on the small porch outside the slightly opened door.

Stapler waited until Bearcat was talking to his people before speaking to Lieutenant Nolan. "The Army is right. We may have to shift closer to Mauritania so they can reach us. I recommend, LT, that while I am at Alpha site, you see how long it would take to get those vehicles out there loaded—just in the event we need them."

The lieutenant bit his lower lip, took off his helmet, and ran his hand through his hair. "So, you don't think we can stay here until help arrives? It looks to me, Gunny, we have everything we need. We got water, food, and plenty of ammunition. We may be able to hold out."

"Then, again, Lieutenant, we may not be able to hold out. If they return with that rocket-propelled grenade launcher and more men, we're going to be up the proverbial shit creek. Especially if they're willing to lose the number they lost today."

"Okay, Gunny. You're probably right."

"I hope not, Lieutenant. All I am recommending is that we be prepared to use the vehicles if we have to. Otherwise, we should remain right where we are until help arrives."

"Who do you think attacked us?"

"Most likely members of the Algerian Liberation Front. It's the same bunch who attacked the evacuation convoy two weeks ago in Algiers and who still hold about fifty American hostages."

"What would they be doing out here in the middle of the Sahara?"

Stapler pulled another cigarette out, looked at the lieutenant, and raised his eyebrows.

Lieutenant Nolan nodded as Stapler lit the cigarette.

"Americans."

"Americans?"

"Sure. They probably came here for the Americans, and we surprised them as much as they surprised us, coming over the hill in those helicopters like we did." Stapler turned and looked out the window at the burning helicopters and thought briefly of the Marines who never made it out of them. "No, sir. It won't take them long to figure out there are no other helicopters coming, and they have us trapped here."

"What then, Gunny?" Lieutenant Nolan asked, moving

up beside the taller man to where he could see Stapler's face beneath the shade of the helmet.

"Then, Lieutenant, they're going to come for us." The image in the movie where the Indians scaled the wall and fought the soldiers hand-to-hand flittered through his thoughts.

The screen door opened, and Bearcat Jordan and Professor Walthers entered. Bearcat pulled the chair back from the radio suite and sat down. Quickly, he had the frequencies changed and was calling Alpha site.

Professor Walthers stopped and spoke to Lieutenant Nolan and Stapler. "I couldn't help but overhear what you said, Gunny Sergeant. You are right. Never count on being rescued in the Sahara. A great French general in the 1900s—believe his name was Lyantey—said, '*In Africa, one defends oneself by moving,*' and at the time he was referring to the Sahara desert. Moving is what we need to do. The Tauregs will not allow us to remain untouched long. Most of those bodies out there are Taureg Bedouins. They'll be back. Maybe not today or tonight, maybe not tomorrow, but once they realize help isn't coming, they'll be back. This is their land; their country, and to them, we are just one more in a long line of invaders."

"Professor, do you think any of them are out there now?" Lieutenant Nolan asked.

"Past experiences by others with the Tauregs—at least, those who lived to tell about it—have shown they remain nearby. Oh, yes, they are out there. They are out there keeping tabs on us."

Bearcat Jordan pulled the chair back. "I've talked with Charlie. They're hunkered down until you get there, Sergeant. As for what the professor is saying, I think that settles it, Lieutenant, Sergeant. By the time you return, Gunny, I'll have a complete inventory of the food and water available."

"Water is more important than food," Stapler added. "We may have to ration if we're going to be here long or if we need to make a run for it. If it's edible and drinkable, take it."

Bearcat patted his stomach. "Wouldn't do me a bit of harm to lose a few pounds." He chuckled.

"LT, I'm going to have the fire teams start breaking down and cleaning their weapons. One or two at a time. Don't want clogged weapons, and with all this dust floating around out here, it is only a matter of time before it penetrates the mechanisms in our pieces."

"Don't we run a risk doing that, Gunny?"

"It's a slight one, sir. We'll have them alternate. One doing it while two others wait. Corporal Heights reports no signs of anyone out there. If there are any snipers, they aren't firing, and if there are any observers, then maybe we can make them move so that the observation lookout can spot them. This will keep them busy."

Stapler looked out the shattered window at the burning helicopters and nodded in that direction. "Eventually, we are going to have to send out a recon team to find out what we have against us."

Lieutenant Nolan appeared to think about it a couple of minutes before answering. "Okay, Gunny, but make sure they know to take no chances, and if it begins to look like they've run into more than they can handle, they need to get back here as fast as possible."

"You won't find anything out there, Lieutenant, Gunny Sergeant. The Tauregs are the true desert people," Professor Walthers mused. "They know this land like you and I know the back of our hands. What you are going to find is nothing. They're out there, but you're not going to see them."

"Thanks, Professor. We appreciate your observations, and please feel free to keep offering them. We still have to do what we have to do. Having you will give us insight into the enemy," Lieutenant Nolan replied.

"When will you leave for Alpha site, Gunny?"

"As soon as the sun drops over the horizon, Mr. Jordan."

"I'll send Peter Karinsky with you. Pete knows the area well and has been here longer than most of us. I'll feel better once I have all the riggers here. Alpha site is nothing but a small trailer with a few amenities for those stuck out there. Not like the Hilton here," Bearcat said, smiling.

This compound was anything but luxurious. Stapler presumed the rooms in the back of the trailer led off to sleeping accommodations, and from the size of the place, those bunks must be shoved right on top of each other. The Marine Corps' open-bay barracks at Henderson Hall in Arlington had better facilities.

Stapler found himself and the lieutenant standing alone as the others moved off. The professor stood near the door a few seconds, looking out, before he pushed it open and stepped into the late-afternoon sun.

"Gunny," Nolan said in a soft voice, "don't you think you're being tough on the Marines? They've been through a lot in the past two hours. . . ."

Stapler nodded and tugged his earlobe a couple of times. "You're right, Lieutenant. I am and they have. And, unless we want their minds to start dwelling on how near they came to dying and on their fellow Marines, whose bodies are still out there, some still inside the burning fifty-threes, we need to keep them busy. I want their minds focused on survival, not death."

Nolan took his helmet off and laid it on the table. He opened his mouth to say something, stopped, nodded twice, and said, "Carry on, Gunny. I think you're right."

"Lieutenant, we are going to have to talk with Home-plate and Base Butler. They need to understand the precarious nature of our situation and work out some rescue ideas." He doubted the LT understood the full impact of their situation. "Though we've been talking about how we would move out if we had to, the best thing to do is remain right where we are until rescue arrives."

Bearcat Jordan thanked a rigger who had entered while the two were talking. As the rigger left the building, Bearcat strolled to where the two stood. "Heinrich is busy on the vehicles. Steve, our cook and supply person, is preparing a ready provisions inventory. Is there anything else we can do?"

Lieutenant Nolan looked at Stapler, who shook his

head. "No, sir, we are doing everything we can right now."

"Thanks, Mr. Jordan," Lieutenant Nolan said. "I want you to know that we will get every one of us out of here. That's what we came to do, and that is just what we will do."

"I hope so. I truly do, Lieutenant. I'd hate for us to discover firsthand if the stories are true about what the Tauregs do to captives who fall into their hands."

"No, Mr. Jordan, and neither do we."

What do they do to their captives? Stapler wondered, but he kept the question to himself. There are some things that you just don't want to know.

"Thanks, Mr. Jordan, and you could help us if you would speak to the professor and ask him to keep his young lady assistant away from my Marines," Stapler added.

He nodded. "I truly understand, Gunny Sergeant. But it won't do any good. I think you'll find neither me nor the professor have much influence on her. Miss Forester is truly a woman of her own."

"I could probably use one word to sum her up," Stapler said, tossing his cigarette through the broken window.

Bearcat turned to Stapler as he turned toward the door and stuck his hand out. "Gunny Sergeant, sorry about how we met. I usually don't fly off the handle like that. You Marines landed at the same time as they launched their attack. I bet you surprised the Tauregs as much as they surprised us."

Stapler shook the offered hand. "There's been too many surprises today."

"Yeah, you're right," Bearcat Jordan said. He shook his head a couple of times as he hurried out of the office, leaving the two Marines alone.

"What now, Gunny?"

"I'll go prepare for tonight's trip to Alpha base." He picked up the lieutenant's helmet from the table and handed it to the young officer. "You're doing good, sir. Keep telling yourself, 'We're going to be all right.' Two reasons: One, it's true; two, we want it to be true; and three, our Marines are looking to us to make it true."

"That's three, Gunny, not two."

"The Marines never said I had to know how to count."

CHAPTER 2

⚓

STAPLER SPAT THE DUST FROM HIS MOUTH just as the humvee bounced over a crest in the road, causing him to bite his tongue. God, he hated this place, and he had been here less than twenty-four hours. He had sand in his hair, sand in his boots, sand inside his shirt, and even sand rubbing in his crotch. He reached inside the humvee and tugged the crotch of the pants down, trying to ease some of the discomfort. He rode standing in the center of the humvee, with his upper torso stuck out of the sunroof. He heard the voices of the riggers inside, but the noise outside of the humvee blurred their conversation.

Before the vehicle headed back down the other side, Stapler saw the shadowy outline of the compound on the other side of the hill. That quick glimpse, at least, looked beautiful after ten kilometers of dust, potholes, and losing the road twice. Safety lay ahead. Starlight shone through the clear sky of the Sahara, providing sufficient light reflecting off the white sands to guide them. The moon would have been better, but it had set an hour after the sun disappeared over the horizon. Unfortunately, the road blended too well with the desert. The outline of the destroyed helicopters had been easily discernible against the sand for a brief moment before the convoy disappeared around the ridge and lost sight of the compound. Stapler did a quick estimate of the distance.

He pulled himself down from the sunroof. "Another couple of miles, and we should be inside the compound," he broadcast into the short-range radio each of the Marines carried. Called a *brick,* the radios allowed them to communicate within a couple of miles. The line-of-sight VHF/UHF radios also served as rescue devices when needed, aircraft being able to pick them up at a much farther range.

"These next couple of miles are not the best, Gunny Sergeant," said Charlie Grant, supervisor of Alpha site, after Stapler had received an acknowledgment from Lieutenant Nolan at the compound and was tucking his brick back in its belt case. "Lots of potholes and drop-offs before we get to the bottom. Never know where they are; they shift all the time. We won't have the light we have now once we enter the ravine down there. This slow, downward drive ends at the base of some small hills that separate this side from where the compound is located. It's a narrow passage through them. Normally, I would never drive in the Sahara at night. Don't much like doing it during the day. One thing you learn early in the desert is to watch the winds. They can whip up without warning, shifting the sands continuously. One moment you know exactly where you are, and the next . . ." He snapped his fingers. ". . . the whole scene changes, and you're lost. We are lucky tonight with the wind. It seems to be asleep—like I wish I was." The Alpha site supervisor pressed his face against the window. "I will feel better once we are inside the compound."

"Ah, Charlie, I know this road like the back of me hand," said Darren Neil, the driver.

"Darren, you're Irish. You think you know everything like the back of your hand."

The humvee hit a hole in the road, tossing everyone up. Stapler bumped his head on the roof.

"See, my fine fellow of a man. I even knew that hole was there."

Stapler figured it was safer with his body outside the humvee. He stuck his head out the sunroof and looked behind him. The other vehicle, an old Volvo flatbed truck similar to the one in the compound, bounced into the same hole. Both vehicles were driving with their lights out. He lifted his hand and waved. From over the top of the cab, Private Garfield waved back. Stapler had taken three Marines with him for the trip to Alpha site and one rigger to show them the way. Alpha site had two vehicles, one of which was this Volvo flatbed and the other, a small extended-cab Ford pickup. Stapler had nixed the idea of bringing the pickup. The gas required to drive it was more than the benefit they would get by using it. He had ripped the distributor cap off and stomped it until it broke so the enemy couldn't use the pickup.

He felt a tug on his pants leg and peered back inside.

"Gunny Sergeant," said Charlie. "Up ahead we have to go through a small, deep gap several hundred yards long before we come out on the other side."

"Thanks," Stapler replied and stuck his head back out. He pulled his M-16 up beside him and thought about switching the safety off when they hit another series of holes, knocking him around the sunroof and nearly throwing him back into the interior of the humvee. He moved his finger off the safety. It would only take a fraction of a second for him to switch to full automatic.

The blast blew the front of the humvee about six feet into the air before what was left of the front end slammed down into the crater. It hurled Stapler against the side of the sunroof, nearly causing him to drop his M-16, even as it knocked the breath from him. Sand, dust, and cursing filled the air.

Stapler pulled himself out through the top. "Get out and find cover!"

He rolled down the slanted top to the rear of the damaged vehicle and dropped flat on the ground. No gunfire. Maybe a mine. Even so, it would only be minutes before the enemy showed if they heard the explosion. They couldn't stay here long. Reload and move out.

"Be careful!" he shouted. "The road is mined!"

"Well, you can have it, me fine friend, if it's going to keep blowing up like that," Darren said from the side of the road where the wiry Irishman had braced himself with his back against the rock wall. Darren looked both ways before quickly leaning forward to push the door shut.

Private Garfield rolled off the side of the flatbed and ran to Stapler, throwing himself down beside the Gunny Sergeant. "You all right, Gunny?"

"Yeah, I'm okay. You?" he asked. Stapler grabbed the back bumper and pushed himself up. The pain from his rib nearly caused him to pass out. He let himself back down gradually.

"Yeah, I'm fine, but are you sure you are, Gunny?"

"Garfield, if I say I am all right, then by God, I am all right," Stapler replied through clenched teeth.

"Well, since you are all right, Gunny, what in the hell do you want me to do?"

"The humvee is blocking the road, Garfield, and there is no way we can drive around it with the high banks on each side." Stapler grabbed the back bumper of the humvee and pulled himself up, grimacing from the pain. It was not the first time he had cracked a rib. If the Marines had a dollar for every time one of them broke a rib in their line of work, the American treasury would be broke. He stood and straightened.

Stapler noticed that those on the flatbed had abandoned it. The riggers pulled themselves up from the sides of the road when they saw Stapler stand.

"What now, Gunny Sergeant?" asked Charlie.

"Anyone hurt?"

"No, just Darren's feelings."

"It was such a beautiful angel, this humvee," said Darren softly. He stayed with his back pressed against the rock wall.

"We're going to have to walk the last mile and a half. Grab your gear from inside, and be sure to bring the water. Garfield, same for your bunch. Then you and Jones take point about fifty yards in front. If you see anything, don't be brave and engage, come back and get me. You understand?"

"Yeah, Gunny," Private Garfield replied and turned to go. "I am sure glad you are all right."

"Stow it, Garfield, you can kiss me later."

"Sure thing, Gunny," Private Garfield said. He hurried back to the truck.

"Gunny, we aren't that far from the compound. We really don't need to take the water and food. We have plenty there," Charlie added.

"We'll take the water, Mr. Grant. A mile and a half can be a long march if we are pinned down or attacked. I'd feel better if we had water along with us."

"I think if they were going to attack, they would have by now, don't you?"

"We've been traveling with our lights out. It is possible they didn't know we were out here. This explosion tells them something different, and most likely, someone is either watching us now or on their way to find out what their mine got. The sooner we get out of here, the better. Don't forget your pieces . . . guns, sir."

Charlie Grant pulled his hat down. The temperature drops rapidly in the desert after dark. He tugged his sleeves down and buttoned them, sliding his Rolex watch up the right wrist and beneath the sleeve. Charlie was thirty-two years old last month and had been working with Loffland Brothers for the past ten. Before coming to Algeria six months ago, he had been rig boss in the middle of the Persian Gulf off Abu Dhabi. A lifelong bachelor, Charlie spent his money on a beach house in Virginia Beach, a nephew and niece who worshipped their wild uncle, and once a year for two weeks of debauchery in Thailand.

"Darren, you and Boot get inside and start handing out the guns, water, food, and anything else we can carry.

Anything left will disappear," Charlie said, referring to the Taureg natives.

"Sure thing, Boss. Come on, me little darling," Darren said to a shorter and older man of about fifty who stood beside him.

The darkness hid the leathery wrinkles of the man's face caused by years of smoking and working in the sun. His face was what gave the American-Greek from New York, Buford Panalopelous, the nickname Boot.

"I ain't yore darling," Boot said, jerking his shoulder away from the laughing Irishman's grasp.

Stapler watched as Darren wrenched open one of the doors and the two of them started to empty the insides.

Garfield and Jones ran up to him. "Gunny, we're ready. I put Raoul out about twenty feet to the rear."

Raoul Gonzales was the third Marine Stapler brought with him. "Good thinking, Garfield. Now, listen to me. We are going to have to walk the last mile and a half. That means keeping your eyes and ears open. You two keep quiet, and no bullshitting as you go. Do not, I repeat, do not walk in the middle of the road. Keep to the sides, but keep your eyes open. I don't think they have enough mines to heavily mine the road. If they had, we would have been blown up long ago. What I want you to do is to make sure we don't stumble into an ambush. That means you need to hear or see them before they hear or see you. I don't know how you're going to do that while walking down the road, but the supervisor here, Mr. Grant, tells me this gully only runs for another few hundred yards. That's less than a quarter of a mile. Once out and on open ground, we should be able to see the compound. Any questions?"

"What do you want us to do if we come under fire, Gunny?" Private Jones asked.

Stapler looked at the tall black man from Baltimore. Jones had been given a choice, so rumor had it, to either join the military or face assault charges. Stapler was outraged when he first heard this, until he discovered what the assault charges were. Jones had nearly killed a drug dealer who dealt a bad dose of crack to his younger sister. Stapler admired the man for not killing the dealer; he would have.

"Jones, I would recommend returning fire. I think that will tell me what has happened, don't you?" Stapler asked. He reached up gingerly and rubbed his side. *Right there,* he said to himself, as his fingers caressed a small bump on the side. *Right there is where the rib is cracked.*

"Ah, all right, Gunny."

"Come on, Jonesy," Garfield said. "Can't you tell the Gunny's hurt?"

"Gunny Sergeants don't get hurt, Garfield," Stapler said.

"Sorry, Gunny. I forgot. *You are all right.*"

"And, don't forget it."

"We're off, Gunny."

"Okay, we're behind you in five minutes." He looked at his watch. "It's five minutes past midnight. At thirty minutes after, you wait for us to catch up. Good luck, men."

"You, too, Gunny," said Jones.

He watched the two walk off into the dark. A minute later, they disappeared around a bend in the road, Garfield on the left side of the narrow track while Jones took the right. Stapler didn't know too much about Garfield other than the boy had been some sort of high school football star in some small city in Indiana or Ohio. He could not remember which. He just recalled overhearing him talking one night aboard the USS *Kearsarge* about playing quarterback. Stapler's luck with football had been limited to the odd win on the bets he always placed on the Washington Redskins or anyone else playing Dallas.

"We're ready," Charlie Grant said.

"Have you got everyone?"

"All ten of us, including those on the flatbed."

"Okay, let me grab my man from the rear, and we'll head out. Mr. Grant, make sure your people know to walk along the sides of the road. This mine was in a rut made by wheels of the vehicles. Hopefully, if there are any other mines, that is where they will be planted."

Gunfire erupted from the rear, sending the men diving for cover. Stapler, at a crouch, ran toward the sound, slipping off his safety. The gunfire was where Private Raoul Gonzales had taken position. Stapler recognized the semiautomatic fire of a M-16: three shots max, then followed by three more. Marines never wasted ammunition. You never knew when the Navy would deem it feasible and safe enough to resupply you. Gonzales was still alive.

"Mr. Grant, get your people moving! Now!" Stapler shouted. He moved hurriedly in a crouch by the end of the flatbed. "Keep an eye to the rear, and don't shoot the first two people you see coming after you. Hopefully, that will be me and Private Gonzales!"

"Okay, color us gone. Come on, guys, let's get the hell out of here. And stay to the sides of the road."

Stapler scrambled around the rear of the Volvo truck, keeping as close as possible to the right bank. He glanced behind him and saw the riggers disappear around the bend where Garfield and Jones had departed five minutes ago.

He inched forward. A renewed round of fire caused him to crouch. He heard the three-shot volley from the M-16 reply, drawing his attention to the outline of Gonzales, pressed against the left bank of the road. Gonzales was about fifty feet ahead.

"Gonzales! It's me, don't shoot!"

"I see you, Gunny!"

Several shots hit the bank over Stapler's head, sending dirt and sand cascading down onto him. Just what he needed. More sand inside his clothes. He ducked instinctively and whipped off a semiautomatic three-shot burst in the direction he thought the rounds originated.

"Gonzales, move back toward me. I'll provide covering fire. Stay to the side and away from the center of the road. Whatever you do, don't step in the ruts."

"Gunny, are you crazy? I ain't got no intention of getting in the center of that road, and if I hug this bank any closer I'm going to be inside it."

"Now!" Stapler shouted.

The Marine jumped up and dashed to the rear, weaving in his run to throw off the aim. Stapler opened fire along the ridge overhead, hoping the gunfire would keep the attackers' heads down to give Gonzales time to reach the front of the flatbed.

About twelve inches above the running Marine's head, a tattoo of bullets laced the bank, missing the Marine but urging Gonzales on to greater speed. Stapler did just what he had told the others not to do. He stepped into the middle of the road and trimmed the top of the bank on his side with bullets. The firing stopped. Stapler ran to the other side, arriving about the same time as Gonzales.

He slapped the Marine on the shoulder. "Let's get the hell out of here, Gonzales."

"Don't have to tell me twice, Gunny." He took off at a sprint down the left side of the Volvo. There, he turned and put up covering fire along the ridges as Stapler ran past him.

Every breath Stapler took sent a wave of pain through him as his cracked rib expanded and contracted. This was not making the trip any easier. It was not a serious fracture, he knew from previous experience, but it is was enough to remind him it was there. Gonzales dashed past him, turned abruptly, and dropped to his haunches.

Stapler caught up and squatted beside Gonzales, drawing an involuntary grunt as his rib rubbed. He touched the man. "The rest have gone ahead. Jones and Garfield are on point, and the riggers are between them and us. You go first. When you get to the bend up ahead, stop and provide covering fire. I'll be coming."

"Okay, Gunny. You all right?

"Christ! Are all you thick? I am all right. I will worry about me. You worry about you and the others."

"Sorry, Gunny."

"Okay. Now take off."

"Got it, Gunny." Gonzales eased around Stapler, touching the gunny on the shoulder as he took off running. An explosion, where they had been a minute earlier, told Stapler that whoever was out there had grenades. It would only be a moment before those grenades got the two stranded vehicles. Gonzales opened up with his M-16. *Good Marine,* Stapler thought, listening to the three-shot bursts.

Without looking to see if Gonzales had made it to the bend, Stapler jumped up and, at a zigzag run, avoided the center of the road as he headed for the bend. He heard the fire coming from above them and saw Gonzales returning it. *Come on, Gonzales,* Stapler thought, *you can use more than three-shot bursts right now!* Ahead, Gonzales kneeled and fired at the top of the ridges. Return fire had stopped.

Stapler passed the Marine and took position behind him. He put his hand on Gonzales's shoulder. "Hold your fire. Let's ease out of here and put some distance between us and the vehicles before they blow them."

"What was that explosion, Gunny?"

"Grenade. Let's go. Let's get out of here before they decide lobbing a few at us is better than firing blindly."

They were one hundred feet down the ravine around the bend, running, when the sounds of two massive explosions reached them. Stapler didn't even glance back; he knew the attackers had blown the two vehicles.

The two Marines rounded a second bend. Gunfire erupted in front of them, tearing up the roadbed and sending both to ground.

"Did you get them?" shouted someone.

"I don't know. I saw them go down!"

"Quit shooting, assholes! It's us!" shouted Stapler.

"Hold your fire, men. It's the Marine," said a voice that Stapler recognized as Mr. Charlie Grant. "Sorry, Gunny Sergeant, we thought you were someone attacking us. We heard the gunfire, and look over there." He pointed back the direction they had come. "Look at that." An orange glow lit up the sky.

Stapler and Gonzales pulled themselves up and walked hurriedly to where the oil riggers stood. "Mr. Grant, I thought I told you to keep walking, to follow my point men."

"You did, Gunny Sergeant, and we were, but then we heard you running behind us and thought we were fixing to be ambushed."

"Ah, we did, mates, and I says to Charlie, 'We'd better get them before they gets us.' So, we turned and waited. Damn good thing we are such poor shots," Darren said, laughing.

"Sir, we need to keep moving," Stapler said. "I don't think we have much time before they follow. Gonzales and I are going to bring up the rear." He looked at his watch. The glowing minute hand showed twenty minutes past midnight. "Ten minutes ahead, you are going to run into Privates Garfield and Jones. For heaven's sake, don't shoot them. When you do catch up, tell them to keep going until you reach the end of the ravine. Then wait for us to catch up. Give them a couple of minutes' head start. Give us ten minutes, and if we aren't there, you start to the compound without us."

"Some of us can always come back to look for you if you don't make it, Gunny Sergeant."

"If I don't make it, there won't be anything for you to come back and get. Just do what I say. Gonzales and I can take care of ourselves," Stapler said, but what he really wanted to say was, *Damn straight, you get your asses back here and help us.*

"Okay, we're gone again," Charlie Grant said. "Come on, men, let's go, and for heaven's sake, don't shoot the Marines in front of us."

"What Marines?"

"You know what Marines, Boot."

"Keep the noise down. Keep quiet," Stapler said.

Gonzales moved quickly to the other side of the road, his head down, watching where he put his feet. He threw himself against the cliff wall, facing back the way they had come, waiting for someone, something, or anything to appear around that second bend. His finger twitched on the trigger.

Stapler leaned against the bank, scanning the top of the ridges that ran about seventy feet overhead. How long did this ravine run? Grant had said only a few hundred yards. How many yards had they come? About two hundred, he guessed. Shouldn't be much farther before they reached the end.

"Let's go," Stapler said to Gonzales after what seemed ten minutes.

The two Marines followed the riggers who, by now, should be a couple hundred yards ahead of them. Behind him, he heard voices and knew the attackers were following at a fast pace. In moments they would be coming down the road or racing along the top. The sooner they were out of this ravine, the better their chances of survival.

Thirty minutes later, the two ran into the rear of the oil riggers. Stapler decided they were close enough to the exit for them to remain together. He was wrong. It took an hour before they passed through the end of the ravine and found themselves on a rocky plain leading down to the desert floor. In all that time, the voices remained the same distance away. Without doubt, those following knew where they were.

"I thought you said it was only a few hundred yards?" Stapler asked softly.

"Well, it seems shorter in the humvee," Charlie Grant answered.

In the distance, about three-quarters of a mile, the faint lights of the compound glowed.

"There it is," Charlie Grant said to Stapler, pointing to the compound.

The two had been bringing up the rear. Stapler had been impressed with the younger supervisor. The man had kept pace with him and never complained—not that it would have done much good.

"Yeah, we may make it after all," Stapler added.

"Had your doubts, Gunny Sergeant?"

"Had this tight feeling around the stomach," he said, smiling.

"You mean your ribs, don't you?" Charlie asked, chuckling.

"Ribs?"

"Gunny, you think you fooling anyone? Too many of us have had cracked ribs not to recognize it when we see it in someone else."

The first few bullets tore up the ground around the bunched oil riggers, sending them scattering in different directions.

"Take cover!" shouted Stapler. *Where in the hell did they come from?* Everyone dove for the rocks poking up through the ground and decorating the slight decline leading down to the desert floor.

He heard the sound of a bullet hitting flesh and saw one of the dark shadows among the oil riggers fall. Two men nearby grabbed the fallen figure and pulled him behind some rocks with them.

A group of figures bunched tightly together, robes fluttering behind them as they charged out of the ravine toward them. Stapler flipped his safety off and fired a semiautomatic burst at the group. They tumbled over, landing on top of each other. The screams from within the tangle of arms and limbs told him some were still alive. He thought a couple of those who went down probably tripped over those in front who were shot. In which case, he had a couple of healthy ones out there within grenade range. Unfortunately, within their grenade range because he didn't have any.

"Mr. Grant, take your people and start working your way back . . . on your belly. These rocks will give you a little cover. We'll be right behind you."

Charlie didn't have to be told twice. He started crawling backward down the hill. As he passed others, they joined him, and soon the hill was alive with oil riggers crawling downhill. Garfield smiled as the riggers moved past. They reminded him of hunting nightcrawlers in Indiana. Sniper shots from the top of the hill sent the oil riggers rushing onward with a new burst of speed. Garfield blasted the cliff overhead. The shooting stopped. Stapler glanced back but couldn't tell if any of the riggers had been hit.

He looked forward at the same time as a *whoosh* sound came from where the road exited the ravine. Stapler recognized it even as he knew the weapon was in flight— RPG—rocket-propelled grenade, the same thing that destroyed the two helicopters. He buried his head in the sand, wishing he was a mole right now, and pulled his arms in as close as he could. The grenade sailed over his head and exploded about fifty feet to the right, sending up clouds of sand and dust. Stapler looked to where the grenade had exploded. Empty desert. Damn good thing, too. If it had landed among them, it would have killed most. Gonzales leaped alongside Stapler.

"Hello, Gunny. Thought you could use some help."

"Private Gonzales, you should be moving the other way."

"Nothing to kill that way, Gunny. You got all the targets up here."

"Well, we can't stay here long. As bad a shot as that RPG gunner is, luck and proximity will grace his aim."

Out of the ravine, a fresh wave of dark-garbed figures, their capes waving in the air, ran toward Stapler and Gonzales, jumping over the dead and dying. Gunshots rang out as the charging figures fired at the Marines. To Stapler's right, another group of enemy fighters rose from the rocks about fifty yards away and charged, waving long, curved knives and screaming something incomprehensible as they neared.

Stapler calculated about thirty-five total. Well, there were three Marines—that should make it a fair fight. He let loose a tattoo of shots at the ones on their flank. They were being cut off and surrounded, as if the attackers had given up on the escaping oil riggers.

Behind him, the M-16s of Garfield and Jones cut loose, firing over his head and wasting five or six enemy warriors who had emerged from the ravine. He hoped Garfield and Jones had enough sense to get the hell out of there.

Gonzales's weapon blazed away at those in front. Suddenly, a figure jumped up from only ten feet away and leaped toward the small Mexican-American. Stapler had his own problems with the approaching enemies from the right. He couldn't get a shot off without shooting Gonzales. Gonzales reached to his boot and pulled out his survival knife. A quick movement of his wrist and, as the attacker drew back a long, curved scimitar to kill the Marine, Gonzales came upright with all his body weight behind the knife. The thick, sharp knife slid into the belly of the enemy. Gonzales pulled up and then jerked the knife to the right before pulling it out. A blood-curdling scream of pain filled the night as the man dropped his scimitar and grabbed his stomach, trying to shove his intestines back inside. Gonzales shoved the man away and watched him fall, the man's hands still trying to push his intestines inside. Gonzales snatched the scimitar as his prize and grabbed his M-16. He fired twice, jerked the ammo clip out, and, patted his ammo pack twice.

"Gunny, that was my last clip."

Stapler reached in his pack, pulled out his last clip, and tossed it to the Marine. "Here. Use it carefully. It's the last one for both of us."

Gonzales grabbed the clip in the air, looked over at Stapler, rammed the clip in, and fired over the gunny sergeant's head, causing Stapler to duck as Gonzales blasted a charging enemy from that side. Stapler had not even heard the man coming toward him, much less seen him. The falling dead man landed beside the gunny sergeant.

"Let's ease back, Gonzales. See those rocks over there?" He asked, pointing to where three rocks formed a one-foot-high triangle. It wasn't much, but it afforded more protection than this open ground. For how long, he had no idea. He felt confident the others had escaped. The M-16s of Garfield and Jones had stopped firing. In a way, he was disappointed, but in another, he was proud. The two were doing what they were supposed to do: protect those civilians. He hoped they made it. Two deaths were enough out here.

Gonzales slid back first, being nearer the rocks. Stapler waited until the Marine reached the defensive position before he started crawling backward a foot at a time, twenty feet to the rocks. Gonzales fired a couple of rounds to keep the enemy heads down and slow their steady encroachment against their position. Stapler rose slightly and threw himself over the largest of the three rocks, tumbling against Gonzales. His breath caught as the cracked rib rolled against something hard on the ground. Stapler whipped around and crawled up against one of the rocks, his weapon pointed into the darkness lit by faint starlight reflecting off the white sands. The numerous rocks scattered around the base of the hill obscured any motionless enemy. They had stopped charging, but dark shadows weaving through the rocks separated the enemy from the terrain. Damn! They were, as Top Sergeant MacGregory would say, *"significantly outnumbered by the bastards."*

A new group of enemy warriors jumped up and charged, their screams on the left drawing their attention. About twenty of them. The tongue-twirling cries of the attackers came from the front at the same time. Then the enemy's cries startled him from behind. This was it, he thought. They were surrounded. He fired cautiously, a burst to the front, whirling to the left, a blast of three rounds; then onto his back, the gun pointing between his combat boots, another three rounds. He rolled over, pointing the gun forward. His rapid rotation of fire caused the attackers to hit the ground. He wanted to save the few bullets remaining. Stapler expected any moment to feel the impact of enemy bullets ripping into his body.

"I'm out, Gunny!" Gonzales cried, too loud.

Stapler wrapped his hands around his M-16. He looked down at the weapon. He figured minimum two more shots, possibly five. Do we go alive or not?

Two Bedouin figures appeared over the rocks on Gonzales's side. Stapler shot them both, then heard a click where the third bullet should have been. Empty. No time for options. He pulled his bayonet out and clipped it on the end of the weapon. Gonzales saw him do it and followed suit.

Stapler shoved Gonzales over and ran his hand swiftly over the front of the Marine's shirt, hoping to discover a grenade or two. Nothing.

The Latino hefted the Bedouin scimitar. "It was such a nice souvenir, Gunny."

The Bedouins shoved themselves up and ran toward them. The waves of flowing robes were about thirty feet away. Stapler rose onto his knees and saw Gonzales do the same. The two put their backs together, ready to push upward with their bayonets when the attackers came over the rocks.

The cries of the attackers faded as the Taureg Bedouins neared. A fusillade of gunfire erupted over Stapler and Gonzales's heads. Stapler recognized it as M-16s. Both Marines dove for the ground. Bodies tumbled, falling, tripping the attackers running behind them. From the rear came the familiar "Oorah," the Devil Dogs' own unique battle cry. Stapler reached over and pulled Gonzales's head down as both friendly and hostile bullets flew across their position. As the gunfire tapered off, he chanced a look and saw the last of the attackers fleeing into the hills and back into the ravine. In seconds, the battlefield was clear.

Behind him, Lieutenant Nolan walked up casually and looked down at the two men. "Evening, Gunny. You two taking a nap? Trying to keep all the fun to yourselves?"

Stapler stood up, brushing himself off. "You have just saved the lives of a lot of natives, Lieutenant. Private Gonzales and I were just about to make a bayonet charge. It would have been unfair, two Marines against fifty enemy, but it was their fault they didn't bring enough."

"Oh, Gunny, I would say about thirty-five is a more accurate count."

"No, sir," added Private Gonzales, saluting. "I would say seventy to eighty."

"Yes, sir," Stapler said, stepping over the rocks beside

the officer and shaking his hand. "I think that number is nearer ninety to a hundred."

"Let's get out of here," Lieutenant Nolan said, releasing Stapler's hand.

"I think the lieutenant is right. We can discuss the numbers back at the compound."

"Over a hundred, now that I include the ones on the right," Gonzales added.

"Good work, LT," Stapler said as the two fell into step with each other. "You don't know how good your young face looked . . . even with that pissant mustache."

"You don't have to say it, Gunny. You would have done the same. Marines don't leave Marines behind. Kind of like the Greek Army?"

"Not funny, sir, but thanks."

Lieutenant Nolan smiled. "Same to you, Gunny."

The other Marines spread out along the way, pulled themselves up as the two men walked past. "How many did you bring, Lieutenant?"

Garfield and Jones ran to Gonzales. A few words, and Garfield handed the Marine another clip, which he promptly shoved into the M-16.

"I brought all of them, Gunny. The riggers are big boys and girls. Let them guard the compound. They need to be involved. We are going to have to use them if we intend to get out of here, or we won't make it. As they taught us in leadership school, we need to make them stakeholders in their own survival."

The LT sounded much older than twenty-six. Amazing how combat not only matures you, it ages you. He rubbed his rib. Damn, it sure as hell was aging him.

Thirty minutes later, with no further attacks, the Marines walked between the barrels making up the walls of this Fort Apache in the middle of the Sahara. Bearcat Jordan and Charlie Grant waited for them, a bottle of Jim Beam being passed from one to the other.

"Lieutenant, what's the word from Homeplate?"

"Homeplate can't help, Gunny, and Base Butler isn't fully operational. They haven't changed their request. We have to move three hundred miles southwest of here, if we want the Army to come get us."

"Lieutenant," said Bearcat. "We've finished. The truck is loaded."

"Loaded?" Stapler asked.

"Yeah, Gunny. Just what you said earlier today."

"Uh, Lieutenant, what was it I said earlier today?" Stapler asked, his mind trying to remember all the advice he had been spitting out to the young officer during these past sixteen hours.

"That we may have to drive out. You said Army CH-47s lacked the legs to get here. You were right. They don't. Therefore, we have to get closer to them. Mr. Jordan and his people have been loading petrol, water, and food into the vehicles ever since I discussed this with Homeplate and Base Butler. We had hoped to use the truck and the humvee you were bringing back."

Stapler knew they discussed the idea, but in the back of his mind, he never really thought they would have to do it. Why? Because he knew not all would make it. Too many others had trekked off across the Sahara desert. He recalled a documentary on the history channel that talked about the number of adventurers who had disappeared into the Sahara. Never heard of again. The odds of them joining that list were high.

"When do we intend to start?" Stapler asked, his mind whirling as he sought reasons for staying here where they had a good defensive position.

"In thirty minutes, Gunny. What do you think? You know, after we just routed them, it makes sense to sneak out now. They won't be expecting us to do anything else tonight, and they are going to be too busy licking their wounds. By God, did you see them run?"

Stapler nodded. "Can I see the plan, Lieutenant?"

"Come into the office," Bearcat said, holding the bottle out to Stapler.

Out of the corner of his eye, he saw the young blond college assistant. She seemed to be waiting for something.

Stapler took the bottle and glanced at the lieutenant,

who turned away. Stapler took a big swig; with the back of his hand, he wiped his mouth before handing the bottle back. The strong whiskey burned going down before Stapler felt the warm glow as it hit his stomach. He would have loved to have taken the bottle, gone off somewhere by himself, and finished it, but it would have to be put off until they got back to civilization—if they got back.

When he looked again, the lieutenant was walking over to the girl. *Just what I need,* Stapler thought, *a young stallion with his hormones raging.*

"Great stuff," said Bearcat. "Melts the wax in your ears."

Stapler looked around the compound and saw the Marines resume their defensive positions at the perimeter. He knew they would remain there until he told them to stand down or they departed. "Mr. Jordan, can you get some food for my Marines?"

"Sure, Gunny. I'll have Kuvashin take care of them right away," Bearcat offered. He waved to the cook and shouted to him to feed everyone. Kuvashin waved in acknowledgment.

He saw the young lady—what was her name? Sheila Anne?—touch the lieutenant lightly on the shoulder. The vision of a shark circling its prey came to mind. He turned back to Jordan. He didn't want to watch the attack against the willing victim.

"I would recommend everyone eat something and drink as much water as they can before we leave. It may be a while before we stop again once we get started. Mr. Jordan, use the food and water being left behind to feed everyone. Don't touch anything you've packed on the vehicles."

Stapler and Charlie Grant continued to the office, arriving there as the lieutenant showed up alone and Mr. Jordan returned. The four men entered the office. Professor Walthers stood in front of the map. *Thirty minutes until we depart,* thought Stapler. Things were moving too fast for his liking. He never really expected them to have to do it. He expected either the Marines or the Army to come up with a plan to allow them to wait here until rescue arrived. They always had the weapons, manpower, and equipment to do it five years ago. Nevertheless, someone somewhere decided that wasn't going to happen.

He was a Marine, and by the time they stopped in front of the map, Stapler had reconciled himself that they were going to convoy. Convoy through hostile territory against hostile people in a hostile climate so they could reach a position where they might be rescued. Who was it that sang that convoy song—Jerry Lee Lewis?

Bearcat leaned across the desk to the chart on the wall. "Here is where we are now. Here is the oasis we have to go through to replenish our water. How much farther did you say we will we need to go after here, Lieutenant?" he asked, turning his face toward Lieutenant Nolan.

Lieutenant Nolan looked for the scale at the bottom of the map and measured it off with a nearby twelve-inch wood ruler. "Recheck it just to be sure." He stood back. "Another seventy miles will make it around two hundred. However, which direction do we go from the oasis? Gunny, one thing we discussed is, do we turn south toward the Army's Base Butler or go west toward our own people?

"Not much choice, Lieutenant. The only CH-53s we had, burned. We need to choose the Army, sir. We also know Homeplate is temporary. As soon as they detect any Moroccan units moving against them, they will vacate Homeplate. In addition, like us with the Tauregs, it may be only time before the Moroccan rebels turn their attention to our presence there. We know Mauritania has allowed the Army to establish a small base about a hundred miles from their northern border."

"Yeah, I heard one of the intelligence officers say that Mauritania is very worried about what is going on in North Africa," Lieutenant Nolan said to the men standing around the table.

Stapler ignored the interruption and kept talking. "If we can get"—he put his finger on a small group of valleys south of the oasis—"through these hills, then we should be okay."

"Those aren't hills. They're valleys, called wadis here," Bearcat corrected. "We don't want to go there."

"It would be very dangerous," The professor replied. "The wadis are a series of small, interconnected valleys that the Tauregs claim as their hereditary home. If we go in there, they will think we are attacking, invading them. They will defend it to the death."

"That wasn't what I was talking about," Bearcat continued. "These wadis were made by water. If we have a sudden rain squall, those wadis will be a death trap."

"When was the last time you had a rain squall in the Sahara?"

"About a year ago, but it does happen," Bearcat said.

"It's a chance I think we'll have to take," Stapler said. "The wadis will provide good cover for us if we have to hide or fight. They are directly between us and rescue. We have little choice."

"It will provide better cover for the Tauregs, who know the wadis like you know the back of your hand," the professor added.

"Regardless, this is where we have to go if we are going to get out of here alive." Stapler jabbed his finger several times on the word Mamluk Wadi.

Before anyone replied, Stapler turned to Lieutenant Nolan. "Sir, you need to contact both Homeplate and Base Butler one more time to see if they have come up with anything that will permit us to stay here. Find out what they're doing to help us. If the final orders are for us to convoy out of here and head southwest, then give them our projected geographical coordinates and path. Make sure they understand we do not have GPS or accurate charts of the area. Give us a plus or minus ten-mile radius around the pickup point." Then, almost as an afterthought, he added, "Sir."

Stapler was impressed with the young man who called himself "only a communications officer." He'd be more impressed if the officer kept clear of the young lady.

Nothing but trouble there. In the six hours he had been gone, Lieutenant Nolan had organized a forced movement that would have taken forever at the staff level. They would depart, crossing the desert to the southwest, avoiding the only road in front of the compound, staying clear of known roads to their west. According to Mr. Jordan, the hard clay to the southwest would make driving about the same as being on a road. If the clay was anything like the road they returned on from Alpha site, then that wasn't saying much. Their first destination, nearly two hundred miles away, the Darhickam Oasis, would be where they would replenish their water.

They all agreed that forty-three people would use up the food and water by then. They estimated three to four days to travel across this inhospitable oven of a country before they reached the oasis.

Stapler walked to the coffeepot and poured himself a cup of the day-old stuff. The strong, night-aged tannic acid caused his mouth to tighten, but he forced it down anyway. It was two in the morning, he had been awake for over twenty-four hours, and he doubted he would get any sleep for another ten.

Behind him, the lieutenant passed last-minute instructions to Bearcat Jordan. The officer had planned well from what Stapler had seen. If he hadn't, it was too late to start changing the plan. Radio contact was going to be the hard factor. When the LT finished his transmission, Bearcat Jordan and a couple of other riggers pulled the radio out from the wall. They soon had the radio disconnected. Bearcat had another team working on a humvee so the radio could be installed on the front seat. The frequency had been sent to both Homeplate and Base Butler. This jerry-rigged radio would be their only means of contact while they traveled. The mobile phones some of the riggers offered were American digital. Even if they worked in this country, without the vicinity of microwave relay towers, they were useless.

Stapler opened the door and walked outside into the cool, night air. His side hurt from the beating it had taken the last few hours, not dulling the pain of the cracked rib but rather spreading it equally around his body. He hoped Carol didn't worry too much when she found out about this, but he knew she would. She would cry, wail, and blame the Marines for sending him here, and then she would calm down and watch CNN for the latest news. That is, if they made CNN news with the other things happening in the world. He wondered briefly if the major offensive in Korea that appeared to be turning back the North Koreans had worked. Shoot! By the time they returned to civilization, the whole world could have changed.

Heinrich Wilshaven, the rigger in charge of vehicle maintenance, walked up to Stapler. "Ach, my nice Marine," he said in a heavy, curt, Teutonic accent. "Ve have a problem."

"What is it?"

"The three vehicles will not carry everyone. The humvees will carry seven for the first one and eight in the second. And the truck; maybe, ve can force twenty, thirty onto it. But, ve do not have room for the supplies ve need and the people ve must carry."

Stapler looked at the man. His bladder was full, and he needed to pee again. Age sure took its toll on a warrior.

Finally, Heinrich leaned forward, his eyes wide, and asked, "So, vhat do I do?"

CHAPTER 3

⚓

COMPARTMENTS ABOARD NAVY SHIPS ARE always small, even those on aircraft carriers such as the USS *Stennis,* CVN-74. A fatigued Clive Bowen, Admiral Gordon Cameron's chief of staff, and Rear Admiral Pete Devlin, the thin crew-cut commander of the Mediterranean Naval Air Forces, had been bumping into each other throughout the morning as they maneuvered around the small staff operations space. Clive couldn't help thinking of balls in a pinball machine as the two men bumped into each other again.

"Damn, Clive, I'm trying to drink this coffee, not wear it," Devlin said.

The lone aluminum table with a lighted top to reflect through the charts also had a low light hanging overhead. The arrangement forced the two men to lean over the plots when they reviewed the day's activities and tried to determine the schedule for tomorrow.

"Sorry, Admiral," Clive said, although it was Devlin who was doing the pacing.

"How is he?" Pete Devlin asked Clive, setting his Navy cup on the edge of the table. He leaned forward with his hands on both sides of the cup.

Clive ran his hand through his thinning gray hair and straightened up from the plot table. "He looked all right when he landed a couple of hours ago. I haven't had a chance to talk much with him, Admiral. He did say the children were holding up well, and his wife's funeral was one of the biggest the town had ever had. I think he appreciated the local community's support for him and his family, considering they have lived away for over thirty years."

"I didn't think he would go."

Clive nodded. "I know. We had originally diverted the *Albany* after the Tomahawk attack so the admiral could disembark. When the top secret message arrived from Naval Intelligence telling us they expected the Algerian rebels to either overrun or attack the embassy, I knew the admiral wouldn't go. I was right. It was good of the family to delay the funeral until he could be there."

"When was the funeral? I forgot."

"Last Sunday. He stayed with her parents for a couple of days and then flew with his son and daughter to Washington. They went their separate ways while he met with the chairman of the Joint Chiefs of Staff and with Admiral Dotson, the new chief of Naval Operations. You know he spent the past two days in Stuttgart, Germany, with General Sutherland going over the situation here."

"Yeah, I hear that Sutherland is sending in an Army general to be the commander of the Joint Task Force?"

Clive nodded. "Yeah, he's a three-star out of Washington named . . ." Clive reached in his pocket and pulled out a three-by-five card. "General Leutze Lewis. According to his bio, his friends call him Rocky."

"Rocky! From what I have heard from some of my former Army classmates from Industrial College of the Armed Forces, working for him is the same way." Devlin paused and sipped his coffee.

"Then you must have some insight I don't?"

Admiral Devlin ignored the question. "Our boss, Admiral Cameron, has been the commander of this Joint Task Force for the past three weeks, as he should be. I mean, by God, ninety-nine percent of this effort is Navy and Marines. Every now and then, the Air Force flies through with their aerial version of an aircraft carrier. Now, when it looks as if we may be pulling out within the next two weeks, they send some asshole from Washington to take charge and soak up credit for Cameron's work. What are they thinking? That Cam and I aren't doing ours?"

Clive didn't have an answer for the mercurial admiral. This was way above his head. He was Admiral Cameron's chief of staff. Where the admiral went, he went. His job was to make the admiral's orders take effect and do whatever else he could to make the three-star's job easier.

But Devlin didn't want an answer. He just wanted someone to listen. Devlin would probably be a three- or four-star now, if he could control his propensity for speaking his mind. Devlin took his half-empty cup of coffee, turned, and walked to the bank of nine televisions that filled one side of the compartment, mumbling under his breath as he moved. The few enlisted sailors and the chief running the compartment moved casually but purposefully out of the path of the pacing flag, almost as if they had a sixth sense as to when to weave and when to dodge.

Most of the televisions were off. The one in the left-hand corner of the third row silently showed flight deck operations from a camera mounted flush with the flight deck. A F-14 was hooked to the forward-port catapult. Clive moved beside Admiral Devlin. Together they watched the afterburner shoot out from the exhaust of the Tomcat. The Sidewinder missiles on both sides of the wings revealed the aircraft was armed for air-to-air combat. The steel barriers raised behind the aircraft deflected the heat and flames up and away from flight deck crewmen, who continued to hurry back and forth behind the aircraft where they maneuvered a waiting aircraft into position for launch. Even this far belowdecks, the noise of the engines revving up to max power penetrated the space. The only thing missing was the overwhelming heat and the thick smell of burning fuel.

"I miss that," Devlin said wistfully over the noise.

"Me, too." Clive was a fighter pilot. Maybe he would get another command tour after this job. Clive never considered himself admiral material. He had been in zone for admiral last year and watched four others—two of them fellow Academy classmates—get selected for their one-star. It was not inconceivable the board could go above zone as they routinely did in the more restricted-line communities like the Cryptologic and Intelligence officers. However, for unrestricted-line officers who made up the warfighters of the Navy, it would be unusual for them to do so.

The pilot of the Hornet saluted the unseen catapult operator to his left. Two seconds later, the catapult threw the aircraft off the deck and into the air at a thrust designed to give the F-14 the ten knots extra headwind needed to be airborne.

Devlin turned to Clive. "Does anyone know anything other than rumors about this new CJTF who is coming? I mean, what is the straight skinny on him, Clive? The only thing I have heard is that he is a bear to work for."

Clive shrugged his shoulders. "Don't know, sir. Just have what we got off the Internet and through official channels. General Lewis is an airborne calvary officer. Before moving over to the five-sided building in Washington, he was the commander of the Old Guard at Fort McNair. He was the deputy J-3 for Operations at JCS before they moved him to some highfalutin job as the Army Legislative Affairs officer. One thing I saw on the Internet is that last year, when the old chief of staff of the Army was retiring, Lewis was being pushed by some members of Congress to relieve him. But he only got his third star last year, so he wasn't even considered by the Army for its chief of staff." He paused. "Oh, another thing is, he is an avid athlete. He has run a bunch of marathons, including every one of the Marine Corps marathons in

Washington. I understand he has finished near the top in every one of them."

"Just what we need: a physical-fitness zealot."

Clive shrugged his shoulders.

Devlin smiled. "If Lewis only got his third star last year, then Gordon is senior to him!" The smile left his face. "Then, why, pray tell, are they sending an Army general to take over control of a primarily Navy and Marine Corps operation?" He raised his finger, waving off Clive's response. "I know, I know: Joint operations, which I wholeheartedly support, as we all should, sometimes doesn't make hell-to-high-water sense to me. As much as I think Air Force officers are prima donnas, they have more forces involved here than the Army."

The grinding noise of the catches on the watertight door leading into the compartment caught their attention. The door opened, and into the Operations space Vice Admiral Gordon Cameron, commander of the United States Sixth Fleet, and until later this afternoon, the commander of the Joint Task Force for Operation African Force, stepped into the compartment.

"Attention on deck!" shouted the chief, who was monitoring an intelligence broadcast system on the other side of the compartment from Clive and Pete Devlin.

"Carry on," Admiral Cameron said.

The Marine guard accompanying the admiral took position in the passageway, with his back to the compartment. Admiral Cameron reached behind him, shut the door, and pushed the long, three-foot handle down, securing the bolts that held the watertight door fast.

"Welcome back, Admiral," Pete Devlin said, crossing the room to shake Cameron's hand. "How's the shoulder and back?"

"Pete, good to see you. They're fine, though if you listen to Chuck Jacobs, our fleet surgeon, you'd think I still need to be in the bed laid up in traction. At least, so far, I haven't seen Kathy Gray living in my outer room again, which is probably a good thing. She is tougher than the doc on telling me what I can and can't do." Kathleen Gray had been the Navy nurse on duty the night Cameron had been shot by terrorists during the car bombing attack against the pier side USS *LaSalle* and USS *Simon Lake* in Gaeta, Italy.

Devlin pushed his aviator glasses back on his nose. "You know how those doctors are, Admiral. If you get well, they're out of a job. For nurses, if you get well, then they've done their jobs."

Cameron chuckled. "Yes, you're probably right. However, to answer your question, the bullet wounds weren't that serious in the first place. They hit at such an oblique angle that Chuck said he could have pinched them out like a splinter if he'd wanted. I heard about the *LaSalle* and the *Simon Lake*."

The car bombing of the flagship, USS *LaSalle*, and the submarine tender, USS *Simon Lake,* had sent sterns of both ships—Mediterranean moored stern to the pier—to the bottom of Gaeta Harbor. Both had been refloated within a week, but the propellers on the *LaSalle* still rested in the mud on the bottom of the harbor. The messages Admiral Cameron read on the short flight to the carrier told the story. According to the Surface Force Atlantic engineers flown out to help, the aged engineering plant of the *Simon Lake had given up the ghost*. Both ships would have to be towed to a repair facility. The Navy had tried to obtain access to a French dry dock, but the French had no space, as their dry docks were fully employed. *At least, that's what they said,* thought Cameron. The Italians were scrambling to see what they could do at their repair facility in Liverno. Since 1990, the Italian Navy had turned into one of the closest bilateral partners of the United States Navy.

Meantime, SurfLant dispatched four oceangoing tugs to bring the two ships back to the States in the event that local repair efforts failed.

Clive stood to the left of Rear Admiral Devlin. Admiral Cameron looked at the two and smiled—a smile with no joy behind it. "Clive, I hope you two haven't finished this little vendetta we have going here. I would hate to miss the end of it."

"No, sir, Admiral. The move from the USS *Nassau* to the USS *Stennis* last week went off without a hitch. A lot of that was because Admiral Devlin's staff covered for us as we did the move, and by the time we arrived, he had the Operations room here up and running."

"Is this all we have here? I rather liked the *Nassau*. They gave us their entire Combat Information Center. Well, at least one of them."

"No, sir. This is more a conference room than an Operations space. We've been holding officers' call in the hangar deck and staff meetings in one of the officer's dining compartments. Two compartments down on the starboard side, we have a mini–Combat Information Center. It's smaller than the CIC on the *Nassau*, but we have access on every information cell on the ship, along with the global information grid to anywhere in the world. We are running our air operations from there."

Cameron pulled out a chair from under the small conference table, positioning himself so he could observe the televisions, and sat down. Both Clive and Admiral Devlin did the same.

Cameron reached up and tweaked his nose. "It's nice to know we have information superiority. Just hope we have the weapons to use it to our advantage. These past two weeks have been very hectic—"

"Yes, sir, we understand," said Clive. "We're very sorry about Susan. I know this has not been an easy time for you."

Cameron waved his hand. "Let's not go down that path. I need to concentrate on what we're doing here. I would like to get the deputy chiefs of staff together as soon as possible to bring me up to date on our operations and status of our forces. As you both know, General Sutherland has identified General Leutze Lewis to relieve me and assume authority as the commander of the Joint Task Force. He prefers to be called Rocky, which is a good thing, considering how I murder his name."

"I'll call him General. Personally, I think it is shitty as hell, Admiral, to replace you," Devlin said. "And—"

Cameron held up his hand. "No, it's the right thing to do, Pete. I have too much on my plate as the commander of the Navy component in this operation to handle the logistics we need and the questions Washington keeps throwing at us. Right now, they have dual-hatted me as the commander in chief, United States Navy Forces in Europe. Admiral Dotson hopes to have a replacement for Admiral Prang as soon as NATO approves the replacement of that damn French general.

"I met General Lewis while in Washington. He understands his role here is to coordinate the forces in the theater to help us finish our mission in Algeria and get the hell out. I know this sounds hard to believe, but I am looking forward to him assuming this burden."

Admiral Cameron's comment seemed to lack veracity to Clive.

Devlin opened his mouth to reply.

"No, Pete," interrupted Cameron, raising his hand higher before dropping it. "I know how you feel, and I can appreciate it, but don't consider this a slam against my or your leadership. With the war in Korea taking new directions, we may have additional forces in that theater within the next three weeks. My goal is to have this wrapped up by then. General Lewis will bring a no-nonsense and objective approach to this campaign."

"If you say so, Gordon," replied Devlin, his voice indicating he didn't believe a word of it. No admiral in his right mind graciously gives up command.

What Devlin didn't know was that the death of Cameron's wife Susan at the hands of the terrorists who attacked the Sixth Fleet officers while they dined at a local Italian bistro in Gaeta had put a new perspective in Gordon Cameron's life. It had not changed his desire to do the best job possible and accomplish the mission assigned, but something his son said to him after the funeral still rang in his mind: *"No matter how hard you work, Dad; no one on their deathbed has ever said, 'I wished I had*

worked a little harder.'" Regardless of what Cameron had
told the two, the relationship with his son and daughter
had deteriorated with the death of their mother—his wife.
They didn't say it, but he knew they believed he was the
cause of her death. Leaving their mother's body in an Italian morgue for three days as he left on the USS *Albany* to
join the fleet seemed to them an insult to their mother. His
daughter, in a moment of candor, told him it was another
indication that the Navy was more important than the
family. The couple of times he tried to make them understand that he did what he had to do failed miserably and
left the three of them angry with each other. Someday,
they might understand. For the time being, the three of
them would mourn separately and, hopefully, they would
become close again.

". . . this afternoon."

Cameron heard the tail end of Clive's comment. "I'm
sorry, Clive. Could you repeat that? I missed it."

"I said that General Lewis is arriving this afternoon."

"What arrangements have we made for him and his
staff?"

Pete Devlin spoke up. "Admiral, billeting has been
arranged. He and his staff will have to share our Operations space. We have integrated some of our staff elements
to make it easier; now we will have three people manning
every watch—"

"Pete, you know we won't do that. We'll work with
General Lewis. In fact, I want everyone on both our staffs
to understand the importance of making the general's job
easier. He is the CJTF, and we will follow his guidance,
recommendations, and orders."

"But—"

"No, buts, Pete. No time for egos to get in the way of
doing our job. If anyone has the right to feel slighted, it's
me. It's my job he's taking, and I welcome it. I know you
find that hard to believe, but someday, over a beer, I shall
tell you why I find it easy to accept." The problems with
his son and daughter had dulled the A-type personality of
Admiral Cameron. He truly did welcome the relief of this

burden from his shoulders and, in the back of his thoughts, he knew his days as an active-duty naval officer were coming to a close.

Devlin nodded.

"Good. There are some staff changes I want to make. Pete, I want to move you up to be my deputy. As you know, Sixth Fleet has always had a billet for two flag officers, but because of constraints, we have never filled that deputy billet. Clive, you have more or less functioned as my deputy for three years, so I don't want you to feel slighted over this."

"No, sir," Clive interjected. And he amazed himself to discover he had no feelings on the subject.

"Admiral, I appreciate that, but I am also handling the air campaign. That may affect my being able to aptly carry out the duties of the deputy."

Cameron nodded. "I know, Pete. That's why the second thing I want to do is to take that duty away from you."

"But who would we give it to? My deputy in Naples? The woman is a flight officer, not a pilot, and her quals are P-three Orions."

"No, but we both know that if we did, Carol Smith could handle it. No, we need her to stay right where she is, managing the logistics tail we need to continue our work here. What I intend to do is to take Dick Holman, the commanding officer of the USS *Stennis,* and shift him over to our staff to run the air campaign."

Devlin thought a minute, nodded, and chuckled a couple of times. "Dick would be a good one. If it had not been for him, we would still be waiting for minesweepers to clear the Strait of Gibraltar and the carrier battle group would still be boring holes in the sea outside of the Mediterranean. He'd be a good one. Do you know him?"

Cameron nodded. "Yeah, Dick and I were classmates at the Academy."

"Good. I wouldn't want to be the one to tell Dick we're taking him away from command and making a staff officer out of him. Whoa! On second thought, I do want to be here when you tell him. If anyone can find an argument as to why something shouldn't be done, he's the one."

"Yeah, I don't expect him to jump up, salute, and move his gear over to Sixth Fleet gracefully . . . much less quietly."

"If you don't mind me asking, why hasn't he made flag? Dick is more than competent."

"Ten pounds."

"Ten pounds?"

"Dick has always managed to be at the edge of the Navy's weight standards, and with age and promotion to captain, he managed to exceed it a couple of times. And you know what that means." Admiral Cameron turned to his chief of staff. "Clive, can I get a cup of coffee? Good coffee. That stuff on the COD, the passenger flight I flew in on, must have been left over from a World War II destroyer."

Clive rose and got the admiral a cup of coffee. Weight standards played an important role in the promotion scheme of the Navy. You could lose an opportunity for promotion as much from being overweight as being caught DWI. He patted his stomach. Already a couple of inches since this crisis started. Less chance for working out, and he hadn't jogged in over a week. He made a mental promise to get down to the gym tonight.

"Dick will assume the air campaign. Carol Smith will fleet up as the commander, Fleet Air Mediterranean, but Dick will become commander, Task Force Sixty-seven." Such a move divided the responsibilities of Pete Devlin between two Navy captains, giving the logistics and administration portion to his deputy in Naples, while the operation responsibilities of the naval air forces would shift to Dick Holman.

Clive handed the admiral his coffee.

The roar of the second F-14 Tomcat catapulting off the carrier vibrated through the compartment. The three men looked at the monitor and watched the aircraft dip slightly at the end of the flight deck and then gracefully rise as it continued ahead of the carrier. At three miles out, the air traffic controller of the carrier would direct the fighter off the departure path and toward its assigned mission or area.

"You're going to get your wish, Pete. I would like you two with me when I discuss this with Dick. The idea of giving up command to be on a staff will go against his grain, and your arguments as to why this is a win-win for everyone may mitigate the sting."

"Let me see: commanding officer of a carrier, or managing flight plans and operations on a staff," said Devlin, grinning as he moved his hands up and down like alternating trays on the ends of a scale. "I can't imagine why he would have second thoughts."

The three chuckled.

"I know it may take a direct order, but we need to use the assets we have available as we wind up Task Force African Force and move on to other more important operations. The offensive on the Korean peninsula has stopped the advance of the North Koreans. More of our forces are arriving every day on that peninsula, creating an opportunity for a major offensive that will drive them back across the border. We are not going to get any more assets than what we have to accomplish our mission here. As soon as those hostages are out of Algiers and we finish the evacuation of other Americans and allied citizens from the oil rigs in the south, we are going to break off and head to the Sea of Japan. With eight carriers off the peninsula, the United States Navy can sustain round-the-clock two-carrier operations indefinitely. Without us, there are three to four days when only one-carrier operations can be brought to bear."

"What will our allies say if we do?"

Cameron pursed his lips. "So sorry. One of the things the chairman passed on—and I do not want it breathed further—is that the French and Germans are pushing for Europe to use its own rapid-reaction force in lieu of NATO. If that occurs, NATO is dead as a military entity. With NATO relegated to a political tool, our influence will wane even further. Something to consider, but the overriding objective of the administration is to put the North

Koreans back in their box. We will continue to receive second attention until that happens, and the consensus of the Joint Chiefs of Staff is that without us, the major offensive required to do it will be harder and more costly."

The bolts on the watertight door squealed in protest as the person entering stooped to step over the six-inch rise. The short, chubby man held an unlit cigar in his right hand.

Captain Richard Holman, commanding officer of the USS *Stennis,* turned to his executive officer. "XO, get some HTs down here, and fix that damn door."

Cameron stood as the man made his way to him. "Admiral Cameron, once again, welcome aboard the USS *Stennis.*" Holman had greeted the admiral initially when the two-engine propeller passenger aircraft that sailors called a COD had landed on board the aircraft carrier. "I trust your accommodations are satisfactory. If there is anything I can do, sir, let me or any of my wardroom know, and we'll make it happen."

Cameron shook Dick's hand. "Dick, I haven't had the chance to tell you how impressed I am with how you got the *Stennis* over here so fast and then to actually sail it through a minefield to enter the Med."

"Thanks, Gor— Sorry, Admiral."

Holman dropped his right hand, realized he still held the cigar in his left hand, and quickly stuffed it into an unbuttoned shirt pocket. "Thank you, Admiral, but I really didn't sail it into the Med. Once we realized the Strait of Gibraltar was mined, the traffic still sailing in the Strait gave us the answer. They were smart mines, keyed for specific magnetic and acoustic readings. So I just had one of the destroyers tow us through."

"That was smart thinking, Dick." Then, in a more somber tone, Admiral Cameron added, "I don't have to tell you how the sacrifice of the *John Rodgers* affected all of us."

"Dick, what if you had been wrong about the mines?" Pete Devlin asked.

"Then you wouldn't have the USS *Stennis* and its battle group here, Admiral."

"Good job, Dick," Cameron added. "Anything Sixth Fleet can help you with?"

"No, sir. I really came down to ensure that everything was going okay. This is my executive officer," Holman said, indicating the taller commander to his left. "Commander Tucson Conroy." Cameron shook his hand and nodded. "If you need anything, just let us know." He motioned toward the watertight door. "I will have someone from engineering up here ASAP to fix that door, Admiral."

"Thank you, Dick, and feel free to consult with me on anything we do that may adversely impact your running of the carrier. We want a smooth interface. You know that General Lewis, the new commander of the Joint Task Force, is arriving this afternoon?"

"Yes, sir. We have put him in adjoining flag quarters beside yours. Both the XO and I will meet his COD when it arrives. When is it arriving, XO?"

"Captain, it is scheduled to depart Naples at fourteen hundred hours and should land during the sixteen fifteen cycle," the XO replied. The cycle was everything to a carrier. Every one hour fifteen minutes was a cycle. In a cycle, aircraft took off, then the deck rearranged quickly by shifting the parked aircraft forward, so others could land. Then the cycle started over again.

"Good. Captain, I would like to meet the general, also. Would you come by and get me and we'll go together?" Admiral Cameron said.

"Yes, sir. Will do," Holman replied. "Come on, XO, we got work to do to keep this bird farm operating."

"Dick, will you sit down with us for a moment? I have something to discuss with you," Cameron said, pointing to the vacant chair at the end of the table.

Holman nodded at the XO, who headed toward the hatch to carry out his orders. Commander Conroy shook his head as he glanced back before stepping through the hatch. He had been in the Navy long enough to know private conversations usually meant more work for him.

"Yes, sir, Admiral," Dick said after the screeching of the watertight door stopped.

"Dick, you're doing an outstanding job as CO of the *Stennis*, but I need you on my staff. There is no easy way to say that and—" Cameron held up his hand to stop Holman from responding. "I know you will hate the idea of leaving command."

"Admiral, you have some of the finest officers in the Navy on your staff. The *Stennis* depends on me, and it is my ship," Dick responded. A cold chill ran down his back as he wiggled uncomfortably in the chair. Even before he argued, he knew he was going to lose against Gordon.

"Yes, they do, Dick. But things are changing, and they will change significantly when I turn over African Force to General Lewis this afternoon." He pointed casually at Pete Devlin. "Admiral Devlin is going to fleet up to be my deputy. A lot of reasons as to why I am doing that, and he isn't happy doing it, either."

Pete Devlin started to object, but Admiral Cameron continued, "And I won't share them with any of you at this time. I am going to give his logistics and administrative responsibilities to his deputy, Carol Smith, in Naples. I want you to assume his operations responsibilities for the ongoing air campaign. You are a pilot like him and Clive, you have the experience. And, most importantly, you have my confidence."

"But what about my ship?"

"You have confidence in your XO?"

"Sure, I do, but he is a Surface Warfare officer, a black shoe—"

"Then he should be able to drive the carrier without running it aground."

"Yes, sir. He can run the *Stennis*, but it's my carrier," Dick said forcefully, tapping himself on the chest.

"Yes, it is, Dick. I am not asking you to give up being its captain permanently. I am asking you to temporarily shift command to your XO and come aboard with me. I need you. The Navy needs you."

Dick sighed. He knew he was going to do it. He obeyed orders. He did what the Navy wanted, even when the Navy sometimes didn't know what it needed. He nodded a couple of times. "When do you want me to shift my colors, Gordon? Sorry, Admiral?"

"I would like to get it done before Rocky Lewis arrives. I want my staff the way I need it to exercise the orders of the new commander of the Joint Task Force."

Dick nodded again. "Yes, sir, Admiral." He slid his chair back, reached in his pocket, and stuck his cigar in his mouth. "With your permission, Admiral, I feel the need of a good cigar before I break the news to the XO."

"How do you think Commander Conroy will take the news?" Cameron asked.

"You mean when he finishes dancing across the bridge or pirouetting through the wardroom?"

They laughed.

"I may have to fight him to take back command when this is done." He grinned again. "No, Conroy is an outstanding officer. Between him, the wardroom, my command master chief, and the goat locker"—referring to the chief petty officer's mess—"the *Stennis* could not ask for a better commanding officer." He paused, took his cigar out of his mouth, and waved it at the three. *"Except for me."*

They stood up and shook his hand. "Thanks, Dick. I know how hard this is for you, but we need you and your experience."

They didn't need my experience when all those past admiral boards met, but Dick quickly dismissed the negative thought. He was not going to fall into that group of malcontent officers who fail to select for the next promotion and then spend their time bad-mouthing and writing negative articles and letters about the Navy. Dick saluted Admiral Cameron as a sign of respect, although saluting inside the skin of the ship was not usually done. He quickly departed, the creaking of the watertight door following in his wake.

The three sat back down at the table as Holman left. Commander Kurt Lederman, the Sixth Fleet intelligence officer, passed Holman at the hatch. Kurt Lederman had been in the bistro the night the terrorists had attacked the officers of the Sixth Fleet staff in an unsuccessful attempt to kill Admiral Cameron. Short and balding, he faced the challenge most at-sea Navy officers did: a growing waistline from putting work above physical fitness. However, Clive knew, as others did also, that Kurt Lederman was a *damn* good intelligence officer.

Ask him, he'll tell you, thought Clive.

Kurt Lederman could give as much ribbing as he took from the unrestricted-line officers. Kurt appreciated the limitations and challenges of being an intelligence officer in the cyber age where what seems is not necessarily what is. He had no adversity to jerking those with the skills he felt were needed to develop the full battle space picture. When he provided the flag a recommendation, confidence in the analysis and the advice was preordained. He also learned early as an intelligence officer to never say, "*I don't know*"; always say "*We're working that, sir or ma'am, and should have an answer soon.*" The sibling rivalry between the Intelligence and the Navy's Cryptologic community still remained an open affair, but Kurt and his Cryptologic counterpart on the Sixth Fleet staff, Captain Paul Brooks, was both a professional and personal relationship.

The technical expertise brought by cryptologists capable of data-mining the information highway like concert pianists kept Intelligence on top of the battle space picture. Despite years of attempts by the Intelligence community to move the Cryptologic officer under the Intelligence chief of staff, Sixth Fleet remained the only United States Navy fleet who, quite rightly, separated the two. Paul Brooks was the head of Operations Command, Control, and Communications' (C3) Warfare department and ran the Information Operations for this theater. Information Operations was the military cover term for fighting the virtual war on the cyber battlefield. Paul, like the majority of Cryptologic officers, knew his expertise was an integral part of the Intelligence picture and worked closely with Kurt to profile the battle space. It helped that the two were friends.

A gray metal door with a small circular window, located along the port side of the staff operations compartment, opened. An aproned mess specialist entered with a tray of fresh coffee and midmorning pastries. Heavily tattooed arms stuck out of the starched white shirt the thin, shaven-head sailor wore.

Cameron smiled. "Mitchell, they brought you over, too?"

"Yes, sir, Admiral," the first class replied, smiling. "Told them you personally wanted me over here, and if they tried to stop me, if you personally didn't whip their butts, it would be because I did." He set the tray down on the table, stepped back, and smiled. "There you are, Admiral."

"Damn, Mitchell! You really know me well. However, I hate to burst your bubble. It's your pastries I like." He pointed at Petty Officer Mitchell's arms. "All I have to do is make sure I don't get blinded by your tattoos. Isn't that a new one?"

Mitchell stood back up and wiped his hands on his apron. His face turned slightly red as he blushed. "Yes, sir, Admiral. I had it done by a fellow first class on board here. He insisted that what I really needed to set off my others was this one of a Tomcat blasting off a carrier. Don't know how I came to have this many tattoos. Must be something in the seawater." He straightened up, coughed once, and said, "Admiral, with all due respect, sir. Me and the others want to offer our condolences on your wife, sir."

The admiral stood and reached out his hand.

Mitchell stared at the outstretched hand for a couple of seconds before reaching forward to shake it. The sailor's palm was warm from the tray.

"Thank you, Mitch. Tell the others I appreciate their thoughts and concerns. The flowers were nice." He dropped his hand. "Now, you sailors get busy, and let's have a nice welcome-back meal tonight." Then, in a voice that seemed to share a secret, he said, "The officers don't realize how long and hard they're going to be working, so I want a nice meal to keep their energy going. They're going to need it."

Mitchell beamed from ear to ear. He ran his hand over his shaven head. "No sweat, Admiral. I have been saving one recipe I wanted to try. It's a—it'll be a surprise. You'll love it." Mitchell turned and walked slowly, head down, as if already planning the meal, toward the door leading back to the small pantry.

Clive smiled as he watched the senior mess specialist mentally going over his planned dinner while physically counting the menu items on his fingers. One thing about the cooks Admiral Cameron brought with him to Sixth Fleet; they were experts. He could not remember another command or ship where he had eaten as well. He touched the small love handle on his waist. Moreover, if he didn't get back to some sort of physical fitness routine, this half-inch roll of fat was going to turn into several; then he and Dick could trade clothes.

"Well done, Cam," said Devlin. "There goes another ten dollars on our mess bills."

"You know, Pete, if you won the lottery, you'd bitch about the taxes you had to pay on it."

They laughed. Even Pete Devlin managed a smile.

"Kurt, come join us," Cameron said to the intelligence officer, who stood talking to the chief petty officer in charge of the operations, while he reviewed the logs the chief had handed him. "How's that leg?"

"Better, Admiral. They took the cast off. Next time I want to scramble down a ladder at night, I will do it slow and careful," Kurt answered, limping to the table. "I was lucky it wasn't a break of the bone. More like a serious fracture."

After shaking hands, Kurt said, "Admiral, welcome back. A lot has been going on since you've been away."

"And I am sure you are going to tell me all about it, Kurt," Cameron answered. "It's good to see you. Your counterpart on Commodore Ellison's staff did a good job for you, but I am glad to have you back with us. Here, sit down," Cameron said, pointing to a chair that, moments ago, Dick Holman had occupied. He preferred to have those providing him a laptop brief to sit across from him. Kept him from turning to the side to look at them, plus he enjoyed trying to read body language. He wasn't much good at it, he thought, though the rest of the staff would disagree with him.

"Okay, boys, time to get down to work. Clive, you told me something when I landed about late-breaking news on our hostages in Algiers?"

"Yes, sir," Clive answered. "Kurt may have more information, so jump in if you do."

As if on cue, Captain Paul Brooks opened the watertight door and entered. A hand reached inside and kept the door from shutting. Two hull technicians from engineering, wearing oil-stained dungarees and sweat-patched shirts, began noisily working on the squeaking bolts.

"Paul, good to see you," Admiral Cameron said.

"Welcome back, Admiral," Brooks said as he pulled a chair out, nodded at Kurt, and sat down.

"Kurt has been putting together a quick synopsis of the hostage situation in Algiers, plus a new development since last night has left a platoon of Marines stranded in southern Algeria," Clive continued.

"Stranded? How did that happen?"

"Sir, I can cover that in the briefing."

"Okay, Kurt. Rather than a formal briefing, why don't you just tell me what's going on, what my options are so we can discuss them, and what I can expect the enemy to do if I do any of them."

Lederman slid three copies of his briefing notes across the table to the three men. "Admiral, the quick and dirty about the Marines is that they flew in from a temporary base we had the USS *Kearsarge* establish at an abandoned airfield in southern Morocco. The base was only going to be there long enough for the Marines to fly into this one oil rigging spot where we had a bunch of Americans. Once we had them back at Homeplate, one of the *Kearsarge*'s ships in the relieving Amphibious Task Force would return and pick them up."

Paul Brooks grabbed a napkin and put a hot cinnamon bun on it. The thin officer earned the envious looks of Clive Bowen and Kurt Lederman. He was forever eating and always looked as if he was starving.

Lederman reached forward and poured himself a cup of coffee. "Unfortunately," he continued as he poured, "the two CH-53s with the Marines landed in the middle of an attack on the site. The two helicopters were destroyed and an unknown number Marines killed. The problem we have is that these were the only two CH-53s left behind to do the evacuation. The others are still on *Kearsarge*." He nodded toward Pete Devlin. "Admiral Devlin detached the USS *Oak Hill* early this morning toward the Moroccan coast to pull out those who are still at Homeplate and recover the four Cobra gunships we have there."

"So how are we going to get those Marines out of southern Algeria? What are the rescue plans?"

The officers exchanged looks, secretly hoping one of the others would answer the admiral's question. After several seconds of silence, Clive sighed and answered, "Admiral, we don't have a plan. We have no helicopters available to go and bring them out. What we do have is an Army Special Operations base in Mauritania, which raises other questions. We don't know why the Army is putting it there, sir. The Air Force have committed to fly in the Army's CH-47 Chinooks this week."

"But the Army Chinooks lack the legs to fly from Base Butler—that's their name for the base—to where our Marines are located," Pete Devlin added.

"The Marines departed the rig site this morning and are convoying southeasterly across the Sahara toward a group of oases. Intentions are for them to close the border area with Mauritania so the Army can effect a rescue," Kurt continued.

Cameron took a sip of coffee. "So I take it the attacks have broken off?"

"No, sir. Last night they were attacked again, and it was only because the Marines made a bayonet charge that the attackers turned and fled."

"Bayonet charge? In the twenty-first century? That sounds a lot like a World War II action."

"Yes, sir. That is what the report said, but I have to tell you, Admiral, that we are not completely sure of the accuracy. What we are sure about is that the convoy may have to fight its way out. Reports are being relayed from Base Butler to Homeplate in Morocco and then on to the USS *Kearsarge*. They are all verbal reports."

"Is there any way we can use airpower to provide some protection for them? How about using the Rivet Joint to guide some fighters to them? At the minimum, we need to be able to air-drop supplies to them."

"Yes, sir," Devlin answered. "We are looking at launching a four-plane operation with two tankers. This should give us the legs to overfly them and, if need be, provide some air protection."

Cameron nodded. Seemed awful tenuous to him. Even if they flew the planes a thousand miles into the desert and found this convoy of Americans, the gas consumption of the aircraft would be so great they would be unable to loiter long. That meant sending tankers along with them, and tankers were awful vulnerable and awful scarce. The USS *Stennis* only had four.

"Let's look at sending in one of the longer-range aircraft, Pete," Cameron said. "Either a P3 or the Air Force's RC-135 or one of VQ's EP-3s. I can't see fighters being much use that far away, and at least we can ferry supplies to them as they work their way across the desert to safety." He leaned forward. "I presume we have air superiority over Algeria?"

"Yeah, that's what we got," mumbled Pete Delvin,

shaking his head. "We got air superiority, and we got information superiority."

Clive nodded in reply to Admiral Cameron's question. "Yes, sir. We destroyed most of their air force while it was on the ground soon after they attacked the evacuation convoy two weeks ago. Of course, some escaped to Libya and Tunisia, and we still have a few scattered at some of the desert airfields. But I don't think they will come out to play."

"Clive, I always worry about air. That's why we wear the wings," he said, touching the aviator wings pinned over his left pocket above his top three medals. "I don't want us to get complacent. Even with the recent successes in Korea, we don't know for sure when more forces are going to show up in this theater. All it would take is one well-planned attack that catches us with our pants down, and we'll have more ships on the bottom of the sea than the two we have already lost."

"No, sir, we aren't being complacent," Admiral Devlin added. "We have an E-2C flying constantly during the day, and it is usually positioned east of us to watch the Libyan air activity. At night, we have the EP-3E and sometimes an Air Force Rivet Joint, RC-135, doing high fives north of us. We are keeping one of them in the area constantly. The British have detached two Nimrod reconnaissance planes to the area, and we have established a data sharing and early warning arrangement with them."

"Good. Are the French playing?"

"No, sir. We have asked the French if they would like to join a rotating reconnaissance arrangement, but they declined."

"Too bad, it's their loss," Admiral Cameron replied. "Pete, Clive, I want a plan to get those Marines out of there. See if the Air Force can give us one of their Puff the Magic Dragon C-130s. It should have the legs to support those Marines until we can rescue them."

Clive pulled his notebook forward. "Yes, sir. We have asked the Air Force for any assets they may have that can help in this situation and are waiting for their reply. European Command is working the issue."

"Let me know the outcome as soon as possible. If necessary, I will call General Sutherland. Kurt, tell me about the hostages."

"Yes, sir," the intelligence officer replied. He flipped over one of the sheets of paper on the handout. "Admiral, the first paper brings you to date on the hostages taken, the number of Marines ashore, and the number of tanks, APCs and humvees landed in the two weeks since we occupied Algiers. Page two provides a list of incidents, including the rioting in the southeastern part of the city that resulted in our Marines firing on a crowd that was trying to overrun them. CNN made a big deal about it; I am sure you saw it on television back in the States. The Algerian rebels have been broadcasting the film clips with their own anti-American spin on them. European television hasn't been too complimentary, either."

Cameron nodded. "Yes, I know, and yes, I did see the CNN report. They made it seem as if we intentionally confronted the rioters with the purpose of killing them."

"Yes, sir. The press is a little upset with the restrictions we put on them within the city. We did it to protect them. Of course, they think we are trying to keep them from discovering some great secret we are hiding. Algiers is not a friendly place for us right now, but the rebels know once they release the hostages, we will leave. The rebels say the hostages will be returned after we leave. It's a Catch-22 situation. Three days ago, they threatened to start killing the hostages if we failed to leave Algiers two days from now. As you know from the news, yesterday they killed and mutilated one of the male hostages and hung him from a streetlight. Our forces ashore received a phone call late yesterday afternoon with the location. Along with the telephone call was the threat that one hostage would be killed every two days, if we haven't left by the end of the week. Admiral." Kurt looked up. "We now have forty-nine hostages and four days until the next one is tortured and killed."

"What are they doing ashore to find them?"

"Colonel Bulldog Stewart is the commander of the landing force, the CLF, Admiral. He has been conducting house-to-house searches in the hopes of finding something. Until the Bedouin appeared early this morning, they had nothing to go on."

Admiral Cameron stood and, with cup in hand, walked to the map of Algeria that someone had taped to the bulkhead. The others at the table stood.

"And what happened today? They find the place?"

"No, sir, Admiral, they still have failed to locate the place, but an Arab who calls himself—" Lederman ran his finger down his notes. "Bashir, has come forward and told Colonel Stewart he knows where the hostages are being kept."

"So let's get in there and free them," Cameron said, turning abruptly to face the three men.

"Well, Admiral, it seems Bashir won't tell him where they are."

"Won't tell him? Why not? Does he want money or something?"

"No, sir. Basically, he doesn't trust us. He wants to talk only with Duncan James."

"Duncan James, the SEAL captain! Isn't he back in the States recovering from wounds?" Cameron crossed to the table and sat down. The others followed suit.

Behind them, the HTs finished oiling the hinges of the bolts and closed the watertight doors. The chief supervising the two operators at the Intelligence console walked over and double-checked the lever to make sure the door was shut tightly. Keeping a ship watertight meant keeping doors shut whenever possible.

"No, sir," Clive interjected. "Duncan and the two officers who came with him from Washington are somewhere in Italy. The other members of the SEAL teams that went into Algeria to rescue the Algerian President Hawali Alneuf have returned to their assigned unit on board the *Nassau*. The most seriously wounded of the bunch was the female SEAL, Lieutenant H. J. McDaniels. She was released from the Navy's Naples Hospital two days ago. The three of them are scheduled for a flight back to Washington in three days. That's the soonest we could get them out because of the paucity of flights out of Naples heading to the States."

"Then tell them to stand by. How soon, Pete, can you have an aircraft pick them up and bring them out here?"

"Almost immediately, Admiral. We have a daily COD flight between Sigonella and the carrier. We just divert it north after it takes off from Sigonella, and an hour later, it lands in Naples, picks them up and, without feathering more than one engine, turns around, and bingo to the carrier." *Feathering* was the navy term for turning off an engine while the others remained on.

"Clive, make it happen. Anything else, Kurt?"

"Admiral," Clive said, raising his hand slightly. "There is a problem with that. We have been trying to locate the three of them, but it looks as if they are exploring Italy. We have left messages at every bachelor officers' quarters in Italy as well as contacting the American embassy in Rome to check and see if the three are touring there. If we don't locate them sooner, it will be when they check into the Naples military airport for the flight home before we can contact them."

"Keep searching for them. I want them out here as soon as possible, Clive."

"Yes, sir, Admiral."

"Kurt, you have anything else?"

"Yes, sir. The Algerian Kilo submarine for one. It is in dry dock at the Oran Naval Base, receiving repairs to its propellers and shafts. A report from the EP-3E indicates the submarine will most likely remain there for the foreseeable future, but cloud cover for the past two days has kept us from obtaining imagery to confirm the report from the reconnaissance aircraft.

"Second is the missing Algerian fighter aircraft. We know they are somewhere south of Algiers, hidden in the desert. We have sent tactical aircraft scurrying over the area, widening their search area and crossing back to search other areas that look promising. To date, we have discovered only two of the thirty-odd Algerian fighters still unaccounted for. We have had a couple of bogies that seemed to spring out of nowhere, and as soon as we direct interceptors toward them, they disappear. I am more concerned with them than with the dry-docked submarine *Al Nasser.* Those are the two highlights right now, Admiral. The rest are minor and can be covered at the staff meeting scheduled for ten o'clock."

"Good, Kurt, you and Paul Brooks keep an eye on that Kilo. We still don't know what submarine attacked the *Nassau* Amphibious Task Force three weeks ago. Is there any way to tell if the damage to the *Al Nasser* is battle damage?"

"No, sir, not without putting someone ashore."

"We have too many ashore now in my book."

"We could send a photo recon aircraft over the area," Pete Devlin volunteered.

Cameron shook his head. "Too many surface-to-air missiles still out there. As long as the Kilo remains up on blocks, it can't hurt us, but if they try to move her from the dry dock, Pete, I want Dick Holman to have his aircraft take it out."

Pete Devlin nodded. He started to suggest they go on and take it out now, but he would wait until later when he and the admiral had some moments alone and then propose the air action.

"Thanks, everyone," Cameron said, sliding his chair back. They all stood. "Clive, why don't you come to my stateroom. Pete, you did an excellent job while I was gone. Kurt, I want an assessment on those stranded Marines, and I want to know what we can expect the rebels to throw at them. I do not want them to disappear into the Sahara as so many others have in the past." He looked at his watch. "General Lewis arrives at sixteen hundred hours. Clive, Kurt, I want a general overview briefing ready for him at seventeen hundred hours. Clive, make sure that Dick Holman is there as our new acting commander of Task Force Sixty-seven."

"Yes, sir."

The admiral picked up a napkin and wrapped two of the pastries in it before reaching into the tray again to lay a croissant on top of the package. He looked up at the men standing around him and grinned. "If I don't take these, you gentlemen will make pigs of yourselves, and I'll have to order all of you to the gym. Not to mention, there won't be any left for me."

"Gym? I think we have forgotten what a gym looks like," Clive added.

They grinned as Admiral Cameron and Clive made their way out of the compartment.

"Anything else, Admiral?" Kurt asked Rear Admiral Devlin.

Devlin shook his head. "No, you and Paul go on, Kurt."

"Admiral, Admiral Cameron made reference to Captain Holman as the new CTF Sixty-seven?"

"Yeah. I'm fleeting up as the admiral's deputy—*Don't ask me why*—and Dick Holman is shifting his colors from commanding officer of *Stennis* to be commander of Task Force Sixty-seven, in charge of the Naval Air Forces in the Mediterranean."

"Thank you, sir."

"Ready, Paul?" Kurt asked his Cryptologic counterpart.

"Sure," Paul mumbled through a mouthful of pastries.

As the Intelligence officer and his Cryptologic counterpart reached the door, Devlin said, "Oh, there is one thing, Kurt. Find out what you can about General Lewis. A bio or something."

"Yes, sir. I'll send it down to you as soon as I get something together, Admiral."

CHAPTER 4

⚓

EVEN AS KURT LEDERMAN WAS PASSING THE information about the Algerian submarine to Admiral Cameron, Captain Ibn Al Jamal, commanding officer of the Algerian Kilo submarine *Al Nasser*, was standing on the edge of the dry dock, watching water fill the void. The Algerian Kilo diesel-powered attack submarine sat upon four huge blocks lifting the warship so the yard workers could finish repairing the damaged shaft. He had been surprised how fast the new rebel government had been able to find enough yard workers to do the job. When the American torpedoes had exploded meters behind the submerged *Al Nasser* three weeks ago, the explosion warped the shaft, causing it to stop turning. The *Al Nasser* had remained motionless at two hundred feet until their passive sonar had shown the *Nassau* Amphibious Task Force departing the area.

Only then did Ibn Al Jamal blow ballast and bring the damaged submarine to the surface. Calls to Algiers to send a tug had gone unanswered, but the Oran Naval Base to the west, from which he had originally sailed, heard his call. When he sailed with the *Al Solomon* at the beginning of the revolution, the two old Soviet-built Kilo-class submarines had departed Oran while the base was under loyalist control. Now, only the city of Oran—twenty kilometers to the west—remained under control of forces loyal to President Alneuf, but the rebels, in a bloody battle, had taken the Oran Naval Base. The decaying bodies of the Algerian loyalists captured during the battle still swayed from the various light poles and cranes, and Ibn Al Jamal even saw one hanging from the balcony of the new rebel headquarters. This was not the Islam he worshiped.

Ibn Al Jamal mumbled a prayer to Allah and continued his walk around the rampart of the dry dock. He had done this every day, many times a day: reviewing concerns that only a fellow captain of a submarine could understand. Bad shipyard work on a surface ship, and the worst thing that could happen was that the ship sat motionless on the surface while everyone scurried about trying to fix whatever was wrong. Bad shipyard work on a submarine, and you ran the risk of never surfacing again.

He visually checked for any last-minute signs of damage, noted minor cosmetic things that needed doing, and directed the boat's crew so they kept busy. He looked forward to refloating the *Al Nasser*. The sooner he was under way and out of the base, the better. He knew he was failing to hide his disillusionment with the rebellion. What a failure he was. He failed in his oath to his country. Like a stupid young man, he had fallen under the spell of convincing orations and ardent exhortations about a new, glorious, Islamic republic, only to realize that true Islam would play no role in the future of Algeria. Just like Hawali Alneuf, the new leaders lived for power.

When he and the zealot captain, who commanded the sister submarine *Al Solomon,* sortied from Oran Naval Base nearly a month ago, Ibn Al Jamal sailed with the belief that the revolution was a religious and righteous one. The two submarines sailed undetected through the Strait of Gibraltar, where he left the *Al Solomon* to guard against an American battle group. When he sailed back through the Strait, the *Al Nasser* had sowed smart mines along the sea-lanes. Smart mines were designed to activate when a certain combination of acoustic and magnetic signatures identified the target as either a large ship or a submerged submarine. These had been the last mines in their inventory. How the USS *Stennis* managed to get through the minefield perplexed him. The aircraft carrier *Theodore Roosevelt* had been sunk in the Red Sea, according to the news report, by the same sort of mines that had been planted in the Strait of Gibraltar, Ibn Al Jamal wrongly assumed.

He turned the corner near the huge gates of the dry dock. The waters of the harbor rose to within a foot of the top of the gates. Soon the water in the dry dock would be the same level, equalizing the water pressure on both sides and allowing the gates to be slowly opened. The stern of the submarine faced him. He leaned forward and put both hands on the heavy safety chains that ran between metal stanchions encircling the ramparts of the dry dock. The bent shaft had been straightened as much as the yard workers could with the limited resources they had. The Algerian Navy had no spare shafts, depending on Russia to provide them. Considering that the Algerian rebels executed the Russian tech-reps assigned to the Navy, Ibn Al Jamal doubted the establishment of a new spare parts contract any time soon. A new propeller to replace the one damaged during the torpedo attack had been discovered in one of the supply warehouses. They had torqued the shaft and propeller yesterday and pronounced the submarine ready for sea this morning. He sensed the yard workers wanted the *Al Nasser* finished and under way as soon as possible. The Americans had to know the whereabouts of the submarine. They were completely perplexed as to why the American Navy had not launched an air attack against it or lobbed one of their many cruise missiles into the dry dock. Maybe they were waiting for the Spanish forces approaching Oran from the west to take the port.

Two nights ago his disillusionment with the rebellion had been completed. Evening prayers had turned into a political call for the heads of non-Muslims and a holy war, death against all Westerners. The passionate discussions included talk about religious cleansing, shocking him; genocide under any name is still genocide. Algeria was a nation of Sunni Moslems, but the words he heard reverberated with the Shiite philosophy prevalent in Iran and Afghanistan. He wanted no part of it. When he met Allah, he would meet Him with a pure heart and soul.

Ibn Al Jamal removed his hat and ran his sleeve across his forehead, wiping the sweat from his eyes. The motion of a waving hand from the submarine caught his attention. His executive officer stood on the conning tower of the submarine, exaggerating a hand wave to catch his attention. He tossed his hand up in acknowledgment. A good man among good men. Ibn Al Jamal had done a good job protecting his officers and crew from the rebel inquisitions. He thought the radical captain on the now destroyed *Al Solomon* had been the exception. Instead, he had discovered that, once the true leaders emerged from cover and felt they had nothing to fear, zealotry was the norm. So many through history had used the guise of religion to gain power. He now believed the new leaders had little religious leanings with the exception of abusing Islamic beliefs to obtain and keep power.

He should have seen it. How could a man his age fall for such guile? Ibn Al Jamal pulled his hat back on and continued his slow walk around the boat, stopping periodically to make an entry in his small notebook. The workers near the bottom moved quickly, scurrying up the various ladders and stairs as the water rose. He looked at his watch. By two o'clock this afternoon, they would exit the dry dock and depart the port. He shook his head. Yes, if he had been the American admiral, he would have bombed the *Al Nasser* while she was vulnerable and unable to escape. The only thing he could figure was that the Americans were unaware it had been his submarine that had attacked them. He knew if he was in charge of the

American battle force, the *Al Nasser* would be in pieces now. This dry dock would be a burning inferno. He looked at the sky, half expecting to see the contrails of an inbound cruise missile. No, the Americans believed in reaction, so they must be unable or unwilling to equate the underwater actions against them as coming from the new Algerian Navy. Never underestimate your adversary, he learned as a junior officer. The Americans never underestimated their adversaries; they just underestimated themselves.

The sound of metal on metal caught his attention. He leaned over the chain and saw one of the dock-worker supervisors beating the safety catch of the starboard aft block away. Yes, he thought, today they would leave the dry dock and head to the open sea again. The rebel leadership had ordered him to attack the USS *Kearsarge,* the new amphibious carrier leading the relief for the American Marines occupying Algiers. The rationale was that if they sank the *Kearsarge,* with its huge two thousand plus complement of Marines, the American public would lose its will for fighting in North Africa. The American public, manipulated by the media, would discover its voice and demand a pullout. Ibn Al Jamal had nearly laughed at the idiocy of the leaders, none of whom was military, all of whom were rebellious intellectual upstarts with miles of aberrant philosophy behind them and not one ounce of common sense or the ability to accept a difference in opinion.

He felt honor bound to carry out the orders. Honor bound as every Navy officer in every Navy throughout the world feels honor bound to the traditions of the sea and the governments who send them onto it. But his heart was not in it. They had miraculously survived the American attack by Allah's grace.

What, for him, had begun as a religious revolution had been revealed as a political rebellion. A political one that would obviate every successful reform the nonreligious government of Hawali Alneuf had implemented. He stumbled over a bolt head jutting a few inches above the walkway and caught himself on the chain. On the other side of the chain lay sixty meters of air and about a meter of water. It would have been a quick death, he thought.

Ibn Al Jamal straightened and brushed his hands on his uniform coat. He reached up and loosened his tie, pulling it down and unbuttoning his white shirt. Before the rebellion, he would never have done such a thing. He would have suffered the heat in silence rather than see a stitch of uniform out of place. What a fool he had been! What an utter, old fool! To listen to words without ever considering them as lies. Now he was committed to the rebellion. He had been a vainglorious fool with thoughts of bringing a religious government into existence, a government raised to the glory of Allah. He even reconciled his traitorous actions with his oath to protect Algeria from enemies both foreign and domestic. The government of Hawali Alneuf had been domestic enemies. He had fallen prey to a rebellion led by a middle class that had lost control to the fanatics.

A shout ahead of him caught his attention. The supervisor of the dockworkers waved at him and motioned him to join him and several others. He headed slowly toward them while recalling the conversation with his executive officer last night after the gathering where the two of them, in a moment of confidence, had shared their private concerns on the rebellion. It had been a slightly nervous conversation between the two until they realized the similarity of thoughts as to what the rebellion had become. Ibn Al Jamal had been surprised to discover the man felt as he did and felt honored to discover that the executive officer never believed in the revolution; he believed in Ibn Al Jamal. Loyalty to him overrode the initial misgivings of his number two. What they should have done when the revolution broke was sailed the *Al Nasser* to Malaga, Spain, as the better officers of the Algerian Navy had done. He mentally saluted them as the true, honorable Navy officers. When the moment arose where honor and loyalty required him to make the right decision, he had failed. His cards had been cast with the rebels, but tonight he sailed to correct this destiny.

The supervisor bowed slightly and took Ibn Al Jamal's arm. The man was very proud of the twenty-four-hours-a-day job done to return *Al Nasser* to service. He went through the motions of congratulating the supervisor and his department heads on a job well done. They had. Before the revolution, nothing like this would have been accomplished. Ibn Al Jamal believed the unsaid threat of an American air strike provided the added incentive for the workers to achieve this event. He looked at the sea of smiling faces surrounding him and cringed at how their beliefs were being manipulated, how they would someday blame themselves for believing the rebel words. He saw several workers glance repeatedly at the cloud-covered sky, probably hoping to be away before the clouds dissipated, and the American satellites were able to see that the *Al Nasser* preparing to get under way.

The supervisor briefed the captain of the *Al Nasser* on the water rate and estimated another six hours before the submarine would float free of its blocks. Six hours meant a slight delay of thirty or forty minutes from the scheduled dry dock departure time of fourteen hundred hours.

He had lines out on both sides of the boat connected to the top of the dry dock, to hold it steady as the water rose. The numbers one and two lines crossed each other like the letter *X* with the numbers three and four lines doing the same. As the water rose, sailors on both sides of the submarine took in the slack on the eight lines, keeping the *Al Nasser* steady in the center of the dry dock.

The voice of the supervisor faded from his attention as his mind turned to how he intended to maneuver the submarine out of the dry dock and into the main channel of the harbor. For the first time in days, he felt a sense of eager anticipation—a feeling he had whenever he set out to sea. The maneuvering of the boat, the precise heading and rudder changes necessary to guide the submarine through the center of the passage. Mariner skills developed from long years of experience. A skill Ibn Al Jamal enjoyed demonstrating. The captain of the *Al Nasser* estimated that, within an hour after the gates were opened, he would be out of dangerous political waters and in the free, open sea of the Mediterranean. He would have more time for prayer and retreat. Above all, it was time for him to recognize his dishonorable actions and reassert his oath as an Algerian Navy officer in the hopes of correcting some of the mistakes he regretted.

Last night, he had been regaled as a true hero of the revolution and had suffered in grateful silence the admiration, back slaps, and hand shakes of those around him for his at-sea feats. No one had taken on the Americans and survived to tell about it, but he had. He had challenged the American Navy on the high seas and won—if surviving means winning. Few could fail to take some pride in that accomplishment, even him.

However, he had his own version of the truth. Allah had protected him for a higher reason than the revolution or for the attack on the American force. How could he be a hero? He took two submarines to sea! Only one returned. He mined the Strait, but the carrier still entered the Mediterranean. He attacked the American task force but sank not one ship, though they nearly sank him. No, the rebels were grasping for heroes. People need heroes. Symbols to rally around and validate their support. Algiers was in American hands. The Spanish invaded Morocco with a massive army that even now bore across west Algeria, heading toward Oran.

Within another week, the Hawali Alneuf forces in Oran would be augmented by one of the strongest armies in the Mediterranean. Since the death of Franco, Spain had truly grown into a regional power worthy of fear, but the rebels last night laughed at the Spanish and believed the boasts that one Algerian in battle was worth ten Spaniards. Had not they once occupied and governed the whole Iberian Peninsula?

Spain came because of the natural gas pipelines. None of the rebel leaders foresaw how Spain would react over a threat to those pipelines. The pipelines ran from the oil fields of Algeria through the Atlas Mountains, over the countryside of Morocco, and beneath the waters of the

Strait to emerge on the Spanish side. The pipelines made their revolution a grand strategic concern to the Spanish. Why didn't anyone see that? Where were the thinkers who led this revolution? Did they believe they could cut off the energy supply to Europe, and Europe would passively sit by, wring its hands, and allow it?

Over 70 percent of the natural gas used on the Iberian Peninsula arrived through pipelines originating in Algeria. No one thought the Spanish would intervene. Not once could he remember ever hearing anyone consider Spain a threat. However, they were here, and in every combat with rebel forces, they had easily rolled over them and continued their advance. They had invaded Algeria—his Algeria! And part of the blame for this rested on his shoulders for betraying his country. If he could turn time back to recapture the moment when he cast his cards with the rebels—

The supervisor touched him, causing him to jump slightly, and asked if he was all right. Ibn Al Jamal acknowledged the concern and passed off the inattention to determining how he would maneuver *Al Nasser* once the boat was refloated. The bedeviled captain thanked the supervisor again, excused himself, and crossed the gangway to the boat. He would rejoin his crew and remain on board until they were under way.

The executive officer met him, and their eyes locked for a few seconds, confirming the new camaraderie established last night. His number two looked so young, with the dark black hair and brown eyes. Even the mustache lacked the gray that speckled Ibn Al Jamal's hair.

For a moment, Ibn Al Jamal's paranoia surfaced as he wondered if his XO was in reality a rebel informer who tricked him to reveal his misgivings. He shook his head a couple of times, touched the XO on the shoulder, and whispered softly, "Thank you." If the XO had been an informer, Ibn Al Jamal would already be in some dark, dank cell somewhere, waiting for the inquisition to begin. As it was, the two of them could be hanging from some unused light pole by the time the sun set if anything went wrong or someone suspected what they planned.

Captain Ibn Al Jamal, lately of President Hawali Alneuf's Algerian Navy, invited the young man below to his cabin, where they could talk. He wanted to talk. He needed to talk. He needed someone who could lift this burden from his soul. Even as they disappeared belowdecks, he knew the burden was his, and only Allah could lift it. It was unfair to throw his guilt onto the shoulders of the young man. As he passed beneath the edge of the top hatch, he also knew the needs of the *Al Nasser* would make whatever they discussed short.

CHAPTER 5

⚓

"ATTENTION ON DECK!" SHOUTED CLIVE when the door to the officers' wardroom opened and the new commander, Joint Task Force African Force marched into the compartment.

The man was impressive. General Leutze Lewis stood nearly six foot four, with a muscular barrel chest that seemed to grow directly from his chin. His small waist seemed ill portioned in comparison. Clive doubted the man could stand on one foot without toppling over. The upper arms on the general stretched the sleeves of the light green Army shirt. Standing at attention with his hands ramrod straight along the seams of his trousers, Clive touched his thighs. The General's arms were about the size of his thighs. The Army high and tight haircut seemed in place with the sharp nose and jutting cheekbones. The general stared straight ahead as he made for the podium as if assaulting an occupied hill.

Most flag officers give an at-ease command upon entering a room. It was not lost on Clive, or the others—*he saw the quick side glances exchanged by the officers near him*—that General Lewis kept everyone at attention as he moved through the compartment. It dawned on Clive, about the time the general reached the raised podium where the lectern stood, that the man was a showman. He didn't walk into the room. He swept across the floor with a calculated cadence to draw attention to himself. Admiral Cameron took a couple of steps forward and extended his hand when the general reached the front of the room.

The tall Army general shook Admiral Cameron's hand and released it too quickly, as if the gesture intruded on his performance. General Lewis spun around and planted both hands on the sides of the only wooden object in the room as if he had scored a goal in a close Army-Navy football game. The lectern accented the general's size. The top of it was even with General Lewis's belt line. *Scene one, act one,* thought Clive.

General Lewis stared around the room, silent for several seconds, before he coughed and ordered, "Stand easy, gentlemen and ladies."

Admiral Cameron moved to the left side of the podium and stood quietly with his hands clasped lightly behind his back. He seemed so small to Clive, standing there beside the general, like a kid in the presence of the school bully. Clive noted the furrowed eyebrows of the admiral and knew Cameron's first assessment of the new commander was not a positive one. Good first impressions were important in a military organization where faces come and go. Make a good impression the first time, and when you screw up later, you're usually able to recover. Make a bad impression, and when you screw up, you meet everyone's expectations and hidden wishes. Even the size of the military won't protect, because reputations, once earned, germinate through a sailor's, soldier's, or airman's community. Clive wondered what the skinny was on General Lewis. They'd find out eventually.

Cameron turned to the taller Lewis. "General, welcome aboard the USS *Stennis*. On behalf of the Sixth Fleet and the United States Navy, we hope everything is to your convenience."

Lewis nodded without looking. "Thank you, Admiral," he answered, his eyes scanning the crowd in front of him. His bass voice bounced off the bulkheads of the compartment.

Was there nothing about this man that didn't shout huge? There was a grated edge to his voice like a deep rumble of an approaching train. For some unexplained reason, Clive thought of it as part of the show.

Admiral Cameron faced the audience. "Before I turn the podium over to General Lewis,"—It wasn't as if he was standing in front of the lectern; the general still firmly held the sides of it—"I would like to give you a quick biography of our new boss. The new commander, Joint Task Force African Force. General Lewis until two days ago was the Army legislative officer to Congress, where he has held the post for three years. Before that assignment, Lieutenant General Lewis was the brigade commander for the Old Guard at Fort McNair. The Old Guard is the Army's premier ceremonial division." Admiral Cameron stroked his chin and grinned.

Clive thought he saw a slight twitch to General Lewis's cheek from the corner of his eye. The deliberate mixing of brigade and division irked Army officers as much as them calling ships *boats* irritated the Navy.

"Most of you may not realize that they hung the assassins of President Lincoln at Fort McNair. Let's hope the good general has better plans for us."

A nervous chuckle echoed from an audience comprised primarily of Navy officers. The two Air Force exchange officers standing near the front looked down at their feet to hide their smiles.

"And we don't join them." He turned to General Lewis, who forced a smile across his tight lips.

This is going to be a fun ride, thought Clive, shaking his head.

"General Lewis is an Army Ranger and earned his combat experience while a major in Liberia and Iraq. He brings a lot of joint experience earned during the tour before his assignment at Fort McNair at the Joint Chiefs of Staff where he was in the J8, formulating war plans." Admiral Cameron paused.

General Lewis stepped forward. "Thanks, Admiral," he interrupted. "I always feel uncomfortable when someone *reads* my biography." He turned back to his audience. "Suffice to say, I have been around the block a few times." He looked down at Cameron. "With your permission, Admiral, I'll take it from here."

Without waiting for a reply, General Lewis continued. "Thank you for coming here this afternoon. It was nice to arrive earlier than expected and jump right into operations. I appreciate the fact that the cooks have turned out some nice finger food for us to get acquainted. Unfortunately, I don't think we have time. I prefer to jump right into this mess and try to straighten it out. We need to move fast to disentangle from the situation we have gotten ourselves into here in North Africa. Before I depart for an executive session with the admiral and his deputies and aides, I would like to pass on some philosophy about how we function in a combat situation. I have never been a strong supporter of all these techno-geeks running around believing that computers will fix everything. There is no substitute for muddy boots on the ground, getting the job done. The same applies to boats at sea."

"Boats! Boats are submarines; surface ships are ships!" hummed Clive, under his breath, to himself.

"I believe in a strong, inviolate chain of command. Too many times, the COC is jumped by well-meaning officers bringing confusion in the ranks over who is in charge and who is running the show. I want no mistakes that I am running this show. You have done an excellent job, and it is up to me to provide the focus and impetus to finish it. This will probably be the last time we meet as a combined group. Things function better when a proper chain of command exists, so I will issue my orders through my staff, most of whom I brought with me. Responses for me please send up via the COC. A good, functioning chain of command ensures military order and discipline. We will have both in this Joint Task Force."

He gripped both sides of the lectern so hard the general's knuckles had turned white. General Lewis knew how to use his size. The Army general casually, and Clive thought purposely, eased Admiral Cameron aside.

Clive noted with surprise a rising anger toward this Johnny-come-lately who just marched in and told them how screwed up they were. The audacity of shoving the admiral aside. Everything Kurt brought him and Pete Devlin earlier this afternoon seemed to confirm his impression of General Lewis as a political general. What they needed was a combat leader. Cameron had been that. Maybe Kurt's friend at the Pentagon had been right about how the general got this job.

Lewis leaned forward. "I know some of you may question why an Army general has been given command of primarily a Navy and Marine Corps operation. There are no easy answers other than we need the forces here restaged ASAP to the Korean theater. The Mediterranean is small potatoes in comparison to the nation's agony on that peninsula. I was briefed by the secretary of Defense before I departed Washington, and Secretary Maddock tasked me personally with doing whatever needs to be done to disengage here. Once that is done, I suspect the Navy and Marine Corps units here will receive new orders directing them to sortie at max speed to the other side of the world, where the real war is happening."

Real war? We have bodies in body bags stacked in the freezer, and he thinks this is not a real war? Clive saw the quick glance by Admiral Cameron at the general.

A visible ripple swept through the audience like a miniature Mexican wave. A few mumbled *bullshits* disguised as coughs brought smiles to the captured Navy audience.

Lewis leaned back, looking at his audience as if evaluating his words. He saw the smiles and interpreted them as agreement. "We are going to be working harder in the days to come than you have been used to, and we will execute the orders of the secretary of Defense as we would the president's.

"Again, thanks for the nice soiree, but—" He turned to Admiral Cameron. "Admiral, where can we go for a private executive meeting?"

"We can use my stateroom, sir."

Lewis shook his head. "Thanks, but no thanks. Staterooms are for sleeping. I prefer an operations space where we can respond instantly to any changes in the military picture."

"Then we can go to the Sixth Fleet staff Operations space, General. It's small, but it has the display screens and systems to monitor everything going on."

Five minutes later, the general sat at the head of the aluminum table in the staff Operations room. The reflective light beneath the charts had been turned off after the general complained about how it affected his vision. Admiral Cameron sat to Lewis's left. Clive sat beside the admiral. Smiling, *puppy-dog* Colonel Brad Storey, General Lewis's executive aide, stood behind the Ranger general. Storey had already interpreted twice to Clive on their way down to the Operations space what the general meant in his wardroom greeting. *Spin doctor* came to Clive's mind as he listened to the fawning colonel.

Near Colonel Storey was Kurt Lederman, standing back as if seeking a shadow to hide in, in this well-lighted compartment. Clive would have smiled if he thought the action would have escaped the darting eagle looks of Lewis. Looks that seemed to say the new commander suspected everyone of being opposed to him, almost paranoid behavior, thought Clive. But what did he know about paranoia? He was a fighter pilot. Then again, just because the general might think everyone was against him didn't necessarily mean he was wrong. Neither he nor Pete Devlin was overjoyed about anyone relieving the "iron warrior," Admiral Cameron. They had been through the entire "mess," as Lewis called it, together. Had their noses bloodied and bloodied a few themselves. Right now, the United States Navy and United States Marine Corps team

owned the Mediterranean, despite the political infighting
by the French to bring Sixth Fleet under their NATO control or the French and Germans screaming at the other European countries to use the European rapid-reaction force.
Clive didn't see any Army soldiers over here with the exception of Lewis and the six he brought with him.

A one-star brigadier named Allen Toon sat to the left of
Colonel Storey. Clive and Pete Devlin had yet to figure
out what Brigadier General Toon's specific function was,
but the man's presence made him pensive over how this
added flag officer was going to fit into the picture.

Pete Devlin would never be a good poker player. Clive
could read the discomfort on the pilot's face. Pete sat beside Toon, silent and fuming. Other than a quick handshake with the two Army flag officers, Pete had kept his
lips together and his comments to himself. Clive knew the
new deputy commander, Sixth Fleet, was probably going
through agony, staying quiet for so long and keeping his
thoughts to himself. He hoped the man didn't bite through
his lips, he had them so tightly clenched.

Clive glanced at Lewis to see if the new boss was
aware of the dissatisfaction around the table. He fought
the urge to look at his watch. The tension around the table
was so thick you could cut it with a knife.

Only Dick Holman, sitting at the end of the table directly across from Lewis, seemed unaffected by the Army
general. He met the general's stare and nod with a slight
nod of his own. It was almost as if Dick viewed the
change of leadership as a common challenge. Captains of
ships endured staffs when they were assigned aboard their
vessels. To Dick, this was probably just one more
headache to sort. Of course, with the impending temporary orders expected from the chief of Naval Personnel
detaching Dick formally from the *Stennis* to Admiral
Cameron's staff, the maintenance of the embarked staffs
would soon become the problem of the current XO.

It would not surprise Clive if Dick Holman hoped General Lewis would return him to his job as commanding officer of USS *Stennis*.

Something was going on behind the scenes that Clive was being kept in the dark about. Admiral Cameron was keeping something back. Clive knew from the moment the three-star returned from Washington and Stuttgart that something happened at either one or both of those places. He initially attributed it to the death of the admiral's wife and the family turmoil in the admiral's life. However, sending what appeared to Clive to be a political general—*junior to the admiral*—to relieve Cameron seemed too ill timed to be anything but previously planned. The recent shuffle to bring Rear Admiral Devlin up as his deputy and shifting Dick Holman to a job normally held by an experienced admiral had further convinced Clive Bowen that something was going on behind the scenes. Whatever it was, he was going to find out, come hell or high water.

General Lewis looked directly at Holman. "We haven't met, have we?"

"No, sir, General. We haven't. I am Captain Richard Holman."

"What is your job, Captain Richard Holman?"

"General, as of this morning, I am the acting commander, Task Force Sixty-seven, in charge of the Naval Air Forces in the Mediterranean. I am also, or was, the commanding officer of the USS *Stennis*, the greatest aircraft carrier in the United States Navy."

Lewis nodded. "This is the *Stennis*, right?"

Holman nodded. "Yes, sir."

"Nice ship, Captain, but I noticed when we landed that there seemed to be several people smoking near the island."

"Well, they shouldn't be. The smoking area is on the stern of the ship. I'll see to that, General. Smoking is only allowed in assigned areas."

Lewis nodded. "That's not what I meant, Captain. I don't like smoking at all. I do not want anyone smoking near me or around me. I do not want to walk through a hallway or near one of these *authorized areas* and smell the rank odor of old, stale smoke. So make sure your crew understands that. Okay? We understand each other?"

Holman reached for his pocket. He started to bring out his chewed cigar and stick it between his teeth, but at the last second, his fingers exchanged it for a three-by-five card. He pulled a Skilcraft pen from his khaki shirt pocket. "Yes, sir. I shall personally take care of that, General. Are there any other odors, other than stale smoke, the general would like to steer clear of?"

Clive looked down at his hands, waiting for the general to explode.

"No, Captain, but from the fuel and oil atmosphere that permeates the ship, I suspect my uniforms will need special attention."

"There is no problem with that, General. I will ensure the laundry will give your uniforms special attention. I will make sure they know your instructions."

"I'll get with you on that, Dick," Colonel Brad Storey said, waving his hand a couple of times to catch Holman's attention.

There were several rules to sea life. Never piss off the personnelmen, who look after the service records; yours could wind up in Timbuktu. Never piss off disbursing clerks, who did the pay; you could find your pay screwed up so badly, it would take years to unravel. And never, ever piss off the ship's servicemen who run the laundry by insinuating they need special directions. Telling the laundry gang to take special care of the general's uniforms would be like waving a red flag in front of a raging bull. Dick Holman looked forward to allowing the general's aide to give directions to the laundry on the general's uniforms.

"Thanks, Richard. I would appreciate that. I like to have a fresh uniform laid out every morning. Nothing makes a warrior feel better than a clean, freshly ironed uniform. I look forward to it after I finish my workout in the gym and my shower. Colonel Storey will get with you later to find out what he needs to keep me going."

Lewis looked at Cameron. "Let's get on with the intelligence brief, and then let's you, I, your deputy, and chief of staff get together with me, Colonel Storey, and General Toon afterward."

Cameron motioned Kurt Lederman forward, and for the next sixty minutes, the men sat silently while the general tore apart Kurt's briefing. Lewis took pleasure in pointing out several grammatical errors on the printed PowerPoint slide. The general was quick to point out the different font sizes on the classification levels of several slides. "Uniformity," the general had commanded as his finger bounced off the paper brief, acting as if the word was a profound quote for legacy. The general frowned continuously as Kurt tried to dodge machine gun questions about the Algerian Kilo submarine and why the Navy was unable to determine whether it was under way or not. The idea that thirty or more Algerian fighter aircraft were unaccounted for and hidden somewhere in terrain that had nothing to hide anything seemed to the general to smack of incompetence. It was the only time that Clive saw Dick Holman shift uncomfortably in his seat. By this time, Pete Devlin looked like a steam locomotive ready to jump the tracks. It would not have surprised Clive if the mercurial admiral had leaped across the table in an attempt to throttle the abrasive general. Unfortunately, the general could probably pick Pete Devlin up with one hand and whip him around as easily as he would a length of lariat. Discretion is the better part of valor when angry.

"I think that about wraps it up as far as I am concerned. I was briefed about the stranded Marines in south Algeria and your inability to help them. So, before I left the European Command at Stuttgart this morning, I asked the Air Force what they could do. Seems they have one of their Aerospace Expeditionary Force flying through the area tomorrow and have offered to divert its route so they can see if they can make contact with the Marines. Let's hope they have better luck with their carrier in the air than you have had with your carrier on the sea," General Lewis said. He looked at his watch. "We have been here for over an hour. Captain . . . what was your name?"

"Kurt Lederman, General."

"Captain Lederman, in the future, let's keep my briefings no more than thirty minutes, and that's to include any questions I may have. We don't have the time to procrastinate or spend in endless briefings and staff meetings. You strike me as very bright for an intelligence officer, so . . . quick briefings and, if I have questions, you be sure to have the answers. Okay?"

Kurt glanced at Cameron, who nodded. "Yes, sir, General. General, is there any special format you prefer for your briefings and any special daily information you want presented? Does your staff have the Microsoft PowerPoint format—fonts and size—that you prefer, *sir?*"

"No specifics, Captain. Just uniform and consistent. Good staff work translates to good combat ops. I want a quick highlight on the plans for the next twenty-four hours along with the current force disposition. Following those two slides, tell me what the current intelligence picture is, what you think is likely to happen, and, if you have any recommendations, I also want to know what the negative fallout will be if I execute any of them."

Kurt acknowledged the general's directions and moved off to one side as he made notes in the small pocket-size green government notebook.

General Lewis turned to Admiral Cameron. "Could I ask you to clear the room for us?"

Admiral Cameron cleared his throat. "Gentlemen, would you excuse us? Clive, will you ask the chief and his sailors to transfer the operations to the ship's combat information center for about thirty minutes and to clear the space?"

Five minutes of awkward silence fell across the table as they waited for the enlisted sailors to depart. Kurt Lederman and Dick Holman eagerly evacuated the space, congratulating each other on escaping the meeting, once they were on the other side of the compartment hatch.

•   •   •

DICK LEANED DOWN TO KURT AS THEY passed the transom into the passageway and said, "Is asshole two words or one?"

Kurt grinned, "I'm not sure, but for this time, it is definitely capitalized."

Dick watched the sailor push the lever down, sealing the compartment with the flag officers.

GENERAL LEWIS LOOKED AROUND THE TABLE, taking muster. Once satisfied that only he, Admiral Cameron, Rear Admiral Pete Devlin, Brigadeer General Toon, Colonel Storey, and Clive remained, he turned to Gordon Cameron. "Admiral, at the risk of being callous, can I ask why Holman is on your staff?"

"Pardon?"

"The man is fat, Admiral. He should have been kicked out when he failed to stay within standards. The military is a fighting organization, and if our officers don't set the example of physical fitness, then the whole organization suffers. You will not find anyone out of standards on my staff, much less fat."

Clive and Pete Devlin exchanged amused glances and waited for the explosion they saw building in Cameron.

Admiral Cameron took a couple of deep breaths. "General, that man is overweight. You are right. But that man is more responsible for us having overwhelming might in this theater than you or I. A lesser officer would still be sitting with his carrier battle group on the other side of the Strait of Gibraltar, scared of mines and waiting for someone else to give him the all clear." Cameron's voice rose as his tempo of delivery picked up. "Yeah, he's overweight, and he's fifty-four years old, but he's more of a warrior than those who spend their time in fancy offices most of their career and take two-hour lunch breaks so they can work out and look physically fit while professionally . . . *professionally, they suck!*" Cameron rose slightly from his seat. He took another couple of breaths as the silence around the table became deafening. He sat back down and put both hands on the table and spread his fingers.

"General," Cameron sighed and in a tight voice continued, "I apologize for my outburst. Dick Holman is a fine officer, and I am recommending him for the Medal of Honor. His battle against an enemy submarine, innovation against smart mines deployed to keep American forces out of the Med, and his arrival with armed and ready fighter aircraft mark his combat accomplishments above and beyond the call of duty. Without him, we would never have evacuated what Americans we did out of Algiers, rescue President Hawali Alneuf, or be controlling the air at this time."

"Admiral, let's you and I have a little talk when we finish here." Lewis said, his voice low and menacing. "I appreciate your loyalty to your officers, but overweight is fat, and fat I do not want on my staff any more than I want someone who smokes. I daresay that another officer in the same situation as Holman would have brought the carrier battle group through as he did. The Navy has to learn that most warriors, when put in a situation, will rise to the occasion and do their duty. I would like a chop on any award packages that go out of the Joint Task Force."

Admiral Cameron's eyebrows bunched in a V, as furrows lined the three-star admiral's forehead. "Yes, General. We had better have that talk sooner rather than later. As for the awards package, it was sent up via Navy channels and not via the Joint Task Force."

HOLMAN, UNLIT CIGAR GRIPPED BETWEEN his teeth, opened the watertight door to the combat information center. The four officers working the tactical air picture stood near the boards and systems responsible for managing aircraft schedules, launch and recover times, and coming missions for the next few hours. As one mission was completed and erased from the board, an upcoming mission farther down the time line was added. If he wanted, he could call up a computer page that had the next forty-eight hours of scheduled flight operations on it. However, there was something satisfying about the old Navy method of using display boards and grease pencils. Holman stood silently observing the action while he chewed on the tip of his cigar. In minutes, he had a feel for what was going on, where aircraft were, and upcoming missions. He had quickly calmed down after leaving the meeting with the general. He didn't expect the man would keep him on the staff long. In fact, he looked forward to regaining his position as commanding officer of the *Stennis*, where he would be out of the joint chain of command that the general dearly loved and back in the real Navy.

The watertight door behind him opened. Kurt Lederman, the Sixth Fleet intelligence officer, entered, saw Dick, and walked over to stand beside him.

"Hi, Kurt. What brings you down to the operational end of the ship?" Dick took the cigar from his mouth and tossed it in a nearby wastebasket. "Not the same as smoking it."

"What did you think of our new commander?"

"Seems to have a lot of confidence in himself to get the job done. Hope he's right."

Kurt nodded. "Yes, I was impressed with his command of the first-person pronoun."

Dick chuckled. "Sure it wasn't his critique of your PowerPoint presentation?"

Kurt grinned. "If I had a dime for everyone who griped and complained about my presentations, I'd be a rich man today."

"So, what did bring you down here, Kurt? I know it wasn't to foment a rebellion against the Army general who has blessed us with his presence."

"You're right. I am concerned about the Algerian Kilo submarine at Oran. Our last imagery of the port showed it in dry dock, but with the cloud covering the Oran Naval Base for the past three days, we have nothing to confirm it is still in dry dock. What I would like to ask, in your new role as commander, Task Force Sixty-seven, is to send a recce bird over the facility to confirm it's still in dry dock."

Dick nodded as he thought over the request. "You know I don't have any photo recce birds on board the *Stennis*."

"There's VQ2's EP-3 at Sigonella," Kurt replied, referring to the premier reconnaissance aircraft of the Navy. The EP-3E was a modified, four-engine, turbo-prop aircraft capable of conducting sustained airborne reconnaissance with a crew of twenty-four.

"Since the bombing of Sigonella and Souda Bay, Kurt, I only have two EP-3Es remaining, and one is waiting for an engine change out. The only operational reconnaissance bird I have is Ranger Twenty-nine." Dick turned to Commander Steve Cloth, the Air Operations officer for Command Task Force Sixty-seven. He was responsible for the orderly scheduling and mission tasking for the Naval Air Forces operating in the Mediterranean. "Steve, what have we got scheduled for the EP-3 today?"

Steve Cloth was one of the hardest working officers on the staff of CTF Sixty-seven. His red hair belied the gentle countenance beneath the surface of this dedicated officer. Admiral Devlin had once jovially remarked that he doubted Commander Cloth was human, because the man never slept. Steve Cloth had developed a reputation for being able to carry the entire air picture in his mind without having to resort to ticklers, grease boards, or computers. With over one hundred aircraft airborne, Dick Holman knew he could never do a feat of that nature.

Without glancing at the air board or the computer presentation nearby, Commander Cloth replied, "The EP-3 is coming off station in the central Mediterranean, Captain. It is inbound to Sigonella with an ETA of 1330 Zulu. We do not have them scheduled again until tomorrow afternoon. Need to give them some crew's rest, if we can."

Dick glanced at the clock mounted on the nearby bulkhead. "They land in about thirty minutes, Steve. How long will it take them to do a hot turnaround?"

"About thirty minutes, sir. But, I recommend against it.

While I don't have the stats right here in front of me, my estimate is that the two crews manning the EP-3 have already exceeded one hundred fifty flight hours for the past thirty days. We are having to meet each crew with a flight surgeon to verify their physical and mental ability to continue flying."

"Like you said, Steve, you don't have the flight statistics in front of you, but I have no doubt that you are accurate in your assessment. The problem is, we only have this one operational EP-3 in theater. Joint Chiefs of Staff have already pulled the RC-135 out and redirected it to the Korean theater. The EP-3 is our only reconnaissance aircraft available."

"That's not exactly accurate, Captain," Commander Cloth replied.

"It isn't? What else do we have?"

"There is an RC-135 in the Azores. It landed this afternoon along with a flight of F-16s accompanying it."

Dick glanced at Kurt, who shrugged. "Why didn't we know about this?"

"We only got notified a couple of hours before they were inbound to the Azores, and as you know, the Azores belong to Joint Forces Command in Norfolk. We got the message only a few minutes before they landed. They are overnighting there and then continuing on to the Persian Gulf theater to conduct a week of operations. After that, they are ordered to continue around the world to the Korean operations area. I think this smacks of an Air Force publicity stunt to show their versatility in meeting any mission, anywhere, anytime."

Dick nodded. "Good. Let them have their publicity, as long as we can borrow that RC-135 while it transits the Med." He turned to Kurt. "We can have it do the recce of Oran tomorrow morning, Kurt, and that will take some of the operations tempo off the EP-3 flight crew."

Commander Cloth cleared his throat. "Sorry, Captain, but the RC-135 and its fighters have been ordered to transit along a southern route that will carry it across the Sahara desert. They have been tasked by General Lewis to find and locate the Marine Corps convoy that is lost in the southern desert area of Algeria."

Dick's eyebrows bunched as he heard the news. "He said something about that at our meeting a few minutes ago?" he asked, looking at Kurt.

"I didn't know anything about it until he did," Kurt protested.

"I looked at the tasking message, Captains, and it was issued while the general was in Stuttgart," Commander Cloth added.

"Well, if he expects me to manage the air picture, then I need to know his orders." Dick took a deep breath. *Actually, what the general ordered is the better option for the RC-135. The Air Force reconnaissance bird can in-flight refuel, unlike the Navy's EP-3E. The Marines stranded in the desert are a primary concern of everyone on the staff. Looks as if the General intends to make them a leading priority of his.* "Never mind. I cannot let my personal ego get in the way of a good decision. Steve, I want to know when that Air Force Aerospace Expeditionary Force takes off from the Azores. Make sure we have comms with them as they transit across our theater." He paused and then added, "Also, make sure we schedule some fighters and tankers to be airborne while they are within range of us. Just in case they meet with some of those missing Algerian fighters we haven't found yet."

"Yes, sir, Captain. I assumed you would want something along those lines, so I have scheduled a four F-14 combat air patrol one hundred miles inside Algeria along with a couple of S-3 tankers for company. It will give them the legs to support the AEF if need be, and we can launch additional tankers to get them back."

"So, does this mean we use the EP-3 now, Dick?" Kurt Lederman asked. "I know rescuing the Marines and their evacuees is important, but that Kilo could make life hell for our fleet if it gets under way."

"What do you think, Steve?" Dick asked the Air Ops boss.

"I am sure VQ can do it, Captain. Would it be all right

if we scheduled them for a hot recce and then ground them for crew rest for two days?" If he could get the aircrews two days' rest, then they would be good to go for a mission a day for thirty days before he would have to ground them again.

"Okay, that sounds good to me. Kurt, what is it you want them to do?"

The Intelligence officer walked over to the chart taped down on the display table. "What I would really like are some photos of the dry dock. Unfortunately, I know that the aircraft would have to overfly the naval base. It's too dangerous for them to do that. Too many shoulder-launched surface-to-air missiles everywhere. However, they have a side-looking optical scanner that can look into the base. It should show us sufficient data for a competent analyst to discern whether the submarine is still in the dry dock or if the dry dock is empty."

"Side-looking opical scanner? How do they do that?"

"Well, you see, first—"

Dick waved his hand. "Never mind, Kurt. I wouldn't understand any of that Intel mumbo jumbo anyway. Steve, contact Sigonella and tell them to have the EP-3 ready for a hot turnaround; then issue the Air Tasking Operations order to them."

"Yes, sir. Will do."

Kurt Lederman straightened up. "Thanks, Dick. I will be in my spaces if you hear anything. We have secure comms with the EP-3, and if I hear anything, I will make sure you are the first to know."

Kurt turned to leave, thought of something, and turned around. "Have you given more thought about our new commander?"

Dick nodded. "I think he is going be a dynamic asset to this team. Some of the things he presented during our roundtable, I am looking forward to seeing how they pan out."

"Sure, me, too." Kurt smiled, turned, and departed the Air Operations spaces, leaving Commander Cloth with his crew making the necessary arrangements to turn the EP-3 around and Captain Dick Holman, the new commander, Task Force Sixty-seven, deep in thought. He wondered briefly as he left what was going on in Dick's mind.

Dick made a mental note to increase the number of smoking areas on the ship. He grinned about the laundry directive. He would point out the laundry to the colonel and let the Army officer pass on his desires to the ship's servicemen. He would give anything to be there when Storey started issuing detailed instructions to sailors as if they were a civilian laundry. Should go over like a lead balloon. He chuckled over what the general was going to say and do when he encountered his first pair of drip-dried, starched underwear.

"Captain, I've taken care of the orders, sir," Commander Steve Cloth interrupted. "They have a projected take-off time of fifteen-fifteen hours with time on target estimate of sixteen-fifty hours. Should give them about five to six hours of daylight at this time of the year."

"Okay, Steve. Let me know when they're airborne. I'd like to be here and observe. Meanwhile, what else do we have up right now?"

Nightly, around nineteen hundred hours, Steve Cloth sat with Admiral Devlin—starting tonight, he would be doing that with Captain Holman—and they decided the missions needed for the next day. They also went over the normal disposition of forces needed for battle group protection. Usually, an hour was needed to review the air plans and approve the next day's operation.

"We still have three pairs of F-14s in combat air patrol, CAP, south of the battle group providing rapid reaction to any threats. Other than that, sir, we have the normal operations going on. Ranger Two-nine is returning from an early-morning central Mediterranean mission."

"Steve, make sure we send a flight of F/A-18s with Ranger Two-nine during her reconnoiter of the Oran Naval Base. Keep the Tomcats where they are."

"Yes, sir," he glanced at the board. "We have a new CAP launching about thirty minutes after the EP-3 is airborne out of Sigonella."

General Lewis was going to be a royal pain in the ass, but at least he was shaking up any complacency they may have on the staff.

"Yes, Steve. Let's hope the Air Force can provide us some up-to-date information on our stranded Marines. The Marines are in a convoy heading southwest to close the distance between them and some Army Chinooks." He looked at the long-range schedule on the board. "I suspect that it will take them another two days to arrive where the Army can make pickup. You have any thoughts?"

Commander Steve Cloth shook his head. "Air Force C-5s off-loaded the Army Special Forces helicopters this morning. According to latest sitrep from Base Butler, they are working on a plan to shorten the pickup distance or do something to get to the Marines sooner. Won't know until they establish direct communications with us. Right now, we send a message, and they send a response; they send a message, and we write a response. Unfortunately, our Navy-Marine Corps Internet doesn't interface with the Army equivalent. It would be nice if we had a direct chat line like we do with the ships in the group and our shore-based facilities."

Holman moved to the board. "When are we going to have the other EP-3 up?"

Cloth ran his hand through his close-cropped red hair. "We are still clearing the damage away in Sigonella and the necessary tools and supplies needed to sustain the shore-based air assets have yet to ramp up fully. Supply is estimating a new engine and prop for the down bird some-time tomorrow, arriving via the Air Force Air Mobility Command flight transiting from Dover."

"Steve, I know I promised to give the crews on the EP-3s two days off, but don't hold me to that. While Kurt is concerned about that old Algerian submarine, I am more concerned about the unlocated Algerian fighters. I would like tomorrow to have the EP-3E fly a southern mission—overland. Put a couple of F/A-18s under her wings, and see what they can find on those missing Algerian fighters. They make me nervous. We got a bunch of fanatics running around North Africa who can't make up their minds whether they are religious fanatics or nationalist fanatics, but they find communal solace against America, *'the great Satan.'* I want to eliminate that remaining air threat. While the EP-3E is airborne, see if they can contact the Marines. I know the aircraft doesn't have the legs to reach their area and return, but I would like to beat the Air Force to reestablishing contact with them. Either way, the EP-3 has a comms suite on it that could be used for relay if the RC-135, Rivet Joint aircraft, does find them."

Commander Steve Cloth grinned. "I would like to beat the Air Force, too, Captain. I will have a revised flight plan for tomorrow, along with a proposed Air Tasking order for you by our nineteen hundred hours meeting."

"Nineteen hundred hours?"

The commander looked perplexed. "Yes, sir. Admiral Devlin and I always got together at nineteen hundred to go over the next day's flight Operations. I presumed you would want to—"

"You're right, Steve. Nineteen hundred would be fine. Let's do it in my in-port stateroom, where we'll have some privacy and quiet."

"Yes, sir. And, I'll contact you when the EP-3 has launched."

Dick Holman nodded. "That's fine, Steve. I am going to the bridge to see the acting commanding officer of the *Stennis* and wipe that shit-eating grin off his face. Plus, I don't want him to forget that I will be coming back." He shook his head as a smile broke across his face. "I hate to see an XO having so much fun."

"DICK, GOOD TO SEE YOU. COME ON IN," Pete Devlin said, pointing the new CTF Sixty-seven to an armchair near the couch. He shut the stateroom door behind Dick.

"I am glad you stopped by. How goes your first day on the job?" the admiral asked as he flopped down on the couch across from him, threw his feet up on the coffee table, and took a sip of the lukewarm coffee in front of him. "Help yourself to some coffee if you want it." He tossed a folder on the table. "You coming by gives me an excuse to skip some of this paperwork."

Dick shook his head. "Half day on the job, Admiral. Thought I would stop by and give you an update on the air campaign and solicit any suggestions or recommendations you may have."

"Glad of that. I rather feel about my promotion up as you do. I enjoyed being the HMFIC—*head mother fellow in charge*—and now, here I am, second fiddle."

"Head mother fellow?"

"Well, we must have some civility in the new job, my fine shipmate. So, tell me what's going on and, as always, whether you need advice from an admiral or not, I will be sure to give it."

Dick grinned. He took the next ten minutes bringing Admiral Pete Devlin, the new deputy commander, United States Sixth Fleet, up to date on the air picture. Pete Devlin flinched when Dick briefed the plans for the RC-135 and F-16 flights tomorrow across the southern Sahara desert.

Dick was gratified when the admiral nodded in agreement over his plans to hot refuel the EP-3E and have it conduct a close flyby of the Oran Naval Base. The admiral mumbled, "Good, good," when Dick briefed him about the plans to have the EP-3E fly south tomorrow with some F/A-18s to both provide a Combat Air Patrol if Rivet Joint encountered any problems and to look for those missing Algerian fighters. The two spent nearly thirty minutes discussing the missing Algerian fighter aircraft that seemed to have vanished into the desert. Their concern focused on the aircraft, both of them being aviators, with little discussion on what they would do if the Algerian Kilo submarine sortied out of Oran. Kurt believed the submarine to be in dry dock, but like all Intelligence Officers, if his sources weren't up to date and he couldn't find it on CNN, he tended to be skeptical.

"Seems to me that you are making me look bad, Dick.

You've already thought ahead as to what needs to be done and executed it. I don't think I would have changed a thing, other than lean over the shoulders of my staff and *granny* them to death."

Dick stood, went to the sink, and poured himself a glass of water. "All that talking made my throat dry."

Pete Devlin reached into the folder on the coffee table and drew out a sheet of paper. "Look at this, Dick, and keep it to yourself—including from Admiral Cameron. I don't think he needs to know this, since it is only subjective."

Dick reached forward and took the paper. "What is it?"

"I asked Kurt to see if he could find out anything about General Lewis. He stopped by about an hour before you did and dropped that off. It's an informal, nonattributable E-mail from a shipmate of his at the N2 at OPNAV. Seems our General Lewis has some powerful friends in Congress."

Dick scanned the half-page E-mail and looked up at the admiral. "What does this mean, Admiral?"

"It means our dear friend, Senator Glendale, on the Senate Armed Forces Committee, plays golf with our general and has for years. They are close friends. Apparently the Army, in their infinite wisdom, passed over General Lewis for his third star, but Senator Glendale put the skids on the flag selection list until Lewis's name was added."

"That means if they added his name, then they had to take someone else's off."

Pete nodded. "Yeah. Right on the nose. Some bright, enterprising two-star major general in the Army is still a two-star major general in the Army, while our new commander of JTF African Force earned his third star the old-fashioned way: politics."

"But, why did they send him out here? Punishment? And if so, for whom? Us or him?"

"None of the above. Apparently, Senator Glendale has made it known that he considers Lewis as a great choice for the next Army chief of staff and eventually the chairman of the Joint Chiefs of Staff. If you believe the candor from that E-mail—*personally, I'd never send anything like this via E-mail; you got no control over it*—this assignment for General Lewis is a stepping-stone to his fourth star."

"Damn. I suspect the general knows this, too?"

"I would be very surprised if he doesn't."

"Even so, Admiral. As much as it miffs us with his tasking the RC-135 to locate our stranded Marines before he even assumed the reins of JTF commander, it was a good action. No offense, but we should have thought of it first."

Pete drew his feet off the coffee table and leaned forward with his arms on his knees. "Dick, we did. Admiral Cameron has been asking for a Rivet Joint in the theater since the Joint Chiefs of Staff withdrew them for the Korean theater. All we got was, *'Sorry, none available.'*"

"Except this one."

"Except this one, but I would bet my gonads that if we backtrack the decision-making process, we would find the Air Force using this opportunity to garner some political support on the hill—"

"I wouldn't want to say that too loud, Admiral."

"Yeah, you're right," he said, leaning back and throwing his arms across the back of the couch before he crossed his legs. "I keep forgetting that in this age of jointness, we aren't supposed to suspect our fellow services of being political and parochial."

"But it wouldn't be the first time. Remember Desert Storm?"

"Who doesn't?"

"The Air Force was ahead of us," Dick said. "Their cameras on the aircraft were compatible with CNN. They could fly a mission, get good footage of bombs going off and missiles hitting, then slip the film to CNN. By the time their aircrews showered and were having a cold beer, the film was live on CNN. As for us in the Navy, we had to rerecord our films before we could share them with the press pool. Our air victories were sometimes two days old before the public saw them."

"I would call that forethought, Dick. At least we learned from that."

Dick stood and looked at his watch. "Admiral, it's around fifteen hundred hours, sir. I have to go back down to Air Operations. I want to observe the EP-3E reconnaissance and then—it's been a long day—I'm going to have a light dinner and maybe a short nap."

Pete Devlin looked up at Dick Holman. "Thanks for coming by, Dick. Keep the story on General Lewis under your hat. I don't think it's fair to Admiral Cameron what they've done, but he doesn't need to be bothered with the internal Washington politics that sent the Army three-star to us."

Dick shut the door behind him, rubbed his eyes, and headed off down the ladders to the Air Operations space. Just what they needed in the middle of the crises here and in Korea, both challenging America's will and military might: politics.

CHAPTER 6

⚓

STAPLER WORKED HIS WAY TO THE TOP OF the rise where Corporal Heights lay watching the oasis through a pair of binoculars the LT had loaned him. Small rust-colored rocks poked through Stapler's desert cammies as he crawled the last few feet to the top. Christ! He was tired. Over forty-eight hours without sleep. He didn't count the few minutes he had gotten earlier that morning.

The swimming movement of his feet left a wake in the brown, sun-baked sand as he worked his way uphill. One more hour, and the sun would be down. The cold of the desert night would replace the scorching heat but, for the first hour, the change would be welcomed. He slapped Heights lightly on the shoulder.

"What you got?"

Stapler rested his M-16 on the crest of the hill, noticing the cracked, sunburned skin of his hands. His thumbs were cracked so badly from the dry, continuous baking heat that the skin around the nails and on the pads had burst, exposing tiny streaks of raw meat, making them tender to the touch. No blood flowed from the small cracks. Stapler cynically figured the white, blazing heat of the Sahara sun was boiling it away before it reached the surface.

He imagined he could almost smell the water at the oasis. He ran his tongue around the inside of his mouth, feeling the dryness, an ache rising from the pit of his stomach, begging for water. The green palm trees ahead shouted *"Water here"* at him. He wanted to jump up and run toward the oasis. The urge quickly passed. He wasn't the only one thirsty. Only a small amount of water remained from the many gallon jugs they had loaded at the compound. Survival manuals called for a gallon of water a day while in the desert, but they had been unable to carry enough to give forty-three people a gallon a day. The truck had to be balanced between fuel, water, food, and the few people unable to walk. Already they had three suffering heat exhaustion. Fuel was the number-one priority. Without it, the vehicles would run dry, and they would never escape this desolate country.

If they had stayed at the compound, they would have had water until rescue arrived. Stapler doubted they would have held out long against any sustained assault. The smoke rising from the burning compound soon after they fled showed it would have been a fight if they had remained. In addition, with no hope of backup or rescue, they stood little chance.

Their intent was to get close to Base Butler. Let the Army rescue them. He'd put up with Top Sergeant MacGregory's ridicule. What was it the gruff old bastard always said whenever some officer used the word *intent?* *"Our intent, Marines . . ."* *"My intent is . . ."* *"The commandant's intent is . . ."* Top Sergeant MacGregory would always mutter, "Intent is a task with a purpose, so *what in the hell* is the purpose, sir?"

"However, a decision made is a decision executed," is what Gunnery Sergeant Leslie Stapler of the Marine Corps fucking Foreign Legion in the middle of the Sahara desert says. What was it the young female government

employee—*and she was nice to look at*—told him about making decisions? It went something like, "Indecision is the key to flexibility." Or, maybe it was, "Flexibility is the key to indecision?"

Visions of Top Sergeant MacGregory mixed up with the cute government employee and, somewhere, Niagara Falls washed over them as they skipped in and out of his thoughts. He licked his dry, cracked lips.

"Gunny? Gunny?"

Stapler opened his eyes and raised his head off his arms. How long had he been asleep?

"Gunny? Gunny, you all right?" Heights asked, reaching over and touching Stapler on the shoulder.

"What'd you see, Corporal?" Stapler asked, turning his head slightly so he could look at Heights. He noticed skin peeling from Heights's nose—raw skin exposed beneath where the flakes of skin had fallen off. "Put some screen on that nose, Heights. You want to see it fall off? Christ, son, have I got to be your mother, too?"

"Sorry, Gunny. I don't have any."

Stapler pulled a tube of government-issued sunscreen from his rear pocket. The Navy stock numbers were larger than the words identifying the product. The end curled on itself from where Stapler had rolled the tube, forcing the cream out. "Here, take this."

"How 'bout you, Gunny. I don't want to take yours. Your nose doesn't look any better than mine."

"You think I'd give you my last sunscreen? Not my fault you either lost yours or forgot to bring it, Marine," Stapler said, knowing it was his only tube. He pulled his helmet down lower. "And keep that helmet over your eyes and forehead. It'll help block out the glare of the sun and protect your face."

"Thanks, Gunny." Heights handed the binoculars to Stapler. He doubted the gunny had another tube, but you didn't argue with gunnery sergeants. They tended to get pissed off when you did.

"You smell it, Corporal?"

"Smell what, Gunny?" Heights lifted his head and took

several deep breaths. "Oh, you mean that smell." Heights pointed to the east of the oasis. "It's those camels, Gunny. I have never smelled shit like that."

Stapler had meant the water, but he took a deep breath and agreed with Heights. "Yeah, that's some stink all right. What else do you see at the oasis?" Maybe he was the only one to smell the water. Maybe he was so thirsty, the scent of water was an illusion—a nostril mirage.

"Gunny, I count two trucks, thirty to forty men. No women or children. Camels grouped to the right—east. See them?"

Stapler swung the binoculars in that direction. "Yeah, Corporal, I see them. About twenty to twenty-five camels, wouldn't you say?"

"But no women and children, Gunny," Heights emphasized. "See?"

"Means they aren't out for a family outing, Corporal. Is that what you're trying to tell me?"

"I was thinking, Gunnery Sergeant, that if they were peaceful, they would be traveling with their families. That many men together, all of them with weapons, tells me they're either bandits or a military force."

Stapler put the binoculars down. "Well, Corporal Heights, I usually frown on Corporals thinking before they've been in the Corps at least eight years, but in this case, I believe we need all the bright ideas we can get." He slapped the man on his shoulder. "I believe you are right. For an old-timer like me, the fact that vehicle down there is a military truck tends to indicate it is a military force."

Heights quickly lifted the binoculars again, twisted the focus a slight turn, and looked. "Yeah, you're right, Gunny," Heights said with a hint of disappointment over failing to notice the Arabic numbers on the side of the truck doors.

"It's been twenty hours without water, Corporal. Got plenty of food for the next few days, but without water, we won't make it. We already have three down—two of the older male riggers and one of the two female riggers— with heat exhaustion. The female rigger lost her hat somewhere along the way and never replaced it. Even a hand-kerchief draped over her head would have been something. It's a wonder she's still alive."

Stapler rolled onto his back so he could look back down the hill toward their camp. "It's a wonder none of us Marines are down there with them, considering we hiked most of the way. Therefore, Corporal Heights, in the best tradition of the United States Marine Corps, we are going to take that oasis. Darhickam Oasis is its name, according to the map Mr. Bearcat Jordan carries. Of course, the professor pronounces it differently. One day, some obscure little historian at headquarters, Marine Corps, will discover this battle and write a little footnote about it for *Naval Proceedings*. Then you'll have a reporter show up at your front door, and your wife will wheel you out to the sunporch with all your grandchildren nestled around your ankles to tell her all about it."

"Gunny, you sure you ain't been in the sun too long?" Heights grinned.

Stapler looked at the corporal and saw the tight smile stretching the sunburned face. Those small cracks on the lips of the Marine must hurt like a son of a bitch. Stapler grinned, too. "Yeah, Corporal. Amazing what the sun will do to you."

Heights nodded toward the oasis. "Lot of open ground to cover, Gunny."

Stapler rolled back over, took the binoculars from Heights, and scanned the oasis. Most of the occupying force were wearing black or white *thobes*. Their heads were covered by a diagonally folded cotton square held in place by a double-coiled cord circlet, the *ghutra*. By the time he escaped the clutches of the professor, Stapler was going to know more about the Bedouin lifestyle than any Marine deserved to know.

The professor, who never stopped talking, said the free-flowing movement of the *thobe* actually helped cool the skin during the day and kept the body warm during the cooler nights. Stapler didn't really understand how—*he didn't care how*. The *thobe* covered every inch of the body with the exception of their hands, face, and feet. He looked at Heights and then himself. Of course, they both had their sleeves rolled all the way down and a helmet shoved down on their heads. Moist blisters covered the backs of his hands. Heights had the same sun-baked blisters on his.

Stapler lifted the binoculars again and focused them on the oasis. This time, he spotted several individuals near a half tent located about fifty feet from the vehicles. He had missed them before because the tent's khaki color blended with the desert sands. They drew Stapler's intense interest. He counted seven soldiers, but others could be resting under the tent or somewhere else in the oasis. They wore light brown uniforms. Regulars, he guessed. He searched the area again for heavy weapons, which for him meant anything larger than a rifle. They could have rocket-propelled grenade launchers, but he didn't see any. If they did have any heavies, they were probably in the trucks. The uniformed men were drinking small finger cups of strong Arab coffee and carrying on an animated conversation. Whatever weapons they had were out of sight. Those occupying the oasis acted as if no nearby threat existed. No perimeter guards patrolling the grounds, nor did he see any defensive measures—no foxholes, no stacked rocks— nothing. They acted as if they had all the time in the world. Well, that time was coming to a quick end.

He handed the binoculars back to Corporal Heights. "I'm going to send Kellogg up to relieve you, Corporal— along with the nightscope. When she gets here, you come down and find me. I'm going to talk with the Lieutenant and see how we are going to do this, then we'll go over it with the Marines. Keep an eye out for any sign of unusual activity. From what I see, I don't think they suspect us of being here, and that is the way I would like to keep it."

"Yes, Gunny," Heights acknowledged. He put the binoculars to his eyes again and swept the small oasis below for a few seconds before putting them down. "Lot of open ground. Lot of camel shit out there, too."

Stapler's eyebrows bunched together, and he wiped

away some sand stuck to his leathery face. "And, Heights, do you think I intend for us to cross that open ground in the daylight? Christ, son, give me some sense."

"Sorry, Gunny. It was just—"

"I know what it is, Corporal. You think I am going to go back down, get the Marines, and we are going to charge across this space toward the oasis. Even I am well aware we wouldn't make it. Marines take time to plan for operations and, by God, this one is going to be no different." Stapler sighed. "Between you and me, Heights, we have been lucky to make it this far without being attacked. There is no going back. Behind us, somewhere, are those who burned the compound after we left. They're out there, Corporal. They're tracking us, and they outnumber us. I'm surprised they haven't stumbled on us yet, considering we've done shit to cover our tracks."

"Gunny, you have a way of putting a dark cloud over a nice day."

"A cloud would be nice. Keep coming up with ideas, Corporal Heights. We may need some of them." Stapler grinned at the young Marine. The spread of his lips pulled the dry, cracked skin apart, causing the grin to disappear quickly. *Good Marine,* Stapler said to himself. *Just hope he doesn't become a dead Marine.* He glanced down at the others in the encampment. Good chance that by tonight some of his Marines would be dead. It was something that continuously intruded on his thoughts and had since the battle last night. Death was always waiting out front. Marines fight and win battles. They don't sit around, afraid one of them was going to die. Death was a frequent traveler with the Marine Corps. It came with the turf, the price paid for honor and glory.

Stapler inched his way downhill until he could stand without danger of being seen from the oasis. The riggers had three ends of a canvas top stretched and tied between a humvee and the truck. The fourth corner seemed to be giving them a problem. Either they had tied the rectangular sheet awry, or the vehicles were parked too far apart. Most of the riggers had crawled under the three-quarters hung sheet, even as the three men working to tie up the last end continued their disjointed effort. If they didn't get it done soon, he would tell them to leave it. Everyone needed to conserve their energy. The other humvee, parked close to the side of the hill, had both advantages of a small half canvas stretched to two rods in the ground and a natural shade created by the setting sun. Stapler saw the professor and his male assistant, Karim, sitting with their backs against the rocks. As he neared, Karim leaped up and began to dance around the area, shouting, "Jesus Christ, Jesus Christ!" while slapping his back.

Hell of a time to become religious, thought Stapler. *And a good thing this large hill absorbs the sounds between us and the enemy three miles away.* The professor grabbed the taller Karim by the arm and beat the back of the young man's shirt with the palm of his hand. "Scorpion," Stapler heard the professor say. Karim ripped his shirt off, threw it on the sand, and stomped it repeatedly.

The only live things seen in the two days since they fled the compound had been scorpions and beetles. He wondered briefly how scorpion would taste. He hated beetles, which he had eaten during his survival, evasion, resistance, and escape—SERE—refresher training two years ago. If you can get past the initial crunch followed by the scrape of their shells on the side of your throat as you swallow, then you can eat anything. If he had to do it again, he would swallow them whole, even if MacGregory said they'd crawl back up if you didn't chew them. Chewing them made him nearly throw up.

Two days crossing the hot Sahara had taken their toll. A few, such as *Miss Sheila Anne Forester,* complained nonstop about everything from being tired to making camp to wanting food to anything else they could think of. He ignored the complaints, forcing the convoy to continue, alternating drivers and guards with those walking, so everyone could snatch a few winks of sleep—but continuously moving, putting distance between them and those following. They were being followed. There was no doubt in Stapler's mind. He would. Therefore, they must.

The three vehicles had been unable to take the forty-three of them on board at the same time. The humvee with the radio held six, the other held eight, and in the truck he crammed three in the cab and ten on the bed amid the water, food, and diesel fuel. If the truck ever took a direct hit, those on board would be immolated by the fireball. He initially assigned the older individuals to the humvees and the truck. The two women riggers, Mary Coblen and Dorothy Meyran—"*Call me, Dot, please,*" midforties, he estimated—had insisted on walking. They said it was a great way to lose weight, and they could afford to lose some. He couldn't argue with that.

The two women walked until yesterday noon when Dot, the younger one, collapsed. Stapler originally thought of them as his Hell's Grannies from the way the two walked and Mary talked. He knew few boatswain mates in the Navy with more skill in the colorful language of cursing than Mary. Mary sat where she had since early this morning on the back of the truck bed, watching over the unconscious Dot. Stapler wasn't too concerned about the three who collapsed. A little water and rest, and they would come around. It wasn't as if they had been in the desert heat for weeks. Christ! It had only been two days. How in the hell were they going to handle another three or four days until rescue arrived?

Stapler reached the bottom of the hill and motioned Private "Catsup" Kellogg over to him. Several nearby Marines sat with their shoes and socks off, doctoring their feet with balm and powder. He needed to do the same. Draped socks over nearby rocks dried quickly in the heat. He told Kellogg to go relieve Corporal Heights at the top of the hill and handed her the nightscope from his pack. Stapler emphasized specific instructions to follow in the event that she saw any hints of new activity inside the oasis. New activity might mean those occupying the oasis had become aware of them.

"And keep your eyes open, Catsup. I know you're tired, but stay awake. I'll send someone up in about an hour to relieve you."

She licked her dry lips and leaned forward. "Gunny, I still have some water," she confided.

Stapler leaned down. "Then while you are up on the hill, you drink it. It's your water. By tomorrow morning, we will have more." He fought the urge to accept the offer, as much as he wanted to.

"I thought, maybe, you might want—"

"Kellogg, get your butt up the hill. Do I look like an old man?"

She grinned. "Well, you do remind me of my father sometimes."

Stapler's eyebrows bunched together, and a grin escaped. "Kellogg, I ain't your father, but if I was, I would put you across my lap and spank the bejesus out of you."

"Oh, Gunny," she said, faking a moan. "You say the most beautifullest things to a young lady. Spankings? And, me without my leather straps."

"Enough, Kellogg. Get your ass up the hill, and don't get it shot off." He turned to move into the bustle of the camp.

"I won't, Gunny. It's made for spanking."

Stapler ignored her. Women in the Marine Corps made combat a little more attractive, but combat wasn't meant to be attractive. Combat meant long periods of watching and waiting followed with a few minutes of racing adrenaline, gut-wrenching fear, and ass-tightening fighting. For him, the vote was still out on women in combat, regardless of what those feminazis, who had never been in battle, thought. He had a quick fantasy about Kellogg involving leather, two mirrors, and a French maid's outfit before intruding thoughts of his wife, JCPenney, and credit cards quickly killed it.

"Don't keep those socks and shoes off too long," he said to the three Marines sitting near the front of the truck, their backsides in the shade of the radiator. He wondered how they stood the heat but then realized the radiator was probably cooler than the surrounding rocks. "And draw those feet into the shade. Last thing you want is blistered feet and ankles. They'll rub raw in minutes when you start walking."

He moved on to a weak chorus of "*Yes, Gunnery Sergeant.*"

He faintly heard two of them exchange comments.

"Why is he smiling?"

"He's a gunny. As things get worse, life becomes more fulfilling."

"Then we must be fixing to die."

He forced the Kellogg-engineered grin from his face. His lips hurt from the effort. Damn, it hurt to smile and it hurt not to.

During the slow but steady pace as they fled the enemy, Stapler had alternated the Marines so they could rest every couple of hours. The survival of the convoy rested on the Marines, not the riggers, and definitely not the professor, Karim, and *Miss Sheila Anne Forester.* He looked around the encampment for his thorn. Griped and bitched the whole two days. How can one woman so young have so much bitching in her? He had hoped the sun would have tempered her. He shaded his eyes and looked toward the blazing orb beating down on them. Not much longer, and it would disappear below the horizon. For a moment, he understood why the Egyptians worshiped the sun.

The trip had been one of constant movement on his part to keep the convoy going. Stapler assigned a Marine to each of the humvees and forced two of the riggers to walk so he could put two Marines in the back of the truck. Their task was to return fire and give the Marines who were walking an opportunity to take cover and join the fray. He and the lieutenant had walked the entire distance.

This lack of capability to put everyone on board a vehicle limited the speed to about three miles an hour. Normal terrain would have allowed them to move around five miles per hour at a fast pace. The sand, uneven terrain, and thousands of small rocks that rolled under the boot with each step made walking atrocious and dangerous. Several had minor sprained ankles caused by boots twisting off the rocks. If they had been wearing anything other than steel-toed combat boots, some of those sprained ankles would have been broken ones.

The rigger wounded during the return from Alpha site had his arm in a sling and rested near the three sunstroke victims. Mary was wiping the sweat from her own forehead and then wiping the wet handkerchief across the face of Dot, who remained unconscious and moaning. They needed water, and they needed it tonight. Without it, he had little doubt that Dot would die. She was the worst of the three. The other two were semiconscious. These two had managed to sip some water and seemed to be recovering. He ran his tongue across dry, cracked lips. They all needed water. Like Kellogg, Stapler had a couple of tablespoons of the precious liquid remaining in his canteen. As much as he wanted it, he refused to drink it until the others had fresh water.

During the trip, the other Marines walked alongside the vehicles with a couple out front and another two bringing up the rear. The first night out had been tense. By dawn, they had only gone about eight miles but had put a few hills between them and the compound. Smoke rising from the direction of the compound told them there was no going back.

The first day started like an excursion. But the rising sun soon burned off the chill of the desert night to bake everything under it. He tried to ration the water, but the riggers drank whenever they felt thirsty, which increased as the day wore on. Stapler had seen the water rapidly disappearing, and when his entreaties went unheeded, he had the Marines fill their canteens to the top. He ordered them to ration the water, but even so, with two days of sweat-sucking heat, the water soon disappeared. At least the Marines had kept water a little longer than the others. With the exception of a few drops scattered through the ranks, the last of the water had disappeared this morning.

The LT stood to one side, talking to someone hidden by the second humvee. Stapler headed in that direction, and as he approached, he heard her before he saw her and felt the hairs on the back of his neck rise. *Miss Sheila Anne*

Forester stood in front of the lieutenant, reaching out every few seconds, touching the officer on the arm or shoulder. Stapler shook his head. If the lieutenant's small head wasn't doing the thinking instead of his big one, she was going to make sure it was before this trip was over.

"Lieutenant," Stapler interrupted as he approached. He had no desire to know what they were discussing. He saw the smile disappear on little *Miss Sheila Anne Forester's* face. It gave him a perverse sense of pleasure that he affected her the same way.

"Yes, Gunny."

"Sir, may I speak with you . . . alone?"

"Oh, we have military secrets out here that only the lieutenant needs to know?" Sheila asked sarcastically, her eyes narrowing with contempt.

Stapler stepped back and stared at the ground around her feet.

"What are you doing?" she asked.

"Just checking where the venom fell. With no water, everything liquid is welcomed."

"Jeff!"

Jeff! She's calling the lieutenant Jeff!

Lieutenant Nolan's face turned red. "Excuse me, Sheila. I'll be right back. The gunny and I need to talk." He touched Stapler's arm, and the two moved off toward the edge of the group, leaving *Miss Sheila Anne Forester* glaring after them.

She stood there a few seconds with her hands on her hips, angrily pouting at the two as they walked away, before she stomped her foot and walked away in the opposite direction.

"Jeff?" Stapler whispered to the young officer.

"Yes, Jeff," Nolan replied, his voice firm.

"I thought it was Malcolm?"

"It is, but Sheila thinks my middle name Jeff sounds better. Who am I to argue with a civilian?" He grinned. "And you shouldn't, either. Her father knows a lot of people in Washington and could make it rough on us when we get back."

"What's he going to do, LT? Make me retire?"

Nolan ignored the questions as Stapler looked away from the lieutenant to hide his ire.

Kids! A couple of seconds of silence passed before Stapler turned to the officer. "Her father paid for this expedition only if they took her with them. I don't think he is going to make any heat as long as his little daughter gets back safe and sound. Come to think of it, most likely, as long as she is safe and sound, he probably doesn't care whether she makes it back or not. Probably why he sent her; to give him some peace at home. LT, a little unsolicited advice: You are the one who needs to be careful. Whatever it is she is up to most likely won't be in your or our best interests. Kind of reminds me of the black widow spider, they eat—"

Lieutenant Nolan held up his hand. "Gunny, I'm a big boy and quite capable of taking care of myself. She is not a bad person once you get to know her. Sure, she's a little rude and, maybe spoiled a little—"

"A little?"

"But it is more a self-esteem problem than a conceit one. She just needs reassurance that everything is all right."

"And I am sure the lieutenant—being a sensitive nineties male—has the right reassurance for her?"

"Gunny, it is strictly in the line of duty."

"Lieutenant, if you believe that, then I have a bridge I want to sell you."

"What you got, Gunny?" Lieutenant Nolan asked, stopping and facing Stapler, a slight edge to his voice.

It's your funeral, Lieutenant, Stapler thought. In his mind, he had a quick vision of the lieutenant marrying this vampire, having several kids, and staying home to raise them while she went partying off into the sunset. *"Tsch tsch,"* Stapler said. He looked up and saw Nolan glaring at him.

"Okay, Lieutenant, you're right. I am out of line. I will leave the reassuring to you." Stapler hooked his thumb toward the top of the hill. "The oasis is crawling with enemy troops. Most of them are natives—Tauregs, as the professor calls them—along with about a dozen military advisors. I only saw seven, but others may be scattered throughout the camp. They are probably the ones in charge. They have made camp for the night. Tents are up, and campfires are burning."

"How many total?"

"About thirty to forty. They have a truck. If we capture it, our men won't have to walk the last hundred miles. No heavy weapons seen. If they have any, they are probably in the truck. Best place to protect them from the sand."

"Think we can take the oasis?"

Stapler reached in his shirt pocket and brought out his last cigarette. He unfolded the package surrounding it carefully, as if unwrapping a highly valuable treasure. He held it to his eyes and searched for any breaks and then, satisfied, he lit it. He had always meant to quit smoking; looked as if he was going to have that opportunity.

"Ought to give those up, Gunny."

"You are right, sir. This will be my last one, and then I intend to follow your advice. No more."

"Good." Nolan hitched his pants up. The gunny sergeant was beginning to listen to his advice. "You'll live longer if you give those coffin nails up."

"You're probably right, LT. Anyway, this is my last one. Got no choice. As for the oasis, sir, it's not a question of can we take it, it's a fact; we have to take it. Without water, we can't go on. We wouldn't last another day. We have a few drops in the bottom of one of those plastic gallon containers. We are portioning it to our three heat stroke victims. When that goes, if they haven't recovered and we haven't secured a water source, they die. We die soon afterward."

Stapler pointed toward the far horizon, back the way they had come. "Somewhere behind us are more enemy. It is not an *if,* it is a *when* they catch up with us. We don't need to be caught between these two groups. We can't hope to win against both of them. This way, we take the oasis, get a much-needed truck, probably find some food, definitely replenish our water and, hopefully, destroy this group before they can combine forces with the other."

"Gunny, this isn't a campaign. We only need to get to the rescue point, not defeat the entire Algerian Army."

"Maybe, Lieutenant. But, right now, it looks like the Algerian Army is trying to defeat us, and we don't have the men and equipment to take it on all at once."

Bearcat Jordan, Professor Walthers, and Karim walked up. "What does it look like, Gunny Sergeant?" Bearcat asked.

"You were right, Professor. There are a lot of people down there. No women and children with them; means they are a combat lot, in my assessment."

"Could be, Gunny," the professor answered. "The Tauregs generally travel with their families unless they are going to a market. They are scavengers, traders, and herders more than hunters."

As the sun edged toward the western horizon, the men continued their conversation about the oasis. Eventually, they moved to the rear of one of the humvees, where someone had placed a bucket of cold beans and Saltine crackers. Munching, they planned the night's raid on the oasis. With luck, thought Stapler, they would surprise the natives, take the critical oasis from them with a minimum of bloodshed, and quickly leave. Of course, pigs have wings, also.

SHEILA ANNE FORESTER PULLED ANOTHER of the empty gallon water containers from the truck. "What is this?" she asked Karim.

He had been standing silently watching her pick up each empty container and check it for drops of water. She jerked another plastic container from the pile, shook it, and tossed it back onto the bed of the truck.

"They only have a few pints left, and they are keeping it for the three heat stroke victims."

"I am sure they have more than that, Karim. Moreover, what do they think we are going to drink? Our piss?"

Karim smiled. "One of the Marines said you can, if it meant surviving."

Sheila turned her nose up and shook her head. "How crass!"

Karim reached out and touched the ponytail as it swished back and forth. A ponytail she had allowed him to pull hard and caress softly for two nights. After that, she had ordered him away. He couldn't help it. He laughed, a sad sort of laugh. He knew he shouldn't have done it as soon as he did.

She stopped and stood absolutely still. "Karim, keep your filthy hands to yourself."

He quickly let the soft ponytail go, rubbing the sand from it between his fingers.

"Where in the hell are we going to get water?" she asked. "The Marines must have some squirreled away somewhere. They just don't want us to have any. *They are protecting us from ourselves like the big brothers they think they are.*" Her hands shoved the empty containers around, still searching for that spare drop or tablespoon of water.

"No, Sheila, I think they are in the same situation as the rest of us." He pointed to the group of men around the humvee. "That's what they're planning now; take the oasis and refill the water jugs."

"That oasis has been over the hill since we got here hours ago, and no one has even bothered to go check it out, Karim."

"I think they said Tauregs were there."

"Well, there you are then! The Tauregs we know, Karim, are petrified of us. I am sure these fourth world primitives will scatter once we get down there."

"Petrified of you, maybe. They walked around the compound like you were some sort of goddess or something."

She grinned. "And, were they wrong?"

He grinned, revealing too-white teeth against his black skin. "Not in my book." He met her gaze until she looked away.

"Well, there you are again, Karim. The question becomes, why hasn't anyone gone and filled up the containers?"

He shrugged. "I don't know. Like I said, they are working on doing just that." A moment of jealousy caused him to spurt out, "Why don't you ask your lieutenant friend?"

She cocked her head to one side, amused at his jealousy. He wasn't the first one and wouldn't be the last, and besides, it amused her and, God knows, she could use some amusement out here. "Maybe I will. Maybe I will." She looked to where Jeff stood with the illiterate, abrasive gunnery sergeant.

Karim stormed away toward the edge of a large canvas tent raised against the hillside. Someone had set up a small stove, heating more beans. Sheila watched him depart; her eyes sparkled with amusement. *Men!* She chuckled. Glancing around and seeing no one, she reached up and grabbed two of the empty gallon containers. Holding them by her sides, she started walking away from the camp. Night falls fast in the desert. She was soon out of sight with only the light from the stars to guide her. Sheila pulled her light cashmere sweater from a small rucksack on her back and wrapped it around her shoulders to protect her from the cool night air. Maybe the men were afraid to get the water, but she wasn't. After all, they were only Tauregs.

KARIM RAN TO STAPLER. "SERGEANT, MISS

Forester is gone!" he gasped, out of breath from his search around the site. He had gone back to the truck after he calmed down only to discover she was no longer there. He spent minutes searching before he returned to the truck and noticed footsteps in the sand leading away from the camp.

Stapler stood up from the group of Marines squatted around him where he had been outlining in the sand with his finger the battle plans for the oasis.

"What do you mean she's gone?"

"I mean she ain't in camp." Karim ran his hand over his hair. "I think she may have gone to the oasis."

"The oasis! Why in the hell would she want to do that?"

"She was thirsty."

"Thirsty! She was thirsty! Is she also stupid?" Stapler turned to Corporal Heights. "Corporal, take three men and see if you can stop her before she gets all of us killed. You have my permission to hog-tie her until we have secured the oasis."

Kellogg came scrambling down the hill, losing her footing and sliding the last few feet. Stapler grimaced, watching the valuable nightscope held aloft in one hand and her M-16 in the other. "Gunny, there's someone out there walking toward the oasis!"

He reached over and took the nightscope from her extended hand. "What are you doing down here, Kellogg?" he asked as she stood up. "You're supposed to be on watch."

"Well, hell, Gunny. How in the hell am I supposed to tell you anything up there when I do see it? I don't have no brick like most of you. Besides, there ain't no one coming this way; just a body signature heading that way," she argued, pointing toward the oasis.

"Yeah, we know. How far is she out?"

"She?"

"Miss Forester," Professor Walthers added.

"About halfway to the oasis."

"Shit!" Stapler uttered. "Lieutenant, we have no choice. We have to move out. Once they discover her, they'll know we're out here, and the element of surprise will be lost."

"You're right, Gunny." Nolan answered, his mind whirling over Sheila walking innocently into the midst of those natives. A vision of a staked-out, naked debutante, begging for her life with Tauregs laughing and tracing their knives along her body, made his stomach turn. He grew embarrassed with himself over the feelings he was experiencing between his legs over the thoughts.

"Corporal Heights, take your squad and head to the west end of the oasis. The lieutenant and I will take our squads and approach from the south and southeast." He looked at his watch. "If we double-time, we can be in position in thirty minutes. Remember, Marines, we want to get there quick, but we have to get there quietly. They outnumber us, so if we can be the first to fire, we reduce the odds."

"We'll be there on time, Gunny." Heights grabbed his M-16, and with the three Marines in his assigned squad, took off at a trot up the hill.

Stapler turned to Karim. "How long has she been gone?"

"Can't be more than an hour. I talked with her, and she was complaining—"

"Sounds normal, so far."

"She wanted water, and if there was water in the oasis, then why didn't someone go and get it."

"The reason no one went and *got it* was because the oasis is crawling with Algerians. *That's why we haven't gone to get water.*" Stapler stamped his foot. "Damn!" The thought of water increased his own craving for the few drops remaining in his canteen.

"We can't leave her out there, Gunny." Nolen shook his head. "You know what they will do to her." The vision of the staked-out *virgin* filled his mind, and the embarrassing stirring in his loins increased. It appalled him. She might die, and he was excited! The stirring stopped.

"We're not going to leave her, Lieutenant. However, we have to move out now. We have twenty-six minutes to be in position before Corporal Heights begins his attack. She'll probably be there in fifteen, if she's walking. We'll have to double-time."

Stapler lifted his M-16, and with the lieutenant running alongside, trotted off. The other Marines followed. "From what I have seen, sir, it is the natives who should be worried," he said as they rounded the side of the hill and began their run across the plain. "If they discover her before we are in position, Lieutenant, it's gonna make the

battle for Darhickam Oasis, a harder-fought one than we
wanted. I would prefer that when the Marine Corps writes
the history of the battle of Darhickam Oasis, it exagger-
ates how hard-fought the battle was than it being an actual
fact."

STAPLER, **AT A CROUCH, SCURRIED FROM**
one withered scrub to another as he edged closer to the
oasis, expecting any moment to hear the sounds of gunfire
coming at him. He heard the caustic voice of Top Sergeant
MacGregory in his mind: *"If your attack is going well,
then it's an ambush."*

Isn't going to be any ambush, Stapler told himself, but
he found himself scrutinizing every bush and tree ahead
of them.

The scrub ran across the plain, growing thicker the
closer they approached the oasis. Loose sand covered the
terrain between and around the scrub, regardless of how
close together the scrawny plants grew. In the starlight,
the sand and brush made the desert look like an unfocused
negative from an old photograph.

Lieutenant Nolan disappeared to the right with two
Marines; Abercombie—the sandy-haired teenager from
San Diego—and Lerfervre, the hell-raising New Orleans
Basque who Stapler had had to discipline a few times.
Their shadowy forms were soon lost amid the whites,
grays, and blacks of the night desert.

Stapler pulled his sleeve back and looked at his watch.
The digital readout showed five minutes until party time.
The attack on the oasis was going to come from three directions at staggered times. Corporal Heights and his
small-fire team to the left would open fire first, drawing
the occupants of the camp across the front of Stapler and
Lieutenant Nolan. He raised himself to a kneeling position
behind the clump of brush in front of him. The first tree of
the oasis was about twenty feet in front of him. He
glanced right and saw Catsup in a prone position, her M-
16 lifted slightly to keep it out of the sand. The other Ma-

rine, Private Jones, was farther away on his left. The
heavy Marine kneeled on one knee, resting his M-16 on it.
Jones's head turned from side to side, slowly searching for
any movement ahead of them.

Stapler hoped Heights and his team were farther forward than where he and the LT's waited. It would be a
short battle indeed if they were directly in front of
Heights's fire. Then, those Marines Heights fail to kill
with friendly fire, the Algerians would finish off as they
swept up their flank. There had been other instances in
history where troops had fired on their own colors.

The plan was a simple one. They would shoot the Tauregs and regulars as they passed in front of them, hopefully stopping the attacks heading toward Heights's
position. When Corporal Heights ceased firing, he and the
lieutenant would lead the Marines forward and secure the
oasis. If it worked as they planned, the enemy would
be disorganized and confused. Those who did not flee the
oasis would journey on to Allah.

Stapler and Lieutenant Nolan were going to roll
through the oasis, mopping up any light—*God, he hoped
it was light*—resistance like grease through a goose.

Stapler motioned his Marines farther apart. Catsup
Kellogg moved a few feet nearer to front and off to the left
side of Stapler. *Yeah,* he thought, *she does have a butt for
spanking.* Even in the starlight, he could see her tongue
sticking out the left side of her mouth as she concentrated
on the view in front.

When he turned to Jones, the Marine had remained
where he was but had shifted to the other knee. Stapler
started to tell him again to move farther down.

Loud shouts from the camp stopped him. All three of
the Marines brought their M-16s up. Even in the thick of
the noise, Stapler heard the safeties being flicked off. He
held his hand up, motioning downward to hold their fire.
All through the camp, the shadowy forms of Tauregs
jumping up and running toward the east weaved in and out
of the palm trees. Several of the shadows crossed in front
of the few campfires scattered inside the oasis. The Tau-

regs were running in the opposite direction from where Heights and his squad waited. They were running toward the east end of the oasis where the well was located.

I think they have found our Miss Sheila Anne Forester. As if hearing him, Sheila's voice rose above the hubbub: "Keep your filthy hands off me, you bastards!" Then Stapler heard the sounds of slaps, grunts, and flesh-on-flesh hits. He hoped they did not kill her. He wanted the pleasure of doing it himself.

Stapler glanced at his watch again. It was time. As if hearing Stapler's thoughts, Heights's squad opened with M-16s on semiautomatic—three shot bursts. Stapler motioned his team to hold their fire. He knew what was going through their minds: fear and the desire to shoot. His stomach tightened with the anxiety of combat. He sensed movement to his right, turned his head quickly, keeping the weapon pointed straight ahead. It was Kellogg's hands opening and closing as she nervously gripped the M-16. Stapler flipped the safety back on.

Heights's attack caught the Tauregs off guard, sending many into the arms of Allah before they realized they were on the journey.

Stapler noticed most of the warriors appeared to have no rifles, though he saw the faint starlight reflect off knives. Probably left the more modern weapons behind because of the distraction at the well. The enemy turned in midstride, running back to grab their weapons. Because they had rushed to the well where *Miss Sheila Anne Forester* was discovered, they ran directly in front of Stapler and the lieutenant. Stapler slipped his finger into the trigger guard and, with a smooth motion, flipped the safety off.

He allowed the first few shadows to pass before Stapler rose to a standing position and fired. Jones and Catsup followed suit, firing into the natives like targets at a carnival rifle range. Nolan's team opened fire simultaneously with his. The Tauregs fell in bunches. Maybe *Miss Sheila Anne Forester* helped the attack through no intent of her own.

Damn if he was going to give her the satisfaction of knowing that.

He heard the Lieutenant shout, "Bayonets," to his right. What in the hell was he up to? Wait a few more minutes, Lieutenant, for your glory. Whatever, the order for bayonets meant he knew the young stallion would go in shortly. The lieutenant probably had visions of saving the beautiful *Miss Sheila Anne Forester* and being her hero. Damn, junior officers were a pain in the ass. Nevertheless, he couldn't let Nolan do it alone. "Fix bayonets, Marines!" Stapler shouted. Top Sergeant MacGregory hated bayonets: *"The law of the bayonet says the bullet wins."*

The firing from Corporal Heights's team stopped. Nolan shouted, "Charge, Marines!"

"Let's go, Marines!" Stapler shouted, and in one movement, he was up and running through the scrub. This was the dangerous moment when friendly fire could be just as dangerous as the enemy's. Bullets whizzed by his head. He pulled the trigger on the M-16, sending a three-bullet salvo into the darkness. He turned the rifle to the right as a shadow passed in front of a campfire, and he pulled the trigger. The shadow doubled up and screamed as it fell into the fire. It continued screaming as Stapler ran past, the fire igniting the long robe, turning the wounded Taureg into a funeral pyre. Lieutenant Nolan shouted some unintelligible order. Stapler turned toward the LT's position.

"Ooorah!" The Marine Corps cry that so emulated the rebel yell of the Civil War filled the air as the three groups of Marines charged the oasis. Heights and his team appeared near the center of the oasis, they, too, running and firing toward the east. The Marine Corps yell encouraged them, while the primitive sound had the opposite effect on the enemy.

Supernatural terror rippled through the Tauregs. Screaming in fear, many ran north, away from the Marines, and disappeared into the desert night, believing devils and demons pursued them. Stapler shot two men wearing khakis who were attempting to put on their pants. He saw rifles thrown onto the sand where frightened Tauregs dropped them in their mad dash for their lives.

Stapler burst through the bushes surrounding the well. Catsup Kellogg dropped to the ground and shoved her weapon through the brush, covering the gunny. Jones dashed into the clearing before he realized he had run out of cover and just as quickly rolled back into the bushes.

Sheila Anne Forester stood at the well, casually drawing water and filling the canister. Stapler was certain he heard her humming.

Four Taureg natives lay around the well, two at her feet. A huge Taureg, dressed in a flowing black robe, crashed through the bushes on the other side of the well, screaming. The Bedouin jerked a curved knife from beneath his robe and ran toward Sheila, raising it as he neared. The *oodalooping* sound the native made by trilling the tongue against the roof of the mouth caused Miss Sheila Anne Forester to turn her head toward the charging giant. *How in the hell do they do that?* Stapler wondered.

Stapler raised the M-16, but she was in his line of fire. "Damn!" Stapler shouted. He charged, running as fast as the shifting sand allowed, his combat boots sinking in the sand, slowing his advance. Stapler brought his bayonet level with the native's midsection. He screamed as he ran, hoping to draw the man to him and away from the unarmed young woman. The native glanced at Stapler, trilled louder with the knowledge that Stapler was too far away to stop him from killing the demon girl. The Taureg raised his knife for the downward slash as he closed the last few feet.

Stapler shouted at Sheila, "Get down!"

She glanced at Stapler and set the gallon jug on the rim of the rock well beside the other gallon container.

The Taureg stopped his trilling long enough to scream something in dialect Arabic.

Sheila took two steps back as the man brought the knife down, the blade barely missing her. She grabbed the man's arm, twisted it under and back. Using his own forward momentum, she stuck her foot out, pulled the knife arm down and around to flip him in the air. She twirled around as the attacker was in midair and jerked the arm toward her. She leaned onto one leg, lifted the other, and slammed her foot into the attacker's stomach as he tumbled down. A loud, short grunt escaped from the native. He landed on his knees. His arm hung at an unusual angle. He grabbed a couple of times for the broken arm. Sheila stepped forward and karate-chopped him across the neck. His eyes rolled back, and he fell forward, spread-eagled and unconscious, his head bouncing off the rocky sand surrounding the well. "I told you I would pay for the water, asshole."

Stapler had slowed his run and stopped in amazement as he watched the last few movements of *Miss Sheila Anne Forester.*

Sheila picked up the two water containers. "Thanks, Gunny Sergeant," she said, taking a deep breath. "They not only don't take American Express here, neither do they take MasterCard or Visa."

Stapler heard moans emerging from the four other Tauregs on the ground. "You did this?"

She tilted the water container back and took a deep drink. "Yes, I did. I tried to explain, but they wouldn't listen. Something about women really bugs the shit out of them! Stupid animals. You do not want to know what they tried to do! They tried to tear my clothes off. How crass!" She grinned and handed the water container to Stapler. "You may want to give this to your men, Gunny."

One of the Tauregs raised his head. Stapler cold cocked him with the butt of his M-16. "Stay down."

"Very good, Gunny." Another one reached up suddenly and grabbed Sheila by the ankle. She spun around and kicked back with the free foot, catching the man on the nose. Stapler heard the cartilage break. The man moaned and fell back on the ground. Across the oasis, the sound of shooting slowed and a couple of seconds later stopped.

He looked at the men on the ground. "You did this?" he asked again incredulously.

"Yes. Hard to believe, I know, Gunny Sergeant. But, you know, once a bitch, always a bitch. And I am a mean bitch, Gunny." Her eyes sparkled. "But you should be happy. I'm the only one you've got." She hoisted the gallon jug again and drank deeply. "Not Evian, but it'll do."

Lieutenant Nolan emerged into the clearing. From the bushes, Catsup and Jones walked out, their M-16s on the five Tauregs who were beginning to regain consciousness. Lieutenant Nolan looked around at the prisoners and nodded to Stapler. "Good work, Gunny. Five?"

"Sir, I didn't—"

"I wish I could have been here to help you. I am impressed. Sheila, are you all right?"

"He didn't do it. Wonder Woman did it. I ain't never seen anything like it before," Catsup Kellogg said, her eyes admiring the young woman. "How in the hell did you do it?"

"I assure you, it was nothing. Just a lot of ballet with about ten years of martial arts training. My father figured with my attitude, I had better have some way of defending myself. I never expected to have to fight for water."

"Well, if you had been a little more patient, *Miss Sheila Anne Forester,* you wouldn't have endangered our lives or yours. You may even have saved some of the enemy casualties we dealt tonight."

Stapler turned and left the clearing. He walked through the oasis, directing his Marines as they sanitized the area. He found Corporal Heights near the far end of the oasis with seven prisoners under guard. The trucks burned.

"What happened?" Stapler asked, pointing at the trucks.

"Asshole here set them on fire before we could stop him."

"Take them over to the well and see what the lieutenant wants to do with them." Heights nudged the prisoners forward. "And don't let him kill them," Stapler whispered. "We don't kill prisoners . . . as a general rule. Bad for morale, Corporal Heights, not to mention the CNN factor."

"Abercombie, you and Garfield hightail it over the ridge and tell those oil riggers to get everything and everyone down here." He looked at his watch. "We have about eight hours until daylight. I want us to be loaded and out of here before then."

"Sure thing, Gunny," Garfield said.

The two Marines started double-timing out of the oasis and toward the slight hill where the civilians waited. "And be careful, you two!" Stapler shouted. "There are a bunch of confused fanatics out there, not to mention the oil riggers. Don't get yourselves shot!"

"We will, Gunnery Sergeant!" Garfield shouted back as the two disappeared into the darkness.

Stapler walked to where the khaki-uniformed soldiers had set their tent. His eyes shifted back and forth, watching for that lone enemy who failed to understand they had lost. Stapler squatted with his M-16 across his knees, opened a trunk, and rummaged through it. He didn't know what he was looking for, but he would know it if he stumbled over it. He wadded up an Algerian flag and stuffed it inside his shirt. Might as well take a souvenir home for Carol. Visions of burning credit cards, caused by too-fast trips through the reader, crossed his mind. He picked up a couple of cans with photos of dates on the front and Arabic writing on the side. He'd better make sure they had toilet tissue if they were going to eat this; then he remembered the briefing about the left and right hands.

A noise like a cacophony of gelded donkeys caused the Marines to lift their weapons and point toward the source. Out of the darkness came Private Raoul Gonzales and Private Cowboy Joe-Boy Henry, leading a line of six camels into the campsite.

"Look what we found, Gunny," Joe Boy said. "Hot dang. No more walking now."

"What the hell are they?" Kellogg asked, walking around the animals. She stepped forward and touched the side of one of the camels. "Gross."

"Oh, you know what the hell they are. They're camels, Catsup. You never rode a camel before? I rode one once at a carnival in Texas. Ain't too hard. Ain't much difference from riding a horse, I seem to remember, except you're about ten feet in the air when you're on the back of one of these things."

Cowboy Joe-Boy and Raoul untied the tethers and wrapped them individually around the various trees and bushes. Joe Boy pulled a camel over to where Kellogg stood. "Watch this, Catsup," he said, trying to impress the diminutive, dark-haired Marine. Catsup was the sweetheart of the company, even though she could fight with the best of them, outdrink most of them, and outcurse all of them.

Stapler watched for a few seconds and then returned to his scavenging. "Christmas," he whispered he turned over a shirt to discover a pack of cigarettes. He shoved it unceremoniously into his shirt pocket. "Spoils of war." He chuckled, his lips hurting in the process. He lifted a nearby canteen, opened it, sniffed, and then took a long drink of warm water. Nothing had ever tasted so good.

Joe-Boy reached up and tugged downward. "Be careful, Cowboy," Catsup said.

"Be careful? Come on, Catsup. I'm from Texas. There ain't a horse or animal living that a Texas cowboy cain't ride."

The camel bellowed as it knelt on its front knees. It paused a second and then bent its back legs and folded up on the ground.

"Watch this," he said, handing his M-16 to Catsup. He crawled onto the back of the camel, shuffled his butt a few times to get comfortable, and then grinned at Catsup as if to say, *See, piece of cake.* Her smile caused his ego to soar and his uncertainty to diminish.

"Giddyap." The camel remained motionless, its mouth chewing whatever it had in it. Joe-Boy kicked the side of the camel. Nothing. The camel remained sitting. "Probably used to Arabic or some other thing to get it started. I heard that camels ain't as smart as horses."

"Yeah, fine job, Joe-Boy. What you got is a living, breathing, chair," Catsup laughed.

"Well, they must do something to get these animals moving," he mumbled just before he gave the camel a swift, hard kick to the backside. "We just ha—"

The camel shot up on his back legs, throwing Joe-Boy over its head, his hand entangled in the tether. A loud cacophony of bellows emerged from the camel, sounding similar to a donkey. Then the animal rose straight up on its front legs, dragging Joe-Boy up over its neck to dangle him a few feet from the ground. A loud bellow tore out of the throat of the camel as the animal stretched its neck. Joe-Boy pushed the tether off his trapped hand and started to crawl down from the neck. The camel began baying and spitting, shaking its head back and forth. It jumped, one foot at a time, its humped body rolling up and down like a series of clashing waves as one foot after the other left the ground, rotating one after the other. The second shake threw Joe-Boy through the air and across the campsite to roll up against a tree. The Marine moaned once and then shoved himself up quickly, brushing his clothes a couple of times. The camel bounded away past Cowboy, baying at the top of its lungs. Cowboy lunged for the tether, missing it by a couple of inches. Behind the stampeding camel, the other camels jerked their tethers loose and took off in pursuit.

"Grab them!" Cowboy Joe-Boy shouted, running toward the nearest camel just as it got the lead lose. He watched helplessly as it disappeared into the dark, baying as it followed the first camel.

Joe-Boy, Raoul, and Catsup took off in pursuit; Catsup laughing and ridiculing Cowboy.

Stapler started laughing and couldn't stop. The remaining Marines laughed, too, and soon the whole site was full of laughing, crying Marines, slapping each other and pointing in the direction their three comrades had gone. Glad to be alive. Across the oasis, the sounds of shouting and camels baying filled the air. No one wounded in the attack. Stapler had fully expected at least some wounded, if not one or two dead.

Stapler patted the golden cigarettes in his pocket and marched off in search of the lieutenant. He now had two packs. Life was good. Jones and Sterling passed him with the five prisoners, heading toward the burning truck where the other prisoners were being contained. The LT and *Miss Sheila Anne Forester* were no longer at the well. He walked around the well, deciding to head back toward the other Marines, when he heard moans coming from behind nearby bushes. Stapler pulled the M-16 up and slipped the safety off. Using his bayonet, he parted the bushes and leaned forward. The white shirt *Miss Sheila Anne Forester* had been wearing came flying through the air and landed on his head. Stapler pulled it off and held it up. Heavier grunts and moans rose from the other side. He caught a glimpse of firm tits, a pink nipple, and the upper crack of tight buttocks straddling the LT before he pulled the bayonet back and let the bushes close around the two. He tossed the shirt back in their direction, hoping it landed on the two of them, and stomped off angrily to where the other Marines were gathering. He grabbed the two gallon containers she had filled and took them with him, hoisting one for a drink.

"Oh, my God," he heard Nolan moan as Stapler stomped out of the clearing, his teeth clenched, afraid they might hear him. *God ain't gonna help you now, boy.*

Looks as if she knows more than just martial arts, Stapler decided, as faint giggles behind him caused the hair on the nape of his neck to stand up. *Nice tits.*

CHAPTER 7

⚓

IBN AL JAMAL LEANED ON THE EDGE OF THE
conning tower, gazing down at crew members topside.
They waited patiently for their sea and anchor stations to
be secured. He intentionally kept the sea and anchor detail
manned longer than normal, wanting to put as much distance as possible between the Oran Naval Base and the *Al
Nasser* before he spoke to them. This way, he knew where
everyone on the boat was located so that when he told
them what the rebel leadership wanted them to do and
what he proposed, he'd be in position to respond to whatever happened. The *Al Nasser* wallowed slightly as it
barely made way in the calm seas outside the port entrance. The other crew members had stations within the
skin of the submarine, waiting for the skipper's orders. A
captain grew to know his boat and his crew. He knew
without anyone telling him that none wanted to go to sea
again. The experience with the previous attack against the
American naval force had left the crew scarred.

Captain Ibn Al Jamal of the Algerian Navy submarine

Al Nasser saw it in the eyes and body language of his sailors and officers. Even if he ignored those signs, the exorbitant number of minor problems that surfaced after the submarine refloated told him the same story. Minor things that each sailor or officer hoped would be the reason or reasons for delaying sailing. He had told none of them about the mission yet. He had asked the XO to keep quiet, also. If he had told them before they left port that the rebel leadership had ordered them to attack the Americans again, he doubted he would have had a sufficient crew to get the submarine under way.

Unspoken, they all realized how lucky they were to be alive. Only Allah's mercy saved them from the underwater damage suffered three weeks ago at the hands of the American Navy. For all the torpedoes they fired, not one connected. Religion and political views are fine things to debate from the safety of Parliament, but when mortality sweeps its scythe across your vision, they tend to become less important.

The tugboat remained reluctantly tied alongside and would remain there until released by him. The burly captain of the tug had already asked twice to be allowed to return to port. The man griped vociferously about having his small tugboat six miles out and argued it was useless for him to remain. The *Al Nasser* was doing fine. No engineering casualties, which was why the tugboat was along—to tow them back to port in the event the engines stopped. The engines were fine on the submarine. Ibn Al Jamal knew it. His XO, below on the bridge, knew it, and the chief engineer knew it. But Ibn Al Jamal had another reason to delay the tugboat. When he finished addressing the crew, then he would release the civilian craft to return to Oran.

Satisfied that the lines were put away and davits stowed, with the exception of the two connecting the tugboat to the *Al Nasser*, Ibn Al Jamal pressed the intercom button. He asked his XO if everything was ready for securing the sea and anchor detail. The XO replied in the affirmative and gave the skipper a quick status report on the engineering plant.

Now was the time, he decided. He and the XO had discussed it, and between them, they identified several in the wardroom who would support the captain. He would discover how many of the remaining crew members would follow him when he told them of his proposal. Ibn Al Jamal knew the rebels would classify the act as treasonous and, if caught, he would be lucky if they only stood him against the wall and shot him. Treason is always transitory in a revolution. It depended on which side of the fence your loyalties fell. President Hawali Alneuf would say he was a traitor. What would he say when Ibn Al Jamal shifted his loyalties back to the democratic elected government of Algeria?

He cleared his throat and began to talk in a low, methodical voice that sounded sad as he expounded upon the reasons for the revolution and the importance of Islam to the Arab world and their way of life. He reminded them of their heroics. And, though they had been unsuccessful in their torpedo attacks against the surface ships, they had forced the American fleet to move farther out to sea. They had accomplished every mission the new government assigned. They had even survived a massive attack by the combined American forces after their torpedo attack. They had done all of this without a single loss of life to the enemy.

Now came the *but* part. For all that, he had reassessed the government role in this grand new country called the Islamic Republic of Barbary and North Africa. "The concept is a great one, with many positive attributes. But we joined this revolution in the belief that our actions would bring glory to Islam. Instead, we have traded a democratic government that respected the right of religious worship for one that demands its own religious views and practices tyranny."

Ibn Al Jamal told how the death of his wife and the following years of loneliness led him to further embrace Islam. A combination of religion, loneliness, and a desire to serve Allah led him to fall for the false words of the rebels and violate his vows to the legitimate government and the nation.

"We have already seen the results in our own boat of what to expect from the new government. We saw the results carried to the extreme and enforced on *Al Solomon* as religious inquisitions by layman leaders decided the life or death of a crew member."

His eyes moved from sailor to sailor as he attempted to read the reaction of those standing below him. Some looked away when their eyes met, while others met his stare. Some of those staring nodded; others looked angry. He had little idea of the effect of his words, but he knew each individual sailor was forming his own opinion.

He cleared his throat and continued. "We have been ordered to attack the American fleet again. To attack the new amphibious carrier that has entered the Mediterranean Sea and force them to withdraw their Marines from Algiers." That got a reaction.

Like the crew, he abhorred the fact that the Americans had occupied their capitol. It was a disgraceful act by what the French continued to call the mighty "hyperpower," but one that could be put in proper context when they considered that their own leaders continued to hold fifty Americans hostage, Americans whom they had guaranteed free passage from their shores.

"If we had allowed those Americans to depart, we would not have the Marines in Algiers or the American fleet off our shores. We would be home with our families and not here, sailing off to what may well be our deaths."

So, where was he going with this speech? Some of the sailors shifted from foot to foot, as they tired of standing in place. He had their attention but would lose it soon. It was time to reach his objective and tell them his proposal.

He keyed the microphone beneath the curve of the bulkhead on the conning tower, pressing the button five times, warning the XO that the moment had come.

He told the crew members how proud he was of them, but after much soul-searching and praying to Allah, he had reached the decision that what they had done in siding with the rebels had been wrong. He could not in good conscience lead them in another attack against the Americans. He could not continue to support the new government. The words of Islam and the guidance of Allah had little in common with the tyranny of the rebel leadership. Maybe the great Satan, America, had the right idea in keeping religion and government separate. He was sorry, and he said so, for failing to realize this sooner and allowing his desire to further his religion to lead his country to where it was today: in chaos and civil war.

The sailors standing in front of him on the bow of the submarine exchanged glances, and a couple of groups whispered among themselves.

Ibn Al Jamal intended to take *Al Nasser* to Malaga and join the other Algerian Navy units that had fled to that Spanish port city. There, he would turn the submarine back over to the government forces of President Hawali Alneuf. A sailor in the back screamed an obscenity at him and, before the sailor could finish, two others on each side slammed the angry man upside the head, knocking him out. They left the sailor collapsed on the deck.

"Many of you remain loyal to the new government," he continued. "I do not want to stand in your way to choose your own path in this time of testing in Algeria. Therefore, those who wish to return to Algeria should get on the tugboat. The tug will take you back to shore and back to the rebel leadership. You can tell them I made this decision, and you fought honorably but were overwhelmed. Maybe they will believe you."

A couple of sailors near the front shoved their way through the crowd topside and picked up the rebel supporter who had been attacked. They glared at Ibn Al Jamal as they helped their fellow supporter to the side of the submarine and onto the tug.

From below, others emerged and worked their way to the tug. Some of the sailors remaining with Ibn Al Jamal hugged those leaving. A couple of the older sailors who he had hoped would stay stopped for a moment at the conning tower and looked up at him. He wished them luck ashore. The taller of the two said that it was only because their families were back there that they returned to Algeria; otherwise, they would gladly go with the captain.

He blessed their choice and wished them the best. He knew some of those returning did so because of fears for their families. Many who stayed did so out of loyalty to him, and he believed most agreed with his assessment.

It took nearly an hour to transfer the rebel faction from the *Al Nasser.* He gave them time to gather their belongings. Even as the tug cast off its lines to return to the naval base, Ibn Al Jamal was wondering if any rebel supporters remained on board. Just as he worried about sabotage by loyalists, now he would have to be concerned about a misguided rebel supporter believing he could earn Allah's blessings by ensuring the submarine never reached Malaga. He didn't know, but they would have to stay alert and be ready.

A shout from the lookout above him drew his attention to the starboard side. He shaded his eyes from the glare of the clouds and the sea. A faint motion in the air caught his attention as an aircraft dropped below the overcast ceiling. It was heading directly for the *Al Nasser*.

He grabbed the radio and ordered the tug to cast off the remaining line and break away—cut it if he had to! A civilian crew member on the tugboat threw the last line overboard. A sailor below the conning tower quickly drew the line on board, hand over hand, almost a blur as the sounds of the approaching aircraft gave added encouragement. Ibn Al Jamal looked upward and watched the approaching aircraft grow larger until he could identify four propeller engines. Other than that, he had no idea what type it was, but he knew it was not Algerian.

He pressed the Dive switch, sending crew members topside scrambling for the hatches. As the last watchstander slid through the conning tower hatch, Ibn Al Jamal followed him. He pulled the hatch down and spun the wheel, sealing off the outside from the interior of the Algerian Kilo submarine.

The XO had the conn and was taking the boat down to periscope depth in the shallow coastal waters. They needed another ten miles before they would have sufficient depth under them to disappear into the sanctuary of the deep sea.

COMMANDER STILLWELL EASED OFF THE throttle of the EP-3E reconnaissance aircraft and began a slow descent. The reducing engine noise made conversation tolerable. The constant engine vibration through the last remaining class of Navy reconnaissance aircraft was augmented by erratic shaking as it passed through the cloud layers in its descent. Stillwell glanced out the portside window and watched the two accompanying F/A-18 Hornets break off. They would orbit overhead the cloud cover with the other two Marine Corps F/A-18 Hornets while the aging EP-3E penetrated to take photographs and video of the Algerian Oran Naval Base. Stillwell estimated they would come out twelve miles off the coast, but the high resolution of the Big Eyes optical system should provide evidence as to the presence or absence of the Algerian Kilo submarine *Al Nasser*. He hoped the gyroscope on the system was operable. The aviation technicians assured him before they lifted off from Sigonella, Sicily, that it had been repaired. Without the gyroscope on the Big Eyes to compensate for aircraft movement, the resulting video would bounce up and down like an amateur film.

"How's the temperature on number two, Jasbo?"

The copilot leaned over and glanced at the gauge. "Still running hotter than normal, Skipper, but still below the red. Should be all right if we don't push it."

"Keep an eye on it. The engine for the other EP-3E didn't make it on the Air Force flight today. Higher priority war materials, they said, for the Korean theater," he sneered. "Not as if we don't have our own war here."

Rachel "Jasbo" Smith reached over and tapped the gauge. She shook her head. "Amazing," she said, smiling.

"That always works in the movies." The deployed squadron had three more copilots than they had qualified pilots, so Commander Stillwell, the officer in charge of the unit, found himself with a different copilot every day. Jasbo was a welcome choice. She was a short woman who barely met the minimum height requirement for a pilot. Jasbo walked everywhere as if she was going to be late and always in short, fast steps, with her head tilted upward as if to add a couple of inches to her height. It was the bounce of her short, brown hair when she walked that first caught everyone's attention. The sparkling brown eyes and quick wit made everyone love Jasbo as you would a sister. She brought out the better qualities in those around her who, through no fault of her own, felt they owed her protection. She had learned to accept this masculine fault, as her liberated sisters would have called it, with grace and aplomb.

The flight engineer reached above the flight team's head and twisted the air-conditioning switch to maximum. The EP-3E reconnaissance aircraft still had the best air conditioner in the shore-based aviation inventory of the Navy. In fact, most times, it was too good, and for the crisis along the North African Coast, this overpowered air-conditioning capability had come in handy.

Stillwell picked up the interior communication system—ICS—handset. "John," he said, contacting the mission commander, Lieutenant Commander John Andrews, in the aft section of the aircraft. "Everything ready to go back there?"

"Yes, boss. We are set up, and the camera is running. Just keep our port side to the beach so Big Eyes can see the coast."

"I'd like to finish this as soon as possible, John. We have a lot of tired souls on board and another mission scheduled for tomorrow. The sooner we return, the sooner they can get some well-deserved shut-eye."

"The only things that could hold us up are visibility, technical problems, surface-to-air missiles, enemy aircraft—"

"Bad joke, John. Tell our cryppie to keep an eye out for hostile aircraft. I don't relish another ass-chewing flight of dodging fighters," Stillwell said, referring to four weeks ago when they overflew the sinking USS *Gearing*. They had no sooner identified the sinking *Gearing* to Sixth Fleet before they had to hit the deck, fifty feet off the Mediterranean Sea, to avoid Libyan fighters flying north to attack Sigonella, Sicily.

"Susan is right on top of it. Her sailors are turning and burning, Skipper. Amazing how a little self-preservation is such a great motivator."

"It is also amazing what a little fatigue will do. Let's get the job done and get back to Sigonella. The chief and I are suffering up here. Jasbo needs to take a bath."

The copilot cut her eyes at Stillwell. "Commander! That's a hell of thing to say to lady."

"What?" he asked, laughing.

"That I need a bath," she said, pretending to be offended.

Stillwell grinned. "I have to admit I am becoming attached to the new perfume you are wearing. What is it? Fuel odor *de jour* mixed with a fine grain of week-old perspiration soaked permanently into the fabric of a Navy green flight suit? Something erotic about that, wouldn't you say?"

Rachel "Jasbo" Smith shook her head. "You're a sick man, Commander. I bet your wife throws a little gasoline behind her ears before you go out, so you'll feel at home."

"Nope. Just when she comes to bed." Stillwell turned to the flight engineer. "Chief, you promised not to tell anyone."

"Moi?" Chief James Henckels answered with an exaggerated look of innocence, touching his chest.

The cloud cover broke. Stillwell glanced at the altimeter. "Two thousand feet," he said.

Everyone in the cockpit looked out the left side of the aircraft. The yellow sands of the Algerian coast marked the horizon. About ten miles farther ahead was the Algerian naval base at Oran.

He pressed the ICS switch. "John, we are approaching the target area. Estimate six minutes. You guys ready?"

"Commander, for the fiftieth time, we're ready. Been ready. Finger on the switch. Get us within sight, and Spielberg will be jealous of our film."

"John, I feel a lot of love in this aircraft. I'm sending the chief back to give you a hug."

John Andrews clicked the microphone twice in acknowledgment.

"What's that?" Jasbo asked, pointing out the front cockpit window on Stillwell's left side.

Stillwell glanced down at the controls, believing Jasbo referred to the exchange with John Andrews. "John? He's being testy again. Doesn't surprise me. He has flown about ten missions in a row—"

"No, no; not that," she interrupted. "There—ahead of us." She pointed.

He leaned forward and looked, trying to follow the direction of her finger. "What? I don't see anything," he asked. He looked up, searching the sky for aircraft.

"On the sea! Look on the sea!" she said, emphasizing her words with exaggerated pointing.

Stillwell looked again. Ahead and to their left, two ships appeared to be outside the harbor of the naval base. It took several seconds before he realized that one of them was a submarine.

He grabbed the microphone. "John! John! The Algerian submarine is ahead of us on our left about six miles. We got her! By George, we've got her!"

"Great! How far out is she? Can we circle her?"

"No, I would say she is about six or seven miles from shore, still within their territorial waters, but her wake shows she is heading out to sea. There appears to be a tugboat alongside her. Maybe she is doing at-sea trials following her dry dock?"

"It'd be great if you could go closer."

"Can't do it. We need commander, Joint Task Force, approval to violate the territorial waters, and we don't have it."

"Sounds kind of dumb to me, considering we are occupying Algiers and flying combat sorties all over the country."

"John, take the pictures. I don't make the rules; I just follow them. I will take us as close as we can, but I am not going closer than fifteen miles to their coast. The submarine should be about nine or ten miles away when we pass her. That's close enough for you to photograph the color of their eyes if you want."

In the aft section of the aircraft, John Andrews and his technicians adjusted the Big Eyes camera system for a closer pass. Ten minutes on-station around the submarine, and they could head for home. The Intel wienies would be happy; the crew would be happy; and the *Rack God*, the sailors' denizen of the bed, calling from the BOQ at Sigonella, would be appeased even sooner than expected.

John turned to see how Susan and her band of cryptologic technicians were doing. They were the keys to survival this close to hostile forces. The submarine was harmless unless they had a couple of shoulder-launched surface-to-air missiles topside. He doubted they did. Intel hadn't said anything about submarines having surface-to-air missiles. They had seen mobile SAMs only with the Algerian land forces.

Susan walked back and forth along the bank of sensitive electronic warfare systems, listening through her own ICS channel to the banter between the CTs. Her role was management of the information, but the highly trained enlisted sailors who sat the positions were trained to collect and analyze electromagnetic raw data to determine threat potential. They had been the primary reason Ranger Two Niner survived the approaching Libyan aircraft four weeks ago.

"Let's take her down to a thousand feet, Jasbo," Stillwell said, simultaneously pushing forward on the steering column.

Jasbo looked at the altimeter. "We're at six thousand now, Commander. Engine number two still wavering at the edge of the red."

"Keep an eye on the number-two engine, Chief," Stillwell said. "I don't like to feather an engine this close to the sea. Not much room to correct."

"Aye, aye, sir. I have it," Chief Henckels said, leaning forward and tapping the glass a couple of times.

"I keep telling you two, that doesn't work."

"It gives us comfort when we do it," Jasbo responded. "Kind of like lighting a candle at church or sacrificing a chicken at a pagan ritual. Passing three thousand."

"Look at that booger! Caught on the top. Nothing a submarine skipper likes better than to be caught with their pants down, sitting on the top."

"Looks to me like the bunch topside are running."

Stillwell stared at the Algerian submarine slightly to their left about ten miles.

"I'll be damned," he said. He clicked on his ICS button. "John, looks as if the submarine is trying to submerge. Three minutes to target."

"Roger, Skipper."

"John, have you relayed this to CTF Sixty-seven?"

"Me? It's not like I haven't been busy back here."

"Temper, temper. I'll do it from up here, John. You just take good photos. I don't want to have to do this again, and we don't want Spielberg laughing at you."

"We always take good photos, Skipper. Remember the one of you with that blond at the Total Motel swimming pool?"

"John, blackmail will not enhance your fitness report. You're testy and being a pain in the ass, so quit trying to get back on my good side. It won't work. In fact, I am thinking of not allowing you to land with us in Sigonella. When Jasbo and I get an opportunity, we will roll the dice up here to see whether you jump before we descend to land or while we are in the pattern."

Without waiting for a reply, Commander Stillwell directed Chief Henckels to connect him to the secure radio. Several seconds passed. They were now four miles from the Algerian submarine.

"The tugboat has broken away, Skipper. It's in a hard left turn toward the shore."

"I see it, Jasbo. Chief, you ready?"

"Got it, sir. Go ahead."

"The wake is increasing. The submarine has increased its speed and remains on course toward the open sea, Commander. I see no one topside. Hatches are buttoned down!"

Stillwell straightened his headset so the earphones covered his ears and called Command Task Force Sixty-seven.

"We've got him," John Andrews said. "Tape is rolling, and we are zooming in on the boat. No one topside on the submarine. Skipper, I think he is preparing to submerge. Bow looks lower."

"SIXTY-SEVEN, THIS IS RANGER TWO NINER. How read, over?"

Commander Steve Cloth, the Air Operations boss for Command Task Force Sixty-seven, lifted the phone. "Ranger Two Niner, this is Six Seven. I read you fivers, go ahead."

"Roger, Six Seven. We have an Algerian submarine on top of the water, approximately seven miles out of Oran on a heading of zero six zero, speed estimated at ten knots; in process of submerging."

Dick Holman shoved himself up from the captain's chair he had been occupying for the past two hours and hurried over to the chart table, where Commander Steve Cloth had turned. The two men's fingers collided on the chart as they touched where the Algerian submarine should be. He wished the *Stennis* had a holograph display unit like the two amphibious ships, the *Kearsarge* and the *Nassau*. It made fighting the maneuvering war so much easier.

"Roger, Ranger Two Niner. What are your position and intentions?"

"Six Seven. We are leveling off at two thousand feet

for a flyby. Big Eyes is rolling. Tugboat escorted the submarine out to sea, but when it saw us, it broke away and is now headed back to port."

Dick Holman turned to the Operations specialist chief petty officer standing to his left. "Chief, have someone call Admiral Devlin and Admiral Cameron. Give them my respects and ask them to join us in the Air Operations space as soon as possible."

"Aye, aye, sir," the chief responded and hurried off to do the tasking himself.

Five minutes later, Admiral Devlin walked through the watertight door, followed immediately by Admiral Cameron escorted by his chief of staff, Captain Clive Bowen.

"What you got, Dick?" Admiral Cameron asked.

"The EP-3E caught the Algerian submarine *Al Nasser* on top of the water as it was exiting Oran Naval Base."

The door opened again, and Captain Kurt Lederman, the intelligence officer, entered. Dick said it again for the benefit of Kurt, who nodded sagely as if he expected nothing less than for the aircraft to catch the submarine on the surface of the water. "I thought something like this would happen," Kurt said, wondering how in the hell the *Al Nasser* got repaired and under way so quickly.

"Sixty-seven, Ranger Two Niner; we are abreast of the submarine, and it is beginning to submerge. Bow is awash."

Steve Cloth clicked the phone twice. "Wait one, Two Niner."

"We still have those Hornets orbiting overhead?" Admiral Cameron asked.

"Yes, sir," Commander Cloth responded.

"Dick," tell them to take the submarine out before it submerges."

Dick Holman moved to the air traffic controller, a first-class petty officer monitoring the air radar screen. "You got contact with Moonlighter flight?"

The operator slid his headset down slightly. "Yes, sir. That's who I'm directing now."

"Good. Are you in secure mode?"

"Sixty-seven, Ranger Two Nine; the submarine is submerging. Expect to lose visual contact within a minute."

"Roger, Two Niner. Let us know when it disappears."

The ATC glanced at his mode switches and nodded. "Yes, sir. I have the Hornets on secure comms mode."

"Tell Beacon formation they have weapons free. We have an immediate surface attack mission for them." Then he continued giving specific directions to be relayed to the Marine Corps Moonlighter squadron F/A-18D Hornet formation.

"Roger, sir, I can tell them that, but their weapons load-out is for air combat. All they've got for a surface attack are their cannons."

"Moonlighter Two Six, this Six Seven. Do you read?"

"Read you fivers, Six Seven. Hey, how much longer we going to be out here?"

Ignoring the question, the ATC operator continued, "Moonlighter Two Six, you have weapons free. Your high-value asset has detected enemy submarine on the surface approximately nine miles north of Oran. Your orders are to sink her." He looked up at the new commander, Task Force Sixty-seven, to ensure he transmitted the orders as directed.

"Holy shit, *Stennis*! We only have Sidewinders and AMRAAMs!"

"Sixty-seven says to use your guns."

Dick Holman touched the sailor on the shoulder and nodded once.

"Roger, Six Seven. This is Moonlighter Two Six. Moonlighter flight Two Six; check master arm on, weapons free. You heard the man, let's make life jolly for the submariner waiting for us below. Six Seven, be advised this will be a guns attack, and you may expect cannon fodder from submarine pieces within two minutes."

Steve Cloth touched Dick Holman on the arm. "Commodore, we do have a P-3C conducting a surface maritime patrol about a hundred twenty miles northeast of the datum. According to the their ATO, they have a full load out of sonobuoys and one Mark-50 torpedo. With your permission, I would like to divert them to the area. If the Hornets fail, the P-3 can track the submerged submarine until we can get ASW forces in the area."

"Roger, Steve. Make it so."

The air traffic controller flipped a switch to pipe the conversation between the four F/A-18 Hornets as they dove to the attack. An electronic screech accompanied the first transmission.

"MOONLIGHTER FLIGHT, MOONLIGHTER TWO Six. Follow me, boys, we're going in for some strafing action."

The four F/A-18s flipped to the right, as one after the other they followed the lead aircraft down through the clouds, depending on their radar system to keep them from hitting each other. Six thousand feet above the Mediterranean, they emerged to a clear sky.

"Ranger Two Nine, Moonlighter Two Six, request your position."

"Moonlighter Two Six, we have you six miles astern of us. Turn right and parallel the coast. Target will be dead ahead of you six miles."

"Roger. Moonlighter flight, master arm on. Weapons free, and for God's sake, don't shoot your wingman."

"I've got a wingman?" one of the pilots asked jokingly.

"Sixty-seven, Ranger Two Nine. The bow of the submarine has disappeared. Stern section is awash. Conning tower remains above water. Target is on course zero six zero with an estimated speed of twelve knots."

"Moonlighter flight, afterburner now!" shouted Two Six as he hurried to arrive over target before it disappeared completely beneath the sea. He wiggled his Hornet fighter back and forth, trying to get a visual on the surface target. Glancing at his heads-up display, he saw they were two miles from target.

"Lead is in hot, follow me," he said, although he had yet to gain a radar lock or a visual on the target. He relied on the data transmission generated by Ranger Two Nine to locate the Algerian submarine.

At two thousand feet, his eye caught a slight movement in the water. He scanned the area where he caught the movement and—*bingo*—there it was, the conning tower still above the waterline but disappearing rapidly beneath the sea.

"There she is!" he shouted over the radio and turned his aircraft slightly toward the target. The other three fighters adjusted their course to match Moonlighter Two Six. A half mile out, he started firing his twenty-millimeter cannon. The odds of missing a target the small size of a conning tower, complicated by it submerging, was high.

"Trail formation," he directed.

The three Hornets maneuvered behind him, increased speed, and came out in a trail formation of four fighters in a row. Cannons blasted away as their aircraft dove on the disappearing target.

The last of the four fighters passed over the conning tower as it disappeared under the water. Moonlighter Two Six ordered the formation to climb and rejoin. They were at two hundred when the formation finished its only attack run.

"Sixty-seven, Moonlighter Two Six. We got one pass, sir. No confirmation if we hit it, but the submarine has submerged."

"Roger, Moonlighter. Request resume combat air patrol. Ranger Two Nine, continue to track the submarine. We have a P-3C en route."

"Six Seven, Ranger Two Nine. Submarine last course zero six zero at twelve knots when it submerged."

ADMIRALS CAMERON AND PETE DEVLIN IN-
tentionally stood back as Dick Holman led the tracking effort against the Algerian submarine. Both men had been in the same hot seat that Dick now occupied, and the one thing they hated most were *powers to be* deciding they had to be involved at the microlevel.

"Pete, better give General *Rocky* Lewis a call and brief him about the submarine. He'll probably want to come down and watch the action. Plus, it will give us a chance to show him how the Navy is exercising its role in African Force."

"Might be better to wait until we finish?" Pete said flippantly.

Cameron shook his head. "As much as the thought might be appealing, Pete, he is the commander of African Force." Admiral Cameron crossed his arms. "Give him a call."

Rear Admiral Pete Devlin crossed to the nearby bulkhead, where a ship's telephone was mounted. With his thumb, he freed the handset from the locked position and, like a normal rotary telephone, dialed the number for General Lewis's stateroom.

"Steve, how soon can we get a couple of S-3s loaded with Mark-50 torpedoes in the air?" Dick Holman asked.

Steve shook his head. "I will have to check, Commodore. We have been using them in a maritime surveillance role. I am unsure if we have the weapons readily available, even if we can turn the aircraft around soon enough." He stopped. "Sorry, Captain. Thinking out loud, I would say we could launch a couple of S-3s with a couple of Mark-50s each in the next launch evolution an hour from now."

"Okay, let's make preparations to do it."

Steve Cloth hustled to the nearby bank of telephones and ship's interior communication systems and quickly relayed instructions to the flight deck officer, the S-3 squadron officer in charge, and the ship's company to arm and launch an antisubmarine mission.

Pete Devlin moved back to the side of Admiral Cameron. "The word has been relayed, Admiral."

"Is he on his way down?"

Pete shook his head. "No, I talked with his executive aide, Colonel Brad Storey. The general is in the gym working out and intends to do a five-mile jog down on the Hangar Deck when he finishes there. Colonel Storey said he will take the news to the general, but unless we hear from him sooner, then expect the new commander in about an hour."

"An hour? Doesn't he know that sea battles move faster than land engagements?"

Pete Devlin shrugged his shoulders. "Guess he has confidence in us to do the right thing."

Admiral Cameron's eyebrows furrowed. "Yeah, he oozed confidence earlier with me."

"You never did say what you two discussed when he asked you to remain behind."

Cameron shook his head. "Nothing important. We continued our discussion on—" He nodded his head at Dick Holman's back. "And about his philosophy on how body fat determines the intellectual qualities and warfighting capabilities of a warrior."

"Admiral, I know how you like to stay above things, but I have a backdoor E-mail from the Pentagon that gives some insight as to why he was sent here. If you are interested—"

Admiral Cameron shook his head. "No, thanks, Pete. I like to develop my own opinions and insights without having Washington politics taint them. The chairman of the Joint Chiefs of Staff would never have sent General Lewis if he didn't think the man was right for the job. Our job is to do everything possible so he can succeed. That means executing his orders expeditiously and without reservations—legal orders, of course—and giving him any advice he may need or ask for."

"Aye, sir."

"Six-seven, Ranger Two Nine. We can see the dark outline of the submarine beneath the water. It is still too shallow for him to go deeper. We are decending another thousand feet to improve the view."

Dick Holman moved to the navigational chart taped down on the plotting table. He ran his finger along the outlined depth contour of the coastal shelf. He looked up at Admiral Cameron.

"Admiral, according to the navigational chart, the submarine will have to remain on this base course for another hour before he gains access to deep water. When that happens, we may lose him."

Commander Steve Cloth crossed over to the plotting table. "Admirals, Commodore. we can launch the S-3s next cycle. They are being armed now. The P-3C should be arriving within the next thirty minutes and can start laying sonobuoys ahead of the submarine. With luck, we should be able to track him for the next hour. We still have plenty of daylight remaining."

Admiral Cameron nodded. He walked over and ran his finger from the Oran Naval Base along a base course of zero six zero degrees. "See this, gentlemen." His finger continued onward for several more inches before it crossed through the middle of the small nameplates identifying the USS *Stennis* battle group and the USS *Kearsarge* Amphibious Task Force. "If he continues on this course—"

"He'll arrive in our vicinity sometime tomorrow morning," Steve Cloth added.

"Correct, Commander. We need to sink that submarine tonight. Meanwhile . . . Pete!" he called. "Alert the fleet to the possible approach of an enemy submarine. I want to move the high-value units *Stennis* and the amphibious ships to the far side of the operations area. Put the destroyers between them and the approaching submarine. Contact the USS *Miami* and USS *Albany* and deploy them . . ." He pointed to two positions north and south of the enemy submarine PIM—position of intended movement. ". . . so our two submarines can bracket him if he makes it this far. Make sure everyone knows the op areas we are assigning to our submarines. The last thing we need is a blue-on-blue incident," he said.

WATER SPRAYED THROUGH THE CONNING tower where the American cannon shells had entered. Blood splattered the depth-control gauges across the bridge area where the three crew members died absorbing the impact of spent shells. Ibn Al Jamal sloshed through two inches of water running across the deck and through the opened hatch leading to the next level. The gauge showed their depth at fifty feet. The sea floor was less than twenty feet beneath their keel, but it was slowly increasing. They had little choice but to either continue on their current course to deeper water or settle on the sandy bottom here. Whichever course of action he chose, the damage to the *Al Nasser* had to be repaired. Ibn Al Jamal straightened up and watched the action around him as he thought about his options. The Oran Naval Base was not one of them.

Crew members rushed to the large holes above their heads with damage-control padding and rubber seals, fighting to stop the flood. Two sailors slid a large rubber pad across one of the larger holes, while another stood nearby with a cone-shaped piece of wood. Behind him, another sailor held a sledgehammer at the ready. This was the tricky part. The rubber piece covered the hole, but the high pressure outside caused seawater to shoot into the submarine from beneath it. The sailor with the cone wedge placed the point in the center of the rubber padding. He barely moved his hand before the sledgehammer slammed down on the top of the wedge, driving the damage control piece, with one motion, into the hole. The water slowed. The hammer came down twice more, driving the wooden wedge deeper into the hull until the water stopped.

The XO turned to another hole. The damage control team hurried with him. The tall XO led the effort, shouting for a crew member to stuff the rubber pad while another fetched a shoring timber to put against the cone once it was driven in.

Ibn Al Jamal knew he could stop the flooding easily by surfacing, but surfacing meant exposing *Al Nasser* to another aerial attack. No, beneath the sea is how submarines avoided air attacks and electronic detection. The damage to the conning tower limited the depth the Algerian diesel-powered Kilo attack submarine could operate. Ibn Al

Jamal glanced again at the depth gauge. They had leveled out at sixty feet. The farther they went down, the more pressure the sea exerted on the temporary repairs to the damaged conning tower. How far down could he go before the sea pressure popped the damage control repairs like a cork on a champagne bottle?

The three remaining holes were repaired using the same method as the largest one. The XO assigned two sailors to remain in the area and keep watch on the repairs. He turned and looked at Ibn Al Jamal.

The skipper nodded back. The two men joined near the navigation table and reviewed the chart.

Ibn Al Jamal briefed the XO and the navigator about the importance of remaining on this course until they reached deeper water. However, even when they reached it, he wasn't sure the submarine could take the increased depth. The XO wanted to know if they had evaded the American forces that attacked them. Were they safe?

Ibn Al Jamal shrugged his shoulders. Since they submerged, the attack had stopped, but they were at shallow depth, making their silhouette easily discernible from the air in the calm sea surrounding the Oran Naval Base. All they could do was pray to Allah and continue on course until they could turn west toward Malaga, Spain.

The other two nodded in agreement.

"OKAY, LET'S GO AROUND FOR ANOTHER pass," Commander Stillwell said to Jasbo.

She nodded, and with the two working in tandem, they put the EP-3E into a left-hand turn. The Algerian horizon slid slowly across their windscreen as they passed through the compass degrees.

"Passing one ninety degrees," the navigator said through the ICS from her position behind the curtains separating the cockpit from the main body of the aircraft. "Recommend course two seventy for three minutes; then, left turn to course zero six zero to line up with the hostile sub."

Stillwell and Jasbo glanced at the gyrocompass simultaneously. "Okay, ease up," Commander Stillwell said, bringing the aircraft level and tapering off the turn as the compass showed the aircraft approaching 200 degrees.

"There she is," Chief Henckels said, pointing over Jasbo's shoulder toward the sea a couple of points off the nose of the aircraft.

The three leaned forward. Commander Stillwell eased the nose of the aircraft forward to enhance their view. Ahead of them, the dark shadow of a submerged submarine appeared under the sea. The tug was to their right, heading toward the harbor entrance.

"Wonder if he knows we can see him?" Jasbo asked.

"If he doesn't, he will soon. Looks almost like a giant whale. One of our VP brethren is on his way. Should be here in the next few minutes."

"You mean one of our VP sisters, don't you?"

"Jasbo, are you going PC on me during this time of war?" he asked, his voice rising in false astonishment. "Give me a goddamn cigarette."

She shook her head, smiling. "Commander, the only thing I know is that you would never survive a visit by NOW."

"NOW?"

"National Organization for Women."

"I thought they merged with Knotts Berry Farm."

"Why would they want to do that?"

"They now call the new organization Knott NOW."

Chief Henckels laughed. "That's good, Commander. I like that. Knott NOW."

"Chief, don't make me call your wife," Jasbo said.

The laughter stopped abruptly, drawing laughs from both Stillwell and Jasbo.

Lieutenant Commander John Andrews stuck his head through the curtains.

"Hi, John. How're things going back there?"

"We may have problems, Skipper."

"You're telling me. I got the *Jasbo* up here, threatening my career, and the chief is having to grovel because of what she is going to tell his wife. If I were the chief, I'd be very very afraid."

"Skipper, Susan and her folks are picking up indications of Algerian fighter activity. Nothing associated with us yet, but if they decide to come our way, we may have little notice this close to the shore."

Commander Stillwell nodded. "Any indications they know about us yet?"

"Haven't seen anything, but that doesn't mean they weren't launched because of us. After all, we are a pretty big airplane, and we've got four F/A-18 Hornets buzzing holes in the sky overhead." He nodded. "Yeah, I would say they're after us."

"We're coming abreast of that tugboat, Commander," Chief Henckels said, touching the two pilots on the shoulders and pointing off to the right.

Stillwell nodded and glanced down at the compass. "Passing two two zero. Let's increase our turn, Jasbo," Commander Stillwell said. "We're getting too close to that tug, and we're way inside the fifteen nautical miles we were authorized." He stretched his head forward to look at the telltale shadow of the submarine. We'll do an aft-to-bow pass over the target."

"John, keep me advised on the hostile air. I will pass the information to the Hornets overhead. Two of them have broken off to refuel, so we only have a couple of CAP aircraft above us. The submarine is outside the fifteen-mile territorial limit, so we can continue to haunt his every movement." He smiled. "Let's us get out of their territorial waters ASAP."

The first missile streaked by the port side of the aircraft to explode overhead about one hundred feet. "Jesus Christ!" Commander Stillwell shouted. He grabbed the controls of the aircraft, jerked the steering column to the right, and pushed it downward. The EP-3E fell into a controlled dive. "Get those Hornets, Jasbo!"

John Andrews bounced off the bulkhead, slamming his head against a protruding piece of metal mounted to hold one end of the curtains. He collapsed on the small walkway, blood pouring from the wound at his temple. The navigator leaned over from her seat located just outside the cockpit, where she was strapped in by a huge seat belt. She pulled the unconscious officer toward her, taking a handkerchief from a flight suit pocket on her leg and pressing it against the bleeding. A trail of blood tracked across the rubber-padded aisle.

The aircraft jerked and vibrated as it descended toward one thousand feet at a forty-five-degree angle.

"Number two is in the red. It's overheating, Skipper."

The explosion shattered the side window beside Commander Stillwell, sending the glass into a thousand small spiders. "What the hell . . ." His eye burned with pain, and for a few seconds his left arm became numb.

"Number-one engine!" shouted Chief Henckels, reaching up and flipping the secure switch.

"Help me, Jasbo!" Commander Stillwell said. "Bring her level."

"We're going to lose number-two engine!"

The sound of the wind rushing by the open window drowned their words.

"Bullshit! I forbid it! You keep number two on-line, Chief!"

"Aye, aye, sir!" he shouted, looking at the redlined temperature gauge of the engine. He reached up and touched a couple of the controls but changed not a one. There was nothing to do. The engine either kept going or it froze up. He placed his palm over the engine temperature gauge. With his other hand, he flipped up the plastic cover covering the fire extinguisher for the number-two engine.

"We got fire on number one, Commander," Chief Henckels said. "Firing extinguisher now."

The plane continued its rush toward the sea. Stillwell shut the damaged eye, ignoring the pain as he fought the controls of the Aries II to bring her back to a level altitude.

The EP-3E had two extinguishers for each wing. The extinguishers could be directed against either engine, but once they were expended, the only other option was a controlled dive from altitude in the hope that the wind would put the fire out. In this case, they had insufficient altitude to put it out.

"What hit us?"

Susan Garner staggered through the doorway. She held a bloody handkerchief to her forehead. She paused momentarily to help the navigator shove the unconscious John Andrews under the navigation table, where she could help control the movement of the unconscious officer.

"Susan, what the hell!"

"SAM, Commander. Someone on that tugboat fired a couple of surface-to-air, shoulder-launched missiles. Infrared. They locked on our engine temperatures."

"Activating second extinguisher, Commander. First unsuccessful."

"Roger, Chief. Jasbo, sound 'prepare to ditch.'"

Jasbo reached over and flipped the signal. A rapid series of beeps penetrated the noise level of the aircraft, sending those few officers and sailors who had not already assumed ditching position when the missile hit rushing into their neck-high flight chairs.

"Chief, status?"

He lifted his palm and peeked at the temperature. "Number two running hot. It's halfway into the red but seems to have steadied; no further increase in temperature. Last extinguisher nearly exhausted. Fire still raging inside number one."

Stillwell turned so he could look out of the side window, but wind and the remaining spiderweb of shattered glass distorted the fire on number one. "It looks as if the propeller has been blown off," he said.

"Skipper, it don't look as if this extinguisher is going to put the fire out."

"Then we'll have to dive, Chief. Jasbo, tell everyone to prepare for rapid descent."

"Skipper, we're at *one thousand feet. We can't dive!*" Jasbo objected.

"Jasbo, we got no choice. We're too low to parachute,

and I'll be damned if we are going to ditch in Algerian waters. I ain't going to be no prisoner."

"Good luck. Right now, we are heading toward shore."

"There are more ways to put out a fire than fire extinguishers and steep dives." He pressed forward on the control, and the EP-3E responded, vibrating, shaking the dive, pulling to the right.

The aircraft shook, straining against the increased self-made turbulence as it passed through the remaining feet. "Jasbo, help me, goddammit! Level off at twenty-five feet."

"Twenty-five feet! Skipper, this bird won't fly at twenty-five feet."

"To hell with the safety manual, Jasbo. Trust me, I am a commander, you know. Quit acting as if I'm a junior officer."

"Passing three hundred feet," Chief Henckels announced.

"At twenty-five feet, Paul," Jasbo said, inadvertently calling Commander Stillwell by his first name. "We won't be able to see for the sea spray."

He grinned. "You're learning, Jasbo."

She grinned. "Sea spray. Shit! Why didn't I think of that?"

"Because I'm the commander and you're the wet-nosed lieutenant," he bantered.

"Passing one hundred feet."

"Start easing up on the control."

The two pulled on the steering column. It refused to budge. "It's not moving, Skipper!"

"Passing seventy-five feet. Pull, goddamn it!" Chief Henckels unstrapped his harness with two quick flips of the toggles. He jumped over Jasbo's shoulders and grabbed the steering column with her.

Commander Stillwell reached over and pushed the number-three and -four engines to maximum power. "Turn slightly to the right, Jasbo, and when you do, jerk the column back. Now!"

The three twisted the column to the right, toward the good engines, and simultaneously pulled back on the steering wheel. The aircraft groaned and from somewhere back near the galley, the sounds of falling metal plates and shattering coffee mugs echoed to the cockpit. The aircraft leveled off.

The vibration tapered off as water on the windshield blinded them. Chief Henckels released the wheel as the aircraft hit a bump in the low altitude, knocking him off his feet and onto the deck. Water blew in through the blown-out window. The low altitude knocked the plane about as the two pilots fought to stay above this unsafe altitude. The chief scrambled up and managed to restrap himself into the raised flight engineer seat above the pilots. The wings of the EP-3E were fifty feet long. Just one hiccup, and the aircraft would Ferris-wheel across the top of the sea, tearing the wings off, and ripping through the fuselage.

"Engine fire number one is out, Skipper. Number two temperature increasing."

Commander Stillwell reached down while keeping his eyes on the altitude gauge. He grabbed the speed throttle for engine number-two and eased it back. The aircraft pulled to the right as the change in torque tried to force it into a spin in that direction. He pushed the throttle foward again. He and Jasbo fought the aircraft, using throttle control and flaps to keep the EP-3E flying straight.

"Course?"

"We are on one eight zero. Christ, we're heading toward Algeria, Skipper."

"Ranger Two Nine, Moonlighter Two Six. What the hell is going on? You're heading into Algeria."

"Moonlighter Two Six, we have taken a missile in our number-one engine."

"Missile? From where?"

"The tugboat must have had a Grail on board. First one missed us but gave us enough warning to take some evasive action. Moonlighter, I am going to try to turn the aircraft. She is acting up, and we have lost number-one engine. We are in danger of losing number-two engine. It's running hot. We are fighting a right-turn spin."

"Ranger, a right turn is going to take you directly over Oran Naval Base."

"I know, but we don't have the power to do a left turn. We are a right-turn-only aircraft, and I have no intentions of ditching this thing near or in Algeria. We are not going to be POWs. Besides, there's no beer available."

"Ranger, we are on our way."

"Moonlighter, maintain distance from us. We are having a difficult control problem with the aircraft, and maneuverability is limited. Be advised Algerian fighters have been detected south of us."

"We'll worry about them when we see them."

"Okay, Jasbo. Chief, need your help in this. You work the throttles. What I want to do is gain some altitude. I hold us at fifty feet now, which means we are going up." As if on cue, the sea spray began to diminish. Ahead, the coastline of Algeria appeared.

"At one hundred feet, I want to start a long, slow turn to the right. Chief, that means you need to be prepared to increase speed on number two and decrease speed on numbers three and four if we find ourselves in an uncontrolled spin to the right. We'll only have a second or two to correct if we lose control, so be ready."

"Roger, Skipper. I've got it. Passing seventy-five feet now."

Over the ICS came the navigator's voice. "Commander, Lieutenant Commander Andrews is still unconscious. I don't like the look of it."

"Roger, Nav. What is our distance to the shore?"

"We are passing the coastline now, Skipper. It will take a bit to get our picture back with all the maneuvering we just did. I will tell you exact location in a few seconds."

"Passing one hundred feet."

Chief Henckels reached forward and flipped on the windshield wipers, clearing away the last of the sea spray. The desert sands of the coast filled the view.

"Okay, here we go. Real slow, Jasbo. Real slow."

The two eased the steering to the right, letting the aircraft pull it along as they fought the torque trying to jerk the controls from their hands. The aircraft pulled to the right. Commander Stillwell watched the shoreline fill the windscreen as they passed over the Algerian coast. He controlled the urge to hurry the turn and escape the landmass below him. "Keep pulling up on it, Jasbo. Let's try to use a nose-up altitude to help control this torque. You're doing good."

"Passing one hundred fifty." Chief Henckels looked at the compass in front of him on the dash of the pilot controls. "Passing two zero zero." He looked out Jasbo's side window. "Land on both sides of us. Sea about one mile to starboard."

"Ranger Two Nine, Moonlighter Two Six. I have relayed your situation to CTF Six Seven. They have ordered the cruiser *Ramage* in this direction. Destroyer *Spruance* is accompanying. USS *Kearsarge* has detached a Marine Corps CH-53 to the *Rampage* to help in the event you have to ditch."

"I am not going to ditch," he mumbled, cursing a couple of times through clenched teeth as the aircraft jerked roughly as it hit the turbulence where land air met the cooler sea air. The tendons on Stillwell's arms stood out against the sleeves of the green fire-retardant flight suit.

"Passing one four zero; altitude two hundred feet."

Susan Garner stuck her head inside the curtains. A medical bandage covered the right side of her forehead. "We've got problems, Skipper."

"What the hell do you think this is?" Commander Stillwell said, his voice choppy through clenched teeth as he strained to keep the aircraft in a controlled turn.

"No, we may have Algerian fighters closing our position."

"Susan, go away. You handle it. I'll fly the plane. You get those Hornets between us and them."

She turned to go.

"Tell Moonlighter flight—shit! You know what to tell them. I can't talk now. Make sure everyone knows that we are not going to ditch this aircraft. We are going to leave this EP-3 Echo like we got on; by the ladder."

The curtain fluttered back into place as she left.

"We're going to have to ease up on the rate of turn. It's too hard to maintain." They eased the wheel slightly to the left, causing the torque to diminish. The tension required to maintain the turn eased from his arms.

"Cockpit, Navigator. John is coming around."

"Passing two hundred fifty feet. Keep her climbing; slow and steady. Passing course one zero zero."

"Roger, sir. At current rate of turn, recommend steady on course zero six five for direct path to Sigonella."

"Roger, Navigator. Keep holding it, Jasbo. We're getting there. I want to come out on course zero zero zero to clear Algeria and then steady on zero six five toward home plate. We are going to take this aircraft back to Sigonella. Somewhere back there, a cold bottle of Nasty Asturo awaits us," Commander Stillwell said, murdering the name of the national Italian beer.

"Commander, we are pegged in the red," Chief Henckels said, reaching up and turning down the revolutions on engine number two. Henckels spun around and started pulling circuit breakers, only to immediately push them back in.

The aircraft jerked as the change in speed caused the aircraft to spin faster to the right.

"Chief, what in hell! Don't do that!"

Stillwell and Jasbo leaned to the left, fighting the sharp increase in torque of the starboard engines as engine number two wound down.

"Shit!" Stillwell shouted. "Hold her, Jasbo. Hold her! Chief, reduce revolutions on engines three and four. Hurry! And get number two back on-line and leave it the hell alone!"

Chief Henckels reached forward and pulled the throttles back. Sweat broke out on his forehead.

What in the hell was the chief thinking? The pull to the right lessened. They had regained control. The tendons on Stillwell's arms relaxed slightly. He wondered briefly how long the diminutive Jasbo could keep up at this physical pace.

"Lieutenant, can I help?" Henckels asked. He unbuckled his seat belt and started to ease out of the seat.

"Chief, get back in your seat and buckle in!" Stillwell shouted.

A horrendous explosion rocked the plane to the left, throwing Henckels backward into his flight engineer seat. A second explosion broke the sky in front of them, immediately followed by a third on the starboard side.

"What the fuck?" Jasbo shouted.

John Andrews stuck his head inside the cockpit. He held a bloody compress against the top of his head. "Antiaircraft guns from the naval base."

"Why are they shooting at us?" Stillwell asked, his attention focused on the instrument panel in front of him.

"Well, Commander, we are overflying their base right now at"—he looked at the altimeter—"five hundred feet. I think they may have seen us."

IBN AL JAMAL INCREASED THE SPEED OF AL *Nasser* to twelve knots but kept the depth at fifty feet. He knew even a half-alert antisubmarine aircraft should be able to see them in these calm seas, but shallow water and battle damage kept him on this course and this depth. Ten more nautical miles he needed before they would enter deeper waters. Deeper waters meant darker waters. The shade of the sea caused by the increased water depth should help them disappear, even if the submarine could go no deeper than fifty feet.

Ten minutes later, the explosive sound of one of the smaller damage control cones shooting out of its hole by seawater pressure caused everyone in the control room to jump. Ears popped because of the change in pressure. Water rocketed through the reopened wound, hitting the far-side bulkhead and ricocheting through the control room. Two sailors slammed a rubber padding over the opening. Water pushed it out of their hands as the increased pressure fought their efforts. They searched frantically for several seconds, groping in the water for the rubber gasket before finding it.

Ibn Al Jamal slowed the submarine to eight knots, and even as the submarine slowed, he ordered it further slowed to two knots. Slower speed meant less water pressure against the temporary repairs. Slower speed also increased the opportunity for detection, but at this moment, the Americans knew where he was, and if they were going to attack, they would have done it already.

Others rushed to help. Two sailors held the rubber padding, while three others fought the cone into position over the hole. They forced an inch of the tapered end of the damage-control cone into the hole, the water fighting their effort, trying to rip it out of their hands. The sledgehammer rose and fell in one smooth, heavy blow, knocking the cone into the opening, wedging the rubber padding tight and sealing the damaged bulkhead. The water stopped immediately.

For the first time, he thought of surfacing and surrendering to the Americans. But would they give him a chance before he could make the offer? He doubted they would accept the surrender of the submarine that attacked their fleet.

He increased the speed slowly until the submarine reached eight knots again. Crew members and officers went about their jobs silently, their eyes continuing to stray toward the three temporary repairs on the bulkhead of the conning tower. If two or all of them failed, the submarine would have little choice but to surface.

Ibn Al Jamal pulled a compass rose from the drawer beneath the lighted plotting table. Placing it over the chart, he and the navigator took a wild guess to their position. He drew a line along their course and added estimated times along their position of intended movement, called PIM in navigationese. The navigator meant to draw a couple of inches, stopping the pencil mark at the edge of the deep water, but his hand slipped, and the line went the complete length of the ruler.

Ibn Al Jamal stared at the line. It went past the deep-water edge, continued on a northeastern path through the last known location of the USS *Kearsarge* and USS *Nassau*

Amphibious Task Forces. It did not stop there; the line passed within fifty miles of the USS *Stennis* Battle Group, which was farther east. The line stopped at the edge of the combined French and British naval forces one hundred miles farther out. The Americans would have already reached the conclusion that he was heading out to sea to attack them. He realized then that attack was inevitable, and if the *Al Nasser* was going to survive, it needed to reach deep water and turn away from this course as soon as possible.

He would turn now, but the risk of hitting one of the numerous undersea mountains or centuries of uncharted wrecks that cluttered the North African coastal sea was high. Wrecks stretching all the way back to the age of the Phoenicians dotted the undersea landscape. Many from the nineteenth century onward continued to raise their masts above their graves to fish for unwary ships passing within their hooks. Last year, two coastal merchants had been lost in this area because heavy seas caused them to collide with uncharted wrecks. He had little choice but to stay the course for another hour.

The Americans knew his position. They would share that information with the British and the French. The French would enjoy nothing better than to sink an Algerian Navy vessel.

The navigator estimated approximately seventy minutes at eight knots before they could turn northwest. They needed a two-hour northwestern leg until they reached the center of the transit lane leading toward the Strait of Gibraltar and far enough away so they avoided the dangerous seas along the North African coast.

Ibn Al Jamal muttered a short prayer to Allah. Before he reached the deeper water, *Al Nasser* would have the attention of the antisubmarine forces of the Americans, British, and French. He hoped they only watched. He shook his head. No, they would be coming after him. The Americans first, if for little else than revenge for the attack three weeks ago.

CHAPTER 8

⚓

THE CONVOY WAS STRETCHED FATHER APART than Stapler wanted. The three vehicles had slowly been increasing the distance between each other for the last twelve hours. He should have noticed sooner. Stapler wiped the sweat from his eyes and shaded them with his hand. He pushed the sunglasses off his nose. The overhead sun glared off the packed clay. He gently touched his swollen lips. So dry and cracked. The terrain was becoming rougher, the closer they got to the wadis ahead of them. The sand had given way to clay somewhere behind them. He slapped the roof of the humvee, causing the vehicle to stop. Stapler pulled his dirty handkerchief from his back pocket and dabbed at his left hand. He had bumped it against the side of the sunroof he was standing through minutes ago and burst several of the sunburn blisters.

His humvee led the convoy, followed by the truck nearly two hundred yards behind. The LT had told the drivers to keep a minimum of fifty yards between the truck, but two hundred? About fifty yards behind the truck was the second humvee with the LT. Inside it, *Miss Sheila Anne Forester* rode with the LT. *Why did she bother him so much?* Stapler stuck his head inside the humvee and told the driver to wait for the others to close their position. This was the second time they had stopped in two hours. This land convoy was a lot like a sea convoy; the slowest vehicle limited the speed, and in this case, it was the truck.

The straining engine of the truck bothered Stapler. It had not bothered Stapler until it bothered Heinrich Wilshaven, the oil rigger in charge of vehicle maintenance, and Bearcat Jordan, the supervisor of the oil riggers. Two hours ago, at a rest break, they passed their concerns to him and the LT. Wilshaven had shared his expert opinion that the old Volvo truck, with nearly two hundred thousand miles on it. "It vas going to give up dat ghost," he had said in a heavy German accent while rubbing an oil drop from the engine between two grease-stained fingers and shaking his head.

The truck carried most of the oil riggers, Professor Walthers, and his male aide Karim. All the food, water, and extra fuel, with the exception of two fuel canisters mounted to the rear of each humvee, was strapped down on the bed. They had made good time since leaving the oasis before dawn this morning, traveling constantly and only stopping for a few minutes every two hours. Modesty for the women consisted of going in front of the humvee, while for some reason the men earned the nearest thing to an off-color comment from Professor Walthers about dogs drawn to the wheels.

The journey had grown easier in the last few hours as the sand gave way to flat, sun-bleached terrain speckled with small, wiry bushes that had forced their way through the brick-hard clay. The heat of the sun never varied. It moved across the sky, beating down on them constantly, a sledgehammer of draining, broiling heat. Stapler glanced up. The same, hour after hour, day after day: not a cloud in the sky to provide a moment of blessed shade. The heat was taking its toll.

Nights provided some relief. The twinkles of the stars lit the crystal sky like lights on a Christmas tree. Night fell quickly, but the heat dissipated within an hour, and the sunburn caused the cool wind to feel colder than it was, forcing them to button collars, strap vests tighter, and some, like Catsup, to seek others' body warmth.

Somewhere ahead lay a series of wadis—small valleys—they would have to navigate. Stapler believed it was less than ten miles to the wadis and safety. Professor Walthers argued ten miles to the wadis and danger. The professor warned that the wadis would be swarming with Tauregs. But the professor had been the voice of doom since they started. If Stapler or the LT had listened to him, they would probably be dead by now.

Once through the wadis—Stapler figured thirty miles through them—they still had one hundred more miles to travel to reach the agreed rendezvous point with the Army. Only then would they be in range of the Army CH-47 Chinook helicopters—if the Army showed.

Three days had passed without radio contact with the Army. The jerry-rigged radio had worked well the first day. Then, for some inexplicable reason, nothing but static. Stapler knew the thing was broadcasting; every one of the Marines could pick up transmissions from the radio on their bricks. Lieutenant Malcolm *"Jeff to Miss Sheila Anne Forester"* Nolan worried about the Algerians picking up the transmissions before the United States Army did. Stapler believed the LT had worried a bit less since the oasis. Couldn't get that shit-eating grin off the officer's face. You would think it was the first time the LT had had a leg thrown across him, thought Stapler. Of course, those were a fine pair of tits from what glimpse he got—definitely pass the pencil test—and with quarter-size, pink nipples. Seemed to Stapler that most tits tended to be various shades of brown rather than any shade of pink. He shook his head. It would be a while before he looked at a quarter the same way again.

The baying of a camel drew his attention. Camels! What a sight! Two humvees, a truck, eleven marines, and eight camels. The baying passed around the camels. Reminded Stapler of turkeys; all you had to do was get one turkey to gobble, and they all joined in the cacophony like dominoes falling. Someday he would be reading about this in *Naval Proceedings*—if they survived. To the right rode two camels, Cowboy Joe-Boy on one with Private Raoul Gonzales on the other. Behind Cowboy, her arms wrapped around his waist, rode Catsup. Stapler felt a slight pang of jealousy but quickly tucked it away in a different part of his thoughts. He was an old man at thirty-seven in comparison to her twenty. What in hell was he thinking?

Cowboy rode his camel nearer the humvee, pushing and tugging on two long ropes leading from the camel's rope bridle. The Marine's M-16 was strapped across his front, so Kellogg could lean against his back.

"See, Gunny!" he shouted. "These camels are great!" Cowboy Joe-Boy Henry pointed to the other side of the humvee, where two oil riggers rode two other camels. Behind them, four Marines rode four more camels.

Christ! Where do they get their energy? thought Stapler. He shook his head at the image of Marines in the middle of the Sahara desert riding camels as if they were on some sort of Disneyland excursion. He would be the laughingstock at the mess, but he'd punch Top Sergeant MacGregory square in the face if he laughed. He thought of the ice machine at the mess—slide that glass under it, lift the lever, and slivers of chewable ice tumbled into it. He wiped the sweat from his forehead, the tenderness of the skin aching from the pressure of his hand. In survival school, they taught that as long as you were sweating, you were okay. When you quit sweating, your hours were numbered. Well, he was definitely sweating.

"Yeah, Gunny," Catsup slurred. "Just think, no one has to walk now. Great, ain't it?" Her head fell back on Cowboy Joe-Boy's back.

"Yeah, Cowboy, Catsup. It's great, but keep your heads down. You two make a tempting target."

"We know, Gunny, but it's either double up or one of us walks."

"Yeah, Gunny, or one of us walks," Catsup mumbled.

Stapler looked up at Cowboy. "Get her back to the truck and under the canvas, Private. Tell them to give her water—lots of it."

Cowboy nodded. "Okay, Gunny." He tugged on the reins, turning the camel around toward the truck. "Come on, Osama."

"You two, be careful! Kellogg, stay awake!"

"I'm okay, Dad."

Grinding sounds from the truck like fingernails down a chalkboard drowned out the last few words. Stapler turned. White clouds rose around the hood of the old Volvo. The truck had stopped. Both doors opened, and Heinrich and Bearcat crawled out.

Stapler leaned in and told the others about the truck. Then he pulled himself out through the roof and slid down the back, careful to keep his bare hands from touching the hot metal. From the rear humvee, the LT headed toward the truck. This might be the end of the road for the truck. Without it, some were going to be walking. How were they going to make it? The two humvees could not carry the water, food, and gasoline they needed to make the rendezvous. He knew it. Heinrich Wilshaven knew it, Bearcat Jordan had already voiced it, and no one had disagreed.

He reached the truck a few seconds after the LT.

Wilshaven had the hood up and his head buried inside. Curses in German bounced off the top of the hood. No one spoke. Stapler nodded at the lieutenant, who returned the nod and said nothing. The group stood, waiting for the verdict like nervous, expectant fathers waiting for news from the doctor.

Stapler pulled on his earlobe as he watched the men around the engine. The M-16 hung loosely in his left hand, the barrel pointing toward the earth. Not having talked with Base Butler in three days made him paranoid the Army wouldn't be there. It reminded him of the time he arranged to meet a distant relative weeks in advance, only to show up on the appointed day at the appointed bar without ever reconfirming the date. The cousin never showed, and Stapler spent the rest of the day getting drunk at a bar he would never have been in except for the anticipated rendezvous.

The two female partners walked around to the front of the truck. All three riggers who had suffered heat exhaustion earlier in the trip had recovered, but the LT had ordered them under the canvas Bearcat had stretched across half the bed of the truck to provide some shade. The younger graying blond, who twenty-four hours before was out cold from the heat, was still unsteady on her feet. Stapler started to say something and then thought, *What the hell! She wants to kill herself, let her.*

Wilshaven stepped down from the bumper and wiped his hands on a rag. He shook his head. "It's gont. It's dead! Dat problem cannot be fixed, I said. The fan belt est broke, and the truck est no can to be fixed. Dirt est in da oil. Dat tubes have leaks. And, there est no spare part. Da Volvo est kaput."

Cowboy Joe-Boy and Catsup rode up behind the group. From the back of the truck came the professor and Karim and, to Stapler's fine pleasure, strolled the fabulous *Miss Sheila Anne Forester* from the other humvee. Bad enough the truck *est kaput.*

"What do we do now, Lieutenant?" Bearcat Jordan asked. "We're about ten miles from the wadis."

Lieutenant Nolan scratched his head. "Gunny, you got any ideas?"

The angry baying of the camel caused him to look. Cowboy said the camels could carry heavy loads. They had eight of the ugly, foul-smelling creatures.

"Camels," he said.

"Camels?"

"Yes, sir, LT."

"Cowboy," Stapler said, motioning the private to him. Corporal Heights walked up from the other side of the truck. He had been in command of the truck and riding in back. "Corporal, help Cowboy get Kellogg down and under the canvas. Fill her up with water. She's got heat exhaustion."

Heights helped get Kellogg down from behind Cowboy. She was able to walk on her own to the truck. The older woman partner helped the Marine to the back, making motherly cooing sounds as they moved.

"Cowboy, go round up the rest of the camels and bring them here on the double."

"LT, we have to strap as much of the water and fuel to the camels as we can. Cowboy, you and Raoul are going to have to be the leaders in this, so get moving."

"What about Catsup, Gunny?"

"Cowboy, what the hell do you think we're going to do with her? Bury her? You get your ass moving, and do what I told you!"

"Yes, Gunnery Sergeant!"

"Corporal Heights, organize a working party to start off-loading the truck." He turned and saw Cowboy still watching.

"Cowboy, didn't I tell you to go get the rest of the camels?"

Cowboy Joe-Boy dug his heels into the side of the camel. "I'm on my way, Gunny."

Stapler saw the glazed look in the private's eyes. *Another heat exhaustion in the making,* he thought. He looked at Gonzales. The Hispanic Marine had taken his T-shirt off and tucked it under his helmet so that the back of it fell across his neck and down his back.

"We've got some rope in the back of the truck," Bearcat added.

"And, der est some heavy tape under the front seat," Heinrich Wilshaven said as he hurried to the driver's side to get it.

"Let's get moving," Lieutenant Nolan said. "We're still ten miles from the wadis. Should be safe once we reach there."

Wilshaven handed the two rolls of tape to Stapler. *"Herz,* my fine Marine friend," he said. Wilshaven looked as if his face had been stuck inside an oven; blisters and faint scabs covered the once immaculate profile. Stapler wondered briefly how the man retained his jovial attitude.

Cowboy came back leading the awkward calvary of baying, protesting camels.

"Cowboy, get everyone off the camels."

"Gunny, do you think they are following us?" Lieutenant Nolan asked.

"Of course they are following us," the professor answered testily. "We are in the middle of the Taureg homeland. They know exactly where we are and when we enter the wadis—and I want everyone to recall that I recommended against this—we are going to be considered more than just invaders. We are entering what they consider near holy ground."

"Gunny, why don't we send out a patrol while we are transferring the supplies to the camels?" Lieutenant Nolan asked, ignoring the professor's outburst.

"On foot?"

"No, let Private Henry and Gonzales—who seem to be the most proficient on the camels—ride back a few miles on our track and see if they can see anything."

Stapler thought the idea was a bad one. *What if they get lost?*

"Yes, sir." Stapler turned to the two privates. "Take your camels and you two backtrack our trail and see if you can spot anyone tailing us. But don't go out of sight of this convoy. There's no reference here in the desert, and we don't want to lose you."

"You want me to go with them, Gunny?" Corporal Heights asked, hoping the gunny would let him. He hadn't gotten to ride the camels yet.

Stapler thought a few moments and then said, "No, you stay here and track them. Keep in contact with them on the brick." The two Marines turned their camels and at a trot rode back along their trail. Corporal Heights crawled back on the bed of the truck to watch them.

"A lot of us are going to be walking now," Stapler said.

"Why don't you tell us the truth?" Sheila blared out.

"We're going to die out here in this godforsaken land, aren't we?"

The men turned and looked, but no one said anything. *What could we say?* thought Stapler. If they were going to die out here, by God they were going to die trying to escape. It'd be a cold day in hell before he curled up and waited for death.

She shook her head. Her arms hung limply by her sides. Stapler noticed for the first time the small, sun-burned blisters on the young woman's lips and a two-inch square abrasion along her right cheek. Her blond hair that swung so freely in a ponytail when they first met was matted by perspiration to her cheeks and neck. For some reason, he never assumed *Miss Sheila Anne Forester* was suffering as much as the rest of the group. For some reason, he assumed she was impervious to the heat and the bad conditions. Stapler tugged his ear. Now, why would he think that? She was as frightened as the rest. The facade was crumbling. In a way, it disappointed him to discover the nemesis of the convoy showing weakness. He liked his opponents strong.

Sheila screamed, "Christ! I don't think it takes a lot of thought to figure out we have ten miles to the wadis, forty miles through its winding ways." Her hand moved back and forth like a snake. "And then still another hundred miles to go? I am not stupid. I know you're not. We started out from the compound with every available container filled with water. We had food for weeks, everyone said. And enough fuel to travel. It's the water. It's the stupid, fucking water. We ran out of water before we had gone fifty miles the first day and a half. We are less than one day from the oasis, and already empty water containers are rolling around in the back of the truck. Those in the back of the—" She stopped, put her hands to her face and ran back toward the humvee in the rear.

Lieutenant Nolan turned to follow but stopped at the last second.

After several moments of awkward silence, Bearcat Jordan broke the spell. "She's right. We're not rationing the water effectively. I know you Marines are; you fill your canteens and then leave the water for the rest of us. We are going to have to ration the water very carefully from here on out if we are going to make it."

Stapler let go of his earlobe and nodded. "We were supposed to be doing that now." He looked around.

"I don't think anyone really took responsibility for rationing the water, Gunnery Sergeant," Professor Walthers said. "It has been more of a you get thirsty, you drink."

Lieutenant Nolan stepped forward. "Bearcat is right, and I think we all understand what we have to do. Since I am technically in charge of this convoy, I am assuming responsibility for rationing the water. From now on, no one drinks until either I or the Gunnery Sergeant ration it out. No more water today. We will ration some out tonight when we stop."

"Maybe we should ration some out now and then do it again tonight," Bearcat recommended.

Lieutenant Nolan shook his head. "No. No more water until tonight." He cupped his hands over his eyes and glanced up toward the blazing sun.

Stapler guessed what was going through the young LT's mind. He hoped he could manage until tonight also, but knew he and the LT would. They had to. Leaders set examples. He learned that as a private, and it was reinforced in Marine Corps Senior NCO School. Marine Corps Officer Candidate School taught the same course to the LT, only they used bigger words.

Stapler nodded, impressed. "You heard the LT."

Stapler stepped around the side of the truck, away from the front. Forty-three of them started this journey four days ago. Forty-three still lived. The white clouds of steam from the engine of the truck had stopped. Not all forty-three would survive the four days needed to reach the rendezvous point, a rendezvous where he expected Army Chinooks to pluck them out. This plucking was to occur in two days, and no way he saw them arriving there in two days. Would the Army wait? Would they come back if they didn't? Some sort of radio contact would

make him feel better. Until then, they had little choice but
to continue. *Which ones standing here won't make it?* He
wondered.

Two hours later, Cowboy and Raoul returned. They
had discovered multiple camel tracks behind them that
crisscrossed over the tire tracks of the vehicles. Nolan
wanted to know if the two could have been mistaken.
Could they have accidentally counted the tracks from the
camels the Marines rode? Cowboy was adamant that the
marks were not ones made by the eight camels of the convoy.

The water, food, and fuel containers hung from the
sides of the camels like so many bumpers along the side
of a ship. Most swung freely as the camels moved. Stapler
had Cowboy and Raoul assign guides to each of the
camels. With the exception of the lone camel that Stapler
allowed Cowboy to keep and to ride, the other seven
camels were fully loaded. They topped off their canteens
and handed the remaining few plastic gallon containers of
water to others among them to carry. Most had some sort
of backpack and, after discarding nonessential items, the
gallon container fit, freeing their hands to carry their
weapons.

The Marines had an M-16 each and two or three hand
grenades. The LT had a Navy forty-five along with his M-
16. The riggers had ten civilian M-16s scattered among
the more gun-knowledgeable of them. The two women
riggers, Stapler discovered, had a small handgun each,
carried in their pants pockets. Personally, he'd never carry
a gun in his pants pocket—too hard to extract and too
much danger of it going off.

Private Raoul Gonzales tied the leads of the camels together and then one to the bumper of the truck creating a
line of small shades where they could sit out of the direct
glare of the sun. The canvas on the back of the truck had
been pulled out and stretched to where it covered the entire bed. Kellogg was sitting up and seemed fully recovered, cursing her Marines comrades who kidded her that
she was just trying to snatch a few winks and using sun-

stroke as an excuse. Stapler noticed she was perspiring as he walked past her. She grinned and held her arms out, palms up. He waved her off and continued his inventory before returning to the lead humvee where Heinrich worked and Bearcat waited.

The radio hadn't done them much good so far—might as well chuck it—but every person in the convoy looked to that radio as their only link to survival. Even water became second when the idea of leaving the radio was voiced by one of the riggers. Without the radio, they only had their limited-range bricks, and for anyone to hear any calls on the bricks, they needed to be within line of sight, which meant fifteen miles to the horizon. The LT had asked Heinrich to check the radio connections before they left, just to make sure everything was okay.

"It's done," Heinrich said, pulling his body out of the front seat of the humvee and sitting down on the clay. He wiped his hands on the cloth he carried tied to a belt loop.

"Have you tried it?" Bearcat Jordan asked.

Heinrich shook his head. "No, dat radio wilt work. I bet *mien* life on it."

"That is just what you are doing," Stapler added.

Heinrich winked at the Marine. "Ah, Sergeant. You must smile more often. Et highlight your face very nicely." Heinrich pulled his long-sleeved T-shirt up and wiped his face with it, exposing a muscular chest and an enviable six-pack accenting his waist.

"Either of you want to try the radio?" Bearcat asked. "I tried every fifteen minutes with no answer. Maybe one of you two will be luckier."

"You go, LT. You're the communicator," Stapler said.

Heinrich pushed himself off the ground and moved out of the way of Lieutenant Nolan, who slid into the small space on the shotgun side of the humvee. He checked the switches, flipped a toggle, and then pressed the Transmit button on the microphone.

"Base Butler, this is Marine One. How copy, over?"

He released the button, and static filled the speaker.

Nolan reached over and turned the volume knob up slightly so those outside could hear the static also.

He tried again. "Base Butler, this is Marine One. How copy, over?"

Again, static answered the challenge. Nolan turned several knobs, changing the bandwidth slightly and increasing his transmission power to maximum. "I just realized that I didn't have the transmission power to maximum."

Stapler looked at Bearcat Jordan. "No, Sergeant. I had it at maximum when I was transmitting."

"I turned it down when I was checking it. I didn't want it going off accidentally *mit mien* ear against it," Heinrich said. He leaned forward, slightly bumping Stapler.

Stapler moved to the other side of Bearcat, so he could see what the LT was doing.

"Base Butler, this is Marine Convoy One. How copy, over?"

Static filled the air, then suddenly stopped for several seconds, and then came back on.

"Did you hear that?" shouted Nolan. He turned and looked at the three men. "Did you hear it?"

"Hear what?" Bearcat asked.

"That moment of silence when the static stopped. That means someone was trying to respond."

Stapler thought the LT was grasping for straws. He and Bearcat exchanged a knowing glance between them. Bearcat shrugged his shoulders.

"Oh, stop it, you two." Lieutenant Nolan pressed the Transmit button again. "Base Butler, this is Marine Convoy One. Do you read me? Over."

Static emanated from the speaker. Nolan turned the speaker knob all the way up. "Base Butler, this is Marine Convoy One. Do you read me? Over." He released the Transmit button.

"Marine Convoy One, this is Heavy Rider Two. I copy you three by five. Keep transmitting, and we shall close your unit."

"It's them. It's them!" cried Nolan, chill bumps rushing up his spine. "It's the goddamn Army."

Bearcat and Heinrich shouted the news to the others, who poured out of their shades, running to the humvee up front, crowding around the door, trying to hear.

"Heavy Rider Two, this is Marine Convoy One. Are we glad to hear you! We have forty-three souls. That includes eleven United States Marines. You should be able to land. We are in the middle of a huge plain."

"Marine Convoy One, sorry, but unable land. We are one Rivet Joint RC-135 aircraft escorted by four F-16 Falcon fighters. Sorry. Wish we could land and take you on. Our job was to locate you and provide that information back to headquarters. Rest assured Army is working rescue. Original rendezvous plans remain in effect."

The cheering and smiles faded as the group realized this was not the CH-47 Chinooks headed their way to bring them out.

"Heavy Rider Two, this is Marine Convoy One. Can you relay to Base Butler that we are four days out from rendezvous point and will not reach rescue point as originally scheduled."

"Roger, Marine Convoy One. Can do, and are doing as we talk. We have you located now. Anything we can do for you?"

"Wait one," Lieutenant Nolan transmitted.

He stuck his head out of the humvee. "Gunny, anything we need to ask them to do for us?"

Stapler thought a minute, tugged on his ear, and then replied, "Yes, sir, LT. Ask them if they can do a quick reconnaissance around our position to make sure we don't have company." He hooked his thumb toward the professor. "The professor thinks they are trailing us and letting the sun do their work for them before they rush us."

Nolan nodded, lifted the microphone to his lips, and pushed the Transmit button. "Heavy Rider Two, can you reconnoiter our immediate vicinity for threat presence?"

The noise originated from the west, gradual at first, growing in intensity, drowning out the radio. Every head turned toward the sound, hands going up to shade eyes from the sun.

"There they are!" cried Karim, pointing toward the line of small hills to the west.

The two F-16 fighters grew in size until they blasted overhead at about five hundred feet, wiggling their wings. The two fighters broke apart and climbed.

A cheer broke out from the crowd as they waved at the departing Air Force fighters. Tears flowed freely down the cheeks of most as they hugged each other. The Air Force presence could do little, but the mere sight sent a new wave of vitality surging through them.

"Heavy Rider Two, nice show," said Lieutenant Nolan, a slight emotional quiver in his voice. Nolan cleared his throat, trying to ease the tightness before he spoke.

"Marine Convoy One, I have the escorts that just passed over you doing a wide sweep around you. If there is anything within fifty miles, we'll know shortly. While we're waiting, would you care to pass a situation report to us for relay?"

"We can do that, Heavy Rider Two." For the next few minutes, Lieutenant Nolan passed a synopsis of their situation. The loss of the truck, the number of people in the convoy divided into civilians and Marines, and his assessment of their chances. He told them briefly about the compound and the trek to the oasis. The battle for the oasis was even briefer, with him giving the impression that their mere presence sent the Algerians running.

"Marine, Heavy Rider. You have visitors about thirty to thirty-five miles behind you. Appear to be around one hundred to one hundred twenty, all on camels. Looks like a Bedouin tribe, a caravan, the pilot says. No soldiers or anything that looks like military. I think if you wait there, they may arrive within the next few hours and can give you a hand getting out."

"Those are the ones who have been attacking us, Heavy Rider! They are not a harmless Bedouin tribe out for a nice trek in the desert!"

Several seconds passed before the Rivet Joint RC-135

responded. "Marine Convoy One, we just had our fighters pass directly overhead, and those natives just waved at them. No shooting. No indications they were anything but friendly. Maybe you're wrong?"

Lieutenant Nolan leaned out of the humvee. "Did you hear that? Those goddamn zoomies have let a bunch of mineteenth-century natives fool them!"

He leaned back in and pressed the Transmit button. "Heavy Rider, trust us on this. They are heading after us, not to help us but to kill us. Can you take them out?"

Nearly a minute passed before the officer on the Air Force four-engine reconnaissance aircraft responded. "No can do, Marine Convoy One. We have no indications they are hostile. Unless they fire on us or show us they are hostile, our hands are tied. Wait one."

That was the ball game, thought Stapler. If the Tauregs were thirty miles behind, then they would catch up to the convoy about the time they entered the wadi. Maybe once the convoy got in the wadi, they could hide from the natives. Then, again, they hadn't been successful yet in hiding from them. What was the difference going to be once they arrived inside the maze of wadis the professor says the Tauregs consider their native home? Those natives probably knew every nook and cranny ahead.

"Marine Convoy One, we have passed on your situation to Base Butler. They relay that they are doing what they can to reach you. They have your new position, the course you are moving, and your new estimate. They request you keep making calls every fifteen minutes, even if there is no joy on making contact. Good luck, Marines. This is Aerospace Expeditionary Force Six Eight departing the area. Wish we could stay longer, but we have to meet a series of tankers at predestined areas to stay aloft. We will be in contact range for about another hour if you need us. Command Joint Task Force African Force wants you to know that they are doing everything they can to get you out of there."

Lieutenant Nolan pressed the Transmit button. Shaking his head, he said, "Heavy Rider, you are making a mistake leaving that group of bandits—rebels—whatever you want to call them—alone. We are going to have to fight them."

"Wish we could, Marine Convoy One, but our hands are tied. I think you are overreacting, but if I were in your place, I'd do the same. As long as we are within range and can do, we will keep the fighters rotating back for a look-see on the caravan. If they do anything we can interpret as hostile, we will take them out. That's all I can promise, Marines. I wish we could do more, but our hands are tied. Good luck. Our prayers are with you. This is EAF Sixty-eight, out."

Lieutenant Nolan threw the microphone down on the driver's seat. "Did you hear that? Did you hear that? They have the enemy in sight and refuse to attack them." He pulled himself out of the humvee. Angrily, the LT spent several minutes discussing the parentage of the Air Force pilots who just flew away, leaving them to the mercy of the desert and the "goddamn ragheads" who followed.

After listening several minutes, Stapler tossed his cigarette down and ground it into the clay. He gripped his M-16 tighter and lifted it to his chest. "It's time, LT. We need to move. The wadi is ten more miles, and the sooner we start, the sooner we reach it." He turned and walked back through the crowd, giving directions to Marines and civilians alike. Sitting around crying about what the Air Force could and couldn't do wasn't going to help their position. This wasn't the first time the United States Marine Corps had to depend on itself in a hostile situation. Why should he expect this to be any different?

Thirty minutes later, the convoy started again. The lead humvee in front was jammed with eight people. Stapler and Lieutenant Nolan walked behind it. Strung out behind them came the seven camels led by Gonzales. Sterling, Abercombie, Garfield, and Lerfervre walked alongside the animals. Cowboy Joe-Boy rode several hundred yards to the right with Private Catsup Kellogg behind him. She had recovered a little from the mild sunstroke but was still weak. Stapler had ordered her to the humvee, but no other

Marines were riding in them, and she refused to be the only one, so he made her ride with Cowboy. The other humvee brought up the rear, it also jammed with eight people. The remaining twenty-five civilians and Marines walked between the two humvees. When they started, everyone bunched together, but within an hour, the spread turned into ones and groups of twos and threes as the convoy moved unsteadily forward toward the setting sun.

Stapler felt the fluid in his boot and knew without looking another blister had broken. Eventually, the sock would stick to the wet sore and rub against the back of the steel-toed desert combat boot. Then every step would send a sharp pain through him. Still, he marched forward, periodically walking to the side and staring back along their path of movement, looking for the Taureg rebels who pursued them.

The sun was touching the horizon when they reached the path leading down into the wadi. From the vantage point at the top of the plateau, the terrain gave way to a series of rough valleys with high red cliffs and sandy bottoms. The valleys were created eons ago from massive floodwaters raging through the area, washing away the softer soils and leaving the exposed granite and rough rock formations to be worn down further by the desert winds that followed. Stapler sighed. How in the hell would they ever find their way out of this maze?

Lieutenant Nolan faced Gunnery Sergeant Leslie Stapler, United States Marine Corps. "Not a nice sight, is it?"

Stapler tugged his ear. "No, sir, LT. Once we are in that maze, about all we can is follow the compass and hope the wadis are open-ended, so we don't find ourselves going into a bunch of dead-end valleys."

"Think we can go around it?"

Stapler shook his head. "It'd be nice if we could. Too far, and not enough water. I doubt we have the food to last, either."

"It's just a thought, Gunny. I don't think we can go around, either. It's over three hundred miles around these valleys, and it is only about thirty to forty through them.

We have little choice. We enter and pray we make it through, or we go around and die."

Stapler tugged his earlobe. "We'll live, LT. We might be thirsty buggers when we come out, but we'll survive."

TWO HOURS LATER, THE CONVOY REACHED the bottom of the wadi and set up camp. The sun had set an hour before, but the sheer walls surrounding the wadi caused the darkness to descend sooner than if they had remained topside. Stapler put out sentries and sent Cowboy back to the top of the wadi entrance to watch for their pursuers. Lieutenant Nolan had taken upon himself the responsibility for calling Base Butler every fifteen minutes. So far, no luck. They had not talked with anyone since the Air Force Aerospace Expeditionary Force flew—blew— through over eight hours ago. Amazing, Stapler thought, the Navy used carriers to keep its air power readily available and able to respond almost immediately. The Air Force had developed its own version of a carrier, one that used the air itself and revolved around tankers. They could send an expeditionary aerospace force anywhere in the world from the continental United States by using a continuous string of tankers.

Of course, Stapler knew if the USS *Stennis* with the Marine Corps Moonlighter F-18D squadron had been the one circling overhead instead of the Air Force, those Tauregs would be greeting Allah right now. The question he had—and one he was sure Top Sergeant MacGregory would ask—was how long could a fighter pilot go without taking a crap. Sure, they had "piddle packs"—small Ziploc bags with a compressed sponge in it a male pilot could unzip, stick his pecker in, and take a leak, but what if you had the trots? And what about women pilots? Those piddle packs wouldn't work for them. He tugged his earlobe. What was he doing? He had more important things on his mind than wondering about Air Force pilots' body functions. They could crap in their pants for all he cared. He had forty-three souls depending on him and a world of doubts that he would reach the rescue point with forty-three.

They tied the camels to the humvees parked in front of the makeshift camp. Several huge boulders in front of the solid wall of craggy, vertical cliffs bracketed the rear of the camp. Stapler warned the riggers, who were beginning to take up residence at the base of the boulders, to be careful of scorpions. When he turned back later, he found no one resting along the rim of boulders. Steve Kuvashin, the Russian cook, was opening cans of beans, dipping the cold mash out into small tin cups, and passing them around. Lieutenant Nolan, after completing another routine, unanswered call to Base Butler, stood beside the short, graying cook and poured out a small cup of water for everyone as they silently marched past to take the meager portions. Stapler would get his later. Right now, he needed to assess their defensive position and get the sentries in the right place. He looked up toward the top of the wadi, where they had entered, hoping to see Cowboy return. Starlight illuminated the area. The lack of a moon and the close proximity of the valley walls made the surroundings a weaving maze of grays and blacks.

The cliffs behind the boulders rose straight up for about two hundred feet before bending at an oblique angle to form a narrow plateau at the top. Stapler eyed the plateau for a long time before deciding it was too narrow for a person to stand on it. If anyone got up there, they could wreak havoc on them before they could blast them out. He had Gonzales, Garfield, Heights, and four of the riggers unload the camels and stack the supplies against one of the larger boulders. The fuel containers he put between the boulders where they were cached away from any firefight—*Lord, don't let there be one*—and the morning sun.

Movement from out front caught the edge of Stapler's peripheral vision. He swung his M-16 toward it and slipped the safety off. His finger traced the switch, telling him he was on single shot. Stapler crouched and moved swiftly to the bumper of the second humvee. He peered around the edge. It was Cowboy. Stapler stood. "Private Cowboy, over here." He waved the young Marine toward him.

"Hi, Gunny. Nothing out there that I saw. Just miles and miles of nothing, except our tracks. You can see them pretty clear in the moonlight."

"Cowboy, there ain't no moon."

"Sorry, Gunny. Starlight. You can see our tracks clear as a bell in the starlight."

Stapler moved forward to stand beside the mounted Marine. "Okay, Cowboy. That makes me feel better. Get off the beast and go have a bite to eat and your sip of water."

Cowboy nodded and tugged on the camel's lead, moving the animal toward the front of the first humvee, where the other camels bayed their discontent. He tugged twice, patted the camel on the neck. Stapler was impressed when the camel folded up like an accordion onto the ground, and Cowboy stepped off.

Stapler turned and nearly bumped into Lieutenant Nolan. "Damn, LT, you want to get yourself killed?" He flipped his safety back on. Should have done it when he recognized Cowboy.

"Sorry, Gunny. I thought you heard me walk up. No joy with Base Butler. You need to go get a bite to eat and your ration of water for the night. Can't go around mothering all of us, you know."

Stapler reached in his shirt pocket and brought out a pack of cigarettes he had requisitioned off the belongings of the dead Algerian regulars at the oasis.

"I thought you gave those up."

"LT, I did. I went two days without a cigarette."

"Two days is two-thirds done, Gunny. Why are you giving up?"

"Because I found some more, LT," Stapler snapped, waving the pack at the LT. "I wouldn't have gone two days if I hadn't run out." He struck a match and inhaled deeply.

Lieutenant Nolan removed his helmet and ran his

handkerchief through his sweaty black hair. Looking back the way they came, the LT pointed at the top of the wadi. "What do you think, Gunny?"

Stapler turned and stared at the entrance. He tugged his ear a couple of times, realized what he was doing, and let go. "I think, LT, that we need to leave early in the morning and try to keep ahead of that group of Ta. uregs the Air Force says are following us."

"Maybe the Air Force is right. Maybe those behind us are friendlies who can help us out."

Professor Walthers stepped out of the shadows. "I believe the Air Force are wrong in their assumption, Lieutenant. They are out there. We didn't need an airplane to tell us. They are out there right now, watching, waiting. They are letting the desert do their hard work . . . tearing our resistance down . . . so when they do make their move, they will lose fewer warriors. This is their country. They know it as well as each of us knows our hometown. And we are invaders, as far as they are concerned. Not only us, but every person who has ever entered this part of the Sahara." He took off his jungle helmet, looked down at it and then back up, shaking his head. "No, they will catch us whether we want them to or not. No matter how hard we try to hide from them. Why? Because they know where we are, they know where these wadis go, and they know where we have to come out. This is probably the widest of the small valleys that we will traverse in our journey. It is a good two hundred to three hundred yards wide. If you noticed when we entered"—he pointed to the west—"the path narrows toward the end of this wadi, and it appears to be only a few yards wide where we enter the next one."

Stapler tossed his cigarette down and ground it into the clay sand. "You know, professor, you have a real knack for ruining a man's first smoke of the day." He moved past the professor and reentered the main camp, looking for Cowboy. With the exception of the Marines and several of the oil riggers, the others had staked out a small part of the ground and had already begun to lie down. How in the hell was he going to move them another 130 miles to rescue? Realization slammed into Stapler like a blow to the head. They were not going to be rescued, because they would never survive the remaining miles. Although he realized it, he never missed a step as he moved around the campsite, where he found Cowboy sitting beside Catsup Kellogg.

Ten minutes later, the young Marine was back on his camel and galloping toward the top of the wadi, his M-16 strapped to his back and his hands out to the side, each with a lead grasped in them. The professor was right, Stapler knew, and he hated for someone to be right all the time, especially when they confirmed his worst fears.

THE GUNSHOT BROUGHT STAPLER'S EYES
wide open. He pushed himself off the wheel of the humvee where he had been napping. The M-16 safety came off—his touch told him it was on single shot—and he positioned the weapon around the edge of the humvee. Night hung heavy on the camp with sunburned bodies accented by the cool desert air.

"Quiet!" he shouted to the camp. Everyone was awake, talking, and asking questions, wanting to know what was going on. Christ! He didn't know, and he couldn't very well find out if they were going to be making all of that noise. The conversations stopped. Several of the oil riggers with their own civilian M-16 automatics moved to the humvees to join the Marines.

Stapler saw Lieutenant Nolan across the campsite, brushing himself off hurriedly and heading toward the rear of the humvee where Stapler had taken position. Stapler also noticed that the person with whom the LT was sharing his blanket was his favorite *Miss Sheila Anne Forester. Probably sharing her pain.*

"Someone's coming!" one of the riggers shouted, his voice high.

The hairs on Stapler's neck bristled as he heard the

noise of a camel approaching. "Be careful, it's probably Cowboy!"

The outline of the camel appeared a few seconds later without a rider. Stapler ran outside of the humvee barrier and grabbed the lead, quickly pulling the camel to the front of the humvee and tying it to another camel's lead. He patted the camel a couple of times on the hump, felt something wet, and looked at his hand.

Lieutenant Nolan came running up. "Where's Private . . . Cowboy?"

Stapler looked up toward the top of the wadi. "Up there probably, LT." Stapler turned his hand over, showing the lieutenant the blood.

"Gunny, let's get a couple of Marines and go see if we can find him."

Stapler held his hand out. The starlight showed a dark smudge running along his fingers and across his palm. "Blood, LT. This was on the back of the camel. If he is up there, he's probably not alive. If a bunch of us go running off into the dark . . ." His voice trailed off. "Better chance if I go alone."

"He could be alive."

"He could be, LT. I hear a gunshot, I see a camel with blood on its back and its rider missing, ergo, I think the rider has been shot. Worst case, he's dead." He pulled his pack of cigarettes out, started to light one, then realized it would give a sniper a target, so he shoved the unlit cigarette back into the wrinkled pack.

"Let's don't forget who's the officer here, Gunny," Lieutenant Nolan replied testily.

Stapler sighed. "Yes, sir, you are the officer. Therefore, you need to stay here and lead the men." He pointed toward the top of the wadi. "Cowboy is one of mine, and I've done this sort of thing before as a buck sergeant when I was with a recon team. I'll go find him."

"Gunny, we can't afford to lose you. Let's send Corporal Heights and Garfield."

"LT, they don't have the experience in night patrol. I will go. And I do not intend to take chances. If he is out there, I will find him." Stapler walked around the back of the humvee, heading up the wide path they had traveled earlier.

He kept close to the wall of the wadi, blending in with the shadows. He checked his safety on the M-16, making sure it was on. He listened intently for any sounds out of place as he moved quickly and quietly from one shadow to the next, inching his way up the incline leading to the top. The LT and the others might not believe it; the professor would. The pursuers were here. The gunshot he heard was not an M-16, and an M-16 was the only weapon Cowboy had—that and maybe a couple of grenades. There had been neither return fire nor grenades, which told 'Sherlock' Stapler that Cowboy was either dead, wounded, or gone to ground. Either way, he would know soon.

An hour passed with Stapler continuing to dart in and out of the gray and black shadows of the wadi, stopping every few steps to listen. A faint breeze blew toward him, carrying any slight noise he might make away from the direction he was approaching. He heard voices before he saw them as he neared the top. He ducked behind nearby rocks, continuing a careful advance toward the voices. Four voices he heard. His foot touched a loose bunch of rocks, sending several tumbling down the side of the wadi. He stopped, waiting for the voices to change in tempo or go silent. When nothing happened, Stapler decided their nonstop conversation drowned out the minor noise he made.

Carefully, Stapler stepped one foot at a time on the small area made up of loose pebbles and stones, trying to keep from dislodging any more. A slight mound of sand rose in front of him. The voices were behind it. He dropped to the ground and crawled forward on all fours to where he could put his head against the bottom of a nearby boulder, blending in with the dark landscape. Christ! He hoped there were no scorpions here.

Four Taureg natives squatted in front of him, less than ten feet away. Across from them, propped up against a wall of rocks, Cowboy Joe-Boy lay, his head resting on his shoulder and his left hand pressed against his stomach. The shirt and the belt line of the Marine's trousers were soaked in blood. He saw a slight movement of Cowboy's hand as if he was trying to stop the bleeding. If Stapler waited too long to do something, the young Marine would die. There was little they could do back in camp, but if he died, he'd die with his buddies and among friendlies. All they brought with them from the compound was a couple of first aid kits, but it was more than Cowboy had now.

No way he could take them silently. He reached down and with his left hand flipped the safety off. Fire was pushed to the burst position. He would have to act quickly and accurately. All it would take would be one lucky shot for these Bedouins to have two wounded Marines—or two dead ones. He had no way of knowing whether these four were by themselves. Others could be nearby. Stapler drew his head back and glanced around, searching for any signs of others. He would shoot, rush in, strap his M-16 across his chest, throw Cowboy across his back and see how far he got before someone creamed him.

Dawn was not that far away. Stapler wanted to be back at the campsite when the sun broke. He wanted to be back inside the safety of the perimeter.

He pulled the M-16 up beside him and eased the barrel over the crest of the small dune. Then, with a Marine Corps shout that brought the four natives to their feet, he pulled the trigger, killing two of them and wounding the other two. One of the wounded tried to bring his ancient rifle around to bear on Stapler. Stapler let go another burst from the M-16, killing the last two. He ran to the other side of the campsite and peered over the rise there. He discovered that he was at the top of the wadi.

Across the plain about three to four miles away, a cloud of dust rose into the starlit night as camels galloped toward him. He slid back into the depression, slid the strap of the M-16 over his head, and bent down beside Cowboy.

"Cowboy, you hear me?"

The eyes of the wounded Marine came slowly open.

"Gunnery Sergeant Stapler, I would like to report the presence of an enemy patrol."

"I know, Cowboy. Listen to me, son. I am going to have to carry you down to where the others are. It is going to hurt like hell. You understand?"

Cowboy reached up with his right hand and touched Stapler's shoulder. "I knew you'd come for me, Gunny. We Marines don't leave other Marines, do we?"

"No, we don't, Cowboy," Stapler replied.

The hand fell limply away.

"Hold on," Stapler said, leaning down, grabbing the wounded Marine under the right armpit and left buttocks. The lean Gunnery Sergeant hefted the 180-pound wounded man across his back. Cowboy's moans were cut short as the Texan passed out.

"Sorry, Marine," Stapler said. He gripped the man's right arm and leg, holding his body across the broad portion of Stapler's back.

No way he could go back the way he came. He would have to move into the center of the trail leading back to the campsite and hope that he made the mile before those crazed fellows on camels reached him.

His foot nearly slid from under him as he duckwalked up the bank leading out of the small depression, leaving four bodies behind. Ten yards later, Stapler reached the trail and began a short-stepped jog down it, knowing each step jostled the wounded Cowboy. He could see the outline of the humvees in the distance. He tried a couple of times to glance behind him, but Cowboy's body blocked his vision. Imagined sounds of galloping camels running him down gave encouraging impetus to his run. His breath came in short, quick gasps as he kept moving, knowing to stop was to invite death from the hordes of sand-sucking scum bent on killing him. Pain in his legs from the weight threatened with tightened muscles. He stopped for a second and straightened up, leaning first to one side and then the other to give each leg a short rest. He turned and searched behind him, seeing nothing. But that didn't mean they weren't there.

When the spasms in his legs and the small of his back eased, he started again down the path. He was no longer running but forcing each foot to take one step at a time. Behind him, angry natives on ugly camels hurried to kill him, but he had yet to hear them, and Cowboy blocked his vision.

The weight of his burden grew with each step. Stapler's eyes wavered on his feet, watching every step as much as his tired mind allowed. Energy to raise his head to see how far he had to go became too much. Somewhere along the trek, he had begun to move off the center of the path. He was walking from one side to the other, weaving a pattern between the funneled sides of the wadi entrance.

He heard voices and said a quick Hail Mary, believing the sounds to come from the galloping hordes of desert nomads bearing down on him, expecting to hear the swish of the blade just before it lopped off his head. He tightened his grip on Cowboy, ready to ease the unconscious Marine to the ground so he could use his M-16. His senses cleared slightly just as he prepared to let go of Cowboy's leg when he recognized the sound of someone calling him.

"Gunny!"

It was Lieutenant Nolan. Fine Lieutenant Nolan, who sent him out to find the missing Marine . . . well, didn't really send him out, but he went, anyway.

Stapler felt hands lifting the burden from his back.

"Gunny, you all right?"

Stapler leaned forward and put his hands on his knees. A cup of water was shoved into his face. He took a swallow of the delicious liquid and then the second and last mouthful he swished around inside, delighting in the plastic flavor of the water. A swimming pool—that was what he was going to have installed when he returned home. Anything that held huge quantities of water, he was going to have.

Lieutenant Nolan reached down and took Stapler's arm. "Come on, Gunny, we have to get back inside the campsite."

Stapler straightened, swayed slightly, and pushed himself away from the LT. "The professor's right. They're coming, LT. I saw them," he said, his breath still coming in quick, rapid gasps.

Lieutenant Nolan pointed to the top of the entrance to the wadi. Faint starlight shadows highlighted the camels that were standing motionless, side by side, with their silent riders in black staring down toward the bottom of the wadi at the Americans.

"You're right, Gunny. They are already here."

CHAPTER 9

⚓

DICK HOLMAN STOOD BESIDE HIS FORMER
XO, now the acting skipper of the USS *Stennis*, as the aircraft carrier prepared to launch the flight of S-3s. *Magnificent* was the word for watching a supercarrier maneuver. The bow turned into the wind. The increasing wind caused him to scrunch his eyes as the ship slowly changed directions. He shoved the cigar to the right side of his mouth so the ashes wouldn't blow into his face. The carrier steadied up on a northwesterly course when the wind was bow on. Wind speed was a combination of natural wind computed against the relative wind created by ship speed and course. The wind whipped across the deck, from bow to stern, to aid launching the high-performance aircraft on board a supercarrier. Only the United States was able to do this.

The French had started to build a similar supercarrier in the 1990s and then cried politics when they were unable to complete their first supercarrier. Dick always thought it was lack of competence on the part of their

Navy. The United States Navy had offered their advice and assistance during the construction phase only to be politely but firmly told it was not required.

He glanced up at the battle flag flying above the fore-castle of the USS *Stennis*, and a swift wave of patriotic pride flowed through his body. It was something hard to describe to someone who had never experienced the same thrill. Pride turned emotional at times. *What a great country we are,* he thought, *for all of its politics and political factions.* He recalled a NATO meeting he attended years ago when a French counterpart joked about how ineffective our government was compared with the well-oiled parliaments of Europe. It was the way our founding fathers—the dead saints of the Constitution—made it.

Our founding fathers were rebels who distrusted governments. Sure, our government was ineffective, but by being so, it scattered the power and responsibilities across three major institutions with distinct powers. The real stakeholders in America's way of governance were the people. They really wielded the biggest power. They determined control of their government. No other government on earth could claim the same rights.

The wind picked up across his face as the carrier steadied on course. The two S-3s, powered up and ready to go, waited on the catapults for the launch officer to give the go-ahead. Dick watched the routine as the sailor monitoring the metal arm protruding from the nose gear properly seated into the catapult. Satisfied, the sailor gave the catapult officer a thumbs-up and ran to the edge of the deck to disappear below the same protective edge.

"Bridge, Deck, ready to launch, sir."

Dick reached for the phone, but the new skipper grabbed it first, ginning at him. "Permission granted."

"Up yours," Dick mouthed as he returned the grin.

"You know, sir, you bubbas on the Sixth Fleet staff need to leave the ship-driving to us professionals."

"Tucson, I'd whip your ass, if it wasn't for the reason it'd take too long," Holman said, a wide grin stretching his face.

The noise of the jet engines increased as the pilots of the antisubmarine aircraft pushed the power to maximum. *Power* was the key word on everything they did, whether it was steaming unmolested through the seas or mounting a major military operation like that of the past four weeks.

The catapult launchers used to be senior petty officers, but the last decade had seen them replaced by junior officers. Both he and the XO leaned over the rampart of the bridge wing, waiting for the magic moment when the aircraft would be jerked off the deck by steam catapults, capable of over 90,000 pounds of thrust, if needed.

Behind the aircraft, the raised blast shields deflected the power of the jet turbines up at a sixty-degree angle into the air and away from the multitude of sailors and aircraft poised behind the two catapults.

Experience told the pilots that, when the catapult officer nodded, it meant the crew chief of the launch team had given his thumbs-up to the catapult officer. The catapult officer looked at the pilot nearest her and saluted. The pilot returned the salute. Two seconds later, the catapult officer hit the red button releasing the mighty mechanisms belowdecks. The S-3 shot forward, and in the space of less than 100 feet went from 0 to 140 miles per hour.

The gravity force from the launch shoved the pilot and weapons officer's heads against their headrests as the plane traveled along the deck, just as quickly releasing the pressure as the S-3 Viking left the end. The plane dropped slightly as it left the carrier. The jets caught, bringing the nose up. The Viking was airborne, heading out to sea. The second S-3 followed ten seconds later.

Dick and Tucson Conroy watched the launch silently. The shrill of the hydraulic lifts lowering the deflector shields joined the smell of burning jet fuel sweeping across the forward bridge wing. The next launch consisted of four F/A-18 Hornets headed out to join the four already on station off the coast of Oran Naval Base.

"Always impressive when they launch," Dick said, trying to blow a ring of smoke into the wind.

"I know what you mean," Tucson Conroy replied.

"Being a Surface Warfare officer, I always watch how the other ships manage to make their way to the farther ends of their assigned boxes when we begin to maneuver."

"Well, you're the one who told me, 'When a carrier maneuvers, all other ships avoid.'"

Tucson grinned. "I heard that Admiral Cameron intends to keep you on his staff, even after this is over," he lied.

"Who told you that?" Dick asked, his voice betraying concern.

Tucson laughed. "Don't worry, Skipper. Just kidding. However, if you decide to stay, I won't argue too much. I have discovered that being commanding officer of the USS *Stennis* is a hell of a lot more fun than being executive officer. Of course, I am considering banning smoking again."

Dick grinned at the taller, muscular XO. "And how well do you tread water, XO?"

"Now, Skipper, if you ever hit me and I find out—"

"Where's the master chief when I need him?" Dick joked.

"So, what now, Captain? Think that submarine is coming out for another run at us?" Tucson asked, his voice serious.

Dick shook his head. "Don't know. Based on the course he is steering, he is headed directly for the two amphibious task forces we have west of us. I dispatched the USS *Rampage* toward them an hour ago with orders to take charge of the surface ASW effort. Clive Bowen ordered the two amphibious task forces to close our position. That should increase the distance for the submarine to travel another hundred miles."

"What does our new general think of all of this?"

"He is still working out. It's been forty-five minutes since Ranger Twenty-nine spotted the *Al Nasser*. By the time he completes his Army remedial training, we should have the boat sunk."

The officer of the deck stuck his head out onto the

bridge wing. "Captain Holman, Admiral Devlin asks that you join him in Flight Operations."

"Tucson, you're doing a good job. Just don't move your bags into my at-sea cabin yet. There is still a chance I may be fired . . . if I'm lucky."

"See you later, Skipper," Tucson Conroy said as Dick departed.

Dick was heading out the hatch leading from the bridge when the voice of the OOD reached him. "Skipper, do you want to maintain this course after we launch the ready CAP?"

Dick stopped to answer before he realized the OOD was speaking to Tucson Conroy. A little pit of disappointment hit his stomach as he continued through the hatch. Tucson was right; there was nothing quite as satisfying as being the commanding officer of a United States Navy warship, especially a carrier and especially when you're doing what it was designed to do: project power. God! He wanted his ship back.

Three decks, two ladders, and four minutes later, Dick Holman entered the Flight Operations space to discover Admiral Cameron and Admiral Pete Devlin in conference with Commander Steve Cloth.

"Admiral, Captain Dick Holman reporting as ordered, sir."

"Dick, glad you're here. Watched the launch on the TV. How long until they arrive on station?"

Steve Cloth answered, "About forty-five minutes, sir. After the carrier launches the ready combat air patrol, we have two tankers launching. The other two S-3 tankers, already airborne, have refueled the four Hornets on station and are low. We'll land them next cycle to refuel and should be able to launch them the following cycle."

"The P-3C is approaching the submarine datum area now."

"What is the status of Ranger Two Niner?"

"It took some shrapnel damage when they overflew Oran Naval Base. The pilot, Commander Stillwell, refuses to consider ditching the aircraft. I concur with his assessment. Number-one engine is destroyed. They may have wing structural damage, but so far, the aircraft is maneuverable, and he is attempting to make it to Sigonella. He has a hole in the back part of the fuselage. As you know, one dead crew member—the communications evaluator—and three with minor wounds.

The hatch burst open, and General Leutze Lewis, commander, Task Force African Force, entered, wearing his PT gear of shorts and a sweat-soaked gray workout shirt with the word *Army* plastered to his chest. *Hairy devil,* thought Dick Holman as the General advanced to where they stood.

"Bring me up to date," he ordered, speaking directly to Admiral Cameron.

Commander Steve Cloth eased away from the group and returned to the Air Operations consoles.

Five minutes later, the general nodded his head. "What are your intentions, Admiral?"

"Sir, the Algerians fired a shoulder-launched SAM and hit one of our aircraft. We have one crew member dead and three wounded. They have also fired multiple antiair artillery batteries against the same aircraft as it attempted to leave the area. We had indications of Algerian fighter aircraft reacting to the presence of our forces. However, they stopped shy of the coast about twenty miles inland and are conducting a racetrack pattern defensive fighter patrol. I have kept our fighters over water for the time being. We have a P-3C with sonobuoys entering the area where the submarine is suspected to be, and a minute ago we launched two ASW-capable S-3s with two Mark-50 torpedoes each. We should be able to sink the submarine, once we narrow down her location."

"Why do you want to sink her?" General Lewis asked, wiping the sweat from his face with the tail of a towel draped across his shoulders.

"Sir?" the voices of Admiral Cameron and Rear Admiral Pete Devlin responded in tandem.

"The submarine hasn't fired on your aircraft, from

what you tell me. It was the tugboat, which has already returned to port. Right?"

"Yes, sir, but the submarine is on a course toward our
forces," Admiral Cameron stressed.

"Yeah, yeah, you told me. But we don't know for sure
it is en route to attack us, do we?"

Dick Holman did not like how this conversation was
going. Bad enough when Surface Warfare officers tried to
learn air combat maneuvers, but an Army officer trying to
learn antisubmarine warfare?

Admiral Cameron shook his head. "No, sir, but we
suspect this submarine was the one that attacked the USS
Nassau Amphibious Task Force four weeks ago."

"I was told your ASW forces sank that submarine."

General Lewis took the towel from his shoulders and
wiped his hands on it. Then he wiped the sweat from his
face again before draping the wet towel across his neck,
holding the ends with each hand. "What I am trying to do,
Admiral, is reduce the conflict. My orders are to disengage and to do that we need to pull back from any new en-
counters and focus on getting your Marines out of Algiers.
Disengagement: That is the key objective. Disengage
throughout the North African theater."

"Sir, the submarine is a threat to our forces. At twelve
knots, it will be within range of the fleet within twenty-
four hours."

"What if the submarine changes its course and doesn't
come our way, but we go on and sink it? Don't you think
that by doing so, we are expanding the engagement envelope?"

Dick Holman eased back and moved over to where
Steve Cloth stood monitoring the air traffic control consoles, away from the flag officers discussing—arguing—
whether to sink an enemy submarine or not. He wanted
the freedom to act by not being privy to what he expected
the new Commander, Joint Task Force, to order. What was
the world coming to?

"Steve, where is the P-3C?"

The Air Operations officer tapped the ATC on the

shoulder and raised his eyebrows, knowing the petty officer had heard Captain Holman's question.

The petty officer slipped his headphones off his ears
and in a low voice replied, "It's five miles off the coast in
a search pattern. It has laid a line of sonobuoys across the
last-known course at the ten mile mark, but no joy as yet."

Dick leaned down. "Son, if they detect it, you are to tell
either me or Commander Cloth before passing on the
news. Okay?"

The petty officer grinned. "Of course, sir." He slid his
headset back on just as a transmission arrived.

Dick Holman moved slightly to the left, blocking the
view of the consoles from the flag officers behind him.

"Ranger Two Niner, this is Sixty-seven. You are
cleared direct into Sigonella approach. You are cleared to
change to channel two zero for landing instructions."

"Before they leave our control, ask them for a status report."

"Yes, sir, Captain. Ranger Two Niner, Sixty-seven
himself would like a status report of your situation."

Several seconds passed before the young petty officer
rogered the transmission and turned to Dick Holman.

"Sir, they have three wounded on board from the AAA
hits they took and one casualty. Engine number one is destroyed, but wing integrity continues to hold. They do not
know status of undercarriage damage, so they intend to
overfly the tower at Sigonella with wheels lowered for
them to do a visual on the aircraft before they attempt to
land. He is unable to pump fuel from the left wing tank
and estimates he will be flying on fumes by the time he arrives at Sigonella."

"Who's accompanying him?" Dick asked Steve.

"I detached one of the empty tankers to go with him,
but the tanker won't catch up for another few minutes,"
Steve Cloth answered.

"Have the S-3 do a flyby beneath the EP-3E and give a
damage assessment."

The Petty Officer pushed his headset tight against his
ears.

"Captain," the petty officer interrupted, touching Dick Holman on the sleeve. "The P3 Charlie has sonobuoy contact and has broken off search. He is en route to the contact area."

"I'll tell the admirals," Steve Cloth said, turning toward the flag officers.

The three flag officers seemed very animated with inaudible whispers being accompanied by emphatic body language.

Dick grabbed Steve's arm. "No, Commander. Let them be while they decide certain issues. Let's not disturb them until we have contact. We have our orders."

"We do?"

"Steve, I am Sixty-seven, right?"

"Yes, sir, but—"

"No, buts. I'll tell you when to tell them."

Dick leaned over the ATC console. "Do we have them on radar?"

"No, sir. They are too far out. The E-2C does," the ATC operator replied, referring to the two-engine prop radar aircraft that circled incessantly above the carrier battle group, continuously mapping the air picture for hundreds of miles around.

"Can we pipe the E-2C's radar picture to this console?"

"Yes, sir, but I will have to shift my flights to the backup consoles."

"Go ahead and do it."

"It will take a few minutes, Captain," the petty officer offered reluctantly. "Control may be clouded as the new ATC and I coordinate the shift, Captain."

Shifting control of a flight of aircraft from the ATC controlling them to a new ATC meant minutes of gaining familiarity by the new controller. Minutes that could be the difference between giving the right commands and the wrong ones.

Dick reached up and pinched his nose. Both the ATC and Steve Cloth waited for him to confirm his orders. He reached out and touched the ATC on the shoulder. "You know something, son, you're right. Leave it the way it is. Who are you controlling?"

"Sir, Ranger Two Nine has shifted to Sigonella control on channel twenty. Four F/A-18 Hornets, Two S-3 Vikings, and one P-3C Orion remain under my control."

"I don't care!" shouted the general behind them. "We are not going to expand this crisis!" He slammed his hand down on the plotting table, unaware tops of plotting tables are made of Plexiglas.

Both Dick Holman and Steve Cloth grimaced as they waited for the sound of Plexiglas cracking and were surprised when the table remained lighted and operable. Pete Devlin leaned forward, put his hand on the table, and said something to the general, who nodded in acknowledgment. The towel, gripped tightly in the general's right hand, bounced around as he made his points. Dick noted the general's executive aide, Colonel Brad Storey, seemed to shift from one side of the general to the other, the smile never leaving his bright face. *Here, go fetch, Fido.*

The two men turned back to the ATC and waited for the word that the Algerian submarine had been located. Dick's eyes locked with Admiral Cameron's for a moment. The admiral nodded as if the two understood what he wanted. Dick raised his hand slowly, and with a salute that could have passed for wiping his forehead, acknowledged the unspoken command of the admiral. What he was about to do might cost him his job, but both of them knew what one submarine could do if it was allowed loose in the middle of a bunch of surface ships. It was always easier to get forgiveness than permission.

"SIGONELLA CONTROL, THIS IS RANGER TWO niner. We are two hundred miles out and request immediate landing clearance. I am declaring an in-flight emergency."

"Roger, Two Niner. We have already been forewarned of your approach. What is your situation?"

"We have three with minor wounds on board and . . .

one casualty. Request medical service meet us on touch-down."

"Two Niner," the Italian operator at Sigonella inter-rupted, "ambulances with medical service are already standing by. We have fire engines at the approach end of the runway. They will chase you down the runway as you land. What is the fuel status and your undercarriage?"

"Sigonella, we are low on fuel. Fuel crossover valve is inop, limiting remaining fuel to the number-five bladder. I would like to make a pass over your position before landing for a wheels-down check. Lights show no prob-lem at this time with the undercarriage. Number-one en-gine is destroyed, and wing integrity seems okay at the moment. We are at two thousand feet altitude. I am re-stricted to less than ten thousand feet because of battle damage to the right rear side of the fuselage. I have a gap-ing hole about three feet across."

"Roger," the Sigonella operator said. Behind the Italian supervisor monitoring the conversation, an American Navy captain walked through the door, followed by sev-eral other American Navy officers. The operator recog-nized the thin, mustached man as the new commanding officer of the American Sigonella Naval Base. He nodded but did not interrupt the operator in his duties.

"Ranger Two Niner, you are cleared for a direct ap-proach. I have you on radar. Come to course zero six two and maintain altitude two zero. All aircraft have been vec-tored away." He paused and then added, "Good luck."

Two clicks on the microphone acknowledged his trans-mission.

"Jasbo, go ahead and have everyone strap in with the exception of the fire watches and those administering first aid. Everyone is to keep their parachutes on. Chief Henckels?"

"Yes, sir. Temperature on number two still in the red. Numbers three and four running within specs. We have fuel for two more hours without regaining fuel transfer ca-pability, Commander." Chief Henckels reached up, pulled out a group of circuit breakers, and reset them. "Fuel transfer pump remains inop."

"Ranger Two Nine, Shell Leader, coming up, on your starboard side, shipmate. Hey, you got some nice scars on that old banger you're flying."

Jasbo and Chief Henckels looked out of the starboard window of the cockpit. The pilot of the S-3 tanker, to their right and slightly behind them, waved.

"Commander, we got company. Looks as if our guide has arrived."

"The S-3?"

"Yes, sir. He is right side, aft position."

Stillwell pushed the Transmit button of his microphone. "Shell Leader, Ranger Two Niner. Welcome aboard. We need an undercarriage check and would appreciate it if you could do a three sixty around the entire aircraft."

"Can do, Ranger Two Niner. We will go beneath—right to left—stop on your left side and then go over you. I got a good look at your tail assembly, and with the exception of some minor shrapnel holes—small, about fist size—I would say you're okay there. Those holes are along the sides and not near the flaps."

"Roger, Shell Leader. I'll be looking for you on the port side."

"Jasbo, tell the crew about Shell Leader. Every little bit of encouragement helps," Commander Stillwell said. The crew would know the S-3 could offer little assistance if they had to ditch the aircraft or bail out, but the presence of another aircraft provided an intrinsic comfort factor while they fought the buffeting aircraft to reach safety.

"Hey, Ranger Two Niner. It's your buddy here on the port side. Man oh man, you know those antennas you guys like to keep hidden under that canoe running along the center of your aircraft? Well, they ain't hidden anymore; but you don't have to worry, because those antennas ain't there, either. Looks to us as if you took a hit—by what, we don't know—but our consolidated professional opinion is that the canoe absorbed the hit and probably saved your butts."

"Did you hear that?" Jasbo asked Chief Henckels.

"Yeah, ma'am," he replied, turning sideways in his chair, ripping open a heavy plastic tarp that covered a bank of hidden circuit breakers. "There are no red lights on, Lieutenant. I don't have a thing showing there is anything wrong with the canoe or its antennas." He bowed his head under his raised arm and looked back at her. "Not a thing."

"Thanks, Shell Leader. Our warning lights failed to show the damage. How do our wheel wells look?"

"Your left wheel well has two shrapnel holes in it that we can see. I see no damage around the nose wheel, and the starboard wing wheel well we surveyed when we approached, and it looked all right."

"Thanks."

"If you want to try to lower them, we can take position aft and see if they lock."

"I am running low on fuel. We have less than two hours of fuel available, and lowering the wheels may affect the flight characteristics of the aircraft. As you can see, we have sustained quite a lot of damage. Several of the avionics packages have already shifted to backup and alternate modes. I am in contact with Sigonella control on channel twenty, and our intentions are to lower the wheels when we reach long final, do a flyby of the tower so they can verify wheels down and locked. Then, we'll do a short pattern and land where beer and women—"

"Don't forget the dancing men," Jasbo added.

"—will be waiting with open arms."

The S-3 moved up alongside the cockpit of the EP-3. The navigator riding in the right-hand seat of the two-jet-engined tanker waved at Commander Stillwell, who threw his hand up in response.

"Ranger Two Niner, we will be with you all the way. According to our calculations, Sigonella is about two hours out with this headwind. You are going to be low on fuel before you hit the coastline. Do you have an alternate airfield in mind, if you have to divert? One closer?"

"Wait one, Shell Leader."

"Jasbo, ask the navigator for the name of that other airfield. The one she said was about five miles closer."

"Commander, she said that airfield was abandoned. It's an old Italian air base that was closed in the early 1990s."

"If it has a runway, we may have no choice, Jasbo. Ask her for the name, and tell the navigator to be prepared to divert there, if need be."

Two minutes later, she had the name of the old, abandoned airfield and gave it to Commander Stillwell, who passed it on to both the chase plane and Sigonella Airfield.

At Sigonella, the new American captain turned to two members of his staff and ordered them to contact the Cantania Airport Fire Department and ask them to send a couple of fire trucks to the abandoned airfield. He then picked up the telephone, contacted the huge hospital complex on Naval Base Two, and asked the commanding officer of it to divert a standby medical team to the old Castelliano Air Base. By the time Ranger Two Nine passed the coastline of Sicily, Sigonella, Cantania, the old, abandoned strip at Castelliano would have fire engines and medical personnel standing by. The options for the EP-3 crew had just expanded.

THE NAVIGATOR ESTIMATED ANOTHER THIRTY minutes before they could safely turn to a northwesterly course, away from the direction of the American and the combined French and British fleets. Just mentioning the presence of the formidable naval forces the *Al Nasser* would encounter if he held the current course made Ibn Al Jamal lean forward, as if urging the submarine to reach deeper water.

The first ping caused him and everyone in the control room to jump. His head snapped right, looking at the sonar operator, who jerked his headset off. It took four long steps for him to cross the control room, shouting for the operator to put the headset back on.

The pings continued. The water was too shallow for a destroyer or another submarine, either of which sonar would have picked up long before they had detected him. No, the source was either a hovering helicopter with a dipping sonar or an active sonobuoy. The helicopter would have to operate from a nearby platform, and sonar had reflected no surface ships within seventy-five nautical miles. That did not mean that it couldn't be a helicopter, just that the flight radius of the helicopter would be stretching its time on station. In the few seconds it took for the sonar operator to put his headset back on and adjust the pads over his ears, Ibn Al Jamal had decided the pings on the skin of the submarine were from an active sonobuoy. The operator soon confirmed his thoughts.

An active sonobuoy meant American antisubmarine warfare aircraft in the area. The aircraft would have to align itself for an attack run. He had—if Allah was with him—a minute before an attack could be launched.

"How much water beneath the hull?" he asked the officer of the deck.

"Another fifty, maybe sixty feet."

"Hit the fathometer and get an accurate reading!"

The OOD hit the button. A faint ping radiated from the *Al Nasser*, bouncing off the smooth bottom of the shallow coastal shelf before returning to the submarine. The OOD stared at the fathometer until the gauge read the depth. "Sixty-seven feet, My Captain."

"Take her down to one hundred feet," Ibn Al Jamal ordered, doubling the current depth of fifty feet.

The shout of the sonar operator, detecting an entry splash, announced the appearance of the American Mark-50 torpedo joining them in their limited sea. He waved his hand slowly in a downward motion, calming the sonar operator, who visibly took two deep breaths before turning back to his console. The operator's voice began a series of steady reports feeding information to the skipper as the torpedo propeller churned the water. The Mark-50, with

its 100 kilos of high explosives, began a circular search
pattern as it looked for an underwater target to attack. The
sonar operator estimated the torpedo to be one kilometer
to the west closing to a half kilometer before it began to
circle back to the west. Every time the torpedo turned
east, the sweat factor in the small control room rose as
everyone waited—prayed—for it to continue its circle.
Ibn Al Jamal's gut reaction was to speed up to maximum
flank in an attempt to reach the open sea before the torpedo locked on them. However, he knew better. At eight
knots, the noise of the *Al Nasser* was low and, so far, the
torpedo had failed to detect them.

Splashes ahead of the *Al Nasser* announced the arrival
of two more American Mark-50 torpedoes to the party beneath the sea. They had landed off the coastal shelf about
two to three kilometers ahead of them. One immediately
commenced a deep-sea search, soon disappearing beneath
the shelf, its telltale noise signature shielded from the passive sonar of the *Al Nasser*. The second started a shallow-
water circular search, each circuit expanding its area until
the torpedo crossed the shelf, making its circuit half over
the coastal shelf and half over the deep water. This torpedo was directly ahead. Ibn Al Jamal had little choice. If
he continued on this course, the torpedo ahead of him
would detect them in a matter of seconds. To his west was
the initial torpedo continuing an expanding racetrack
search for the submarine. East was the only open area.
The very direction he wanted to avoid. The very direction
that carried him closer to the Western forces operating off
the coast of his country and farther from the sanctuary of
Malaga, Spain.

He eased the *Al Nasser* into a slow, easterly turn,
avoiding cavitating the water behind him. Cavitation
churned the water and attracted torpedoes like blood attracted sharks.

The *Al Nasser* was twenty degrees farther east on its
course when the sonar operator—in a breaking voice—
tried calmly to announce that the torpedo ahead of them
had broken off its search. It was locked on the *Al Nasser*

and headed their way. The pings of the torpedo replaced the pings of the active sonobuoy that had disappeared moments before the first torpedo entered the water.

Ibn Al Jamal shouted, ordering the *Al Nasser* into a hard left turn and increasing the speed to fourteen knots, cavitating the water behind the old surplus Soviet submarine. The torpedo changed direction slightly, drawn to the higher decibels of the churning water and away from the submarine propellers. He regretted the shout. If the captain loses his cool, then the crew soon follows. He kept the submarine in a hard left turn until the bow approached slightly off center to the approaching torpedo. He steadied the submarine on a bow approach. Decoys rocketed from the rear of the *Al Nasser*. The noisemakers hit the water, clanging away, distracting the passive sonar of the torpedo. Ibn Al Jamal simultaneously ordered "All stop," stopping the rotation of the propellers and shaft. The submarine continued moving forward on the remaining momentum as the giant propellers slowed.

The sonar operator turned and reported ten seconds to impact. He raised the headset away from his head but held it near his ears. Everyone watched the clock . . . eight, seven, six . . . and then the torpedo was past. The sonar operator let the earpieces slap back onto his ears. The torpedo was traveling down the port side of the submarine, only a few feet away. Those in the control room heard the spinning propellers through the hull of the submarine as the Mark-50 traveled the length of *Al Nasser*. They held their breaths for the next few seconds, praying silently that the torpedo would fail to detect the faint rotation of the propellers as it passed. The emotional response of the torpedo operator praising Allah, his mother, his father, and the captain told everyone the torpedo danger was past and locked on the decoys. Ibn Al Jamal brought the speed back up to eight knots.

An explosion rocked the submarine slightly. Ibn Al Jamal looked to the sonar operator, who reported the explosion was of the torpedo that had disappeared beneath the coastal shelf. "Must have hit something . . ." he offered, his voice trailing off.

They were not out of danger yet. Two torpedoes remained active in the water. One, Ibn Al Jamal believed, was too far to the west to be an immediate threat, but he knew to never discount anything in the water. The one they avoided—a second explosion rocked the *Al Nasser*—just hit a decoy. He grinned. Only one threat remained in the water, but by now, the attacking ASW aircraft had had sufficient time to complete a circuit and align for another attack. Ibn Al Jamal suspected a minimum of two American aircraft attacking him. Most ASW aircraft possessed the capability for at least two Mark-50 torpedoes; therefore, three dropped that close together told him he had at least two above him. He turned the *Al Nasser* to port, back into the underwater channel leading to deep-sea water. *One-quarter kilometer to go—250 meters.*

"WHAT IS GOING ON HERE?" SHOUTED GENeral Lewis, overhearing the excited ASW ATC operator tell Captain Dick Holman of the launch of the third torpedo.

Two steps brought the sweat gear–garbed Army three-star General beside Dick. He looked up at the Ranger general, towering over him by a good eight inches.

"Sir, the P-3C and the two S-3s we launched off the *Stennis* a half hour ago are in combat with the Algerian Kilo submarine, the *Al Nasser*." He glanced toward the console. "Looks very good right now, General. We have three torpedoes in the water. Two have made contact and exploded. We are waiting for confirmation of the kill."

It seemed to Dick the flow of blood to the top of the general's head was a visible wave that crept up the neck, past flaring nostrils, across blazing eyes, bunched eyebrows, and furrowed brow before disappearing under the short cropped hair. He would have not been surprised to see steam rolling out of his ears.

"Admiral! I said I did not want to engage! Does the reticent service ever listen to orders? I want the attack broken off now! I mean now!"

"Yes, sir," Admiral Cameron responded politely. He touched Dick Holman on the shoulder. "Captain Holman, have the aircraft disengage. Have the P-3C set up a sonobuoy pattern between us and the enemy and the S-3s establish an overhead orbit for the remainder of their flight."

"Yes, sir. When would you like it done?" Dick asked, knowing he was pushing the envelope.

"Enough of this bullshit, Admiral. Stop the attack, and stop it now, Captain."

Dick Holman turned to the young petty officer who had been listening intently to the confrontation. Sweat on the sailor's wide-eyed face streamed down to a neckline that was quickly becoming soaked. It wasn't the temperature in the air-conditioned space causing that.

"Stay calm, Sailor," he said softly. "Order the aircraft to break off their attack."

"Sir, Hunter Three One—the P-3C—reports no joy on the torpedoes. One exploded. They suspect on a decoy; the second exploded for unknown reasons and the other ran out of steam. The submarine maneuvered to avoid but has returned its original course of zero six zero."

General Lewis leaned down, pulling the towel back and forth across the back of his neck. "What does that mean, Captain?"

Dick straightened up. "It means, General, that you got your wish, sir. The attack failed, and the submarine has returned to its original course directly toward the Amphibious Task Force. With luck, sir, we may be able to throw hand grenades at it from the flight deck when it arrives tomorrow."

"Don't go too far down this road, Captain," General Lewis warned.

The lieutenant general turned to the two admirals and included Dick Holman in his words. "Gentlemen, don't think just because I am Army that I don't know what you tried to do right now. Admiral, you have every reason in the world to hate these people. You just buried your wife. Rear Admiral Devlin, you are an aviator and a P-3 jockey, so I know you have the instinct to kill a submarine when your aircraft discover it. You, Captain Holman, besides being overweight, a smoker, out of shape, and insolent, used to be captain of the USS *Stennis* before being involuntarily transferred to the Joint Task Force staff. You fear for your ship and the ships out here. In fact, all three of you do. I know I am abrasive. Sometimes it stimulates rebellion, but understand this; I am under orders to disengage us from North Africa. Those orders came from above the chairman of the Joint Chiefs of Staff and above the secretary of Defense. Do I make myself clear without saying specifically that the president himself wants our people off the beach, onto the ships and the hell out of here? Do I?"

Behind the general, the low voice of the ATC arguing with the pilots of the three aircraft to break off contact could be heard. The P-3C pilot begged for one more pass; he had the submarine dead on and could drop his remaining Mark-50 directly on top of the bastard. Dick Holman heard the exchange and shook his head at the operator, who relayed a "Permission denied" to the pilot. The sailor grimaced over the response. Dick had a fair feel for what the pilot probably said, but he knew the pilot would obey the order even as the aviator cursed the stupidity of the battle group commander.

"I know there is resentment over me coming in here and taking over a Navy show. Believe me when I say that I did not volunteer for this, but I did not try to get out of it, either, when they ordered me forward. We are professionals. We will act as professionals. We will work together toward one end: extricating ourselves from the beach and from contact with the forces of this new country. Can we do that?"

When he received no answer, he turned to his aide. "Let's go, Brad. I need a Navy shower, clean shorts, and a pressed uniform. I will see you gentlemen at dinner. My quarters, my invite, twenty one hundred hours. Okay?"

Admiral Cameron spoke for the three of them. "Yes, sir, General. It will be our pleasure."

"Good, I would like someone to have some pleasure from today's events. We have gotten off on the wrong foot, gentlemen. Let's see if we can start over. Captain Holman, I will have the cook prepare a dieter's special for you. The only other thing you need to pursue further is finding that missing SEAL captain and getting him and his cohorts off Italy and into Algiers. The sooner we recover those hostages, the sooner we vacate this quagmire. The Marines aren't having much luck in finding them, so use this bastard who won't tell anyone but this Captain James where the hostages are being held." With that comment, he turned without waiting for a reply and headed toward the hatch.

Colonel Brad Storey remained behind for a second and spoke to Admiral Cameron. "Sir, that invitation also includes Captain Bowen, sir. The general looks forward to an engaging and pleasant dinner. Thank you for coming."

Admiral Cameron nodded and watched General Lewis's executive aide rush to catch up with the Ranger flag officer, arriving at the hatch as the general stood in front of it, eyeing the mechanism to open the door before attempting it.

"He can't have both," Rear Admiral Devlin said.

Cameron looked at him. "Both what?"

"Engaging and pleasant. We just had an engagement with him. What do we do now? Present him our swords and lower the flag?"

Admiral Cameron thought a few seconds before he spoke. "We have our orders. Our focus is to identify ways to disengage our forces throughout our operating area. Pete, put the word out that no naval or marine forces are to engage the enemy unless in self-defense. They are to avoid confrontations as best possible. The general is right, gentlemen, and we are the ones in the wrong. He has been ordered to disengage us from this theater. If we cannot support General Lewis, then we need to be up front and step aside so he can get someone in here who can. Understood?"

Dick Holman and Pete Devlin acknowledged the admiral's words.

"Good," Admiral Cameron said. "What is the status of Captain James? Have they located him and his two traveling companions?"

Pete Devlin nodded. "They have flight reservations on a military airlift out of Naples tomorrow to Washington. We'll intercept them at the airport and divert them here, to the *Stennis*, to pick up the rest of the team."

"Let me know when we have them. Shouldn't have given them the weekend off to see beautiful Italy. Gentlemen, I'll see you tonight at dinner. I am sure it will be engaging, if not pleasant."

The two stood side by side as the admiral strolled to the hatch to leave. He reached it as Captain Clive Bowen opened it from the other side. Admiral Cameron and Clive spoke a few words before the two departed the Air Operations space together.

"Well, I guess that's the ball game," Pete Devlin muttered.

"How's that, Admiral?"

He shook his head. "Nothing, Dick. Just thinking out loud. Go ahead and set up an ASW barrier between us and the Algerian Kilo submarine. Just because we can't attack him, doesn't mean he won't attack us." He paused for a moment. "Anything else?"

"Ranger Two Nine should be entering the Sigonella pattern in the next few minutes. If her wheels lower and lock, it should be an easy landing. Otherwise, could be asshole tight for the crew."

"RANGER TWO NINE, SIGONELLA CONTROL; you are clear to join pattern. Report over beacon Bravo Sierra. You are authorized to descend to fifteen hundred feet."

"Okay, we have clearance. Jasbo, I want to lower the

wheels in two minutes when we pass over Bravo Sierra. Be prepared to jerk up on the landing gear controls if I holler. Chief, if we start an uncontrolled descent, I want throttles on numbers two, three, and four pressed forward to maximum. The Jasbo and I will attempt to regain control. Jasbo, if that happens, we'll have about ten seconds to correct. Chief, you count. If I shout, it'll mean we can't correct. You then flip on the automatic controls, and at that moment we pray to the God of technology and computers to bring us out."

"Ain't nothing going to happen, Skipper."

"Sure, Chief. I know that. You know that. And the Jasbo knows that. But, who knows what this aircraft is thinking after getting the beating it just got southwest of here. I don't want Ranger Two Nine to decide because the wheels are down, it can land anywhere."

"She."

"She?"

"Yes, sir. We all know that Ranger Two Nine is a she, not an it."

"Well, right now, she's having a bad case of PMS."

The plane shook as it descended through the hot atmosphere above the cacti and brown grasses of the Sicilian hills. As he watched the altimeter needle slowly creeping downward and listened to the flight engineer's voice calling off the feet, Commander Stillwell mentally reviewed the procedures to drop the wheels. *Naval Aviation Training and Operations Safety* manual, commonly called *NATOPS*, governed the safety, performance, and emergency procedures for every aircraft in the Navy inventory. The one for the EP-3E was written by Fleet Air Reconnaissance Squadron Two out of Jacksonville, Florida, formerly of Naval Base Rota, Spain. Stillwell was the operations officer for the squadron when not deployed. The continuous updating and revising of the EP-3E *NATOPS* manual fell under his responsibilities. He knew the *NATOPS* manual like a priest knows the Bible. For the tense crew aboard the war-torn Aries aircraft, no better pilot could have been on board.

"Fifteen hundred feet, sir!" Chief Henckels announced.

Stillwell pulled up slightly on the stick, leveling the plane at slightly under 1,500 feet.

He pressed the Transmit button. "Sigonella Control, Ranger Two Nine, past beacon Bravo Sierra. Permission to join circuit?"

"Permission granted, Ranger Two Nine. Turn right to course zero one zero. Distance to runway ten miles. You are cleared for pass by the tower for a wheels check, then short circuit, short final for landing."

The American captain in the Italian control tower picked up a pair of binoculars he brought with him. He and the other American officers moved onto the small observation deck where others had crowded to watch the damaged aircraft land. He scanned the skies with his binoculars, searching for the EP-3E reconnaissance aircraft.

"OKAY, GUYS, IT'S THE MOMENT OF TRUTH. Everyone prepared?" Stillwell asked.

They both rogered his question. Jasbo grasped the wheel, stretched her fingers briefly as her palms rested on it, before gripping the column so tightly her knuckles turned visibly white against the tan skin earned by her off hours poolside at the Total Motel. She knew she would have little opportunity to correct if the plane lost its maneuverability. She rolled her shoulders. Her entire body, from her feet on the pedals, through her legs, up her abdomen, and out through her arms, was one tightly wound mass of feminine muscle prepared to exert every ounce of her 130 pounds to save this plane.

Chief Henckels reached down and tightened his seat belt before leaning forward, putting both hands on the throttle, prepared to increase the speed of the engines. His right hand held the throttles to engines three and four, while his left gripped the one for engine number two. The fourth throttle for engine number one remained in the off position. The chief glanced at the gauge for engine num-

ber two and relayed to Commander Stillwell the fact the
engine was operating in the lower edge of the red. If they
lost engine number two during their final approach, the
plane would roll hard to the right. At the altitude they
were flying, he doubted the three of them together would
stop Ranger Two Nine from diving right wing first into
the dry soil of Sigonella Airfield. *What's the last thing to
go through a bug's mind when it hits a windshield? Its ass.*

Stillwell flicked the switch on his helmet microphone
to internal ICS. He briefed the crew on what they were
going to do in the next fifteen minutes. First, they were
preparing to lower the wheels, and he told them the hard
truth of what could happen. He also told them that if the
worst happened, they had to remain in their seats and not
panic. They would be unable to recover the aircraft if
every crew member decided it was time to run and shout.
Stay calm, and they would get through this.

"Okay, here we go," he said.

He reached beneath the chief's hands and pushed the
levers controlling the wheels down. The sound of hydraulic machinery opening the wheel well doors reverberated throughout the aircraft, drowning out normal
conversation. The three red lights in the middle of the cockpit console showed the wheels up and secure. In the back
of the aircraft, the lowered wheels bent the sounds and the
wind coming through the flak hole at the rear, sending
both rushing through the fuselage like screaming ban-
shees demanding their sacrifice. John Andrews made the
personal observation, strapped in at his senior evaluator
ditching station, that there seemed to be a lot of eyeballs
sweating in this heat. He touched the bandage on his head,
thankful the wound was only superficial.

"One green," Chief Henckels said. "Nose gear down
and locked."

Stillwell and Jasbo took their eyes momentarily away
from the cockpit window to glance down at the lights.
Two remained red, but the port and starboard wheels were
always several seconds behind the nose gear wheel.

"There's the tower," Jasbo said, nodding toward her

side of the front cockpit window. No way she was going to release her death grip on the wheel.

"Let's maintain current course, speed, and altitude until we get greens on the last two wheels. Then we'll turn slightly to the right so we can pass over the tower."

The red light for the starboard wheel blinked to green. The aircraft rocked and vibrated, straining to turn farther to the right. Chief Henckels slid the belt out on his seat belt and stretched forward until he could touch the port light. He tapped it twice, more in wishful thinking than expecting it to miraculously glow green.

"No joy, Skipper, on port wheel. We have two greens; nose gear and starboard wheel."

"Chief, increase speed on number two," he spat out through clenched teeth.

"Hurry," Jasbo stuttered, her arms straining to hold the aircraft against the increasing right-hand torque.

Chief Henckels pushed the number-two engine forward all the way, his eyes looking up, watching the heat indicator.

The two pilots glanced at the wheel indicator lights briefly. "Could be a faulty connection," Stillwell offered as the aircraft eased against the right-hand pull of the aircraft. Maybe the AAA damaged the indicator line on the port side. It was on the same side as the engine hit by the SAM. Could be a multitude of things. Just because the light indicates the wheel failed to lower and lock doesn't necessarily make it so.

"Could be," Chief Henckels agreed.

"She is pulling a lot harder to the right with the wheels down, Chief. Keep an eye on number two."

"Sir, number two is still in the red. The needle is easing upward. If we continue on maximum power, we run the risk of her freezing up."

"Chief, she can freeze up and frost over for all I care as long as she waits until we're on the ground. Since we are relying on faulty indicators for the wheels, let's hope we have one on number two. If she has been operating this long in the red, she can do it a little longer." He crossed his fingers on his left hand briefly without removing it from the steering column. God, he hoped he was right. Aviation mishaps usually don't give pilots a second chance. You make the right choices the first time, or the second time may be in another life.

Engine number two operating at a higher power setting raised the decibel level slightly in the cockpit.

"Jasbo, let's edge the aircraft over a couple of degrees so we can fly by the tower. When we reach the tower, I want us to turn left. It's going to be hard to do against the pull to the right, but we need to expose our belly to the tower. At least long enough so they can see our complete undercarriage."

"Anything I can do, Ranger Two Nine?" Shell Leader asked. The S-3 tanker was flying an overhead orbit at ten thousand feet to stay out of the way of the damaged EP-3E as it attempted to land.

"No, thanks, Shell Leader. You may want to hop down here and land before we go in. I do not know how the runway will be afterward."

"Ranger Two Nine, Shell Leader. Thanks, shipmate, but as soon as you touch down, I am off to the carrier. Only four of us, you know, and those gas-hog fighters need us gas stations to do their job."

"Shell Leader, I look forward to buying the first round when our paths cross again. Ranger Two Nine out."

The flashing small red light on the starboard fuel bladder went from blinking to a steady red. They had less than ten minutes to land.

"Commander," Chief Henckels started.

"I know, Chief. We're empty, flying on fumes."

"I can turn off one of the starboard engines, sir. That would give us a couple of more minutes."

Stillwell shook his head. "No, I don't think one good engine with our number two would keep the plane airborne. Cross your fingers, Jasbo, Chief."

• • •

THE AMERICAN CAPTAIN STARED AT THE approaching aircraft through binoculars pressed against his eyes. His fingers meticulously twisted the lens as he tried to focus on the bobbing aircraft. The several seconds he had the aircraft in his vision, he saw the two wheels down Ranger Two Nine had reported. He failed to spot the port side wheel, but it was hard to take in everything through binoculars when your target was bobbing, weaving and approaching. He did not envy those pilots. From his own experience, he knew the adrenaline surge going through their bodies and the fear they were fighting to contain. He lowered the binoculars. One minute to truth time. He turned to the operations officer behind him and told him to check again and make sure those Italians were prepared to foam the runway. He wanted the foam laid as soon as they were sure the wheels did not fully extend. Further, he wanted his people to rig the barrier at the end of the runway. There was little he could do to help the plane recover. The foam padded the runway with fire retardant chemicals that expanded on contact with the air. If Ranger Two Nine had to belly in, the foam reduced the chance of the aircraft exploding from sparks or catching on fire. The barrier was a grid of metal wires running between two steel stanchions, designed to stop a plane from cartwheeling off the end of the runway. Barriers were used on carriers to trap a plane that has problems with its tail hook. Most airfields had smooth ground past the end of the runway, but in Sigonella, the runway ended abruptly, and rough, uneven cacti plains speckled with deep drainage ditches began. The barrier was not designed to stop a plane the size of the EP-3E, but even so, it would slow it down and maybe keep it on the runway with the foam. Three hundred yards farther, in the direction the Aries aircraft was going to land, a paved civilian highway, on a high bank, crossed the T of the runway.

The noise of the approaching plane made the American captain think of a sick bird. He had over twelve thousand hours of flight time in fighter aircraft before the beloved

medical corps decided his flight years were over. He
glanced at the men and the two women officers standing
with him to see if they heard what he did. They gave no
indication, and he said nothing. There was a slight hiccup
in one of the engines, a background noise that only an experienced pilot could recognize. He knew Commander
Stillwell, and he knew as surely as he stood here waiting
for the aircraft to pass overhead that the vibration of that
slight sound the pilot would feel through the steering column.

Several of the officers put their hands over their ears as
the plane headed in its last 200 feet. Ranger Two Nine
turned slightly to the left and then seemed to turn too far
to the left before it whipped back to level flight. In that instant, when the belly was fully exposed to the Americans
and the Italians standing in the crowded tower, everyone
saw that only two wheels were fully deployed. The port
wheel was barely visible out of its cradle, as if it tried to
deploy and then locked up. He knew the wheel would not
reset. They could try pumping it down, but they had insufficient fuel with their transfer fuel pump broken to
have the time do it.

"Ranger Two Nine, Sigonella Tower; your port wheel
is not fully deployed. It appears to be wedged half in and
half out of the wheel well. What is your fuel situation?"

"We have no fuel. I am going to climb above fifteen
hundred feet and allow the crew to bail out. I know it is
low level for a bailout, but within parameters. I have no
choice, Sigonella, I am coming in. Request—if possible
and you have time—foam the runway for us."

The American captain snatched up his walkie-talkie
and transmitted the necessary instructions. Even as
Ranger Two Nine climbed to higher altitude for a bailout,
two large fire trucks raced down the runway, pouring out
the white foam chemical across the tarmac. At the farther
end, sailors, chiefs and officers raced back and forth as
they raised the barrier. The foam expanded, growing from
a foot-high layer to two feet, to three, and in places as
high as five feet. Two fire trucks moved to the edge of the

approach end of the runway. Two more spun into positions halfway down and off the runway about 100 yards and at the end, past the barrier, two more waited.

One of the officers touched the American captain on the shoulder and pointed to Ranger Two Nine. White parachutes blossomed as EP-3E crew members jumped from the side door of Ranger Two Nine. The American captain overheard the operations officers ordering pickup trucks and official sedans toward the fields outside the base to recover the crew members. One of the four ambulances broke off and sped off toward the field where the bulk of the parachutes appeared to be heading. The bailout stopped as Ranger Two Nine turned to port. He took a deep breath and let it out slowly, willing the constriction in his throat to loosen. He relived his own crash and muttered a short prayer for the three who would try to bring it in.

The bailout continued after Ranger Two Nine leveled off, flying parallel to the runway about one-half mile out. The aircraft would continue on this path for about four miles, make a left turn, and then a last left to line up on the runway. The decisive moment would be about two minutes after it lined up.

"Sigonella Tower, Ranger Two Nine. We have completed bailout. Request short final."

The captain leaned forward, putting both hands on the railing. Those parachutes of the last group to bail out were being blown toward the runway. Shit! They were going to hit the runway about the same time as the aircraft touched down. He grabbed his walkie-talkie again and passed urgent instructions to those along the runway. Get those crew members off and away from the runway and under cover before the aircraft touched down. He passed the effort onto his operations officer, who stepped inside the tower to tell his Italian counterpart what was happening. They had seen the same thing and had passed similar instructions to their people on the ground.

"Ranger Two Nine, Sigonella Tower. We have a slight problem. Some of your people who bailed out are being blown toward the runway. How long can you delay landing?"

"Sigonella Tower, I cannot delay. I have no fuel! I am flying on fumes now. I have a fire warning light on engine number two. No visible flames yet, but the light is on. I can't turn it off. If we cannot land ASAP, then we will have to ditch the plane."

"Roger, continue with your approach. We are working to clear your crew members off the runway before you land. It will be close, but we can do it. Left turn, for short final."

Two clicks acknowledged the instruction.

The first two parachutists landed in the middle of the foam. Silver-garbed Italian and American firemen rushed across the runway, grabbed them, their parachutes, and hurried them off the foamed pavement. Two more landed, one on each side of the runway. Firefighters snatched them under each arm and, more dragging than carrying, ran with them to a position behind nearby trucks.

Only three parachutists remained in the air. Two of them would touch down before Ranger Two Nine. The American captain saw it was going to be close for the last crew member who bailed out. He doubted the man would land before Ranger Two Nine started its controlled crash along the runway.

"This is Ranger Two Nine. Five hundred feet and descending."

"Ranger Two Nine, you are on glide path. Continue gradual descent. One minute to touchdown. Just prior to touchdown, cut engines and secure unnecessary electronics."

"Roger, will do."

Dark, oily smoke erupted from engine number two, sending a black trail behind the injured aircraft. Flames leaped up, surrounding the engine.

The parachutist tugged on his strands, fighting to maneuver his descent away from the runway. In so doing, the wind caught the parachute and caused it to rise slightly, delaying the time to impact even more. It had been close, but now his unsuccessful attempt to avoid the runway had increased his chance for landing on it as the plane touched down. The captain estimated the parachutist was at 100 feet. He seemed to have ceased trying to manipulate the parachute, probably realizing his attempts only worsened the situation.

The sounds from Ranger Two Nine's engines abruptly stopped 300 yards from the runway. Flames spewed out of engine number two, moving up the wing toward the fuselage.

"Don't cut them yet!" shouted the transmission from the tower.

"We didn't. It's on fire!"

"Hit your extinguisher!"

"They are empty on port wing side."

The plane moved forward another 100 yards before the nose dropped abruptly. Flames shot up suddenly, wrapping around the fuselage of the aircraft for a moment before dropping back. The American captain watched the flaps as Commander Stillwell attempted to coast the last 200 yards to the Sigonella runway. Without hydraulic power, the flight crew would have to use muscle to move any of the flight controls. His throat constricted as he watched the burning aircraft approach the runway.

The EP-3E nose lifted slightly, but the plane was dropping fast. "Just get on the ground," the captain muttered. Several of the officers near him agreed. If the aircraft would just stay together a few more minutes.

"That's it, Sigonella. Fuel's gone!"

Ranger Two Nine tilted to the port side for a moment before righting itself. Fifty yards. *Come on, fellow.* Fifty more yards, and then suddenly, the nose wheel touched the end of the runway, followed by the starboard wheel. The two starboard propellers were winding down. The propeller on number-one engine was missing. Fire was blazing from the number two engine, obscuring the port side.

"That must have been the one shot off by the SAM,"

the American captain said aloud, musing over the missing propeller of the number-one engine.

The port wing remained aloft several seconds before slowly folding toward the runway. The tip of the wing disappeared into the foam, and the sound of horrendous wrenching, the tearing away of the undercarriage and the ripping of the number-two propeller from its shaft, filled the twilit atmosphere. The detached propeller spun about fifty feet into the air before falling back down to disappear into the foam behind the aircraft. The starboard wheel was invisible beneath the foam. Suddenly, the starboard side of the plane fell onto the runway as the wheel gave way. Flames roiled out of the foam, wrapping the Aries II reconnaissance aircraft in a moving pyre. Only the cockpit seemed free of the flames.

The aircraft began an uncontrolled skid along the pavement toward the barrier, sparks flying behind it to be quickly smothered by the foam. *Why isn't the foam putting out the conflagration?* the commanding officer of Sigonella asked silently.

The nose gear collapsed next, burying the nose of the aircraft into the foam. Foam shot up and over the cockpit windows, blinding the cockpit crew inside. The only visible parts of the aircraft were the top of the fuselage and the top portions of the wing. The tail looked like a shark fin charging through white waters as the momentum of the aircraft shoveled the foam ahead of it, building a wave over ten feet high traveling down the runway, the burning fuselage marking its path along the runway.

The aircraft spun clockwise, its tail rotating to port. Behind the aircraft, shooting more foam at the aircraft, sped the two fire trucks that had waited at the beginning of the runway. The foam fell ineffectively behind the aircraft. The trucks were unable to get close to the aircraft as it skidded down the runway because of the heat. Two fire trucks midway down the runway came in from the side to join the chase. Other vehicles, trucks, ambulances, and maintenance vehicles that had earlier converged toward the barrier began to move away as the EP-3E approached.

At the barrier, the people began running, seeking safety, knowing the fate of the crew inside the aircraft rested in that thin strip of steel. It was the static barrier against the declining momentum of a heavy, spinning, crashed aircraft it was never designed to stop.

The captain glanced up. The parachutist was ahead of the EP-3E. He watched the man in the parachute frantically tug at the canvas lines running to the canopy of the parachute, trying to gain altitude above the uncontrolled aircraft rushing toward him. The crew member jerked his feet up to his chest at the last moment. The tail passed beneath the parachutist, missing his butt by what seemed to the captain to be inches. The edge of the parachute canopy caught on fire as it passed over the burning middle of the aircraft. He had not realized he was holding his breath until that critical moment passed, and he heard the others around him let theirs out, also. The man in the parachute hit the center of the runway behind Ranger Two Nine and disappeared under the foam, only to emerge several seconds later at a dead run toward the near side of the runway. That would be one sailor who would have tales to tell his grandchildren.

Ranger Two Nine hit the barrier with its port wing first, breaking through two of the steel cables before the tail section hit it. The barrier strained, the two stanchions bent, and when the captain thought they were going to give, they straightened. Ranger Two Nine had landed. The two fire trucks behind the barrier rushed up and trained their foam guns on the aircraft. The explosion knocked the captain and the officers with him back against the concrete side of the tower. They quickly pulled themselves up.

Pieces of the aircraft hurled outward and up. Flames, smoke, and burning fuel rolled into the air with the fuel raining down on the firemen and others who had run toward the aircraft in a valiant effort to save the crew. A fire truck behind the barrier was on its side, burning.

The American captain wanted to rush down there. He forced himself to watch, to witness. He could do little at ground level other than get in the way. Two firefighters in their silver fireproof gear emerged from the foam and fire, one pulling the other, who appeared to be unconscious. Their suits were speckled with small dots of flame where fuel burned on the fireproof suits. Nearby firemen returning to the blackening hulk of the Ranger Two Nine blasted the two with fire extinguishers. Two of them grabbed the injured one and carried him away toward a nearby ambulance, removing his helmet along the way. The second man dropped to his knees for a moment and then fell face forward onto the tarmac as two other firemen wrestled with his helmet, freeing it.

He let his binoculars drop, turned to the officers beside him, and suggested they go see what they could do, though he knew there was little. He ordered the operations officer to have all the surviving crew members taken immediately to the hospital. Also, no press were to be allowed around them until he received instructions from Washington, next of kin were notified, and the intel had their chance with them.

What a brave bunch of crew men on that aircraft, he thought, and then, in a kind of a by the way, he wondered who in the hell was the last person to bail out of that plane.

JOHN ANDREWS LAY IN THE DRY GRASS BE-
side the runway. Everyone was so focused on the exploding and burning aircraft that no one noticed him. He ran his hands down his sides, checking himself, even though he knew if anything had been wrong he never would have been able to run off the runway. His breaths came in short, rapid gulps. That tail nearly knocked him from the sky. He thought he was dead when he looked down the runway and saw the EP-3E, aflame, spinning toward him and there wasn't a thing he could do. Several minutes passed before he managed to stand. Two sailors watching from a nearby pickup truck pointed at him. They rushed out of the vehicles and soon had Lieutenant Commander John

Andrews resting against some boxes in the back of the maintenance vehicle as one of the sailors transmitted on the pickup radio his presence. The other one passed a half bottle of water to him.

An ambulance sped up to the scene, the tires leaving a trail of rubber when the driver slammed on the brakes. The white-garbed medics threw open the doors and rushed toward him, leaving the siren blaring on the empty ambulance. Everything seemed to flow in slow motion. It was as if he was a third party, watching things happen. Seemed to him a lot of sirens and horns were blaring across the runway. He turned and looked toward the end of the runway, expecting to see Stillwell, Jasbo Smith, and Chief Henckels. What he saw was a cockpit with flames licking through the side and the tail of the EP-3 burning on the other side of the runway. The thought passed through his mind that the tail shouldn't be that far from the nose. As the adrenaline high ebbed and things returned to normal speed, tears began to flow. He couldn't stop them. He shut his eyes, screwing them together as tightly as he could. Dead. He felt hands on him. Where were the others who bailed out with him? Where were they? He cried. Cried like a baby. Tears streamed from beneath the closed eyes. He had never been so scared in his life. His throat was so constricted, he couldn't talk when the ambulance attendants picked him up gently and strapped him to the stretcher. Never so scared.

CHAPTER 10

⚓

STAPLER MOVED CAUTIOUSLY BUT QUICKLY around the dug-in positions of the Marines. He touched each of the Marines and oil riggers manning the defensive line. They stopped long enough to acknowledge his few words of encouragement before continuing to dig. Shoveling the sand and rocks to the front of their positions, building small walls to better protect themselves. Where he had placed a Marine, Stapler had interspersed one of the ten, armed riggers. What was coming their way would need the combined firepower of everyone.

The unarmed, such as the professor, Karim, and *Miss Sheila Anne Forester,* who bitched and moaned the whole time about being ordered to take cover, demanding she be given a weapon, he moved behind the large boulders to their rear. He ought to give her to the Tauregs; they'd surrender after a couple of hours with her. But he noticed that even she was stacking rocks around the positions nearer the base of the wadi cliff, creating some sort of half-built, waist-high fort. They would be safe as long as Stapler and the others held the front position. When he had looked back at what she was doing after an hour, he had to admit the girl had some intelligence.

What she had done was build them a fallback position if they had to abandon the humvees—a fallback position he knew that, if used, admitted they wouldn't be leaving the wadi. The efforts reminded him of an old Western movie where the settlers ring their wagons to fight off the Indians; only they were the settlers, and he didn't see a happy ending to this story. There was no calvary to charge over the horizon at the last minute and still no contact with Base Butler.

The rest of the night had passed uneventfully, except the nightlong vigilance gave everyone a chance to count the small campfires of the Tauregs above them and build their own conclusions and anxieties. Professor Walthers said they burned dried camel and goat dung to make the strong tea the Tauregs enjoyed. Sometimes there was more information than you needed from this man who'd pass for Colonel Sanders if he had a white suit to go with that beard. The thought of fried chicken made his stomach growl.

The small fires flickered along the top edge of the wadi cliff and down along the broad path that lead to the bottom, several hundred yards away from their camp. Stapler believed there were more campfires than needed and said so. The Air Force fighter jocks had estimated the size of the force opposing them at around a hundred. If the campfires were any indication, then there were more than that number surrounding them. The Algerians were confident, Stapler knew. Why else would they feel safe enough to light campfires? They lit the campfires to confuse and frighten us. Well, goddammit, it worked.

Stapler knew what the others probably suspected but refused to admit. The only way out of the wadi was to kill enough of their attackers that the remainder fled—kill them completely, utterly, and without regard to the moral platitudes. If they didn't, then they would be the ones killed. Nathan Bedford Forest, that fine old Southern general from the Civil War said it best: "War is fighting and fighting is killing." In the fog of battle and the fiction of combat, individual soldiers—Marines—never stop to review the rules of war as they fight. No, they fight to survive and to keep faith with their comrades fighting alongside them. Whatever happened here in the wadi during this approaching day would never be reviewed by those black-robed assholes in the Hague like they did the NATO forces who bombed Kosovo back in the late 1990s.

"Abercombie, that as deep a hole as you can dig?" Stapler asked the young, sandy-haired Marine from San Diego.

The Marine stood up, pushed his shovel into the sand in front of him, and reached under his helmet to scratch his head. The new Marine Corps tattoo on his shoulder, gotten just before they left Camp LeJeune, North Carolina, showed in the faint false dawn. "Gee, Gunny, It's up to my waist now. If they overrun, I want to be able to get out of the hole, not be buried in it."

Stapler nodded once, quickly. "Okay, Abercombie. Just wanted to make sure you knew what you were doing."

"Sure, Gunnery Sergeant, I know what I am doing, but I don't think those people up there know what they are doing. Do you think they know there're eleven Marines down here, including Cowboy? Ain't gonna be a fair fight; a hundred of them and eleven of us. In a way, I kinda feel sorry for them." The Marine grinned. "Yeah, Gunny, I kinda feel sorry for them." Abercombie picked up his shovel and, with lip-biting concentration, continued arranging his foxhole and the rocks above it into some sort of personal sense of order.

After watching a few seconds, Stapler sighed and said, "Well, don't feel too sorry for them, and pull down those sleeves before the sun rises. Protect your skin, Abercombie."

"Sure thing, Gunnery Sergeant." He squatted back down in his desert foxhole as Stapler moved off. "Gunny, protect yours, too!" he said.

Stapler grinned. "Oh, I intend to, Abercombie."

The false light of approaching dawn filtered into the

darkness of the wadi. The dark outline of the top of the cliffs separated from the night skies. The stars twinkled out one by one as the sun neared the horizon. Stapler suspected the first attack would be around dawn. If not, then it meant they intended to wait them out. Let the sun do the work for them. It's what he would do. Why risk lives when a little patience could do the job for you?

Gonzales and a couple of the riggers had unloaded the camels and the humvees last night. The supplies had been stuck with those unarmed behind the boulders at the rear of the camp. The water was buried near the boulders. Awry bullets could hit the plastic containers, draining their sparse water supply and making their untenable position more untenable, if such a thing could be. If he were going to die, he'd would prefer not to die thirsty.

Private Cowboy Joe-Boy Henry had been doctored the best that they could do with the limited first aid kits they had. Abercombie had recovered the corpsman's first aid kit before the Tauregs liberated it from the dead at the rig site. The Marines sometimes reminded Stapler of the French Foreign Legion, though he would have been hard pressed to explain. Sometimes those joining the Marines did so to escape something back home, something in their past they wanted to expunge. Of course, the Marine Corps never offered opportunities to change names or earn citizenship like the Legionnaires, but some still had secrets they kept to themselves.

One such secret surfaced with the wounding of Private Henry. Funny how nicknames have little relevance when someone is dying. Private Eric Sterling was a dropout of Virginia Institute of Medicine. Six months into medical school and he hung it up! He had a bachelor's degree; he could have gone to Officer Candidate School, if he had applied. The older private had never said a word about his medical training, nothing about his degree. In fact, when the man joined the platoon four months ago following boot camp, Stapler had interviewed the heavyset, dark-haired man from Newnan, Georgia. The interview had gone like a trip to the dentist; any information Stapler wanted, he had to pull out of the quiet Marine. There was a story somewhere in why Sterling left the medical field so near to becoming a doctor and joined the Marines. Stapler's curiosity would be satisfied, but he knew it would be long after they got out of this fix—if they got out of it. Whatever the reason, it was probably not a nice one, which piqued his curiosity even more.

Sterling did what he could. He pulled the sides of the wound together, put in a few stitches to close the opening, and sprinkled antibiotic powders over it. He even gave the moaning, crying Henry—who muttered "Momma" over and over, until the man slid into unconsciousness—two shots: one for the pain and one for the infection. The bullet still lay somewhere in Cowboy's left side. Sterling said from the way the blood ran, he believed the bullet missed the major veins and arteries. However, that was speculation, according to Sterling and, besides, he had no way of knowing how much internal damage the bullet had done to the insides of the thin Texan.

What Stapler was sure of was that Henry had lost a lot of blood. He knew because his cammie shirt was soaked with it. He could have squeezed the shirt like a dishrag, and blood would have run out of it. The drying shirt lay across one of the two huge boulders behind him. Streaks, where Henry's blood had seeped out of the shirt, ran down the red sides of the boulder. Stapler had little choice but to wear the shirt later. The other choice was to remained exposed to the Saharan sun and watch his tender, lily-white skin bake and burst until every bit of him looked like his hands. He picked it up. Even in the cool Saharan night, the shirt had dried. Where the blood had soaked it, the fabric bent between his fingers. *Ah, to hell with it,* he thought, and he braced his M-16 against the rock and put the shirt on. Hell of a time to be thinking of hygiene.

"Morning, Gunny," Lieutenant Nolan said, approaching from behind the boulders.

Where have you been all night, LT? he asked himself, already knowing the answer.

Stapler acknowledged the greeting without saluting

and turned toward the perimeter. Nolan fell in step with him.

"Miss Forester is very scared, you know, Gunny," Lieutenant Nolan said softly. "I know you haven't hit it off with her, but she is probably the youngest person we have in the convoy. I tried to reassure her everything would be all right. If you get a chance—"

"If she gets much more scared, you may not be able to walk," Stapler interrupted. He spat to the side, pulled the last pack of Algerian cigarettes from his pocket, and cupped his hand to hide the flame as he lit one. The flame wouldn't show with the sun about to crest the ridge. *Christ, give me strength.*

The lieutenant stared at Stapler, his looks questioning Stapler's remarks.

Stapler shook his head. "It isn't her who should be scared, LT."

"Who then?"

He took a puff and blew the smoke away from the young officer. "It's those goddamn Tauregs if they capture her. I think there is a Geneva Convention war crimes thing about civilians like her. We aren't allowed to give them up voluntarily, and the enemy has to keep them."

Stapler saw the LT open his mouth to speak. "Besides, LT, Catsup is the youngest. She just turned twenty last month. *Miss Sheila Anne Forester* of Boston, Mass, is twenty."

"It's Philadelphia, Gunny, and she is two."

Stapler leaned over the boulder where Private Henry lay on a blanket among the noncombatants. "How is he?" he asked Mary Coblen, one of the women riggers. He had discovered a lot about the two partners during this journey. Most of it while Mary's friend was suffering sunstroke. Mary and her partner Dorothy—call me Dot, please—Meyran were from a small town in Ohio near Akron. Some place called Compact. Dot had been a teacher at a junior high school when word circulated among the parents about them. With the loss of her job looming in the near future, the two opted for elsewhere.

He never truly understood how the two came to work for Loffland Brothers in Algeria.

Nevertheless, he had an appreciation for what Mary told him. Stapler spent as little time as possible in his hometown of Concord, North Carolina. Three days were about the maximum he could handle before cabin fever set in. Small towns roll the sidewalks up at nine every night—some places even earlier than Concord. If you didn't have a job, weren't involved in some sort of church function, or didn't live close to your family, then you were one isolated son of a bitch. He took a deep drag on the fag, wondering what their situation would be if they survived until nightfall.

"Hi, Gunny, " Mary and Dot replied almost simultaneously. Dot looked at Mary and smiled.

"He's still unconscious, Gunnery Sergeant," Mary continued, patting Dot on the hand. "Dot gave him a few drops of water a couple of minutes ago. We don't know if any made it down; some ran out of the corner of his mouth."

He turned to Private Eric Sterling. Sterling leaned against the larger boulder to the right, the M-16 cradled in his lap. The Marine was cleaning his weapon with a torn-off piece of green T-shirt. "Sterling?"

"He's still unconscious, Gunny," the Marine replied without stopping his cleaning or looking up at Stapler. He glanced at his watch. "Been out for about six hours now, but his breathing is steady and his pulse seems normal."

Stapler waited for the ex-intern cum Marine to continue, and when he didn't, he asked, "Well, Sterling, would you like to tell me what that means?"

Sterling looked up. In the growing light of day, Stapler saw the twinkle of moisture in the eyes of the Marine. Sterling stuck his hand up and gave Stapler a thumbs-down. The hand shook slightly before Sterling lowered it. "That's what it means, Gunny, unless we get him proper medical attention, and I don't see us getting it out here, do you?" the private replied, his tone shaken and slightly belligerent. Sterling tossed the piece of cloth aside. "Gunny, what in the hell are we doing here?" He rammed in the magazine, pushed it once toward the front until a click told him it was seated.

"Sterling, you know the answer to that as well as I do, and I don't have the time to reply." What in the hell were they doing out here? They weren't supposed to be here. They were supposed to be back on board the USS *Kearsarge* by now, relieving the Marines occupying Algiers. *Shit, Sterling, I don't know the answer any more than you do. It is times like these you wish you could turn the clock back.*

Professor Walthers slid out of the nearby shadows. "Gunnery Sergeant, maybe it would help if I went up there and talked to them? I do know a little about the Tauregs. Maybe I can convince them we are leaving their country. I can appeal to Islamic principles."

"And what principles are those, Professor? They've already shot one of my men."

Unperturbed, Walthers continued, "Islamic precept says that when a visitor shows up at your abode, you are obligated to give him three days of hospitality and make sure he has provisions to continue his journey before he departs."

Stapler tugged his left earlobe. "You think they believe we are visitors here?"

Professor Walthers ran his hand through his gray beard as he thought about the answer. "I don't know, Gunny, but it may be worth a try."

"Professor," Stapler said angrily. He ran his hand under his helmet and over his short, graying hair. "I'll tell you this, sir, if the opportunity presents itself and we are still alive, then you can have your chance to try the 'We come in peace' routine with them. If you think they are going to buy it, you are living in an idealistic world, Professor. This is the real world out there." Stapler's voice rose, causing others to look. He stopped, took a last drag on the cigarette, and stomped it out. "And that real world wants to kill us."

The Professor's mouth moved, but no reply emerged.

The LT stared at Stapler. There was no reason to go nuts on the professor. He took a couple of deep breaths. Keep calm. The Marines depended on him.

Stapler reached out and touched the elderly gentleman on the shoulder. "Sorry, Professor," he said, shaking his head. He exhaled a deep sigh. "I shouldn't have lost my temper, sir. I know you mean well, but let's face it; they attacked us first and, since then, we have sent a lot of their kinfolk and friends onward and upward to Allah. We both have a blood debt that has yet to be fully collected. I don't know much about how folks here in the Sahara react toward that, but where I come from, North Carolina, we wouldn't believe a word you said."

"Jeff, are we going to get out of here?" Sheila asked, stepping carefully from behind the boulder, one hand on the gigantic rock to keep her balance in the sand. The sun and sand had taken its toll on the young woman's natural beauty. Her hair hung disarrayed in strings matted to the side of her head. The petulant lips that so captivated men when they first saw her were covered with blisters, and the dirt from her face, washed off at the oasis, once again caked her cheeks.

Lieutenant Nolan smiled. Stapler's stomach growled. He wondered if Sterling had a shot hidden in that medical kit for stopping raging hormones.

"Of course we are, Sheila. You are protected by the finest the Marine Corps has to provide. Right, Gunny?"

"I'm protected by the only Marines provided," she mumbled.

"Don't worry, Hon . . . Miss Forester, I am always within shouting distance and will personally keep an eye on you."

Gag! Stapler rolled his eyes. He was going to throw up if this thicker-than-honey shit lasted much longer. "Sterling, keep an eye on Private Henry. You stay here; protect the noncombatants. We are going to be concentrating on keeping them out. If any get through, you take them under fire. Understand?"

Sterling nodded. "Sure, Gunny."

"Just don't shoot any of us. I'll send an armed rigger back here to keep you company. If they get through the perimeter, there's nothing to stop them except you until we can fall back here."

"Thanks, Gunny. I work good under pressure," Sterling replied unconvincingly.

"Good luck. And try not to shoot us while you're shooting them." Stapler turned and continued his round.

"Good luck to you," Sterling mumbled.

Private Cathy "Catsup" Kellogg's foxhole was next. The young woman Marine had dug one six feet long in the sand and rocky clay. The uncovered rocks and those that surrounded her hole had been neatly stacked around the front of the pit. The hole was deep enough for her small frame. The two riggers—one on each side—were digging away the back so they could lie down behind the makeshift wall in front.

"Gunny, how is Cowboy?" she asked as soon as she saw Stapler approaching.

"Not too good, Catsup, but Sterling is doing all he can." Done all he could is what Sterling had done and, *Sorry, young lady, I don't think Cowboy is going to be with us much longer. What a hell of a place to discover young love,* he thought. But gunnery sergeants were paid to be positive. Let's not complicate her thoughts about Cowboy Joe-Boy right now. Not this close to combat. Not before a hundred pissed-off Tauregs rode down on them like some apparition out of *Lawrence of Arabia.* A week ago, he didn't even know what a Taureg was. He wished it had stayed that way.

"Kellogg, make every shot count."

She patted three grenades at the bottom of the foxhole. "Ain't they gonna be surprised when we begin playing baseball with these things, Gunny."

"Wait until I give the signal before throwing them, Kellogg, and make sure they go farther than the one you threw six feet at LeJeune."

"She will, Gunny," Bearcat Jordan said from the left side of her. "And we'll make them eat lead."

"Sorry, Mr. Jordan, I didn't recognize you."

Bearcat pulled the loose shirt away from his body. "Story of my life, Gunny. I finally lose this potbelly, and look where we're at. Not much of a chance to impress the women of Denver with it," he said, laughing. He stopped digging, wiped the sweat from his forehead and leaned on the shovel as he talked with Stapler.

"I'm sure the women in Denver will be waiting when we get back."

"But, at my age, will they have their own teeth?"

"How are those civilian M-16s holding up?" Stapler asked, squatting down beside the three. "And what is our ammo status?" The Marines had flown in with a normal packout of five cartridges per Marine. Thirty bullets per cartridge. The destruction of the helicopters had stranded them with only the supplies in their packs.

The oil riggers had ten civilian M-16A2 5.56 mm rifles, making the ammunition compatible with the newer variant of the M-16 the Marines carried.

"We still have the one crate with fifty cartridges in it, Gunny. I talked with the lieutenant earlier. The crate is against the front wheel of that humvee," Bearcat said, pointing to the second one in line. "The top is just lying on the crate. All you have to do is lift it and take out a magazine."

"I thought we had another crate of 5.56 millimeter bullets so we could replenish the magazines."

"No, I don't think so, Gunny. If we did, I don't remember. All we had was the one crate."

Lieutenant Nolan caught up with Stapler. "I think they'll be all right, Gunny. I've told them not to worry."

Stapler looked back at the LT. "I'm sure that will do it, sir," in as serious of a tone as he could muster.

He stood up, hoisted his rifle, and strolled off to the next foxhole a few feet away. "Good luck, Bearcat. Kellogg, look for the whites of their eyes."

"They have whites?"

Corporal Heights's and Private Hank Jones's two-man foxhole, about six feet away, ran parallel to Catsup Kellogg's. Three riggers balanced the two Marines like matching bookends, with one in the center.

"Hello, Gunny, LT," said Heights when the two approached.

"How's it going, Corporal?" Lieutenant Nolan asked.

Heights raised his hand to salute, realized what he was doing, and dropped it. "We're fine, LT. Just waiting for an opportunity to kick some native ass."

"Yeah, that be what we gonna do all right," Private Jones added sarcastically. "We gonna kick a hundred native asses before they kick ours." He looked up at Stapler. "Gunny, I wanna put in for a transfer."

"See me once we get back, Jones."

"Naw, Gunny. I wanna do it now so I can get the hell out of here before they get the hell down here," he replied, elbowing Heights and laughing. "We in one hell of a mess, ain't we, Gunny? One hell of a mess."

"Marines have been in other situations and won the day, and we will this time, Private Jones," Lieutenant Nolan answered. "We will win the day, and never forget that."

"Oh, I ain't forgot it, LT. The problem I have is that I remember it all too well. And, I tell you this, LT, Gunny, when those assholes get down here and discover we are United States Marines, it is gonna be one Kodak moment in their memory." He elbowed Heights again and laughed. "Yeah, man, it gonna be one hell of a Kodak moment."

"Keep those shirtsleeves rolled down, Jones," Stapler said. "The sun will be up soon, and if they are going to attack, they may do it then."

"You're black, Jones. You don't sunburn," Heights said, grinning.

"Yeah, man. Just like all us Afro-Americans are hung like horses. Another myth shot to hell."

"We have to conserve our ammo, Marines. Make each shot count."

"We will, Gunnery Sergeant," Heights said. "Good luck, sir."

"Good luck, Corporal Heights," Lieutenant Nolan

replied. "And, Private Jones, we are going to make it one hell of a Kodak moment for them."

Just hope we live to see prints, thought Stapler.

The two moved along the line to where Privates Darren Garfield and Luc Lerfervre had dug in. Along the front of the foxhole, the two Marines and the two riggers had stacked rocks like the others to make the position more defendable. The foxhole butted against the front wheel of the lead humvee. Under the humvee, an oil rigger—Stapler tried unsuccessfully to recall the man's name—had taken position. He wasn't sure, but one thing he knew, the boots sticking out from beneath were not Marine Corps issue. Private Gonzales had dug his own foxhole in the narrow space between the two humvees. The foxhole was on the far side of the two vehicles. Stapler bent down and looked underneath the humvees. No one was there.

"Where's Gonzales?" he asked.

"He's with the camels, Gunny," Heights replied, pointing toward the base of the cliff behind them.

The day had lightened considerably in the past few minutes. The sun chased the shadow downward on the cliff behind them as it rose into the sky. A few minutes, and the hot, dry heat of the Sahara would rush across them.

Stapler looked to where the camels had been moved and saw the silhouette of Gonzales moving among the animals, forcing them to their knees and a resting position. Even Stapler knew once gunfire started those animals would bolt.

He looked back between the two vehicles. Gonzales's position in the center of the two humvees limited the coverage area to forty-five degrees on either side, but that's what he wanted. Just a small amount of overlapping fire. Each Marine's area of coverage was a ninety-degree angle projecting from forty-five degrees to the left, revolving to forty-five to the right.

On both sides of Gonzales's position, an oil rigger lay beneath the humvees. The one on the far side Stapler recognized as Heinrich Wilshaven, the maintenance guru for the vehicles. Heinrich saw Stapler and gave a halfhearted salute. "At least here, Gunny, I haft the shade."

"LT, we are about as ready as we are going to be."

"Where should you and I position ourselves, Gunny?"

"LT, I recommend you take position near the front of the first humvee when the battle starts, and I will be over near Corporal Heights's and Private Kellogg's positions. I think they will try to come through there first. There is little to stop them other than firepower. You may even want to try the radio while we wait to see what they are doing."

Nolan nodded. "I'm trying to conserve the battery as much as possible." He saw Stapler's eyebrows bunch even as the Gunnery Sergeant tugged his earlobe. "I see, Gunny. Won't matter about the battery if we don't get out of here."

Stapler nodded. "We can always jump-start from the second humvee if we have to, LT."

"Okay, Gunny," Lieutenant Nolan replied. He looked down at his combat boots and then back at Stapler and whispered, "Gunny, I don't mind telling you that I am scared shitless."

Stapler grinned. "Ain't we all, LT. Ain't we all." Stapler left the lieutenant to squat beside the ammo crate. This small crate was going to determine how long they lasted. Behind him came the sounds of radio static as the LT tuned the radio and began calling Base Butler. He looked down at his watch. Stapler had little hope the LT would establish contact. Even if he did, Base Butler could do little for them. They were still a hundred miles from reaching a point where the Army's CH-47 Chinooks could reach and extract them. But the key to good military organization was consistency and hope, even when the odds against you were poor and getting worse.

Stapler removed the lid. The loaded magazines were stacked neatly on top of each other. All anyone had to do was reach in, grab a magazine, and ram it home. But everyone couldn't do that. Someone had to keep these bullets going to those who needed them.

"Gunnery Sergeant," someone said from behind.

Stapler looked up. Karim Abdul Washington stood there. "Yeah, Karim?"

"I want to help. What can I do? I am not used to standing back and letting others do my fighting for me. So, if you've got a spare pistol, rifle, even a knife, tell me where you want me, and I'll be there."

Stapler looked down at the crate. His hand went automatically to his ear. "Squat down here beside me, Karim." Five minutes later he finished explaining what he wanted the Baltimore native to do.

"And, this is all we have left?" Karim asked, hefting one of the cartridges, turning it back and forth to look at it.

"That's it, Karim, with the exception of one other thing. It's not a pleasant thought but a simple fact of battlefield life. A weapon not firing is useless. If someone is wounded to the point where they are unable to fight or if someone—we don't like to think about it—is killed, then we need to get that weapon back into the fray as soon as possible. At the minimum, we want their ammunition recirculated. That's your job."

Karim put the cartridge back into the box. "Bummer, man."

Stapler nodded. "Yeah. A real bummer."

Stapler stood and wiped the sweat from his brow. Night had gone while he was talking with Karim. The daytime temperature had already chased away the cool, desert night. Sunlight had chased the shadows from the cliffs like shades rising inside a house. He tilted his helmet back on his head and searched the surrounding countryside, looking for signs of an advancing enemy. The campfires were gone in the light of day. There was quiet stillness to the morning. It was going to be a hot day with the walls of the wadi blocking any breeze from the desert.

Nothing but waterless terrain marked the transition from flat desert to this first in a maze of small valleys. Where were they? A hundred warriors do not just disappear. He tugged his ear slightly. Let the fight decide the outcome rather than a siege. Don't let the sun win the battle. He hoped they felt the same way.

"Gunny! Gunny!" shouted Private Lerfervre, motioning rapidly for Stapler. The others looked in his direction.

Stapler pulled his helmet down and advanced to the foxhole where Lerfervre and Garfield lay between two of the riggers. Stapler didn't know the names of the two riggers, though the American Legion tattoo on the arm of one of them indicated the man was a veteran.

"What is it, Lerfervre?"

"Gunny, look out there," he said, pointing toward the front.

Stapler looked. "Okay, I've looked. What am I supposed to see?"

Everyone had gone quiet, trying to hear Lerfervre. From the humvee the sound of the LT calling Base Butler filtered over the alert Marines and nervous oil riggers.

"The rocks, Gunny. We didn't have any *boulders* out there last night."

Lieutenant Nolan backed out of the humvee and threw the microphone into the vehicle where it wedged against the seat belt buckle, the Transmit button lodged in the open position. "Not a damn thing, Gunny. Just for a moment, I thought someone might have been trying to respond, but it was only ghost."

The edge of the desert sun burst over the top of the cliff, blinding Stapler briefly as he cupped his hand over his eyes. He shut them for a moment as they became accustomed to the morning rays. When he opened them a few seconds later, it seemed to Stapler that the rocks surrounding the encampment were moving.

"Here they come!" shouted Corporal Heights from the other side.

The rocks weren't rocks. The Tauregs had curled up on their sides and draped their abas over their bodies so that in the shadows of the night they blended into the rocky terrain of the wadi.

"Hold your fire!" Stapler shouted. "Make each shot count." The Taureg charge was several hundred yards away and uncoordinated. Now that the battle had begun, his anxiety eased. The years of exercises, training, and combat experience burst forth within him.

"Get down, Gunny!" the LT shouted from the humvee.

Stapler turned to the order. A loud *oodalooping* noise rose from the desert, cascading across the encampment, as the war cry of the Tauregs increased in volume and sound. Stapler raised his M-16. The sun was in their eyes, aiding the attackers heading their way.

"Gunny, get down, I said!"

A bullet went past his ear so close he felt the breeze.

Stapler dove to the side, rolled twice, and came up against the front wheel of the lead humvee. A moment of pain shot up his side from the cracked rib. *Won't try that again.*

The static from the radio bled into the battle sounds. He lifted his weapon and flipped the safety off to burst as several Tauregs reached the perimeter. He fired two bursts of three bullets, killing the three. The Marines and riggers, who waited for the gunny's command, opened fire together, sending a wave of bullets out to greet the Taureg horde.

One Bedouin fell on the rigger to the left of Garfield, who shoved the dead man off. As the rigger turned back toward the front, an attacker jumped across the small barrier, drew back, and brought a huge knife down into the man's back. Stapler shot him. The rigger's screams filled the air, his hands grabbing for the knife sticking out of his back. Garfield jerked the man down, and he thankfully passed out.

Stapler looked over at Heights's and Kellogg's positions. A wall of Tauregs charged, screaming their weird war cry, like a rushing tidal wave of black water. The Tauregs didn't aim their old rifles but fired from whatever position they held them. Enough bullets went in the same direction that one of them was going to hit something.

Two attackers rolled across the hood of the second vehicle, their sandals exposed as their robes rode upward. Stapler flipped onto his back and shot the first one. A third and fourth attacker followed, knocking the second one off his feet and saving him from Stapler's next volley. The burst meant for him hitting the three behind, sending them tumbling into a bleeding pile of wounded rolling and shouting in the Taureg dialect. Stapler whipped the M-16 back and forth racking the wounded Tauregs as they stood up.

A shadow crossed his eyes. He glanced up into the eyes of two Taureg natives as they crawled over the top of the lead humvee. The barrel of a gun never looked bigger to him.

A moment later, Stapler was opening his eyes. He was in the center of the encampment, about twenty feet from the boulders. How did he get here? The LT and Karim stood over him. Gunfire filled the air. He recognized the distinct popping sound of the M-16 and even recognized the slight difference of the older variant the riggers used. He looked at the LT and saw the young officer's lips moving, but for some reason he couldn't make out what the LT was saying. It seemed the inside of the perimeter was covered in unmoving bodies dressed in black, like an overdone scene in one of those Hong Kong karate movies.

He tried to move his lips, but nothing emerged. His arms felt like lead weights, and then pain rippled through his body, seeming to center on his left side. Stapler lifted his hand to discover it covered in blood.

Another face emerged into his vision. *Sterling, my medical school dropout*, he thought. *So tired.* The LT's lips moved, and the officer disappeared.

A voice filtered through the haze of gunfire. "Don't you go to sleep on me, you old bastard!"

Sterling! Calling me—a gunnery sergeant in the United States Marines Corps—a bastard! Only Top Sergeant MacGregory called him a bastard and only jokingly. *Sterling must know me better than I thought. Even so, I'm going to have to whup his ass.*

He felt pressure on his chest and coughed. Stapler turned his head to the side and spat out red fluid. He

opened his eyes and for a brief moment wondered about
the red stuff soaking into the sand.

"Gunny, can you hear me?" Lieutenant Nolan asked.

Where did he come from? Stapler nodded his head.
God! His head felt so heavy.

"Gunny, I'm leaving you with Sterling. I have to go."
The LT's face disappeared again from Stapler's vision.
When was the officer going to realize he didn't have to
ask Stapler's permission for everything?

He took a deep breath, and pain whipped through his
body, starting on the left side of his chest and rippling up
to his brain. *Fight the pain,* came the thought, and it
sounded like that asshole Top Sergeant MacGregory
shouting it at him. *MacGregory needed to stay at the club
and leave the fighting to us younger men,* he thought.
Somewhere he had heard that pain travels at 325 feet per
second. He felt this pain exceeded that speed.

"What happened?" he mumbled, surprised at how the
words sounded slurred.

"You old bastard! You got yourself shot is what you
got. Man, you supposed to be leading us, and you got
yourself shot! What the fuck are we going to do now?"
Sterling spoke more to himself than to Stapler. The Marine cum medic's hands moved fast as Sterling jerked
gauze off a roll in long strips, ripping with his hands, folding it rapidly, and applying it with pressure over the chest
wound.

The bullet had entered Stapler's chest at an oblique
angle, piercing his lung before exiting on the left side.
Only three inches separated where the bullet entered and
where it exited. A more modern weapon and bullet would
have ripped half his back off during the exit.

Stapler looked past the Marine turned corpsman, raised
his hand slightly and pointed. "Look out," he said.

Sterling rolled onto his back, whipped up his M-16,
and shot two attackers rushing toward them. His head
turned from side to side, searching for others. Satisfied,
Sterling turned back to Stapler.

"And, you know what, Gunny? Naw, you don't know,

but I'm gonna tell you anyway. You gonna live. You gonna live because, by God, I ain't scared of losing any patients. I ain't scared."

"AMMO, I NEED AMMO!" CAME THE SHOUT from Garfield's direction.

Karim stood and ran to the ammo crate. He snatched up four of the cartridges. Bent over, he hurried around the perimeter, dropping them off to those who needed them.

Little puffs of sand followed him as bullets traced his steps.

Karim slid to the ground, like a base runner sliding into home plate ahead of the ball. A slight sting in his left leg grew into excruciating pain. "Damn," he said, bringing his hand to his face and rubbing the blood on it between his fingers. "I've been shot."

Garfield leaned back and glanced at the wound before facing forward again. "Don't worry. It's just a flesh wound. You'll live," Garfield said, holding out his hand. "Give me another cartridge."

Karim slid over beside the still rigger, the knife still stuck in the man's back. He put his fingers to the man's neck.

The firing of the M-16s and the ancient weapons opposing them drowned out the normal level of conversation.

Karim passed two more cartridges to Garfield and pointed to the rigger. "Dead," he said. Karim lifted the idle M-16 lying to the side, recalling what Stapler had told him. "He ain't gonna need this, and they've pissed me off now."

Garfield fired a couple of bursts over the top of his position and heard the magazine click on empty. He pulled the magazine from his weapon and automatically shoved in a full one.

Karim pulled himself back to the magazine box. He sat down, his back against the back wheel, waiting for the next call. The amount of ammunition they were firing, they would run out soon. Probably minutes. He took his handkerchief and wrapped it around the wound. The salt soaked into the cloth burned the open wound. He hefted the lightweight M-16, leaned around the side of the humvee, and began firing. *Just like Baltimore on a Saturday night,* he thought.

"Help me up, Sterling," Stapler said.

"Gunny, you can't stand. Your legs won't hold you."

The firing increased in tempo. Stapler turned his head to the right. Four Tauregs, their robes flapping like black flags, jumped into the encampment. The huge five millimeter plus bullets of multiple M-16s hitting the attackers created a macabre dance of death as the bodies rocked with each impact. So far, they had protected the interior lines of communications. . . . Now why did he say that? His mind seemed to jump from one thought to the next. He needed to move; clear his mind.

"Help me up, Sterling, or neither of us will be around for me to recover." Stapler spat another mouthful of blood out. He wiped his sleeve across his mouth and surprised himself to find a long streak of blood along it.

He looked up at Sterling. "How bad is it?" Stapler asked, lying back on the sand, all thoughts of standing up gone.

"I already told you, Gunny. You gonna live. You got a punctured lung, but the bullet went clean through. If you don't get infection—and where in the hell would you get infection in the middle of the desert—then you gonna live."

Sterling glanced back toward the rear of the camp. He leaned toward Stapler. "This is going to hurt, Gunnery Sergeant, but I am going to pull you over to the boulders and brace you up against them. The wound is in the lower part of the lung. Bracing you up should keep the blood from flooding the upper part . . . or at least slow it down."

Stapler coughed. "You have such a great bedside manner, Sterling."

Sterling crawled behind Stapler and put his hands under Stapler's arms. "You ready?"

"Yeah," Stapler said.

The pain caused dancing spots of whiteness and stars to cross his vision. Involuntarily, Stapler closed his eyes. Pain sent waves of white sheets across his eyes. He held his breath for several seconds against the mind-numbing pain. Sterling pulled and tugged him the few feet to the boulders.

"Gunny, you ready for the difficult part?"

"That wasn't it?"

"Christ!" Sterling shouted, rolled to the side, and brought his M-16 up. He fired a three-shot burst at another Taureg who had jumped the perimeter.

"Hurry, Sterling, get me up!" Stapler gasped through the pain.

A few seconds later, with a lot of pain and several quick seconds of unconsciousness, Stapler found himself propped against the huge boulder behind him. He felt guilty over the pain of his wound when he thought of the gut-shot Cowboy only a few feet away behind them. The young Marine had yet to regain consciousness since Stapler carried him in, and he asked about him. Sterling leaned down and whispered that the Texan was dying. He guessed he should be grateful for the pain because it showed he was still alive.

"Sterling!" Lieutenant Nolan shouted. "Wounded here." The LT was pointing to a nearby oil rigger who was holding his arm.

"Gunny, I'm gone. You'll be all right as long as those pressure bandages stay in place. Don't move too much, and they'll stay in place. It's a serious wound but not a deadly one. At least, it ain't yet," Sterling said, handing Stapler his M-16. The Marine quickly checked the safety to make sure it was off. "It's on burst, Gunny. And, now, you don't shoot me, okay?" He patted Stapler twice on the arm, and he was gone, heading toward the front. Stapler tried to grin at the thought. He was only a few feet away from the front himself.

Sterling ran past a rigger just as a round penetrated the

man's head, splattering gray matter and blood over Sterling.

Stapler pulled his M-16 to his lap and pointed the weapon toward the front. Behind him, he heard the noise of the unarmed civilians and farther to the rear the frightening bellows of the camels fighting their tethers to escape the chaos in front.

From this vantage point, he watched their small group of defenders fighting against the tide of the main body ebbing closer and closer to the edge of the perimeter. *More than a hundred,* he estimated. *Guess they flew in more last night,* he thought with morbid humor at the idea of the Saharan natives having wings to fly like a huge flock of human buzzards to feed on American roadkill.

He lifted his M-16 toward Corporal Heights's position. A wave of Tauregs swarmed up the slight incline toward the five men occupying that strategic area. Catsup Kellogg shifted her weapon, bringing it to bear on the charging wave. Bearcat rose to one knee, exposing himself above the small rock mound that protected them. Little puffs of dirt jumped into the air around the oil rigger supervisor, as it seemed hundreds of bullets fired at the man missed. Kellogg reached up, grabbed Bearcat's belt, and jerked the off-balance supervisor back into the foxhole.

Another shadow broke the sun from Stapler's face. Above him stood a screaming, wide-eyed Taureg with his gun pointed at Stapler. He tried to bring his gun around even as he watched the native fumble for the trigger.

A foot appeared to the side of his vision, swinging through the air to connect with the Taureg's face. Teeth flew out of the native's mouth as the attacker, his eyes rolled up, fell away, the ancient rifle falling on top of Stapler's legs.

Miss Sheila Anne Forester jerked the native's gun up and tossed it aside. "Gunnery Sergeant! What the hell are you doing? You're supposed to be protecting me; not me, you! Give me that damn gun!" She jerked the gun from Stapler's fingers.

"Give me my gun back! What the hell do you think you are doing?" he asked weakly.

"Saving your life, old man." Her eyes roamed over the M-16. "How does this thing work?" she asked, turning it back and forth.

He raised his hand, and she handed it back to him, shaking her head.

The wave broke. All along the perimeter the Tauregs were breaking off and running toward the other side of the wadi. Sterling leaped over the boulder, ripped out a hypodermic needle, and jammed it into Stapler's leg. "Shot of morphine, Gunny. It'll ease the pain a little." Sterling rose and ran toward the perimeter defense line, not waiting for Stapler to reply.

Movement at the top of the path leading down to the floor of the wadi drew Stapler's attention. As he watched, camels with riders began to congregate at the top, lining up abreast of each other. First a few, then ten, twenty, and now he estimated about thirty. He couldn't hear the shouts, but he knew they were shouting up there from the way they were waving their rifles up and down. Building up their courage for an attack.

The firing slacked off as Lieutenant Nolan shouted, "Cease fire, cease fire!"

White steam curled from the engines of the humvees, and long streaks of oil ran out beneath the vehicles. They wouldn't be driving out of here, thought Stapler. He fought against a wave of despair that threatened to rush over him. He thought of his wife, daughter and son and how they would feel when word reached them of his death. If word ever reached them. With the exception of the Air Force bunch that overflew them yesterday, no one had any idea where they were. They would become like so many other expeditions that ventured into the Sahara desert to disappear and never be heard of again. Several things washed through Stapler's thoughts as he watched the growing camel calvary at the top of the trail. He didn't want to die, but who does? He wished he had paid more attention to Carol. It bothered him to think of how his shy Carol would react to the reporters who would swarm over her when the loss of this expedition became apparent. He wished he had made more arrangements for supporting her after he died. The Marines would watch after her for a while, but life moves on. The United States government would give her some nice papers, a flag, and maybe even an award for his death. Then they would slip her a check, a small pension, and fight her every inch of the way on wanting free medical.

Lieutenant Nolan ran over to Stapler. "Gunny, how are you feeling?"

"Like shit, LT," Stapler said softly, nodding toward the top of the path. "It don't look too good, does it?"

Nolan shook his head. "Gunny, we are into the reserve cartridges already. I just counted the remaining ones in the crate—ten. We used what we had and have dispersed forty of the cartridges out. We have only two grenades left."

"LT, see those camels up there?" Stapler asked, nodding toward the top of the trail.

Nolan shielded his eyes and looked to where Stapler pointed. "Yeah. You thinking what I'm thinking?"

"Probably, LT. When those camels start down here, those others we just turned back will attack also. Where Heights, Jones, and Kellogg are dug in seems to be our weakest point. It's the broadest point for those camels to get in here. If they get inside the perimeter, then we're gone."

Sterling, crouched over, came running up. "LT, Gunny, the rigger's dead. Bullet pierced his temporal lobe and stayed inside. Scrambled brains. Abercombie took a bullet in the left arm; Kellogg has a scratch where, I think, a ricochet caught her on its way by. Gonzales is wounded but refuses to move away from between the humvees so I can treat him. He can talk, so I don't think it is too serious."

"That it?" Lieutenant Nolan asked.

Sterling hung his head. "No, sir. I wish it was. Garfield is dead. Don't know when. Must have been instant because Lerfervre and the two riggers with them didn't even realize Garfield had been hit until the fighting was over. Sorry. I can pull his body back behind the boulders."

Lieutenant Nolan nodded. "All right."

"No," Stapler said. "Leave him where he is. He's dead, but the enemy don't know that. It's one more target for them to shoot and one less bullet shot at the living when they do it."

The *oodalooping* war cry of the Tauregs escalated, echoing off the walls of the wadi. Within the noise was the galloping sound of camels as the native calvary charged down the trail.

"Good luck, LT," Stapler said. "Sterling, get behind the boulders and take care of any who get inside the perimeters."

Stapler looked across the field of battle and saw the native equivalent to infantry running toward them. He was a little impressed on how illiterate Bedouins had managed to synchronize their attack. From this vantage point, he estimated the two attacking forces would reach the perimeter about the same time. As expected, the camels were veering toward the defensive positions of Heights and Kellogg.

"Hold you fire! Hold your fire!" Lieutenant Nolan shouted. "Wait! Wait!"

Stapler grinned. The LT had turned into a good warrior—lousy taste in women—but a good warrior. He turned his M-16 in his lap and saw the safety was still off. He would never have done that before. . . . It was second nature to him to flip the safety on when he finished firing.

"Prop me up," he said to Sheila Anne Forester.

She reached behind Stapler and pushed him farther up into a sitting position. Then she scrambled behind him and braced her back against his with her feet against the bolder to hold him upright.

"Don't get yourself shot while I am doing this, Gunny. It'll piss me the hell off."

He raised the M-16 and pointed it toward the charging calvary. Holding his fire, waiting for the LT to give the word. The LT stood in the center of the perimeter, small bursts of sand rising around the young officer as bullets missed the easy target, hitting the ground around him. The LT was offering himself as a target so the limited firepower of the Marines and riggers dug in around the perimeter would have less receiving fire.

Kellogg rose on one knee, pulled the pin on one of the two remaining grenades, and heaved it overhand toward the charging Taureg infantry. The explosion blew several into the air and caused those behind them to hesitate. Bearcat's M-16 blazed through the staggering line.

An explosion on the other side drew his attention as Lerfervre hurled his last grenade against the charging natives, stopping the charge momentarily on that side.

There were only seconds until the attackers regrouped and charged the perimeter. He heard the click of an empty rifle and saw Abercombie shift his stance, positioning his knees so that when the moment came, the force of his body would shove his bayonet up and through the enemy.

The galloping sound changed as the camels got nearer, almost a *whup whup whup* tempo. Reminded Stapler of helicopters. He lifted his M-16 and fired a short burst across the top of the second humvee, killing two Tauregs who had appeared there. The camels were less than a hundred yards away, most of the screaming riders waving swords while the others fired their rifles.

The ground exploded in front of the enemy calvary as missile after missile hit the ground, blowing camels and Tauregs into the air. Thousands of puffs of sand and rocks filled the air in front of the charging infantry as thirty-millimeter cannon shells whipped through the horde.

"We don't have thirty-millimeters or missiles," Stapler said aloud.

"What's going on, Gunny?" Sheila asked. "You're one heavy bugger, you know."

Over the top of the cliff behind the embattled Marines and riggers, eight United States Army Apache helicopters erupted into the valley, filling the enclosed space with death. The few riders who survived the initial attack turned their camels and fled for their lives up the trail, away from the valley. The Tauregs afoot ran screaming up the trail as four of the Apache helicopters dove and blasted the enemy like hornets from a disturbed nest, raining death and destruction. About fifty Tauregs, unable to escape, took position three hundred yards away against the farther side of the wadi. They fired their rifles ineffectively against the Apache helicopters, which wove and dodged as they blasted the cliff side, sending cascades of rocks to fall onto the Tauregs.

As if cued, the four Apaches pulled away from the stranded Tauregs and took off up the trail in pursuit of the other Apache combat helicopters that were chasing the camel calvary.

Behind the Apaches, six CH-47 helicopters rushed up and over the top of the cliff. Two of the helicopters combat landed—in fast, landed hard, slam dropped the gate— to the west of the Marines. United States Army Rangers rushed out, conducting an immediate attack against the remaining Tauregs in the valley. The helicopters accelerated back into the air and disappeared over the rim, leaving the battle to their riders.

Cheers erupted from the Marines and riggers as they stood and waved the soldiers on. In a few minutes, the Rangers rode over the lose perimeter the undisciplined natives arranged. The gunfire slacked as one after the other the Tauregs threw their arms into the air, surrendering. The battle was over. The Ranger force stood in a circle with the prisoners in the center.

Lieutenant Nolan walked over to Stapler. "Gunny, looks as if miracles do happen."

Stapler shut his eyes to keep the moisture from leaking out. "Let's hope it ain't a mirage, Lieutenant." He reached out and touched the LT's arm. Blood came away on his hand.

"What's this, LT?"

"Just a scratch, Gunny."

Stapler surveyed the young officer. Lieutenant Nolan's cammies were torn in several places where bullets had grazed the man. He counted three on the left pants leg and several on the right. Ribbons of cloth hung from the officer's shirt where bullets had ripped through him. Blood stained every place where bullet after bullet had nicked his skin.

"You are one lucky mother, LT."

"Are you two done? I'm getting tired in this position." Sheila Anne complained.

Lieutenant Nolan helped her move and eased Stapler down to the ground. White wisps of color decorated Stapler's vision as pain ripped through his body.

"Now, don't go and pass out on me, Gunny," Nolan said.

A tall soldier, followed by three more, advanced toward the encampment. The Army officer reached behind him to his RTO and said something. Stapler turned his head slightly so he could watch the soldiers. The RTO spoke into his radio. A minute later, the four CH-47s reappeared, hovering over the cliff before settling gently into the valley. They touched down about the time the tall gentleman stepped across the foxhole where Garfield had died.

The darkened eagle of a full colonel became visible when the man raised his head and looked around the camp.

"Colonel, I am Lieutenant Nolan, United States Marine Corps," Nolan said, saluting the Army officer.

The Ranger colonel looked at the young Marine officer, reached out, and touched him. He turned to one of the officers with him. "Chuck, get the medics up here ASAP." He then returned Nolan's salute. "Lieutenant, Colonel Dusty Cooper, United States Army Rangers. Seems we arrived just in time."

Army Rangers filtered into the camp. A medic rushed over to Stapler and asked questions as he checked the dressing. Stapler ignored the man. *How in the hell does he think I feel?* He was more interested in listening to what the colonel was saying. He wanted to know how in the hell they got helicopters this far and how in the hell were they going to get them back. The Army didn't have the legs.

"Lieutenant, good idea to leave your radio keyed. If you hadn't we never would have located you as fast as we did. I can't tell you how the sounds of your fighting echoing over the airwaves affected every one of us."

"Keyed?" Nolan asked, glancing toward the open door of the lead humvee where he could see the microphone wedged against the seat belt mechanism.

"Yes, sir, keyed. I don't think I would have thought of that in the heat of battle." Colonel Cooper said.

"Yes, sir. We try to think of everything in the Marines," Lieutenant Nolan replied straight-faced.

The colonel grinned. "I'm sure you do, son. And from what I've seen here, young man, you have had one hell of a battle." He sighed. "But, we don't want to stay here any longer than we have to. You need to have those wounds seen to ASAP, Lieutenant Nolan."

As if on cue, the eight Apache helicopters returned. Two went to the west end of the wadi and hovered about ten feet off the ground, while two took position near the entrance. The others disappeared. Stapler figured they were conducting patrols around the area so they wouldn't be surprised.

Colonel Cooper walked toward where Stapler lay. "Colonel, this is Gunnery Sergeant Stapler. Without him, I don't think any of us would have made it this far."

The colonel squatted beside Stapler and the medic. "Got yourself a little wound, Gunny."

"Only way the LT would let me lie down and rest, sir."

Colonel Cooper patted Stapler on the leg. "We'll have you out of here and back at the base within the next three hours. You just hold on until then, Gunny." He looked at the medic.

"Colonel, whoever did his dressing did a good job. There's nothing else I can do until we get him back to Butler. The bleeding has stopped." A shout from behind the boulders for the medic caused the soldier to excuse himself. Stapler knew it was Cowboy drawing the medical attention.

"Save him," Stapler said to the medic before the soldier hurried off. He hoped they weren't too late. Cowboy was a fine Marine.

The colonel started to get up, but Stapler put his hand on the man's arm. "Colonel, curiosity is going to kill me before this wound. Tell me how in the hell you flew Chinooks and Apaches this far. I thought we had to go another hundred or so miles to be in range."

Colonel Cooper stood up. "You did, and you do. When we arrived two days ago and got an update on your predicament, we knew we had to extend our range. We had to find some way to get to you sooner. Waiting for you to come to us was unsatisfactory. You've heard of FAARP—forward area arming refueling point?"

Stapler hadn't, but he nodded as if he had.

Cooper continued, "The Marines have used this tactic for extending the range of your Cobras. We forward-staged fuel and water in a leapfrog method. We flew Chinooks with fuel bladders and extra water as far as we could and left the supplies in the middle of the desert. I mean, who in the hell is going to steal something in the middle of the desert? The next day, we flew to those supplies, refueled, and flew another leg, where we off-loaded more fuel bladders and supplies. While that second bunch of helicopters was doing the second leg, another bunch restocked the first logistic stop. See? We are just leapfrogging from one makeshift fuel dump to the next. While we are here, other forces are restocking the two stops we have to make on the way back. At the second stop, we are going to be met by a full medical team. The one doctor I brought is back there with your young Marine."

A Ranger ran up to the colonel and whispered something in his ear. The colonel nodded and turned to face Lieutenant Nolan and Stapler. "Sorry, gentlemen, but one of your Marines is dead as well as two of the civilians. We'll take their bodies with us when we go."

"Yes, sir, we know. Private Garfield was killed in the first attack. The same one when the gunnery sergeant got wounded."

Stapler removed his hand from the colonel's arm. "Leapfrogged all the way here, Colonel. I'm impressed and thankful that you did."

Around them, Rangers helped the Marines and the civilians toward the four empty Chinook helicopters. Two Rangers appeared with a stretcher behind the colonel.

"We have to go, Lieutenant, Gunny. Fuel constraints, you know. In the event I don't have an opportunity to see you two together again when we get back, I want you to know you have my utmost respect." He waved his right hand, encompassing the wadi. "You fought a battle here against overwhelming odds, and like thousands of Marine Corps battles in history, you prevailed. I would like to shake your hands now because I think in the near future, it will be very hard to get close enough to you to do so later." He shook Nolan's first and then bent down to shake Stapler's as the two Rangers hoisted the wounded gunnery sergeant onto the stretcher.

"Overwhelming odds, Lieutenant," Colonel Cooper continued as he walked with Nolan and alongside the stretcher with Stapler. "I want to hear all about this adventure on our trip back, if you could find the time to debrief me."

Sheila Anne Forester walked up to the gunny. "You get carried, while I have to walk?" she asked, grinning, and then she leaned down and kissed Stapler on the cheek. "Thanks, Gunny. For an old bastard, you aren't so bad."

Stapler laid back and let his eyes close. Things must really be bad if Miss Sheila Anne Forester was kissing him. *Nice tits, though.* The pain was still there, but the second morphine shot the medic gave him worked quickly as the adrenaline faded from his system. Maybe he should have mentioned the earlier shot Sterling gave him. The bouncing of the stretcher soothed him in his drugged state more than aggravating the wound. By the time the two men walked up the ramp of the turning CH-47 with Stapler, the gunnery sergeant was asleep and smiling. It was a scary sight.